WILD LIFE

Also by Molly Gloss

MOLLY GLOSS

WILD
LIFE

SAGA PRESS

LONDON SYDNEY **NEW YORK** TORONTO NEW DELHI

SAGA PRESS

AN IMPRINT OF SIMON & SCHUSTER, INC.

1230 AVENUE OF THE AMERICAS, NEW YORK, NEW YORK 10020

SAGA PRESS and colophon are trademarks of Simon & Schuster, Inc.

For information about special discounts for bulk purchases, please contact Simon & Schuster Special Sales at 1-866-506-1949 or business@simonandschuster.com.

The Simon & Schuster Speakers Bureau can bring authors to your live event. For more information or to book an event, contact the Simon & Schuster Speakers Bureau at 1-866-248-3049 or visit our website at www.simonspeakers.com.

Also available in a Saga Press hardcover edition

Interior design by Vikki Sheatsley

The text for this book was set in Cormorant Garamond.

Manufactured in the United States of America

First Saga Press paperback edition February 2019

10 9 8 7 6 5 4 3 2 1

Library of Congress Cataloging-in-Publication Data
Names: Gloss, Molly, author.
Title: Wild life / Molly Gloss.
Description: First Saga Press paperback edition. | London ; New York : Saga Press, 2019.
Identifiers: LCCN 2018022757 | ISBN 9781534414990 (paperback : alk. paper) | ISBN 9781534415003 (hardcover : alk. paper) | ISBN 9781534403109 (eBook)
Subjects: LCSH: Frontier and pioneer life—Fiction. | Wilderness survival—Fiction. | Women pioneers—Fiction. | Wild men gsafd | GSAFD: Adventure fiction.
Classification: LCC PS3557.L65 W5 2019 (print) | DDC 813/.54—dc23
LC record available at https://lccn.loc.gov/2018022757

For my sister, Pat Zagelow

AUTHOR'S NOTE

The events in this book are entirely fictional, all its people imaginary. Certain thoughts and attitudes shared by many turn-of-the-century women writers have been shamelessly placed in Charlotte's mouth or upon the pages of her journal without attribution to the actual women who thought and wrote them.

Though much diminished from their heyday at the turn of the century, Skamokawa and Yacolt, as well as other named towns of southwest Washington State, are yet living communities, to which, in both history and landscape, I have been largely faithful. Certain bits of gossip and anecdotal stories (dates and details often recast) have been gathered from a variety of local sources, including especially *Battleground . . . In and Around*, by Louise McKay Allworth, and *Skamokawa: Sad Years, Glad Years*, by Irene Martin.

I am indebted to Robert Michael Pyle for his nonfiction exploration of the mystery of wilderness, *Where Bigfoot Walks: Crossing the Dark Divide*, and to the poet Pattiann Rogers for "Rolling Naked in the Morning Dew," and to T. H. White for *The Bestiary: A Book of Beasts, Being a Translation from a Latin Bestiary of the Twelfth Century*.

There were giants in the earth in those days; and also after that.

GENESIS 6:4

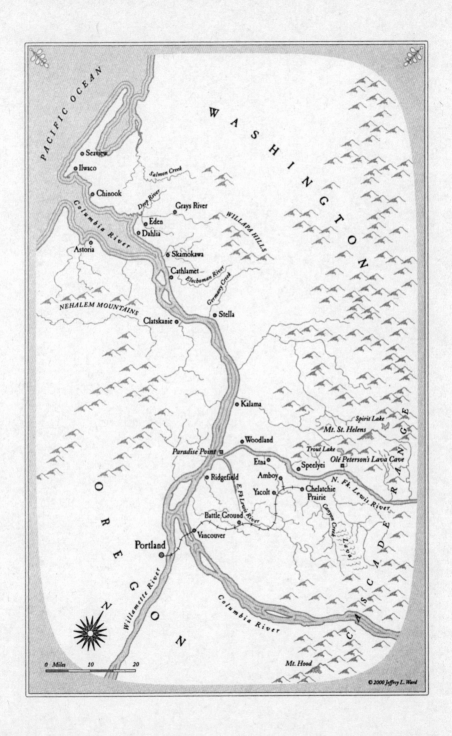

April 5, 1999
Sara,

You said you wanted to see the whole thing just as I found it, so it's unmessed with, except I'm the one who rubberbanded it with cardboard. The notebook, when I found it, was tied together with rotting string inside a rotting manila folder and lying in a bottom drawer, along with tax returns and receipts dating back to the sixties, in one of my dad's five (five!) highboy dressers. (I saved the string and the folder, in case you meant the "as is" literally.)

It's mostly (apparently) a diary. Some of the diary pages were torn out and stuck in at other places, so the dates are not entirely consecutive; and there's a bunch of other stuff interleafed too. Some of this "stuff" I know you'll recognize as coming from Grandmother's published writing; some others I think might be pieces of unfinished stories of hers (early drafts or experimental writing), but I could be wrong about that. The smaller scraps of paper shoved in between the pages are mostly quotations from various people, newspaper clippings, that kind of thing.

I almost started in rearranging the diary by the dates and pulling out the little scraps of paper, so I'm glad I called you first. After we talked, I sat down and read the whole thing through, just as it was, which you'll find is uphill work, her handwriting always scrawly, of course, but some of this the worst I've seen, besides age-faded, water stained, and so forth, and even the diary has a lot of scribbled revisions between the lines and in the margins (which I guess should have tipped me what I had). Anyway, I did start to see a kind of order to the arrangement of it all, which is why I think your first guess was right and this was something Grandmother was working on—whether as memoir or allegory or novel or who knows?—and for whatever reason, it never was finished, and obviously never published. (If the diary isn't a fictional invention, but her own, her *actual* diary, and she was thinking of using it as the foundation for a memoir, then I can imagine a couple of good reasons she may not have gone ahead with it, and why Dad kept it in a drawer and didn't tell me he had it.)

I know you said any papers I found among Dad's things should probably go to the university for their archive, but now I'm kind of thinking somebody—a feminist press?—might want to publish this if we could get it into a little better shape. I know Grandmother isn't as famous as Kate Chopin or "that other Charlotte" (as Dad used to call Perkins Gilman), but I would think people would find this story interesting just on its own merits.

Of course, we don't know whether she meant this as a true account of what happened (as in socks knocked off), but why should we have to answer the question? Unless you think people would think she was crazy, in which case maybe someone (not naming any names, but you know who you are) could write a biographical introduction. We could say Charlotte was apparently planning to use her "great adventure"—searching for little Harriet Coffee—as the basis for a novel, a metaphysical (metaphorical?) adventure-fantasy, maybe, which was certainly popular in those days. (Or something else; I would leave it up to you.) That would bring in the women's studies angle, the "glimpse of a writer's creative process," and so forth. And of course you could point out (again) that it was after Grandmother went up into the woods looking for Harriet—or rather, after she came home—that her writing turned a corner and her reputation as a serious writer was made (though by now she's not on anybody's radar screen except yours, and the vaunted few in women's studies, and don't get me started on that).

Anyway, it's just a thought. If you don't think it will interest a publisher, you should tell me (I trust your judgment), and we'll go from there. You've already written the Great American Dissertation on Charlotte Bridger Drummond, but at the very least there should be a journal article in this stuff somewhere, which might help you get tenure. (Ha!) Call me when you've finished reading it.

Best,

J

❦ *To write, I have decided, is to be insane. In ordinary life you look sane, act sane—just as sane as any mother of five children. But once you start to write, you are moonstruck, out of your senses. As you stare hard inward, following behind your eyes the images of invisible places, of people, of events, and listening hard inward to silent voices and unspoken conversations—as you are seeing the story, hearing it, feeling it—your very skin becomes permeable, not a boundary, and you enter the place of your writing and live inside the people who live there. You think and say incredible things. You even love other people—you don't love your children and your husband at all. And here is the interesting thing to me: when this happens, you often learn something, understand something, that can transcend the words on the paper.*

C. B. D.
September 1905

Sat'y 25 Mar '05

The death of Jules Verne was reported in the morning papers—a great loss to France and to the world. When I read this news,

I confess I was briefly startled into tears—just had to sit down and cry. Generally I am not much of a one for tears, and so my youngest son, named Jules for that very man, came and climbed on me, pulling at my hair and whining the way children will do, and dogs the same way, they'll climb on you and lick your eyes because they want things to go on being understandable, they don't want you to sit down suddenly in a kitchen chair crying.

I won't tolerate having my hair pulled, which my children know very well, so I stood up and tumbled my son right out of my lap. "Don't grab on my hair," I said, and discovered, upon sitting down again, that I was already finished with crying. There followed a theatrical burst of sobbing from Jules where he lay on the floor at my feet, but as quickly done with—a long wet sigh—when I pulled him onto my knee. He settled his bony little spine against my bosom and began to twist a forelock of his own hair around his pointy finger while I held the newspaper out in front of us and read:

Death Relieves Jules Verne

Calmly Foresaw His End and Discussed It with His Family

He had suffered from cataracts and deafness and diabetes, this was something I knew. And seventy-seven. Well, it shouldn't have been a surprise; I don't suppose it was. But something about it was unexpected, a jolt. Indeed, he leaves large work, long years of glorious writing; and now is dead. The world is changing, he told us, and in my strong opinion Verne predicted very nearly every one of the major mechanical developments of this century; his ideas have obtained a kind of technological immortality. The world is changing but people go on dying in the usual ways, is somewhere near what I was thinking, now that the prophet himself had arrived at the limits of personal mortality.

"Bird of six weeks kills her self with gas," my son read

solemnly. My children all are smart as whips, which I have written in these pages many times, but this last one an uncommon case: not yet five years old, but for more than a year he has been copying his letters from books and reading to me the captions of the daily newspaper.

I looked where he pointed. "Bride," I said. "Bride of six weeks."

"What's a bride?"

"A woman with a romantic inclination which has led her into reckless behavior."

This answer might have seemed sensible to him if he hadn't taken up from his older brothers a mistrust of anything I am likely to say about women. And my children are parlor artists, every one of them: he breathed out in a dramatical fashion and tipped his head backward against my breast, staring upward with the expectation of a revised reply.

"A woman newly married," I said.

"What's married?"

"Enslaved to a man," I told him truthfully. At four years of age he has no appreciation of scrupulous truthfulness nor understanding of irony, and withal has learned from his brothers to question anything I am likely to say about *men*. "Ma!" he said, in the particular way of all my children, exasperated and demanding.

I said into his turned-up face, "When a man and a woman decide to live as husband and wife, that's marriage. Like Otto and Edith."

He considered the idea, studying upward with his eyes evidently fixed on the little dark caves of my nose; then he said seriously, "Like Jules and Charlotte."

Well, boys are prone to confuse the mother with the wife; in fact, husbands are prone to this same thing. So I only said, "No, not like you and me. We are mother and son."

I expected him to follow this line of questioning to its next natural point—to ask me if I had a husband, and who was he, which is related to, but not the same as, *Do I have a father, and where is he?* (heard and answered many times); but his mind does not work like mine and shortly he had circled round again to another issue. "Why'd the bride kill herself with gas?"

With a child as young as Jules there is not much point in carrying scrupulous truthfulness to the edge of the abyss. "I don't know," I said. "It may just be she was very, very sad." Both of us considered this poor sad bride for a moment. *The world is changing but people go on dying in the usual ways.* Then I said, "Get up now, I have work. So do you. I want you to find the dog and a scissors and cut the hair away from his eyes, but not too short, and don't poke his face nor yours, and put the scissors away after."

This was something he had attempted without instruction on two occasions in the recent past, for which reason I had hidden the scissors thoroughly and cautioned the dog against cooperation. But I had lately been wondering if Permission would cut the desirability right out of that particular adventure, and in any case Horace Stuband would be rowing Melba up the slough by this time, and it might be, if Jules went on searching out the scissors for a quarter of an hour, Melba would be standing in my kitchen tying on her apron and I'd be locked away in the shed when the matter came to a climax.

Jules popped out of my lap with a little shout and went off at a gallop, calling for the dog.

"Ma!" Frank said from the very air aloft. "Lightning's hid her kitties up here, Ma, there's a hidey-hole under the eave. Look!"

Someone has taught that cat to count, is my belief, for she has never failed to notice when we have sneaked off with the weaklings and the crooked-born of her kittens, and she has become more and more wily with each successive litter, determined to raise them all, runts and mutants all, in a behavior that to my mind must be proof of the basic tenets of Darwin, or disproof; which, I cannot as yet decide. For more than a week my children have been looking for Lightning's new litter in places as unlikely as sugar bowls, desk drawers, and rooftops.

"Where?" I called to Frank, and went out in the mud of the yard to see where he was pointing from his slippery toehold on the gable of the kitchen porch. "Oh my Lord, Frank. Can you see them? How many are in there?"

"She's in there with them. I ain't reaching in. It smells like puke and she'll bite a hole in me and I'll bleed to death."

I school my children as to the rules of absolute construction, agreement of the participle, and placement of copulative conjunctions, but ignore the colloquial as a matter of principle. Ignore, as well, certain subjects of interest to Frank, whose inclination is to direct people's attention toward blood, purulence, and excrement. I said, "Just look in there, Frank, for heaven's sake. Count them."

"I don't want to put my face up there! She'll tear my eyes out and I'll be blind."

Parlor artists, every one of them—which is something their departed father unjustly blamed on me. "Well, then, come down from the roof and go look for Lewis; he's left the woodpile in a jumble. Let Lightning keep her mutant, godforsaken children, only I won't be held responsible for what comes to pass. It's inevitable, I suppose, that a Cat Monster will someday take over the earth."

I shook the newspaper as interjection, but having given up
for now any hope of reading the dying words of Jules Verne, I
returned the paper to the parlor, to the teetery stack at the end
of the davenport bed. If I'm to follow what is happening in the
world, and what's being said about this writer or that book,
and the details not only of the book industry but of biology
and archaeology, chemistry and medicine, the latest debates
over the conceptions of Schopenhauer and Nietzsche, and
arguments to do with socialism, feminism, evolution, eugen-
ics, insanity, disease, not to mention what it was exactly that
Jules Verne said to his family before he died, and if I'm to go
on living three thousand miles from the centers of science and
politics and publishing, it always will be necessary to rely on
a barrowload of subscriptions to publications of all sorts, and
books through the mails. It's a very lot of reading, and for four
days of each and every month there's no keeping up, as Melba
never can be persuaded away from making a monthly visit to
her daughter, Florence, in Yacolt, leaving my children and me
to manage the household without her; and since the U.S. Post
Office continues to bring my mail to the dock at Skamokawa
every day with the flood tide, the stack of unread newspapers
and periodicals always will build up during my housekeeper's
monthly absence, until by the fourth and last day it slides off
the arm of the davenport bed into a loose mountain on the floor
beside it: a direct result of Melba's stubbornness and the continuing inability of my children to manage their lives without
subvention and stewardship.

As if in perfect demonstration of this truth, I discovered Jules
in the kitchen standing on his toes on a high stool so as to peer
through the deep dust along the top of the Wilson cabinet, while
his brother stood below, jiggling the stool legs beneath him.

"Oscar, quit that. Jules, climb down from there. You won't find the scissors in this kitchen, Jules, I've looked myself and I know for a fact they are not here. Look out in the potato cellar for them, that would be my advice. And failing that, try along the garden fence; someone may have left them lying on the grass there."

"I never did," Oscar said in a righteously aggrieved way.

"Did too," Jules told him automatically, and the two of them fell to wrestling on the kitchen floor. Oscar, at barely seven, is small enough to present Jules, who is big for his age, with a challenging but not impossible opponent. They wrestle daily over important matters, such as whose arrow came nearest killing a particular Indian or slavering wolf, and trivial matters such as who wiped whose snot on whose trousers.

"I haven't said that Oscar left the scissors out by the garden fence; I said you ought to go look there. In fact, both of you ought to head for the garden straightaway and search the fence line thoroughly."

I stepped around their thrashing arms and legs and began to clear away these last four days of table scrapings. My personal belief is that a woman's worth doesn't lie in the cleanliness of her house; and at the commencement of each of Melba's absences I always am determined, on principle, to let the housekeeping pile up. It is Melba's belief, though, that a woman who neglects her home is unnatural, an abnormity more horrible than Frankenstein's monster, and on her return there is a particular look she will give me as she surveys the disorder. I believe it's dread of that look that sometimes moves me at the last moment toward a cursory sweep of the carpet, a symbolic neatening of dirty plates.

"Ma, I can't find Lewis." Frank was breathless, roseate. "I

think he's disappeared. There's tracks and blood. I think he was maybe captured by Indians."

"I wouldn't be surprised. But if Lewis has disappeared, Frank, it'll fall on you, as his twin, to neaten the woodpile."

"Ma!"

"Go and ask any Indians you see skulking about whether they have seen your brother. Look in all the mine shafts and secret caves. Follow the blood trail. I'm serious, Frank. I want you to find Lewis and I want Lewis to put straight the woodpile."

"Ma! He won't do it, Ma! He's out in the woods digging a bear trap and he says he won't come."

"Go tell Lewis I'm giving his clothes to the orphans in Panama and his pocket-knife to Oscar. Tell Lewis, since he's got bear meat to eat, he surely won't be needing a place set for him at the supper table. And tell Lewis that Melba is in a fine temper; if she sees the woodpile like that, she'll box his ears off and he'll bleed to death."

Frank's face brightened; he went off to deliver these warnings to Lewis. Oscar went off to claim Lewis's pocket-knife. Jules went off to look for scissors in the deep grass along the garden fence. I stood briefly in an empty room.

Just as Samuel Butler is said to have stopped everywhere and anywhere to write down his notes, it is my habit to snatch up every moment of quiet and solitariness for myself, to sit right down in these circumstances and turn out a few lines, a paragraph of deathless prose, while none of my children are underfoot: I keep a little notebook in the pocket of every apron and wrapper for just such momentary occasions. But I expected Melba; and I am as liable to be governed by my housekeeper as any woman. I went on scraping the plates bitterly and carried the pail out to Buster, who has taken up the prudent doggy habit of hiding under the floor of the toolshed whenever summoned by a child below a certain age.

The shores of the Columbia River at this lower end are crowded with small and flat islands divided from one another by the narrow slackwater of the sloughs—that is to say, by the river's back alleys as it finds its slow way round and among the islands. Price Island and Tenasillahe are so low lying as to be barely suitable for fish-seining sites, but this island (having no name, and therefore just the Island) is a great wedge of rolling pastureland and arable fields, as well as wood-lots of black cottonwood and red alder, engirt by the Steamboat, Alger, and Ellison Sloughs. I should be surprised if the highest hillock on the Island stands ten feet above the flood tide of an average spring freshet, for which reason this house and several of its outbuildings perch upon high stone piers in the hope (usually vain) of getting through our periodic out-of-the-ordinary tides with merely draggled skirts.

When Buster scooted out for the pail of scraps, I peered into the great muddy vacancy beneath the shed and called, "George," for my oldest sat in the dim dampness there, with his back reclined to the rocks of a corner pier and his head not visible to me unless I bothered to circle around to another corner and lean in. He said, "What," in a flat and sullen way as if it were a reply.

"What are you doing under there? Reading a book? Consulting the stars?"

George, having the advantage of years, has long since reached an understanding of irony, but continues without any appreciation for it. "Ma," he said, from the very mountaintop of Impatience, "will you leave me be."

He has gotten to be fourteen with no encouragement from

me. I believe the perfect age for any son is a certain week in his
eleventh year when he balances briefly at the triangular inter-
section of self-sufficiency, unconditional love, and eagerness to
please. If Science is to be believed, nothing in the universe actually ceases to exist, but I have begun to wonder: Whatever happens to all that affection, those years of motherly attachment,
when a son determines to discard them?

"I'll do exactly that," I told him, and I removed the empty
pail from under Buster's nose and carried it back to the house.

At this time of year the path between the kitchen and the
shed is always a perfect trench of mud, for which reason I had
gone over there barefooted and with my hem pulled up into
my belt. I've read that the Wahkiakum and Kathlamet Indians
of this coast never wore a shoe, and the sensibleness of that has
stayed with me ever since. While I stood at the kitchen door
stroking the bottoms of my muddy feet along the rag rug, I discovered Melba standing in the front hall taking stock of the
clutter. Horace Stuband had delivered her and silently rowed
himself home.

Her look went round the rooms while her hat came off and
then her gloves. "I see you've left all the work to pile up for me,"
she said in her usual way, which is Aggrieved.

Melba has failed to age well and suffers from an unlovely
overbite as well as an unsympathetic nature, but I believe I
understand why men once found her attractive. She is a small
woman, under five feet in her shoes, generous of bosom, with a
waist that suggests it once was narrow as a boy's; it would be in
a man's nature to consider a woman's figure ahead of her character. But she has made unlucky choices: two husbands have died
young, and the third, Henry, is a terrible drunkard and a wom-
anizer. Unlucky, too, has been her experience of childbearing:

a miscarriage, then a stillborn son, then a daughter borne hard and born early, and a surgeon's hysterical removal of her womb. Then, I suppose, Melba's daughter married and left the house before Melba felt herself quite finished with raising her up; this would account for the way in which she goes on trying to direct Florence's life from afar, in daily letters shored up by these monthly visitations.

There is an approach I have learned from the dog, who will always pass by a warlike cat by pretending not to notice her. "Frank has found Lightning," was what I briskly announced. "It seems she's been hiding her kittens in the eave of the kitchen porch roof." Melba, catlike, received my information with a certain narrowing of the eyes and a throaty, wordless warning; but her coat then came briskly off and was hung upon the hook, after which she brought down her apron and tied up the strings. So if she was briefly distracted from my insufficiencies as a housekeeper, my purpose was served. "Frank is searching for Lewis, who may have been killed by Indians," I said. "Oscar is in the house playing with knives. Jules is in the garden looking for scissors. George is lying under the shed with the dog." I went about the business of gathering up my newspapers and digests while I delivered this household report to Melba; and while she was still standing in the front hall gathering up her dander, I was carrying my armload out the kitchen door and through the mud to the shed.

Every writer needs a time and place in which to work. When some or all of my children were yet unborn, there had been space in this house for me to claim as my own: an unused bedroom, a sunporch, the rib-roofed third-floor attic. But it has been a terrible task to write books underneath the same roof with five irrepressible boys; this house is full as a tick and peaceless. When push came to shove, I was forced to look to other buildings for a room of my own.

When her own children were young, it had been my mother's habit to lock herself in the outhouse with her embroidery, and in certain seasons of the year when the deer were likely to come down into the yard to browse the tender lawn with our cow, Mother kept a rifle with her and developed a deadly aim from two hundred yards. I never did consider following my mother's example, for our two-holer stands like a bastion upon its high stone foundation and is a favorite stronghold of my continually warring sons; they have made a particular science of scaling its ramparts, from which vantage they ambush their unsuspecting brothers with missiles of various kinds, or fire on their enemies with wooden guns. I briefly gave thought to the little barn the cow stands in to get relief from the rain, but refused it on the grounds that it's three-sided (open to weather from the south), frequently lies in flood, and is home to certain of Lightning's misconceived offspring. When I first looked to the shed, it was full up with stove wood and tools and broken things waiting there for repair, but numbered its walls at four and had a door that would shut and latch. I instructed the boys to bring the stove wood outside, where it was a-rowed between the stone footings under cover of the shed floor, and our broken things out to the yard, to rust or rot or be made over by one boy or another into a steam launch or a cannon; and then the tools and I were able to come to an amicable division of space. When I had fitted a lock to the inside of the door, the place became proof against my children. Horace Stuband, when he saw what I was doing, took it on himself to reboard the floor against mice and mud and reshake the roof against rain and draught. I have forty acres for no good reason except Wes had a childish notion of himself as a Gentleman Farmer; and with Wes gone, I have leased the greater part of these acres to my neighbor for his cows. Of course, Stuband long has conducted himself as no mere neighbor, instead a prospective husband, which I don't encourage; but I accept the tangible tokens of his courtship with a sensible and silent gratitude.

The shed is windowless and dark, hot or cold with the weather, but if cold, Melba will send one of the boys over every long while with a heated brick for my feet to rest on, and if hot, a cake of ice. As for the lack of outlook, I consider I am driven inward to fanciful mountain-scapes and lost continents, and no worse for it, though in certain weathers I find I must take a breath when I go in the little dark room, in the manner, I suppose, of a hard-rock miner going down in the shaft; and sometimes, coming out, I am surprised by the light, by the absolute green of Stuband's pastures, or a sky unexpectedly huge and blowsy with cloud, or the receding purplish ridges of the Nehalem Mountains. This, I imagine, must be the surprise felt by someone who comes up from years in a dungeon; or by Mountain Mary, returning from the black heart of a volcano where she has discovered blind pygmies living in a secret civilization.

On the other hand, I rather like the rain striking the roof of the shed, the unpatterned drumming, and on those days there is comfort in lantern light, the little room become snug and golden. Inasmuch as rain is what we commonly have for weather, I am able to get along.

I climbed up the ladder to the high doorsill and while I scraped my soles free of mud I said to George or the dog, "Don't thump around down there while I'm at work," and someone, George or the dog, made a sound of grievance. I toppled my

papers and periodicals onto the maple secretary, which once
was my husband's, lit the lamp, locked the door, and put the
chair under me. The dying words of Jules Verne notwithstand-
ing, it's my habit when I can escape to this study to keep my
morning hours for reading, my afternoons for writing. Being
as it was already (though barely) afternoon, I dipped the pen
in the ink pot and drove the nib across the page with a pent-up
fury. *The horrible sight,* I wrote, *so clouded her mind and bound up
the winds of reason that she nearly cried quits with Fate and gave up
the battle of Life.*

Melba always has complained of her son-in-law, Homer,
that he torments his daughter in a man's careless way by bringing down with him from the log camps horrid tales of Wild
Men of the Woods, and so forth. I don't believe a child is spoiled
by the telling of monster stories; I've told them myself, in such a
way as to make the boys jump. But Homer will swear every story
is true, and that he has been a witness of great barefooted tracks
in the mud, twenty inches from toe to heel, and night screaming
of a bestial sort which is not the roaring of bears or lions, which
he claims he would recognize. He brings to his family gruesome accounts of monstrous hairy men stepping forth from the
shrub-wood to crush an empty oil barrel, or bend back the iron
top of a donkey engine, or brandish an uprooted tree, and long
recountings of stories other men have told him, of women captured from sylvan picnics and toted miles across the mountains
on the shoulders of stinking man-beasts. (Such is the nature of
men, I am sure in their own camps, outside the earshot of wives
and children, these timbermen tell one another the lascivious
details of the ways in which these creatures force their sexual
attentions on captive women.)

Melba, I'm sure, wishes that her son-in-law would bring

home to his wife and daughter gentler tales of the sort she told her own young child: St. Augustine's fables of men whose ears are large enough to sleep in, and fanciful tales of griffins and centaurs. The Wild Man of the Woods strikes her as altogether too near to the real, and consequently dreadful. It is a discredited feeling in civilized nations, but I believe we are all still afraid of the dark, and here in this land of dark forests the very air is imbued with such stories; indeed, the loggers had the tales first from the Indians. The realness of them is another matter. As the woods are daylighted, and wilderness gives way to modern advances in education and technology, I expect to see the end of the Wild Man, exactly as faeries and gnomes disappeared with the encroaching of the cities in Europe.

I also frankly wonder why Homer's stories remind me of certain of the white man's fearful fictions of other races. It seems to me men always have endowed the Indian, the Negro, the Hottentot with savagery and a strong reek, with apelike looks and movements, and with a taste for white women, and my own belief is that it's not a matter of other races but a matter of fear. There is a bestial side to human nature, basic and primitive impulses in the bodies of men which clamor for satisfaction, and it must be a Christian comfort to ascribe such things not to oneself or one's tribe but to hairy giants and savages. It may be the Wild Man of the Woods is but a ghost of the wild man within.

I am forgiving of poor, dull Homer, though, inasmuch as I'm always on the lookout for the seeds of my novels and have begun to make these wild-man tales over, turn them quite on their backs and fill the shells with my own turtle stew: the brave Helena Reed, Girl Adventurer, has come face-to-face with a secret race of hairy mountain giants, and in particular with a single example, the great and fearful Tatoosh of the See-Ah-Tiks (whose civilization, of course, will prove more enlightened than our own).

Today I wrote straight through—brought the dear girl to the very gates of their great secret cavern—2,000 words in rather more than five and a half hours. Of course, by then it was long since dark. If it suits Melba, she will sometimes send one of my sons down with a sandwich at midday, but she never will bring my supper to the shed; she's stubbornly of the opinion I should quit my work as the night falls, whether I've got to a stopping place or not. So when I went up the path to the house, I discovered Stuband sitting with my children at the supper table. Melba is determined that he should have a wife, and I'm determined that it never will be me, but standing on the porch looking through the kitchen window to the sight of my sons happily plying their forks, and sweet, sad Horace Stuband sitting with them, neatly tipping a glass of milk to his mustache, I admit I was pierced with loneliness. There is something about a lighted room when you are standing outside it in the cold night.

His hair has gone gray early, his whiskers gray, and his lean, pensive face just short of pleasing to the eye. He is indulgent of my children and kind with his cows, a man largely self-educated, and I believe he's a bit in awe of me; in fact he seldom looks at me when he speaks, which I suppose is due to abject fear; all of which may very well be good qualities in a husband. And any woman might wish to console him for a sad life: years ago, his baby son drowned in the bath and his wife afterward fell into a long melancholia from which no one, least of all Stuband, could deliver her. When a second child died on the day of its birth, the poor woman began a habit of walking the fields and pastures all night and falling to sleep outdoors in the daylight, very often lying on the graves of her babies. One day she lay down in Hume Sandersen's hay field, asleep or not, and the blades of Sandersen's new reaping and binding machine passed over her. It always has struck me that the woman was careful not to lay herself down in her own husband's hay field; and that Sandersen is well known as a man of cold feeling. People say he cleaned out his machine and went back to work the same day.

But it's marriage I mean to avoid, not poor Stuband.

While I wiped my feet at the kitchen door I said, "Hello, boys, it's gotten cold as hell," which was true, the mud on the path having gone hard and glazed. Melba, standing at the stove with a pancake lifter held up like a scepter, clicked her teeth in irritation. She objects to my cursing, on the grounds that women should defend the purity of children's minds. It's my argument that a child's happiness and well-being decreases in direct proportion to the degree of his civilization.

"Snow, Ma?" This from Oscar and Jules both at once, raising their faces to me hopefully.

We are always more likely to get rain in this quarter of the world than snow, and I have seen winters pass here with no more than a brief flurry in January, but Stuband, who is as childish in that way as any of my sons, gave back the boys' eagerness. "I've seen it snow this late in the year," he said. "Look here, boys, I've seen it snow in May. In ninety-two, we were skating on the sloughs and driving wagons out on the bosom of the river, it was that froze."

I placed myself on the bit of bench between the twins and lifted a finger of mashed potatoes from Lewis's plate. "I believe you've missed the question, Stuband," I said. "The boys want to know if there's snow in this particular bit of cold weather, and since the sky has now gone clear as a windowpane, I should think the likeliest answer is No."

Stuband is used to my glibness, I suppose, or might have

pitched me a crestfallen look. It was Melba, deliberately serving
the boys' coconut hermits ahead of my cold supper, who rattled
the plate warningly with the edge of her spatula.

I said to the boys, "In any case, if you're yearning for snow,
you should yearn for it on a day of the week when it will do you
some good."

"What's 'yearn'?" Jules whispered to Stuband, and Stuband,
who is an amateur reader and has taught himself the rudiments
of vocabulary, said, "It's to pray after something."

George corrected him mildly, "Ma doesn't pray. She's a
Freethinker."

Stuband then said, "It's to set your heart for it," and got to
the real point: "School's called off if it snows."

This brought a light into the faces of the two youngest,
quite as if the news pertained to the moment, though an entire
Sunday divides them from their next possible encounter with
the schoolhouse. In these isolated precincts the school term is
intermittent at best, commencing when a teacher can be found
and ceasing when one cannot, so my sons have become more
than a little spoiled from home schooling. When the six of us
are left to our own devices, I teach the children Thucydides &
Co. in the mornings, and then—having encouraged them to
form museums, to collect fossils and butterflies and to dissect
worms—I let them run wild in the woods and fields for the rest
of the day while I scribble, which is, more or less, the curriculum
famously advocated by Seton and his fellow Woodcrafters as
being advantageous to the active minds and bodies of the young.

Melba at last brought round my plate, and while I bolted
down the cold roast and mashed potatoes, the lima beans, the
new bread and butter, the boys brought up memorable snow-
falls and then memorable teachers. The Island School, having

lost a string of teachers to the custody of lonely bachelors, has lately taken to hiring girls whose principal qualification is their seeming unsuitableness as brides—hard-featured and repellent girls of vicious disposition and shiftless intelligence. I expect my sons to become wise through teaching one another the canny sufferance of inept teachers.

Stuband kept out of this discussion—he has a quiet center, which I suppose is due to the difficulties of his life—but then he cleared his throat and made an attempt to speak across the boys to me. "I'm glad to see the sky clear off some," he said. "There's no good to plow while this rain keeps up." He said this in an interested way, but one of his shortcomings is a notable lack of conversational themes. The boys were arguing about whether Miss Parrish kept a thumbscrew in her desk drawer, and whether the little vial in the deep pocket of her duster contained itching powder or arsenic, and I'm afraid my ear must have been taking this in with somewhat more attention than poor Stuband's weather talk. He went a few words further, seeming to speak to the fork as he pushed it along the edge of his empty plate; and then reversing his fork to travel the opposite way around the china, the poor man lapsed silent.

In the following silence—well, not silence, as the older boys began to give the younger an elaborate account of a girl whose fingernails had turned black from a teacher's hammering them with a handy piece of stove wood—I studied the shape of Stuband's big gray mustache, a smoothly down-turned and pleated crescent very like the horns of an Arctic musk ox, and when he became aware of this, he looked up. There are times when I feel under his scrutiny: as if he has taken me into his hands like a book and is studying the pages.

I was driven to say, "You know, Stuband, there are some very strange things going on in the world today, and the world is flying forward just as fast as it can." His look became startled, so that I was freed to plow ahead. "Encke's comet," I said. "Blindness cured by a miraculous drug. Moons circling Jupiter. A tunnel under the Hudson River. We shall soon be piping natural gas from the sloughs into our houses for lights and for cooking." I then began at some length on the future of agriculture: in our lifetime, plants rendered microbe-proof; farmers raising isinglass roofs over their fields, just as if they were circus tents—but miles in expanse—and growing their crops under those transparent covers without the suffering of bad weather.

I suppose I thought this would leave him fazed. He is always dim and earnest with respect to my knowledge of the future and of the advances of Science; it is principally for this reason I suffer Melba's practice of asking him in for dinner. But when he had considered things—drawing one horn of his mustache up into his mouth thoughtfully—he said, "I wonder the wind wouldn't take hold of such a roof, Mrs. Drummond. A circus tent won't stand much wind, I know that."

Finding that our interview had turned suddenly interesting again, Oscar said, "I saw the roof fly off the Renegade Queen's Wild West Fair and Bavarian Exposition!" On the instant, the other boys pushed in with their own recollections of that memorable event, when we all had stood in the streets of Astoria and watched the striped and flounced pavilion of the Renegade Queen sail over the roofs of town and flatten quietly on the backs of thirteen sheep, who were caught by surprise standing dreamily in their own field. It was Frank who remembered: those ewes had gone into a kind of nervous prostration from which they never had recovered, and word had reached us afterward that the farmer had been forced to slaughter every one of them to relieve them of their anxiety.

I kept to the point of my argument: "Not isinglass," I told Stuband, "which I meant only as a similitude. We should expect to see the invention of an artificial resin, clear as glass but plastic in its consistency, like putty or wax, which will therefore hold up to the wind and keep out every kind of scourge from cutworms to rabbits. The world is in a terrific flux, Stuband, and astonishing things are in the air all around us."

The boys by then had gone on from talk of slaughtered sheep to other memorable and bloody animal encounters: a hog that had run amok in the neighborhood with the butcher's knife stuck in its throat; a dog whose eye was pierced with a porcupine quill; a drowned gopher found inexplicably high in the crotch of a hemlock tree. Finally they had come round to arguments about the length of time a headless chicken might go on running around a yard spurting blood from its neck hole, and plans were being made to conduct a scientific test of the question.

"I believe you must be right about that, Mrs. Drummond," Stuband said to me, and he spread his mouth again so the edge of his teeth parted the mustache in an abstracted smile. "I never have felt so in a flat spin."

🍂 *The prosperity of the last century has had a curious effect upon literature. As every slum and hamlet has embraced compulsory schooling, unprecedented numbers of literate adults have risen among us, to form a great audience of readers, and though Montaigne has said that books are the only masterpieces of Art the poor can have as well as the rich, it must be these Great Unwashed who are to blame for the commercialization of the publishing industry. Of course, one could argue that publishers have ever worshiped the Dollar more than Art, but with the rise of a large, and largely undiscriminating, audience, publishing houses have raced toward mediocrity as pigs to a trough. Of the immense outpouring of novels, how few will be alive in ninety years? Think how many hundreds of books are never heard of (and justly) after their first editions.*

If at the present moment literature looks discouraging—where is the successor to Verne?—not Wells, surely—I suppose we need not lose sleep over it; such states have prevailed in the past and will in the future. But the higher form of Romance is the highest form of fiction and it will never desert us. Such men as write them (and I should say women, if there were any) write as artists and give little consideration to the editor's requirements, being always first concerned with expressing important Truths, though they be unpopular. It is the rest of us who write to earn a living, and if we are to succeed must please the editor, who in turn is driven to please the public.

The Beadle Half-Dime Library refused my little novel The Magic Helpmate: A Romance of the Seen and Unseen *on the grounds that it advocated women's natural superiority, and therefore was bound to fail in the popular market. In that book Lettie Porter is transformed by X rays and develops the ability to influence others' thoughts. Following her husband's cowardly suicide—he cannot accept that she is superior to him in intellect—she founds a meditation center where selected women come to learn this ability from her, and as her movement grows, these women influence the course of world events in such a way that war and violence of every kind very nearly disappear from the earth. In the final chapter, Lettie, though much loved by men and women of all nations, dies a martyr's death at the hands of the incorrigibly malevolent Count Madeira, whose murderous act results—of course!—in his own death as well. In the final scenes, Lettie's serenely beautiful daughter Edith receives the honorific title Empress of the World.*

In the world of book publishing, there is an axiom that what is good cannot be popular and what is popular cannot be good; from that, I suppose, I should believe The Magic Helpmate *better than it is. The poor orphaned manuscript was finally taken by Tosh and Thompson, which printed fewer than a thousand copies, of which more than half were discarded for want of readers.*

Fiction could go along slowly in the old days, when it took two weeks to get news from across the Atlantic; now we like our novels to barrel along. And the principal wish of the multitudes is to hear repeated the established views, beliefs, and emotions, without regard to the truth (though even the Great Unwashed will recognize him, I hope, when the successor to Verne, to Kipling, to Poe arises from out the Ordinary Sea; I mistrust the individual man but have faith in the community of them).

There are, of course, considerable practical difficulties to a woman being a great and artful writer while at the same time mother of five children; more profitable and less arduous to write pot-boilers. I therefore have no particular objections to the readers' lowering of standards, having been a beneficiary of it myself. Several books of mine— trivial novels of moon voyages, African adventures, time travel, stories of Black Wizards with mysterious powers of invisibility—have had a surprising popularity and deliver an income sufficient to support a family of six.

If I pander to popular taste with romantic tales of girl heroes who are both brave and desirable, crack shots, and cunning horsewomen who "clean up well"—if my plots are selected from the ordinary stock of forged letters, birthmarks, disguises, accidental meetings, mistaken identities, babies exchanged in the cradle, newly discovered wills, lost heirs—well, I have been encouraged in it by the economics of the literary marketplace and the necessities of supporting a family. I should have no reason to apologize.

And while I would never put myself forward as a likely successor to Verne—I shall never be as popular—my intrepid heroines are perhaps too lively for the common rabble—I can amuse and digress with the best of them, and have an imagination that gives way to no man.

C. B. D.

November 1903

Still Sat'y (midnight)

This is past midnight, with the boys in bed and Melba below me in the kitchen, though the hour for baking pies is long since past.

I have been in the grip of a jealous muse, so rose again after Stuband had been banished to his own house and everyone here abed, to take up the brave Miss Helena Reed. In the manner of the infamous and popular George Sand, it's sometimes my practice to sit up very late, scratching my pen quietly by candlelight on the tiny *escritoire* in my bedroom, with my cold feet drawn under this chair, which was once my husband's mother's, an ersatz French desk chair with a stiff silk cushion and a carven, inhumanly shaped back—a chair which entirely suits my purposes, as I have a mind that inclines toward wandering if I am too comfortable.

Tonight I believe I was silent as Coleridge's shadows, but shortly I heard the attic floor take Melba's weight. From my mother I've received unbroken health, together with an iron constitution and the gift of getting by on little sleep, but this late-night writing is a practice Melba objects to, believing strongly herself in knitting up the ravell'd sleave of care; she never has been an admirer of George Sand, on the warrant of that woman's queer and scandalous habits.

The attic stairs creaked, and then Melba spoke with her face pressed against the face of my door. "The clock has struck twelve," she whispered, hoarse and irritable, "an hour at which any respectable woman ought to be asleep." Practicing her impertinent habit, she then swung the door in and followed her words through. With her feet planted and her candle aloft, she was the very picture of Umbrage.

"Or working," I said sourly, "if the woman is so inclined," and I went on doing it. I was at an important point—Helena at the very heart of the great cave city of the Mountain Giants, and her attention drawn to a scene of great animation and excitement transpiring in the arcade.

It is Melba's usual practice to carry on with her objections, and my habit to resist them, until all impulse to write has been lost in the marshaling of my arguments and I am badgered into a kind of surrender—customarily a promise to retire at the next strike of the clock. But tonight she stood a few moments fixed in my doorway, gathering herself for battle, and then gathered the hem of her nightgown into her fist and went silently out. *My work supports this entire household, and ever has,* I had been preparing to tell her, which is true, and an argument she always will ignore.

I went on with my writing—Helena not alarmed, the dear girl, inasmuch as she has caught a particular gleam of amusement in the eyes of the noble Tatoosh. The boards of the first-floor staircase tightened and released in a familiar way, and shortly I heard a rattling of the kitchen stove. I considered, and wrote, and considered, and then put my feet to the cold floor and wriggled them, and when they had woken enough to bear my weight, I went stiffly after Melba down the narrow stairs to the kitchen.

She had lit the lamp and stood in its high shadows with a bowl pressed up to her ribs, cutting lard into flour with the blade of a knife. There were winter apples, little yellow knobs withered and spotted with brown, piled up in the sink.

"What are you doing?" I said. It was clear she had begun to make a pie; I expected her to know I was asking another question entirely.

"I am working," she said sullenly, "as any woman may do at any hour she's so inclined." Her mouth was drawn up in a little pucker. She had hung her apron from her neck without tying its strings, and much of her hair had escaped a disheveled braid. Horned and yellowing toenails were ranked below the edge of her gown.

"What do you think? That this example will shame me?"

She bristled up, her chin pushing toward me until the crepey skin of her throat was tight on its cords. "I don't think nothing of that, I'm just making a pie, and that's all. Go on back to your own work." She shook a palmful of water over the dough and drove a fork briskly around the bowl. "Go on," she said in another minute, without lifting her attention from her work.

I said, as a kind of warning, "Don't expect me to take your pie from the oven, once you have gone off to your bed."

"I'll get the pie out myself. This is my work, it's nothing to do with you." Her face had reddened suddenly with the heat of fierce and honest anger. She shoveled flour to the breadboard and tipped the ball of dough onto it, but before taking up the rolling pin she held her bare hands out tenderly for a brief, frowning self-examination. This gesture before beginning one's work always will make me think of Mother, who had the same odd habit, though Melba's hands are small as a girl's, reddened and split and peeling from excessive dryness, and my mother's hands were of another sort, big and blunt and tanned, toughened with callus across the palms and at the joint of the middle finger. In the last year of her life the baby finger of Mother's right hand was crooked and swollen, and I suppose, had she lived into old age, she'd have been troubled with arthritis, but her hands went on seeming to me strong and well made until the day she died. I consider there is something vaguely afflicted about Melba, and when she spreads her small bleeding fingers for that little inspection, I'm inclined to think it arises from her hands.

The air in the kitchen was crackling cold. I went to the stove and shook the wood about, for that stove is pettish, very like a man, and must be coaxed into doing the woman's bidding. When I determined there was sufficient smoke in the room, I took up a paring knife and stood at the sink peeling apples. If this disagreed with Melba, she didn't say. She had by then taken after the dough with the rolling pin, in her typically short, radiating blows.

We are unlike each other and get along chiefly by the favored method of couples who have been long married: there is very little conversation between us. But it's the way of those couples, I suppose, that a small alteration of habit raises a kind of signal of alarm, like the watchman's rattle of the knob.

"How is Henry?" I asked her eventually. Her husband frequents low places and is a pathetic drunkard. She has long since given up living under his roof but goes on delivering his supper on Sunday afternoons, and in addition stopping by to see him on the occasion of any errand that takes her into town, for he lives alone in a rented house not far from the Skamokawa steamer landing.

"As always," she told me in some disgust. The pie dough had

become a great circle, soft and elastic, springing against the pan.
She lifted it neatly into the pie tin and began to slice the apples
as I peeled them.

"And Harriet?" Until this moment, I had rudely failed to ask
for the most recent news of her family; and her granddaughter,
Harriet, is frail, a peaked little girl whose skin bruises violet at
the mere touch. She is Florence's only child, a thin, shy thing
born in the same month and nearly on the same day as Oscar.
My older boys often have declared they would have preferred a
trade.

Melba pursed her mouth. "She's thin. I would put weight on
her if it was up to me." This was ground we had covered often.

"And how is Florence?"

"Oh, Florence is just fine." She delivered these words in a
mutter which I determined to be begrudging or concealing.

Florence is prone to Female Complaints, and I have released
Melba from my house more than once for the stated reason of
nursing her daughter back to health; so I pressed Melba on this
matter. "Is Florence not feeling well? I suppose you shouldn't
have come away if she needed you." I have a thorough dislike of
my housekeeper's absenting herself from my house but never
have been among those Utopists who advocate the severing of a
woman's ties to her children.

"If they have a need for me to be there, well, then, they'll just
have to ask me," Melba said in a disgruntled way.

"Someone is sick, then? Who is it? Is it Homer?"

She made a quick loud noise, a release of aggravation. "He
never goes sick, no, it's not Homer." Then finally she let loose of
the first part of her pent-up news: "He means to take Harriet
up in the woods with him come Monday morning and keep her
there all the week long, which he evidently has made out to be

a great adventure for the child, though up until now he's always said it was a great danger, and his very life on the line from dawn to dark. I argued with Florence over it, but the truth is she has no say in her own house, it's all Homer's way and ever has been. He's evidently determined to do it, and of course he's got Harriet wanting it too, though she'll be among a pack of dirty timber beasts with not a single woman to see that she washes her face and eats proper."

"Where is this camp of Homer's, Melba?"

She gestured wildly with the paring knife. "Oh, it's way back in the greenwoods. They was working in the burn, but when the rains come, it got to be all a mud slide, and so they moved far up there on Canyon Crick."

A great timber industry flourishes in Yacolt just now, but most of it is a frantic rush to salvage dead trees; the great burn of '02 has left that forest over there a wasteland of ash and cinders and blackened poles for twenty-five miles to the east and south, but I took Canyon Creek to lie out in the saved woods.

"Is there not housing for the family men up there? Why is it Florence didn't move up there with him when the camp was moved?"

"Oh, there's homeguards right there in Yacolt as walks out to their work every morning, but he wouldn't have none of that, had to go out in the almighty tules, where there's all men and no whistle to tell them when to eat and when to sleep."

I don't know Homer well, but my general opinion of men and their childish posturing has not suffered any from the stories Melba has brought down from Yacolt. To marry and make himself the father of a child, and then arrange to keep himself up in the woods among other men for six days out of seven, is entirely the thing a man would do.

"Well, you shouldn't worry," I said, since the adventure was evidently already decided. "I've never seen a crew of loggers without a soft spot for a child, and I expect they'll watch over her like a spoiled dog. You ought to know she'll never go hungry, for there's more food in a log camp than on a maharani's table."

Melba had no answer for this, beyond the disgusted expelling of her breath. We went on turning and paring and slicing the apples in silence until she said suddenly—a burst of bitterness—"And his wife. My Florence. In all the months she never has said a word to me about it, I had to see it for myself, that he's got her in a delicate condition. I don't know why I had to learn this like any stranger on the street, and not from my daughter's own mouth."

Florence, very like her mother, had suffered a hard delivery, and it had been darkly hinted that the Yacolt surgeon had forbidden Homer to share his wife's bed; that Harriet, in the manner of her mother, was to be an only child.

I said, "Well, you shouldn't be surprised a man would put his sexual appetite ahead of his wife's health, Melba."

I suppose in some domestic novels this frankness of speaking might have brought on a fainting swoon, but Melba has an unflappable demeanor, and in any case she never has been the sort of person to tie her corset too tight. She is stubborn in her convictions regarding a woman's language, though, and I always expect to be taken to task for my lapses. It was a great surprise when she answered fiercely, "That don't surprise me at all! Men are no different than toms and roosters, when it comes to it! But Florence should have told me he'd gotten another one on her. I'm her mother. I wish she'd told me, and not let it go on like this until I had to see it for myself."

She never came to the edge of tears, but there was a distress in her voice that I had not looked for. I'm not clever in these cases, but after a bit I said, "Oh, she was just afraid to frighten you, Melba," and that may have comforted her. She said, "Well, maybe so," and we lapsed again into silence. She began to pinch up the rim of the pie crust with a fissured, reddened thumb and forefinger. "I'll just sit down here until it comes done," she said when we had put the pie in the oven, and then she said quietly, "Go on, now," and her face, which had been drawn up, gave way to tiredness.

I went up the stairs, but I soon came down again and told her from the last step, "Now, Melba, don't be worrying over Florence and Harriet."

I had surprised her, coming down again; she had already pulled out a kitchen chair and was sitting in it, stroking back the yellowy gray hair from her brow. "No," she said with a little note of astonishment, and she dropped her hands down in her lap and twisted the chapped fingers together. Her look when it finally passed over me was softly forbearing. "No, I won't if I can help it," she said, which of course she cannot.

Florence

As her husband's hands came to her in the darkness, as he came pulling at her nightgown, as he turned her on the bed, the woman whispered briefly not a protest but something like a resigned inquiry. He believed his use of her body was an entitlement, which was something she believed herself. In any case, though he was not generally a brutal man, she had learned that in sexual matters he was deaf to her objections. In the early days and weeks of their marriage, her repugnance and painful cries had secretly quickened his sexual appetite, so that his possession of his bride had been all but indistinguishable from the rape of an astonished child. Now, after nine years of marriage, she was largely indifferent to the act of copulation, and he accepted her indifference as natural and unavoidable—regrettable only for the loss of a certain heated ferocity.

As he opened her legs and covered her, he said in a hoarse murmur, "Just this once, just this one time," which was something he said every time, and which he may have meant as a kind of apology; they both had been warned if he got her with child again, it might be the death of her. She had borne him one living child and twice had discharged a formless embryo resembling the infant body of a bird or of a fish. Her husband had pressed his conjugal rights upon her even while she was still shedding blood from those losses, and this may have been the cause of the present troubles with her womb.

As he beat his heavy hips against the open bowl of her pelvis, he began a low brutish grunting such as she had once heard bears make—it might have been bears—in the dark woods where she had played as a child. She lay still and silent beneath her husband, as she had once lain still and silent, alone under the heavy branching trees, waiting to be eaten or taken by the monsters whose heavy dark bodies moving past her, grumbling and gnarling, she had merely glimpsed against the obscurity of the forest; only when his ragged fingernails came scraping at her breasts did a lisping whistle rise through her teeth, a birdlike sound, thin, a woodnote—merely glimpsed.

He had become convinced that he could prevent his wife from suffering further pregnancies by wetting two fingers of his hand with his saliva and swabbing the semen from her vulva after intercourse. In another month it would become apparent to him that she was carrying again, and he would cease this well-meant gesture; but for now he still believed in it, and as soon as he had finished using her he rose to his knees above his wife and ritually cleaned up after himself. The moon lit his wife's pale belly and the pale flesh of her thighs, though not the damp run where his fingers searched, thorough and thoughtful as a man destroying blind whelps in a dark wolfish warren of the earth.

Sun'y 26 Mar '05

I meant to let the boys run wild while I gave the day over to writing; if we had enjoyed our usual poor weather, all lowering clouds and sheets of rain, I would have held to that intent. But when the fog lifted off the water, it was a fine sunny day, and a scrubbing westerly breeze drove out the frost. In the month of March such days are infinitely rare, a gift of grace and glory, and so the boys and I, together with Stuband and the Eustlers, took a boat up to the mouth of the Elochoman River and spread a picnic lunch on the grass. Melba, on Sundays, is in thrall to the Lutheran Church, and though our little diversion would surely have taken her mind from her worries, she held stubborn against my coaxing and rowed herself to town on the Sunday morning tide, where in the silence of prayer I imagine she fell to contemplating her daughter dead of childbirth and her granddaughter killed by a rolling log. Horace Stuband is a Methodist and a regular churchgoer himself, but the boys evidently persuaded him to thank God for his infrequent gift of fair weather by actually taking pleasure in it. Otto and Edith Eustler, who have the farm northeast of Stuband's, are backsliders from the Catholic Church, and for this, as for their readiness to pack a lunch, they are the perfect picture of good company on a Sunday.

We raised the sail on Otto's fine little skiff so as to catch a following air, and coasted upriver into the Elochoman Slough, then George and the twins rowed turn and turn about, a winding course amongst the tiny clay-bank islands of the river delta until we had agreed on a mote of prairie fletched with red huckleberry bushes and bare legs of viny willow. The ground was soft and wet, the grasses laid flat by the months of rain, but we overspread a tarpaulin before putting out the picnic cloth, and built a fire up from driftwood and dead clumps of alder thicket, and were comfortable lying about in the thin sunlight munching roast beef sandwiches and sour cream cookies. The boys disappeared into the bushes as soon as the food was eaten, and the men cast their fishhooks into the river; Edith and I lay on the picnic cloth with our shoes off and our belts unbuckled and put the whip of gossip to various and sundry Skamokawans.

Edith is a woman of about sixty whose children are long since scattered about the world: Blanche, the oldest, became a schoolteacher and settled on an island off the shore of North Carolina, where she is a contented spinster; Myrtle married a seiner and followed him to Alaska, where I suppose they must spend their summers on a scow in one Alaska river or another, and their winters in Juneau or Prince Rupert in a drafty rented house. Adelin, who is a carpenter and boat-builder, lives a bachelor's life on the beach near Eureka; and Jim, who was once Edith's baby boy, has taken up law in Portland and has recently settled upon a particular woman to wife. I believe there were others, who died in their childhood, but I report this from hearsay, for Edith never speaks of any but her living children. She and Otto had a farm in Montavilla and sold it to settle here. The house in which they raised their children was "rattle-can empty," she told me, as if that should explain it.

Otto is entirely an educated man, a Prussian who held a place as professor of music at an institution in Berlin. This was during the war between Prussia and Austria, the reign of Bismarck, and it was partly to escape the army that he came west. Edith's father was a person of conscience who by then had already brought his family out of Prussia—as soon as Bismarck robbed Denmark of the province of Schleswig-Holstein. Edith is fond of telling me that she and Otto lived in the same Berlin street at one time but they had to come to Montavilla to make each other's acquaintance. She had been a gifted student of music herself and wished to be a composer, but of course, when she became a student of Otto's, all that was forgotten. They were married and she gave up the violin in favor of raising her children.

The story of my mother's death, that terrible sinking of the *Gleaner*, and so forth, is still told hereabouts, and I think Edith must know of it, although, like her vanished babies, it's something we never speak of. If my mother had gone on living she would now be sixty, and I believe Edith sometimes imagines I am one of her daughters, as sometimes I imagine this myself. I am fond of her as I am of few women. She is clever and funny and has an easy manner about her, as if nothing discomforts or surprises her, least of all my vulgar immodesty and the scandal that still attends Wes Drummond's forsaking of his wife and family. And of course, there is the matter of the clay pipe which Edith goes on smoking against Otto's express wishes—a habit of many years' standing. She was encouraged in it as a distraction from hard labor by the midwife who attended Blanche's birth—I encourage her in it myself.

I told her an amusing story about Arlie Shoup, who is a Freethinker and never has stepped foot in church, though his wife, Grace, is Catholic: when the priest arrived rain-soaked for his once-a-month Mass, and Grace lent him her husband's clothes, the priest told his congregation there was hope for Arlie yet, since his clothes had made it inside the church.

And she told me of the Fuger brothers' recent row-de-dow, in which Fred sank his front teeth into one of Karl's hands and held on like a bulldog, all the while thumping the daylights out of Karl with two fists, while Karl, with but one free hand to smite with, yelled bloody murder, so as to make the neighbors wonder which of them had finally killed the other.

We thoroughly aired our opinions about that purse-seiner whose body washed up at Jim Crow Point with an axe mark in his shoulder. The principal industry here, aside from lumbering and dairying, is fishing, and there is the same kind of traditional feud between the gillnetters and purse-seiners on the rivers as occurred between the sheepmen and cattlemen on the Western range. It is a perpetual vendetta—many a gillnetter has disappeared from his boat in a heavy fog. Edith and I are agreed that men, in the matter of territorial disputes, are little different from bears and other wild beasts of the woods, which idea we return to on the relevant occasions, such as this one.

We had been telling our stories and heaping dirt upon the male sex and consequently laughing so hard that Otto and Horace came wandering back to us, feeling a bit left out, I think, and we laughed when we saw the two of them, their faces a bit pathetic, anxious to discover what they were missing—laughed until tears stood in our eyes.

I suppose I should report that in the afternoon there was a bit of a scare, the twins coming at the run to say Oscar had fallen into the river and drowned. I am used to my children bringing false reports of tragedy, and by the lights of the new mind sciences, I believe my natural complexion must be Sanguine, for I'm not one of those women who watch the horizon in dread of tornadoes and I am phlegmatic as regards small cuts and bloody noses. But the boys' faces were white, and their pants sopping past the knees, which gave my heart a cruel turn. Calamity has been delivered regularly to my door, so whenever I stand at the divide where terrible events in my life may yet come out well or badly, I generally expect to hear the dead-man whistle blow. I dashed off without my shoes, with my belt flying from its loops, following Frank and Lewis through the brush and thickets to a muddy and caved-in bank where Jules was standing wailing, but no sign of Oscar, and it was minutes of agony before I could get a coherent story from the boys, a disconnected narrative of slingshots and pebbles—a cry and a splash when Lewis let fly his missile at an obscure target in the bushes—he was sure it was Oscar. But they had not seen him go in the water, this much became clear. Where was George? There was disagreement. Frank swore he had heard George give a heroic shout—*I'll save you, Oscar!*—but Lewis thought it was Oscar himself, crying to be saved, and George must still be hiding in the shrubs—it had been a wide-ranging game of stalk-and-shoot.

By this time Horace had caught up to us—he made a show of inexcitability but was grim and white about the mouth, which frightened me as much as anything else—and then Otto and Edith, who were trailing and out of breath and entirely alarmed. We four, hanging on to the three undrowned boys, began a search. It was a small river island, perhaps two acres in extent, and you would think it an easy matter to cover every inch of ground, but it was grown over with shrubbery and thickets of alder, willow, and dogwood, and there was standing water and seepage at every hand. We had to beat tediously through every grove and woodlet, look beneath every bush, wade each and every pond; we were at it a good long while.

My first rush of unholy dread had tailed away upon hearing the whole story, and I was sure of another false alarm; but as all our shouting went unanswered, and no boys came flushing from the trees, my heart began to fidget again. I have an energetic imagination and no trouble imagining the worst: George had jumped in the water to rescue Oscar, and now they were both dead. But of course, it was all a flash in the pan, a quick bright light and a clap of thunder, but no consequence. George had cooked up the scheme to fool and scare his brothers, and engaged Oscar in it; they were hiding in a lovely deep logjam at the upstream tip of the island.

He said he was sorry, and pointedly apologized to Edith and Otto and Horace. But he is too old to whip and too smart to intimidate, and has a desperate pigheadedness which arrives by way of the male line: while I bellowed and lambasted, he sat on his driftwood and gazed off across the water with a finely conceived frown.

We trailed back to the boat in a straggling, dispirited column. Stuband walked with George—he afterward said he was trying to make him realize the pain and worry he had caused me—and so I brought up the rear, where I fell into an irrational dejection, as if the outcome of the adventure had been unfortunate. When I climbed up from the little mud beach, there was the *Telephone* on the uphill run from Astoria, passing along the far side of the island. I stood and looked.

The stubby little boats plodding by on their daily tasks get my short attention, but the big white steamers with their great stacks throwing pennants of smoke and the national ensign snapping at the king post and their chime whistles moaning, oh my, they put on a fine show, worth watching. The *Telephone* is long and lean and clean of line—she can give even the renowned *Potter* a run for the money—and from a wide outlook such as Pillar Rock or the tip of Nasset Point, I would have seen how she cuts the water away on either side, leaving long arrowheads of waves making toward the shore and a straight wake of froth behind; but from that brushy island in the Elochoman Slough there is a peculiar foreshortened view, and the packet looked to me quite as if she were floating over the island's mudflats and tidal grasses. A man was on the afterdeck, a little dark figure in a black coat, in a cloth cap, and from this distance I wouldn't have known if it was the Pope; but something in his posture started an unfortunate chord of memory, and that, together with the relief of worry, made my throat close up suddenly. The fellow was leaning his forearms on the railing and looking off across the boat's wake toward the passing shoreline, and when he saw me watching, he lifted his hand. After just a moment, I lifted mine.

> Bodily offspring I do not leave, but mental off-spring I do. Well, my books do not have to be sent to school and college and then insist on going into the Church or take to drinking or marry their mother's maid.
>
> SAMUEL BUTLER

Thurs p.m.—
Mother—
Something has come about. Dont worry. Harriet has gone missing but they are all looking for her and will find her soon,

*as she cant have gone far. She went up to the camp with Homer
on M'day morn and on W'day night was lost, which I did not
hear of until now, and all the men there are looking and say
they will find her. I am sick, but try not to worry. What can I
do? Dont come, Mother, as theres nothing to do but wait and
worry, which I am doing enough for both of us. I will send
word when shes found. Homer must he worried and very beat
in from looking for her but I should be glad if he never had
taken her up to Camp, and I would look too if they would let
me. What can I do here? I am praying for my baby girl and
ask you the same. Its in Gods hands and so I try not to worry.
I pray God is watching over my little angel. I will write when
shes found.*

Your daughter—
Florence

*The mails so slow I am sending this letter with Henneng
Sunstrom who is going out tonight to look for work in Astoria.*

Late, Fri'y 31 Mar

It seems Melba's fears have summoned up the event. We have
had a letter from Florence which is a distraught announcement
that Harriet has gone lost in the Yacolt woods. Of course, Melba
expects to be indulged in her overanxious worry, but I have a
sensible mind and have told her the affair will all be ended by
tomorrow. Since Harriet evidently went missing on Wednesday
night, and Florence did not get word of it until Thursday afternoon, she has by now already been found, and we will have the
news by tomorrow on the early boat: this is only sweet reason. And I reminded Melba of the outcome of the boys' picnic

escapade on Sunday, which is the usual outcome in such cases. But I am a poor friend, I suppose, to sit at the kitchen table and drink my coffee as deliberate as a churchman taking wine, while Melba goes on in a terrible state of nerves.

I argued with her that she ought to follow her daughter's clear advice to stay home and wait for word. "Do you think the child will be found quicker because you travel over there to Yacolt and pray from Florence's house instead of this one? Word's on its way by this time, Melba, and will pass you on a boat going downriver as you go up."

"Well, that would be all right," Melba said with her usual stubbornness and her eyebrows drawn up in a look of nervous strain and perturbation. "I guess I could stand the trip anyway, to hear that she's found. But if she's found killed"—a trembling mouth—"then I guess I would want to be there for Florence's sake." She stood and then sat again restlessly, the tips of her fingers capturing and releasing bits of twig and walnut shell and litter from the tablecloth.

She had been in midst of cracking walnuts when the news found her, sitting at this work at the kitchen table with an ear toward our reading of Elizabeth Phelps Ward's *The Silent Partner*. When the boys came to a particular moment in the reading—Mr. Hayle, the senior partner, bringing to Miss Kelso the dispatch with news of her poor father's death—this scene reminded Lewis and Frank, and they asked Melba suddenly of her news from Florence, which Melba claimed not to know, and then the story came out: Florence had sent her own dispatch not by the U.S. Mail but delivered hand to hand, first by a logging tramp who stepped off the afternoon boat only long enough to pass it to the hand of Joe Wells, who was loading fish and broke from his work to carry the folded note down

the pier to Clarence Evansen in the mill office, who brought it
from the pocket of his coat and passed it on to the twins as they
sauntered past the wharf on their way home from school. And
of course, they laid the folded and sealed sheet on the front hall
table until Melba should come in from hanging out the laundry,
and she failed to notice it, and they failed to think of it again,
believing she had read it long since. This they made up for, but
late. And poor Melba, breaking from her walnuts to read the
letter, cast me such a wild look—I suppose in that moment we
both knew: if it was an apology and peace offering intended to
smooth Melba's ruffled feathers, or a note to say Harriet had
come through her week in the woods without the loss of a limb,
it would doubtless have been posted in the usual way.

"Oh! I just knew this was bound to come to a terrible end,
this trip into the woods," Melba said dramatically, and her chin
shook with the strain. "I've had an awful, awful feeling in my
bones."

"You speak like this is Tragic Opera and you are a Gypsy
soothsayer," I told her flatly. "I daresay Harriet's not dead. We
have had a glorious week of warm and dry weather, and a child
won't be any the worse from spending a night in a hollow tree,
for heaven's sake."

It was, of course, quite easy for me to be heedless and
untroubled, this being not one of my own children; and I might
have considered Melba's feelings. She reddened in silence until
finally getting out, "That girl of Florence's is no older than your
Oscar," which rebuke was enough to shame me.

I believe her anger may have done her some little good,
though, for she then took up her nut pliers and, grim-faced,
cracked a walnut into the lap of her apron and fiercely picked
through the broken shell for nut meats; which action, from

habit, I suppose, or fretting or irritation, caused her to keep on with the shelling. A peck of unshelled nuts lay on the tabletop, nut meats filling one mason jar and half another; the emptied shells were heaped in a pan. The snap of the pliers, the hollow rattle of the shells dropping into the pan, the small dry rustle of the nut meats going into the jar became methodical, and vaguely a comfort. While I sat with my coffee and watched her at this work, I believe she forgave me for Cold Logic; and of course I also forgave her for Excitable Worry.

"Lord, I wish'd they'd been working in the burnt woods," she said in a miserable way, and I took Melba's meaning: a child lost in a fire-scorched forest was likely to be spotted, while one lost in the green brush and trees might go on hidden in that rank jungle to the crack of doom. "Lord, Lord, what was he thinking, taking Harriet up there without other women to watch out for her?"

I had no answer for this. She has spent the last many years complaining about the failings of her son-in-law, but to blame him for the loss of his own child seemed to me a heartless cruelty.

"Well, we ought to hear something more in the morning," I said firmly, and this awakened Melba's irritation.

"It's a good four days or five to get a letter between us. They shuffle that mail back and forth across two hundred miles to cover but seventy."

"Oh, I know the mails are slow as hell. I don't mean by the Post Office, Melba, of course not. But word'll be sent out with someone who's going downriver, as was done with Henneng Sundstrom. You'll hear something in the morning, from someone on the *Lurline*. You know Florence wouldn't let you go on wondering and worrying."

She said nothing in reply, and it was clear to me that she

was unpersuaded. Melba is strong in her opinions and quick to make up her mind to something; it wouldn't have surprised me if she'd stood up right then and packed her duffel and hurried off to catch the evening boat to Portland.

"Well, you'll do as you feel best, Melba, but you have my opinion. You ought to stay put until the boats have come through tomorrow. I expect word will come on the *Lurline* in the morning, but if not, then the *Potter* will bring it on the afternoon tide. Here is the hard truth, which you know as well as I do: If Harriet is to be found safe, it must happen in this first little while. If there's no good news on the *Potter* by tomorrow afternoon, well then I agree you ought to take yourself to Yacolt and wait with your daughter, because the search is liable to go on for the long haul."

Her chin began to dimple again. "That's an unfeeling thing to say," she told me, but did not deny it. In the silence that followed I began to see that I had turned her from going.

"We baked a sour cream cake, me and Harriet, while I was over there this last time," she told me desolately. "And we sung rhymes together, and I darned up the holes in her dolly."

If there was an answer for me to make, I did not discover it. I thought of putting my fingers around Melba's hands to still them from their worried shelling, but feared this might start her weeping. I'm a notoriously poor friend wherever tears are concerned.

> Many years ago a small tribe of Indians went huckleberrying on a certain prairie and some of their children were mysteriously lost. Since they could not find the children they concluded that

they had been stolen by the wild spirits of the forest. Thereupon they called the prairie Yacolt, meaning "haunted by spirits."

"ABORIGINAL PLACE NAMES
IN THE STATE OF WASHINGTON,"
American Anthropologist 9 (1907)

3 p.m. Sat'y 1 Apr '05

I have been strongly of the opinion the *Lurline* would bring things to a quick end—that word would come saying Harriet had wandered back into camp with a dirty face and a hole in her stockings; and this delay (I admit) is worrisome, though I would not say so to Melba. While the waiting goes on, I find I can't keep my mind upon my writing—made only the briefest attempt following lunch, and have now abandoned the shed and come into the house, where I am sitting in the front parlor making these notes, keeping out of the way of Melba as she carries on with her violent scrubbing of the kitchen floor; though of course we may both be interrupted if the *Potter* brings word on the evening tide, as we all expect. (Of course we will get favorable news this afternoon; I fully expect it.)

It is the *Lurline* which delivers and takes the regular mails daily on its route from Portland to Astoria, and on most occasions I'll wait for Stuband to bring or take my letters— he rows a boatload of cream to town every day, and the post office is directly on his course. We are two miles from town, but as my house sits at the eastern entrance of the Steamboat Slough, I am able to keep a close eye on the *Lurline*'s approach, and therefore if I'm anxious—in particular expectation of a posting—I can always send one of my boys in a boat as soon as she whistles, and depending on the direction of the wind and which boy it is, he may reach the wharf before they have tied up the steamer, and row back with my letter before the *Lurline* has cleared the river beacon on her way west to Pillar Rock. But with this worry about Harriet hanging over the house like a sword, I told Melba this morning that I would ride into town and meet the *Lurline* myself, as I was sure she would bring a note from Florence on the early tide. Of course, even in such circumstances as these, Melba has an abhorrence of wasted steps, so she pressed on me other errands—a pair of shoes crying for new heels, and a little list of notions to be bought—which relieved my guilt about carrying on with my own usual concerns and habits. I dressed for town with no more than ordinary irreverence, put a batch of my outbound letters and an installment of a story for *Leslie's Illustrated* in the saddlebags with Melba's shoes, and thus outfitted dear Margaret between my knees, and we pedaled off across Stuband's lumpy cow pasture and onto the downriver trail.

Just as anyone will name a steed, I have called my bicycle by the name of Margaret Le Long, a woman I read of who pedaled alone from Chicago to San Francisco in two months, carrying no more than a change of underwear and a pistol, and firing the pistol but once, when it became necessary to break up a stubborn bunch of cattle that had overrun the road somewhere west of Laramie, Wyoming. I try to take my Margaret onto the trails regularly, as she relishes a good brisk run and will not gladly suffer the weakness of a sedentary woman; but of course on the first day of April I believe I'm the only fool in Wahkiakum County attempting to ride a two-wheeled conveyance.

Given that the rain falls here for hours and days and weeks at a time, and the ground consequently is a quagmire nine months of the year, and inasmuch as the state of Washington cannot be persuaded to let hold of its fistful of tax money for such superfluity as road building in remote precincts such as ours, the principal roads hereabouts are the running streams, sloughs, and rivers. Every child of five is a crackerjack boat handler. I'm as lively a sailor as the next man but continue my practice of bicycling year around on the principle of modernity and the hope of scandal, and for the further reason that a bicycle depends on neither the tides nor the wind, and my experiment with walking on water has proved a failure—I could not correct a troubling tendency to overbalance upon the pontoons and end up on my head in the slough.

The greater part of our local Indian trails must surely be 2,000 years old, for so long has there been continuous settlement at the mouth of Skamokawa Creek, but such proven tracks run upon the ridges and uplands, whereas the two-mile track from my yard to town runs beside the Steamboat Slough, which is tidewater, and the trail only barely passable at certain times of the day and certain seasons of the year. Of course I have necessarily made myself used to riding in mud and I never give up holding tight to the handlebars and keeping a sharp eye on the ditches and potholes; I've flown off my saddle and laid open the skin of elbows and knees from coming down that imperfect path with too little caution.

Conversely, there is nothing that points up the modernity of these times so much as the miles of wooden causeway various Skamokawans have built right across mud, marsh, and slough in a spider's web of boardwalks connecting one neighbor with another, church with parsonage, mill with mess hall, boat works with float house. Old Peder Goehring's place, while yet a mile from town proper, is the nearest outpost of boardwalk, and at

Goehring's I am able to leave the Steamboat trail, lift Margaret onto the boards, and be finished with mud.

Poor old Goehring is a Finn and a Republican, and consequently a man of considerable conservatism. He was standing on his boat landing when I pedaled by him, and so, for effect, I made of his boardwalk a bicycle speedway; and having raised up a fine wind, I thrust out my boot heels and went freewheeling. His shout of contempt, when it came to me on the spring air, was a particular pleasure on a morning grievously short of them.

There's a great deal of foolishness been written about the dangers of the bicycling craze. As regards women, the intoxication of flying through the streets under ones own power is said to lead to unspecified, doubtless shameful, acts of immorality, and on those worrisome grounds I frequently bicycle into town wearing a man's getup and smoking a cigar. If I had foreseen the poor outcome to the morning, I might have adopted a more solemn decorum in respect of Melba's situation, but as it was, I rolled down to the town limit and stood a minute, holding Margaret to my trousered leg while I nipped the end from a cigar and got it puffing. Two men were surveying a field there between the boat works and the shingle mill, and they gave me a little inspection; Bob Vandewater, who was sitting on a stump watching them work, took me nonchalantly. News of Harriett's misadventure has been kept very close within the family the boys given strict instructions and threatened with torturous consequences should they tell, as Melba does not wish her husband to learn the news and use it as an excuse to loudly drown in his beer. So Vandewater, being therefore ignorant of events, said only, "Hullo, Mizz Drummond, you need a light?" without much looking away from what interested him. It was his field that was being measured. The log business is booming just now and the town with it, as may be evidenced by the Alger Slough bridge, which is a wondrous piece of work with a 135-feet draw; I suppose Vandewater, with that bridge in mind, will make this cutover land into town lots and sell them for an unseemly profit. He is a man of commerce.

"No, Vandewater, I'd never take a light from a man," I said to him with no more than my normal disaffection, and soon afterward Margaret and I were mounted up again and rolling over the boardwalk to the U.S. Post Office.

Until lately, the Skamokawa post office had made its home in the sawmill, where it occupied a corner of the mill company's store, but in recent weeks has come into a leased building at the narrow, downriver tip of the island, on the wharf between the sawmill and the boat works. These are swank accommodations, sporting new shelving and counters, fine coal oil lamps, and a long porch for sheltering postal customers out of the rain, as well as a handsome sign locating the place for the ever-transient population of loggers, seiners, and cannery crew. We might have had, as well, a cancel machine of the very latest design, a quite glorious mechanical marvel, if we had not had at the time a postmaster with a deep distrust of mechanization. He received the thing with suspicion and promptly gave it to the mill, where others more mechanically inclined, and having no qualms about the progress of technology, made it over into a lumber planer.

Belva Gardner is now the postmistress. She is a widow woman of about fifty or so whose three grandchildren have been left in her care. The mother of those children was killed by mud slide on the Deep River trail, and Gardner's son, who had fathered them, brought them to his mother to keep until he could acquire another wife. Seeing as how he's a faller who lives in the woods among a population of other men, everyone's expectation is that those children are now Belva Gardner's to raise. The youngest of them, Lucille, was seated on the post office floor with her shift hiked up to her hips and her elbows pinched between a pair of skinned and scabby knees. This is a girl about Harriet's age, thin and pale like Harriet, which must be why it gave me a little jolt to see her doll-baby resting lightly in her lap, its several holes neatly darned. "Hello, Lucille," I said. Being Oscar's age, she has often played in our yard, but she bent her head shyly when I spoke to her, and her lips and eyes directed a murmury stream toward the doll: secrets in a secret language.

I put the big *Leslie*'s envelope on the postal scale and dug pennies from my pants pocket after the fashion of a man, while Belva Gardner stood behind the counter in green eyeshade and sleeve protectors, pushing the little weight along its bar to the balance point. "This must go out on the boat as soon as possible," I said to her, meaning the envelope for *Leslie*'s. She said, "It will," in the disinterested and negligent way of civil servants everywhere, which encouraged me to say, in the vain hope of impressing her, "They're waiting for it in New York, and it must go to proof by the twenty-eighth of April." Belva is a petty despot, who gave me a second look as flat as the first and said, "It'll go out on the *Lurline* when she comes," as her hand pushed the entire of my mail carelessly out of sight under the edge of the counter.

There being as yet no sign at all of the steamboat, I retrieved Margaret from where she leaned at the front of the post office and we pushed on around the sawmill and behind the mess hall and the office of the *Skamokawa Eagle* to the bridge. When you have come around the end of the island to face Nasset Point, then you can see that Skamokawa is laid out in a rather pretty way, built on pilings over the water and meandering along the several river sloughs and up the several forks of Skamokawa Creek.

All the business buildings face their fronts to the water so that, without a street between, the waterways are the streets, and the high wharfs the sidewalks. Narrow wooden causeways, railed to save drunkards from falling off, span the low places between the pilings, and on the mainland a string of boardwalks run upward from the waterfront to houses on the higher ground behind the stores. Little Venice, people are wont to call this town, which I believe is from an excess of civic pride. Nevertheless, whenever fair weather graces a Regatta day, I find I must shout "Huzzah!" with the rest of them when the decorated boats parade up the little bright harbor into the water streets.

The Skamokawa anchorage is both deep and sheltered; log booms lie in the sloughs in bad weather, and there are a few small hand-logging outfits who skid down to the river and hang their booms in the Columbia River, east and west of the town. We are long in years, as Western towns go, and in the self-conscious manner of the logging West, much is made of the "old days" before the donkey engine—the days of ox teams and bull-whackers and monstrous trees so immense as to challenge the imagination. Now the big trees have all been cut for miles around, and there is a packet that stops daily on a westbound trip to Astoria, and another on an eastbound to Kalama, Ridgefield, and Portland, and we get every kind of local river traffic—tugs and trawlers as well as rowboats and barges. We are, if not entirely civilized, entirely modern, and consider ourselves at the center of Western commerce and industry.

The walks this day were overrun with men. The first day of April, which might be considered at the outside edge of the logging season, had brought to town an early swarm of loggers and millmen, cruisers and pulp-concession men, and this rare spate of sun had brought them out of the saloons and promenading along the wharfs. I had put on wool pants and lace-up boots, together with a collarless logger's shirt and woolly vest, and outfitted thus, pedaling muddy Margaret over the bridge and into town, I was gawkingstock. There's not much point in dressing outlandishly if it goes unnoticed, is my belief, and so I've refrained from cutting short my hair, which has been advocated by certain Feminists as being both liberating and sensible. I have a big and squarish sort of face, very strong around the chin, and my eyebrows, by a woman's standards, ought to be plucked, as they're thick and dark without the least delicacy of an arch; in men's clothes I would fear being taken entirely for a man if not for my hair, which is a womanly crown, thick and with an inclination to wave, and of a chestnut red not yet gone to gray. When I put on men's clothes, I pin up my hair in a proper Psyche knot, loose and charmingly curled at the nape, so there's no mistaking my sex, and this gains me the desired effect when displayed against the cigar and clothes of a workingman. On the wharf, men who had newly come to town just stood and took a long look. Skamokawa people are hardened to my ways, though, and as a sign of their Western liberalism will make a show of imperturbability. Shopmen and farmers I knew tipped their hats with aplomb; which courtesy I returned by briskly dipping my lit cigar with my clenched teeth.

There are two bootmakers on the wharf, one a Swede named Orvil Jurgensen and one a Chinaman whose name is unknown to everyone and believed irrelevant, since he has always answered to China Sam. China Sam is the only Celestial in Skamokawa who does not come and go with the cannery season, a distinction sufficient in itself to inspire my confidence. When I had left

Melba's shoes with him, and gone to Thatcher's for the needles and matches and baking powder on her list, and wandered in and out of the confectioner's on my own account, and put the little paper packages of notions and candies in the basket at Margaret's head, we went (merry as a cricket, I'm afraid) down again to the wharf to await the *Lurline*.

And when the packet came and went without news of any kind, well, it took me aback. Of course, we will get a favorable letter this afternoon—I am fairly sure of it. But watching the *Lurline* steam away without word at all from Yacolt—just for that moment—I suffered a sudden terrible misgiving as to how this adventure might come out. And I suppose that moment of misgiving is to blame for my poor behavior afterward.

I should have gone (of course) straightaway back to Melba with word that there was no word (and for not doing it, I have since been vehemently condemned). But I imagined she would come to this discovery on her own when the *Lurline* steamed past the house and I did not come flying back at once with a wild look of triumph or of grief; and in my lowered mood, I frankly dreaded returning myself to the orbit of her overanxious hysteria. When I had stood some little while in disorder, watching the *Lurline* out of sight, I took it suddenly into my mind to go up the hill and see Joseph Sheets.

He has queer ways, old Sheets, and the common run of the rabble is that he is a lunatic. Since I am held to be something of a lunatic too, I consider the old man a confederate. He has a little shack on top of a high hill that overlooks the three forks of Skamokawa Creek, and the light from his cabin at the summit can be seen from nearly any farm up the left, right, or middle fork—a night beacon for travelers. He is a recluse in most respects, though he will come down from his hill to lay in rice and flour, and on those occasions has been known to involve himself in a card game or two and play on through the night. He grows tobacco and strawberries on a couple of acres he has cleared at the top of his hill, and will sell to anyone who comes up there to buy them. Mother sent Teddy and me up that steep trail every strawberry season, and it was old Sheets (though he must not have been old in those days; do you suppose he was forty?) who taught my brother and me to roll tobacco leaves and smoke them, the most vile kind of cigars.

It's always my intent to conquer Sheets's hill without dismounting, and I believe this is something I will one day accomplish; but it will have to be on a day when the mud is not sticky. In April, of course, it's a hopeless ambition. I went up resolutely, standing on the pedals, but after a short, sweaty exercise, I stood off and pushed Margaret heavily up through the long aisle in the trees. That trail of his, not being of Wahkiakum Indian origin, is laid out in the White Man's imperfect way, plunging almost directly up from the river bluff to the hilltop. The trees all grow straight from the sidehill, while the ground bears off sharply beneath them, and of course the rain gathers itself and shoots down the trail to the river just as if it were a log flume. In certain weathers, a person laboring uphill against the muddy stream can't stand and get her wind, or, standing, she'll begin to slide down again; and going down the hill the hind end of a bicycle is liable to slew around and pass the front end.

At the edge of Sheets's cleared field I put Margaret to rest against a tree and went on, as broken winded as an old horse, until I had come out on the highest point. I stood awhile getting back my breath, and then I just stood and looked, because I had come up for the clear day, the view, as much as the old man. And here is the truth: I had come also for the irrational purpose of "looking" for Harriet, which doubtless some people will think is a species of prayer from a woman who does not believe in prayer, and which of course I deny.

From that certain point at the top of Sheets's hill, in limpid air, you can see the Columbia from Cathlamet Head to Grays Point, the bright water littered with islands and scalloped with little inlets. You can see the drift logs piled white along the narrow beaches, and the gray ribbons of the sloughs looping across the lowlands in a deep-laid design that from the water is unknowable. You can see bristling dead poles of burnt timber showing against bare mottled rock amid the immeasurable forests of the Nehalem Mountains as they break in long blue ridges southward across the sky; and the unapproachably distant peaks of Hood and St. Helens adrift like pyramidal icebergs at the edge of a purplish sea. From the top of Sheets's hill, if the weather is soft, you can hear the low moan of the Columbia River bar more than twenty miles to the west.

But in that immensity of woods and mountains and waters a person can also see the horses and men laboring on the fish-seining grounds at Welch's Island, and gillnet boats upon their drifts upstream and down, and salmon traps near Puget Island, and columns of smoke from a dozen sawmills and from the Altoona Cannery. There are cleared fields and the dark dots of houses all up and down the valley bottoms, and of course everywhere the high flaring stumps of cut trees and shattered small timber where the loggers have been at work. I was struck, suddenly, by the sense of a human presence upon the wilderness, which was a reassurance and comfort more rational to me than any prayer.

When I had taken in about all the reassurance there was, I called for Sheets and walked down through the berry rows to his little place, calling again. He will come out to you with a tender grin or hide in the trees and wait until you've looked, and called, and gone; this is Sheets.

I had about given up and left a little folio of peppermints tucked into his door latch when he evidently made me out from his hiding place in the brush and broke cover at last. "Well, see who that is," he said to the air, "it's Mr. Charlie Bridger," which is an old childhood name he has always attached to me, and I replied, "Yes, it's me, Sheets, I'm glad to see you," and I gave the peppermints into his hand.

He has a rank smell of tobacco about him, and I suppose it's tobacco to blame for the yellowing of his beard, but he is strongly built, his old features clean and angular, "shaped with an axe," as my mother would say about him, and I believe he must have been catmint to women when he was young and sane. Skamokawa gossip has Sheets coming west as a result of a broken engagement, and though he is now quite unmarriageable, a thoroughgoing hermit of odd habits, suppose there are women who would accept him nonetheless on the strength of rumors: he is thought to keep a box of gold coins buried in his yard.

I offered him one of my Kentucky cigars and lit my own stub again, and we smoked together companionably. "Well, Sheets," I said, "here are your dry spring days," for Sheets's foretellings of the coming year's weather have always been widely celebrated, and the *Skamokawa Eagle* annually has sent someone to ask after his predictions. Last January's clipping is still pinned to the wall of my kitchen. *"Sky'll clear up a good week in all, around the end of March,"* pronounced the Skamokawa Weather Prophet, *and upon being reminded that the town receives an average fifteen inches of rain in the month of March, replied, "Well I guess rain will fall hard on the other twenty-five of the days."*

He solemnly pulled on the cigar while he considered my remark, and then, with a practiced slanting motion of his head, released a plume of smoke toward the sky. "It's a mystery of the Lord, I expect."

I have heard of hermits more intent on their solitude than Sheets. There is a couple living eight miles up the Left Fork who grow their own garden, hay field, berries, and fruit, and have been to town only twice in anyone's memory, each time the wife arriving in her wedding suit and high-topped old shoes. And my dog, Buster, may be crazier than old Sheets: he is afraid of certain dread spots in the front hallway and the kitchen, and will go to any lengths to keep from stepping upon them. What I believe may be Sheets's singular glory is his raising of tobacco in a climate such as this one, where the sun arriving on the first of April must be pronounced a mythic creature, and a sign of God's wonders.

While we strolled up and down admiring his rows of strawberries, the small rosettes of new green growth among the brown and withered leaves of the summer past, I asked after his prospects for a good crop and listened as he told the coming weather and in his customary way tolled the names of the dead, among them his sisters and his mother and old acquaintances of his childhood. He lives alone, and I've always understood his lunacy to be a kind of loneliness. But when he walked me back across the hill to Margaret he began suddenly to give me his advice about the little witches who will come and live right under the floor of your house if you let them, and must be driven out by pouring boiling water through the cracks; and this brought me up a little.

In my childhood, if Sheets had carried a pistol in his belt and cited the old poets, I suppose Teddy and I would have made him over into a Hero, but as it was, we thought he was a holy oracle, a Wizard. Sitting with him at the top of his hill, the three of us soberly smoking, we would often ask for his prophesies on matters more momentous to us than the weather: *Will the flood get as high as our house? Will Pearl's calf be a heifer? Will Lester's runt puppy die?* And without knowing who Lester was, or any of the other circumstances of our question, he would simply take the cigar from his mouth and answer yes or no; and the future, we knew, would be sealed.

Of course, it's been years since I've asked for one of Sheets's divinations or believed in them. But walking back across his hill—I don't know why—I had meant to ask the old man whether Harriet would be safely found. And I suppose it was his quiet rant which closed my mouth; or I had a qualm of good sense, or of dread.

> When anything in [my books] is rather strange and *outré*, it is probably drawn straight from nature as close as I could draw it; when it is plausible, there is probably no particular and especial foundation for it.
>
> SAMUEL BUTLER

On the boat landing (Skamokawa), Sat'y night

I write this hurriedly while the *Telephone* is making her approach.

It is a mild paradox, I suppose, that plots taken from real life often are the harder to believe. In the dime novel, misadventure and misfortune are discreetly foreshadowed; one expects a heroine to suffer adversity and equally expects the outcome to be favorable. In real life such events are more often defined by

their absolute unexpectedness and the indeterminacy of the outcome. Extraordinary things happen in real life and extraordinary
coincidences occur, but I daresay a deft pen must make them
plausible before they can be delivered to the pages of a novel. I
should not have dared to write a fiction so improbable as this:
on the *T. J. Potter* came word that Harriet, after all, may not have
wandered away lost; that she may have been seized by a giant
wild ape and carried off to his lair in the woods, which possibility was at first kept from Florence to spare her from torment.

Melba and I fell out entirely over this news. She received it
as a ghastly truth and collapsed prematurely into horror and
grief; I would not take the story seriously enough and made of
it a barbarous joke. "Jacko the Chimpanzee has made his escape
from Barnum's, then," I said to her, "and has come back to the
woods to take his revenge on little children."

She turned to me a wildly rabid look, which I felt I must
parry with reasonable theories: "This was a bear, Melba, or some
hirsute old tramp in his flapping rags."

Inasmuch as Harriet continued missing, these words were
both blind and cruel, which I knew as soon as they were out of
my mouth. Melba's whole face folded inward and I could not
think how to recover my damn-fool mistake. We stood in the
front hall, bound in a malignant silence.

"What is 'hirsute'?" Jules whispered. I had forgotten him
standing there, with his fists wrapped in my skirt, and children have an instinct for understanding when argument has
transcended the ordinary and become dangerous: his eyes were
round and white with alarm. "Hairy," I said, and rested my
palm on the crown of his head. "'Hirsute' is hairy. Run over to
Eustler's and ask Edith to come and see me. And then run over
to Stuband's and ask how his mother cows are doing. Tell him I

sent you over. You can help him pull calves, if any of his mother cows are so inclined."

Though pulling calves has been denied to him in the past on grounds of his young age, he was not distracted from his fear. He took a deeper grip of my dress and screwed up his mouth to cry.

I stooped and took his face firmly in my two hands. "Go get Edith and then go over to Stuband's," I said, in the voice I reserved for Serious Matters Involving Punishment. I peeled his fingers from their clench and pushed him to the porch. When the door closed between us, he burst out crying and went off in the general direction of Eustler's.

"You aren't right, the way you deal with that boy," Melba said bitterly. "He's high strung."

"He's thin-skinned, and will have to get over it," I told her. Then I said, "We'll take the *Telephone* on the flood tide, Melba. I'll farm the little boys out to Edith, and Stuband can look in on George and the twins, who ought to be old enough to fend for themselves."

She was evidently startled. "I don't need you to see after me."

"What you need is someone of a clear mind and fit for a tramp afoot and horseback, who can go out from Yacolt to that deepwoods camp and learn the truth of what has happened to Harriet."

Her clenched face examined me with considerable distrust. I would not have been surprised by further argument, but in a bit she wrung her chapped hands together and began silently to weep.

"Oh now, Melba, don't," I said.

"Well, I try to consider your comfort, but you can't always be spared other women's tears," she said crossly. She pressed her knuckles to her eyes and went on standing with her hands at her face, sobbing quietly. At long last she withdrew an embroidered hanky from her pocket and wiped her eyes with it. "There," she said, folding the handkerchief to a precise square once again, "I'm finished for now. I'll go up and pack my duffel." Which I took to mean I should go up and pack mine.

Of course, there was considerable alarm and argument from Horace Stuband, who is entirely a man of his times, that is to say hidebound and proper. If he was scandalized at the prospect of my traipsing into logging camps unaccompanied, he did not say so, but made his argument—that he should go in my place— by raising foremost the question of danger, as if a woman may not stand up to a wild, fierce life as well as a man; and of course the question of strength, and stamina, and heart, in case the search should go on long or lead to horror. I blame a too-narrow imagination for his failure to mention death at the hands of an orang-utan. I said to him, "A woman can and should do everything a man can do, and do it without ceasing to be female," which he has heard me say before. "Waiting For Word," I further told him, "has often been the female portion but shall never be mine if I can help it."

And here is the boat. We are off.

WHAT IS IT?
A Strange Creature Captured Above Yale
A British Columbia Gorilla
Yale, B.C., July 3rd, 1882.

"Jacko," as the creature has been called by his capturers, is something of the gorilla type, standing about four feet seven inches in height and weighing

127 pounds. He has long, black, strong hair and resembles a human being with one exception, his entire body, excepting his hands (or paws) and feet, is covered with glossy hair about one inch long. His fore arm is much longer than a man's fore arm, and he possesses extraordinary strength, as he will take hold of a stick and break it by wrenching or twisting it, which no man living could break in the same way. Since his capture he is very reticent, only occasionally uttering a noise which is half bark and half growl. He is, however, becoming daily more attached to his keeper, Mr. George Tilbury, of this place, who proposes shortly starting for London, England, to exhibit him. His favorite food so far is berries, and he drinks fresh milk with evident relish. By advice of Dr. Hannington raw meats have been withheld from Jacko, as the doctor thinks it would have a tendency to make him savage.

The Daily Colonist
(Port of Victoria, British Columbia)

On the Telephone, early a.m., 2 Apr

At the front of my mind is a thicket of worries to do with Harriet, of course, and Melba, and my children left behind; in the middle ground there are half a hundred lesser concerns, such as the state of our pregnant cow and whether the Brussels sprouts standing ripe in the garden will go neglectfully to seed in my absence; what lies dimly at the back of my mind is a small, irrepressible tremor of excitement. As the *Telephone* bore us away from the Skamokawa landing in foreboding midnight darkness, there was a whispering, ignoble voice within me which said, *We are two women entering on a wilderness adventure.*

We have not been tempted to waste money on a berth, for all the little cabins are taken, and in fact several men are sleeping on the passage floors. The women's saloon is crowded and restless with children, which is the worst situation for Melba, so we are sleeping sitting up in the smoking room, or rather we drowse there, for a number of men play cards all night, and their murmury voices and the soft ripple of shuffled cards, as well as the spitting of tobacco, keep up without cease. Once, when I had dreamt in a shallow way, I woke to find Melba asleep in the deck chair opposite to mine, displaying a clenched frown that pulled her eyebrows right in to her nose. I am well acquainted with her black look, for it's brought out at every tedious aggravation, but just then with her body slumped in the chair, seeming shrunken and aged with this bad news from Yacolt, it struck me that her face was engraved by sorrow. My little writerly fancies, my childish plots involving the two of us in bravery and derring-do and perilous rescue, all of that was beaten back suddenly by a terrible clear vision of Harriet raped and strangled. I put my hand to my heart, the quick drum-drumming, and then I had to stand as quietly as I could manage and creep out through the cigar smoke, past the frank inspection of the card players, to the afterdeck, where the cold rain was a distraction and there was no sound but the steady thumping of the engines, and I stood a long while, heavy, leaning as against a brute force, staring across the black water, the black wind, to the dim moving line of the river shore.

This was, after all, not the best thing for my state of mind, as I never have learned to ride the river at night without falling into an old morose train of thought. I began to follow my misgivings about Harriet down a dark and secret path, and shortly I was brooding about Wes. Why is it, do you suppose, we are so at the mercy of Memory?

"Is you feeling ill, miss?"

I said no, I most surely was not, and what I was feeling was the need to be Alone, all this even before seeing who it was, a broad-necked old Swede of the sort to grow a beard in winter and shave it when the weather warms up, a line of thick blond brows shading his eyes, a florid complexion. I had an intent to be rude, but he failed to take notice of it and settled his big arms on the rail to the left of me. "Well, good then. I seen you go pale and wondered if it was the boat gived it, or the smoke, or what."

"It was the What," I said, which made him blink and smile in confusion. But shortly he took another run at the situation and began to entertain me with information on the keeping of bees—I recall fire-weed spoken of with approval. These bee stories gave way at last to fish stories, for his honey deliveries all up and down the river evidently leave him with sufficient time to dig clams and to fish for perch, and he is proud minded as regards his long casts off the rocks at Seaview.

The greater number of these old Scandinavian bachelors are a quiet type who must be poked and whipped before they can be made to speak, but the odd one will be burdened with an excess of energy and a sore need for female company, and this was evidently such a one. Without so much as a word of encouragement from me, he gave an account of the major events of his life, including the cracked skull he suffered from falling "arse over tea kettle" while shoe-skating on the frozen mud-puddles of Tenasillahe Island; events of the Great Flood of '92, in which he hooked and landed an entire house filled with all its possessions

as it floated by him on the river; and the heartbreaking accidental death of his dog Frazer, a brown-and-white spaniel which he
had unknowingly rolled over with the wheels of his own wagon.

These stories might have been entertaining if he'd had the
knack for telling them, but he was the sort to argue with himself over every small detail—*It was We'nsdee the ninth, no, musta
bean the tenth, no, I's right the first time, was the ninth, morning of
the ninth, or shortly after I'd had m' lunch*—and as a result I lost
patience the longer he kept at it, and became flat-out surly in
my responses. It could be that rough treatment is wasted on
a man of his good nature, for he wore on at a deliberate pace,
emptying his sack of stories, and presently I gave up listening.
While the old Swede prattled, I began to get our ducks in a row.

My experience of traveling is an odd mare's nest: I have
twice crossed over the nation, and have a passing familiarity
with the Capitol Building in Washington, and the Metropolitan
Opera House in the city of New York, but on the other hand,
after nearly thirty years' acquaintance with the logging and
fishing country of the lower Columbia, I never have been in
Yacolt, indeed few places in the state of Washington aside from
the Skamokawa environs, and few in Oregon save Astoria and
Portland and the steamer landings between them. Howsomever,
every mill town resembles every other, and getting into the
backwoods requires a private understanding of bad roads rather
more than anything else.

The *Telephone* will deliver us to the foot of Alder Street, city
of Portland, where we must then hire a cab to the train yard
and get onto a lumber train bound over the bridge and through
the woods to Yacolt. This will be the easy part, for the trains
run three or four times a day in and out of every booming log
town, bringing down the logs and trailing a Daylight car for the

millmen and loggers, timber cruisers, and the occasional wife or mother; we are likely to gain Florence's doorstep by lunch.

Beyond Yacolt, the way is less clear. They will have laid track out into the timber and built camps at the ends of the spurs, a great pin-wheel of industry and destruction, and one or another of those rails will bring me more or less in the direction of Homer's camp at Canyon Creek. From there I shall have to try to catch a ride with a millman supplied of mule or horse; and failing that, I must walk. In either case, I've every expectation of deep ruts and mud holes, narrow embankments, and wicked steep climbs. These backwoods camps are notorious for their remoteness.

From the Canyon Creek camp, if the search has not come to a pass by then, I fully mean to make myself part of it. Beyond that is impossible of imagination.

I have not met a man with better feet than mine, but my neck is wobbly and won't take a heavy pack. I have come away from the house with clothes and boots for a tramp, and my purse crammed with soda crackers and cheese, but a full provisioning waits for Yacolt; while the Swede sang on, I exercised my brain with a thoroughly abstemious list of rations. And when at last he cheerfully lifted his cap and sauntered off in search of another feminine audience, I found I had quite recovered my spirits. I have a mind that relishes a plan.

> For the trip one needs to be as unhampered by clothes as possible. Men always seem to know what to wear; or at least, they never confess that they are uncomfortable; but all women have not learned the lesson yet. An active woman can get

along well for a month's tramp with two short
skirts and one jacket of some stout material, as
corduroy or denim; bloomers and leggins of the
same goods, or at least the same color; strong
shoes, not too heavy, but with a thick sole con-
taining Hungarian nails, for tramping, and a
lighter pair to rest one's feet in camp; a sunbonnet
and a soft canvas hat; a few darkish shirt waists of
cotton crepe which will wash easily and not need
ironing; some stout gloves; two changes of underwear; one flannelette nightgown, and a golf cape,
or a heavy shawl. She will need hairpins galore to
keep tidy and all the necessities of a workbag.

"HOUSEKEEPING IN THE SUMMER CAMP,"
Sunset Magazine, May 1902

Wesley

The man put his folded newspaper in the pocket of his coat and
his hands into his trouser's pockets and stood with his shoulders
hunched, waiting for his wife to stop fiddling with the boy's
shoelaces. The wife had released her infant son into the arms
of her eldest, and then, to guard against the possibility of the
boy stumbling with the baby, she had squatted to tie up the
muddy laces trailing rearward from his muddy shoes. The boy
was ten. He twisted his shoulders anxiously, shifting his eyes up
and down the wharf in fear of being seen while his mother, with
her skirts gathered around her knees, was crouched at his feet.

Their other sons were with them on the boat landing. The
youngest—that is, the one who had been youngest before the
birth of this last child—stood between his next-older brothers,

gripping a hand of each. His brothers, who might usually have squeezed and twisted his fingers until he cried, assumed an uncommon attitude of nervous solemnity, and all three stood in a tableau, shifting their feet restlessly, watching the wood go aboard, and the transfer of the mail, eyeing the pilot and the passengers. Their manner was fueled by a kind of foreboding. Sometime in the dim and distant past—months ago—their father had used to take a boat regularly, but the boys viewed those earlier days as if through a long lens, and understood their father's departure now to be unusual and exotic, a cause for gravity and formality.

The restless dignity of his children made the man anxious to be gone. He wished to jump straight over this moment so that he might be sitting in the stove heat of the *Hassalo*, unfolding his newspaper, arguing mildly with other men about the coming currency crisis, the dogs of Wall Street, the doings of Harriman and James J. Hill. He fingered the coins in his trouser's pocket and gazed off across the water to the cloud mass dragging past the mountain slopes, its rooster tails of mist. The river was ridged with whitecaps in the path of a wind slanting eastward into the gorge.

"Do you have your sandwich?" his wife said to him, standing finally between her oldest son and her husband. Dinner on the *Hassalo* was lavish and cheap—Jerusalem artichokes and smoked chicken, plums, peppered steak—an entire smorgasbord for four bits; but he and his wife were guarding their money, and his coat pockets were weighty with Grape-Nuts and cheese.

"Yes," he said irritably, and his small bristling-up caused his wife to tighten her smile. She touched his sleeve, which she meant as a kind of apology.

In a moment he pulled his hands from his trousers and took

her hands in them. He had, in the days before this, helped his neighbor with dressing his hogs, had traded this labor for hams, and the work had coarsened his palms. He was conscious of it, and of his wife's palms, smooth and cold and slightly damp. She had held on to her housekeeper through the months of their money troubles, which he understood was necessary; he didn't understand why his wife's hands, which were not work-roughened, caused him to feel bitterly used.

"All right," he said irrelevantly, and she mistook this for *I'll write*. "No novels, please. I shouldn't want the competition." Her teasing of him was ineluctable, one of the wry and clever things that had endeared her to him and now was sometimes a provocation. The man was glad to be escaping his wife for these several days. But he understood, also, that he would inevitably begin to yearn for her opinion of things, and that he would begin to save up the small events of his days in order to share them with her.

"Whether they hire me or don't, I'll get home on the Sunday boat," he said. They had been over this, and he could see that she was unwilling to go over it again. He had meant it as a kind of signal, an indication of his affection for her, and so he understood her impatience as a kind of signal too, and realized suddenly that his eyes had filled with tears. She found his tears amusing, or shameful, and kissed him with a light laugh. "It's not the ends of the earth," she said.

Marriage, the woman had discovered, was nothing close to what she had imagined when she had been newly wed: was less romantic, more mundane, made up of small compromises and irritations, agreements and misunderstandings, and a gradual accumulation of common memories. They were both romantically inclined, but her husband had a more sentimental nature

than her own, and he viewed their marriage as having lost a
good deal of its passion. The woman was not aware of his feeling
and considered the loss of passion in their marriage to be the
natural and unregrettable order of things.

He picked up each of the younger boys in turn and squeezed
him to his chest; he touched his lips tenderly to the infant's
cheek. He and his wife had lately agreed that their oldest son
was too well grown for his father's embraces, and so he only
cupped the boy's head briefly, a hand around his cold ear. Then
he put his arms around his wife and briefly placed his mouth
against her temple, before escaping over the planks onto the
steamer.

The *Hassalo* was wallowy and slow in foul weather but
nicely fitted out with brass lamps and Brussels carpets, polished
chrome stoves, stewards in white coats. Bundles of dead grouse
and pheasant hung in the cool shadows of the boat gangways.
He pushed up the stair and through the warm, smoky air of
the men's cabin, out to the afterdeck, where he stood watching while the mooring lines were cast off. His wife had taken
the baby into her arms, and their oldest son now stood with
the bunch of littler boys, affecting a manly posture of hands in
pockets. When the boat began to slide away from the landing,
his wife shifted the infant's weight in her arms, holding the baby
more upright as if displaying it for him, or allowing the baby to
send him her last greeting. He looked away over the choppy
water, distracted by a flurry of birds hoisting their bodies into
the damp air, and when he looked again his sons were scattering up the wharf, running and shouting, but his wife was still
standing with the baby, watching after the boat. The wind had
brought some of her hair down from its chignon, and she bent
her head to one side slightly, attempting to capture the loose

lock against her collar. It was already impossible for him to see the features of her face, but this gesture was so particular to her that his throat swelled suddenly with familiar, abiding affection. She swayed a bit, and then he realized that she had freed her arm, was lifting it to him, waving; and after just a moment he raised his own.

There was a cold wind on the afterdeck, and as he straightened, gathering himself to go in the cabin, he realized he was basely happy—delivered, briefly, from the strains of ordinary living, which in recent months had been not ordinary but in extremis.

The woman went on standing on the pier after her husband had taken himself inside the cabin of the *Hassalo*. This was not due to any inkling or premonition, but from a wish to put off returning to the house—the five boys demanding her continual attention. She was a spirited young woman who enjoyed solitude and reading and writing but found herself engulfed by the demands of her children. She considered herself an unnatural mother, lacking in the native affections and patience she believed to be given to other women. She had only recently come through the tiring, insistent first weeks of caring for the baby, the physical absorption of it, and had fallen into—not suffering, really, but feeling unloved and put-upon and irritable. At night, with the baby crying and miserable with colic, she had grown tireder and tireder, and the anguish of having no time for herself, not even the time necessary to keep a diary—of finding her day cut into small and smaller pieces—this anguish visited her at night. She was half inclined to cry at being unable to devote herself entirely to her work, though she considered the work only a means to an end, which was the support of her family. In later years she would discover that the work was everything to her—everything—but now she tossed and tossed, trying to explain and defend something that shifted and was elusive; and at such times she had secretly—horrifyingly—wished for a calamity that would free her of the weight, the otherwise inescapable burden, of her maternity.

She believed that she had lately carried another weight, which was her husband—as if he were drowning and she must save him; as if she were swimming hard toward a distant shore with both her husband and her children depending from her arms and shoulders, and her legs scissoring through the water as she labored to keep all of them above the chop of the waves.

❦ *My mother was a single-woman homesteader for twelve years after her husband's death and knew a thing or two about independence, which prepared me to take an uncustomary view of women's roles. And after all, I lived far back on the frontier, very far from the artificial restraints by which most girls are hedged in. I had the good fortune to "run wild," which is exactly the activity that develops a good physique and an unconventional mind.*

Of course, after my mother's death my life as an unbroken colt was brought to its end; I was sent out east to live with my mother's sister. I recall little of the rail trip save that I was bridled and saddled in cumbrous long skirts, corsets, and high heels, my hair bound up with pins, and so forth; and that I spent a good deal of energy in tirades against fate, and in daydreams which I suppose were despairing attempts to find some outlet for my wildness. I would flee to Paris, or to Alaska. Run off to the Territories and marry an Apache. "If only I were a man," I wrote in my diary, "I would mount an expedition and conquer the South Pole."

In my first days and weeks in New York, I lay on my bed at night

and imagined myself captured by Indians, and through my bravery and derring-do winning a place as their woman chief. When I
explained the Indian political view to the white generals, they were
moved to tears and set aside the richest lands as a sovereign Indian
nation. My photograph appeared in Eastern newspapers above the cap-
tion "She likes to ride hard and speak her mind." And then I was in
love. The man I loved was a Frenchman come west to study the Indian
languages, and for his health. He placed himself in my tutelage and
was soon bewitched by my prowess as a horsewoman, as a leader of my
adopted peoples, and as a communicator with animals and the spirit
world. When I had overseen his return to health, we were married,
though shortly afterward he was killed by men who had meant their
bullets for me.

Then I went to New Orleans and surrounded myself with intelligent men—artists and writers—with whom I talked, discussed, and
argued, and female friends who were my confidantes in matters of
romantic love. What is the meaning of love? we asked one another, and
the answer was always: Suffering. Love means sorrowing and suffering. My friends cast meaningful looks in my direction; my poor dead
Frenchman qualified me to speak in this manner.

As things fell out, I discovered New York to be a center for
Freethinkers, women's rights, muckraking journalism, artistic and
musical experiments of all kinds. My aunt ran a shelter for battered
wives and in those days surrounded herself with militant suffragists—
women who were the lesser-known habitués of New York's literary and
cultural worlds and devoted themselves to intellectual clubs and social
reform. In their early lives, as in my mother's, these women had had
more control over their own destinies. They had not been (as now) a
class of idle women supported by wealthy husbands, but had worked
hard, and therefore had expected and received the right to be eccentric,
to smoke and play cards and tell stories, and to make fun of hypocrisy.

*By all rights I should have become a bluestockinged wildwoman—
an artist of pseudonymous fame and freakish habits; but it is a notoriously difficult thing to throw over the chains of the world's expectations of females. I had seen my own mother as an example of what a
woman could accomplish without a man, and my outrageous notions
of male and female relations were cemented at the feet of those wild-
women friends of my aunt's. If I had been born a man, I would have
created for myself a world full of work and egoism and imagined that
my whole life belonged to me. But since I was born a woman, I suffered
the usual girlish desires and aspirations; and I believed that my life
should eventually be joined to a husband's. It went on seeming to me
that the whole aim of Feminism must be to get the vote and to place
a woman in the free position to marry whom she will—to ensure that
her marriage relation never was one of owner and chattel but a part-
nership between agreeable companions.*

*I meant to wait before marrying, to be clearheaded and rational,
to consider coolly the pros and cons of (doubtless) several proposals;
but of course that was all thrown over when I met Wes. I was nineteen. In a manner somewhat like Edith and Otto Eustler, we had spent
our childhoods rowing up and down the same rivers and sloughs but
never had stood face-to-face until three thousand miles from the lower
Columbia, seated at a Thinking Club of the New York Public Library.
I should remember this meeting—what we were Thinking about—but
do not, beyond the astonishment of learning that Wesley Drummond's
home and mine lay nearly within gunshot of each other.*

*His family had a fish receiving station and cold storage plant on a
rocky point just to the west of Dahlia, from which they shipped frozen
sturgeon and caviar by rail to the East Coast. I told him about my
mother's farm up Skamokawa Creek, which now was rented out to
neighbors. We went over the names of people we knew in common and
told certain gossip which had not made it across the intervening nine*

or ten miles. I remember that he was passionate in his belief that the
wealth of capitalism would shortly abolish poverty. I had just begun
to see my stories into print, and he encouraged me to write, stating his
belief that women's minds should be satisfied as well as their hearts.
We had read the same books. His eyes were a delicate green.

By the time I was twenty, I was a mother in addition to a wife,
and within the next ten years would be the mother of five, and alone.

I have always been of two minds on the matter of Love. In one of
them I am a fool for the romantic hero in buckskins, and the heroine
who is a crack shot and binds up the poor boy's wounds without
swooning; they marry and live happily unto The End. But when I am
in my other mind, I know that love is a longer, more difficult, and
more interesting story.

The lower Columbia is a wilderness of gillnetters, horse-seiners,
salmon boats, and fish traps, which the steamboats must negotiate
without tangling their wheels. I have been aboard boats that lunged
suddenly to one side or the other to avoid disaster—passengers thrown
to their knees, china sent flying, lamps swinging crazily. Every now
and then when a boat makes an urgent hairpin turn, someone is
thrown over the rail.

Twenty-three days after my husband's failure to return to his wife,
a man's body washed up near Stella, at the mouth of Germany Creek.
This news was brought to me by a sheriff's deputy, who stood with his
hat in his hands, turning and turning it by the soft brim as he brought
the words out laboriously. I suppose he expected me to fly into hysteria.

I was excused from viewing the body—Horace Stuband and Otto
Eustler went in my place. Evidently the face, as well as body, were
much destroyed, and the clothes remaining to the corpse were ragged
and muddy remnants of blue serge such as Wes wore, along with half
the men plying the river routes. Nothing remained of the pockets.

The lower river, of course, is home to numberless migrants, army

deserters, tramps, and ship jumpers, any one of whom might disappear
without notice or report. Who was to say this was Wes's body when it
might just as well have been a friendless Bavarian hop-picker headed
for the Finnish baths in Astoria?

When it was suggested to me that I might wish to claim the body,
I said that I did not. I understood what was being offered: inasmuch
as a deserted wife is held to be discreditable, here was the dignity of
widowhood. But I always have preferred scandal to sympathy; and I
had had twenty-three days to sound out my heart and to discover its
druthers: I would rather hate a living husband than grieve a dead one.

C. B. D.

October 1906

There is nothing in the whole world so unbecom-
ing to a woman as a Nonconformist conscience.

OSCAR WILDE

Sun'y afternoon 2 Apr '05 (Yacolt)

I am told there are a dozen mills within a two-mile radius of
this town, and no proof can be more telling than the occasional scrawny young tree standing forlorn amidst the stumps
and shattered brush either side of the railroad right-of-way. At
sight of this shorn countryside, I have begun to relent a little in
my opinion of Homer traipsing off into the tules to work. The
homeguards here have a long walk and then some to bring them
to uncut timber, burnt or green, and the big trees are sure to be
away back in the deepwoods, for the nearby hills were hand-
logged and re-hand-logged in days before the boom.

The town is unremarkable except for its late flowering. If

there were settlers here before '03, then the greater part of them were taking up claims in the best interests of the timber companies, would be my guess. Now that the railroad has brought the logging industry to town, there are a few hopeful souls who have scratched at the ground between the stumps and planted hops, but I should be surprised if the town much survives the falling of the last tree.

Florence has her house very near the train yard—Melba pointed it out to me as soon as we had stepped down on the landing—but the mud was deep in the streets and Melba could not be persuaded to shuck her shoes and cross directly, which meant we must keep to the boardwalks where possible and take a tedious way around, which I'm afraid I did chafe at, being anxious to get past this necessary visit and deliver myself into the woods.

All the business buildings a-rowed beside the tracks are of a raw newness, and Florence likewise lives in a new little shack cobbled together of rough lumber and shakes. I have seen worse, and lived in them too. Melba called, "Florence," against the shut door, her voice breaking a bit, and then with her usual impertinence promptly lifted the latch and stepped across the mudsill.

Upon every horizontal surface in that room sat a woman, her hands busied with needlework. Half a dozen faces lifted to us with strained, anxious attention. The girl who let her embroidery fall and came weeping onto Melba's bosom was not Florence, surely—could not be, for Melba's girl has a rosy round countenance of the sort people call a Sweetheart Face, and not this face all bone and ash—but oh, oh, and my heart sinking in my breast. There was a terrible moment, a quick shying away, an unreasonable dread for my own children left behind: I was run through by a blind impulse to break and turn back. In such ways does a body defend itself from an unbearable pain.

Our entrance roused a little bustle of activity, and directly a lunch was brought forward and urged especially upon Florence, who sipped coffee and touched the chicken with her fork. Melba, sitting beside her, patted her knee from time to time, which invariably started them both into tears.

I sat over my own plate beside a woman with a no-nonsense look to her, and shortly I had as much news as there was to be had, though the crux of it is rumor and thirdhand tale: Evidently Homer and others heard Harriet's cry of alarm, and following a trail of freakish big footprints, they came on tufts of coarse hair from bear or beast or wildman, and a scrap of Harriet's shift. In the rain and mud the trail was lost, though, and now every man in that part of the woods is engaged in looking for sign. At Camp 8 they have shut down the logging show, which is an uncommon event; the injury or death of a man might only call for poles run through the sleeves of a coat and two men to haul him down from the woods when the boss declares there is sufficient time. But rough old fallers and buckers and heartless boss-loggers will weaken where a child is concerned, and men in camps lying miles away to the east and south are keeping a look-out. There have been a dozen sightings of "monstrous forms," and three men claim to have seen little Harriet carried upon a hairy creature's back like a yoke.

Of course, it is typical of men not to think of sending detailed and accurate information back to the waiting women, and every scrap of news reaching Yacolt is delayed and distorted by the distance. Generally Florence must wait for news to come to town with the occasional injured man. The country being rough and rock-ribbed, it is seemingly every bit as risky

to mount a search for monsters as to carry on with logging: four
men have been carried down from the woods so far, of which
two suffered from broken bones and two were shot by their
nervous fellows in the deep brush. Homer evidently has not left
off his searching even to comfort his wife, being unwilling to
surrender the greater part of a day to travel here and back again.
In any case, I should wonder what he would say to Florence if he
came. That she must prepare herself for the worst?

"There is a general hope that if the beast's den can be tumbled
on, Harriet might yet be found alive."

This last was said to me by a sober mind, and with a solemn
face.

From the women in Florence's house I have gained a better
notion of how one must travel to reach Homer's camp in the
deepwoods, and this only confirms my belief that the trek is
beyond Melba's capabilities. In the morning (for I have missed
the afternoon run) I shall have to hitch aboard a log train the
six miles to Chelatchie Prairie at the terminus of the regular
line and catch a little Shay engine up the spur line to Camp 6
on Canyon Creek. Evidently one must then walk five miles of
flume to Camp 7 and two miles of footpath to reach Camp 8,
away up the canyon. Since Melba is too weak and old for a hike
of that kind, she'll remain here with her daughter while I go on
alone.

Immediately on finishing lunch, someone instigated a prayer,
and every woman in the room went down on her knees, even an
old lady of eighty or eighty-five whose joints crackled when she
knelt. Melba and I are both stubborn in our separate beliefs,
and I generally will neither bow my head nor kneel for prayers
and devotions; but to coldly stand while Melba and Florence
were on their knees praying Jesus to return Harriet harmless

would defeat even my own expectations. I let myself down to the floor and examined my clasped hands briefly before taking my glance around the room. Eyes were tightly shut beneath earnest frowns, lips were moving in devout silence. At length, a heavy woman with moles on her face, whose name had been told to me but which I'd promptly forgotten, opened her mouth and importuned the Lord on Harriet's behalf in a series of platitudes and prescribed phrases which the others seemed to think well of. Then we stood again, and the women picked up their needlework and resumed the solemn business of Waiting For Word. When I have caught up these notes (I suppose I mean now) I shall go into town and buy my provisions, and tomorrow at the crack of dawn shall be off into the woods.

Once we were awakened in the middle of the night by the screams of a wild beast that sounded like the yells and laughter of a demented man. I took my rifle; it was moonlight; I went in to the field, but could not make up the animal; I let go a shot in its direction, for conscience's sake. Never heard anything like it ever afterward. We thought it might have been a hyena; it may have been only an unusually gifted coyote.

Later, at another time, a large beast came to the edge of the cleared land, and would utter a scream that sounded like a frightened colt. I took my rifle, and a lantern, but the beast disappeared. My idea is, it was a cougar.

EDGAR ROTSCHY,
Early Days in Yacolt

C. B. D. (1889; unpublished)
FEMALE EMANCIPATION

It's my belief there are only a few necessary conditions for female emancipation.

First, food preparation must be removed from the province of the home: I dream of a nourishing meal to which one adds only water; cheap and plentiful cafés; and refrigerated produce.

Then there must be a transformation of domestic duties through technology—principally the mechanization of heat and laundry. Freed of the labor of chopping and splitting wood, hauling and heating water, scrubbing and soaking and hanging up her family's clothes, a woman's real self will be able to have its day.

With the public spread of health care and birth control, women will be relieved of the unending cycle of maternity and nursing—freed, after raising through their infancy one or two or three children, to develop occupations suitable to their inclinations. And if there is available public education for all children unto the last degree, then every woman's mind will be a fertile field for ideas and she will have been properly prepared for the life she chooses to occupy.

Lastly, of course, women need the vote.

We are already "free" in the sense of being considered no man's possession. Of late there has been some improvement in a woman's rights to property and to children in the case of divorce. But we are still politically disenfranchised and economically dependent, undereducated and—this is my belief—overpampered. With suffrage and these very few improvements and scientific advances, there will be no economic necessity to marry; and if a woman chooses to marry, she will have been cut loose from onerous domestic responsibilities and will still retain her independence. I envision a day very soon when women as a class shall be guaranteed happiness. We lack only the technology.

Evening of the 2nd (Yacolt)

The hotels and saloons here, as in any lumbering town, are crowded in winters and on weekends, when loggers are forced out of the woods by bad weather or by the Sabbath, and this being a Sunday, men were scuffling on the sidewalks or sleeping drunk in the gutters when I passed uptown to find a store. I am at home in any village where the storefronts all trumpet the price of beer—was put at ease to find a few men, in the rumpled clothes they had slept in, standing before employment office chalkboards, gazing upon listings for axemen, rigging-slingers, buckers, and swampers.

Of course, with the uncommonly early spring weather, all the mills and shows are working twelve-hour shifts, and consequently the shops in town do the bulk of their trade on the weekends and do not trouble to close in honor of the Lord's Day. In the Worthington's store the shopkeeper was a Swede whose name was not Worthington, and he took my list between thumb and forefinger and examined it in wonder, as if it were the schematic of a ship that would sail to the moon.

"What's we got here, eh? What's is this?"

Having formed a clear idea of what lies between Yacolt and Camp 8, and how I might get from here to there, I had refined my little list of sustainables to a miserly few. At Camp 6 I can expect to receive the cook's fare for lunch before stepping off the end of the rails into the deepwoods; and once I've reached Camp 8 a cook supplies board to all that great search-party of men. Therefore I meant to pay Yacolt's dear prices for only matches in tins (many matches, for this is wet country), plug tobacco (for, paradoxically, cigars may not be lit in the woods without risk of runaway fire), dried apricots, hardtack, choco-late, and coffee, which ought to keep me alive for the tramp from Camp 6 to Camp 8 and replenish me when I'm engaged in the grim business of the search. I asked also for a map of the Yacolt environs, especially a Company map marking off every spur line, backwoods camp, flume, and trail. It was evidently these items, one or all, which had confounded the shopkeeper; or it was the tin pants in a small man's size, which I had put onto the list from an expectation that I'd be bucking brush and crawling into caves.

I should have told the fellow truthfully that I was on a ter-rible errand with bleak prospects, but in recent years have made it my habit, wherever tender or wretched feelings are concerned, to put on a show of coldness and disregard. Naturally I went on in my old jog-trot way, saying to the Swede, "As you see, they are stores for a flight to the moon."

This facetiousness bewildered him no more than before. He swung his eyes to me with a slight frown and then posed a ques-tion and three more in a murmur of Swedish—inquiries evi-dently directed at his own ears—and upon hearing the answer, brightened considerably. "Sure, sure," he said, and thumped the list with a blunt, blackened thumbnail. I supposed this to mean all had become clear to him: the ship in question would fly to the moon by helium power, after first being launched from the isle of Majorca by a giant rubber strap.

My small pile of stores appeared slowly on the counter. From

the shopkeeper's frowns and gesticulations it became clear that
I must settle for a general map covering half the territory of
two states, which does not suit my purposes very well but is
evidently the only map to be had. And he carried on a sporadic
discussion with himself, arguing both sides of the question of
chocolate: whether it was to be cake or powder. I know a word
of Swedish here or there, but since my Swedish does not include
"Majorca," I kept still and waited for the man's finding; and it
fell out correctly that a lunar journey is better served by cake
chocolate than by powdered.

I confess without shame, this little shopping expedition
uptown was a bright, brief escape from the terrible unhappiness
in Florence's house, and when I came out again into the bustling
street—men carrying on their affairs in the fine sunlight quite
as if nothing were amiss in the world—I found I was short of
the necessary courage for going into that cave of despair again. I
am a hopeless lilyliver, evidently, and if there had been a hermit
sitting on a hill nearby, I suppose I would have set out for the
top. In the event, my groceries and I made a vagrant and cowardly return through town, west to the end of the business district and then north among the little houses and chicken yards
and stacks of cordwood, until we chanced onto a baseball field
where three men were attempting to burn out a yellowjackets'
nest in the ground, well out from the first-base line.

A boy with a wooden leg sat on the three-tier bleachers
between third base and home plate, watching this activity with
interest. He sat on the lowest bench and rested his elbows back
on the next high, with his wooden leg and his other one out-
stretched before him. An east wind had sprung up and cleared
out the smoke of burning slab, sawdust, and mill-ends, the great
piles that go on burning day and night for years in such towns as

these, and the sun shone through for a moment. The bleachers struck me as a fine place to enjoy the improbable spring sunlight and several minutes of free entertainment.

The boy wore a police uniform with brass buttons but no insignia, which is a get-up I know loggers are fond of wearing, seeing as they are inexpensive and warm and known to wear well. He was half a dozen years older than George, I thought, and with George's smart look to his face. His name, he said, was Dick Musch. When we had shared our opinions of the proper way to eliminate a yellowjackets' nest and speculated happily on what might happen in the coming minutes, I leant back and rested my elbows on the bench beside him and commented upon his wooden leg in a mild and roundabout way. "I believe I've seen half a dozen crippled men in coming four blocks through town," I said, which didn't seem to offend or surprise him.

"Donkey boilers blow up," he said easily. "People fall from flumes, band saws break, a tree walks, a leg gets caught in the bight of the donkey cable. I guess there is about a hundred ways to get killed or hurt in the woods and the mills."

While the hornet hunters fumbled to place their firepot in the hole and cover the hole with a big homemade sheet-metal hood, Dick Musch and I exchanged one-legged-man stories. I told him about the old Russian whose leg was lost in a fishing accident, and when he applied to the Columbia River Fishermen's Protective Union for help, they bought a wooden leg and leased it to the fellow, for fear that an outright donation would set a dangerous precedent.

The boy knew an old man, a chute-flagger, who had ridden a runaway car down the hill into Yacolt. When he was thrown off and his friends came running to ask if he was hurt, he said no, he wasn't, not unless you counted that he had broken his leg; and he brandished the shattered wooden foot.

"Here is what that old man give me," he said, "when my own leg was cut off." He pulled from his pocket a limp and dog-eared postcard of a one-legged tramp, hat in hand at the back porch of a fine house. *Kind Lady, I had the misfortin ter loose me leg,* was the tramp's line, and the lady's firm reply, *Well, it's no use lookin for it here, I ain't got it!*

"It cheered me up considerable," Dick said, looking down fondly at the card.

"Are you twenty yet?" I asked him.

"No ma'am, I'm seventeen."

I had supposed him to be young, but this news—seventeen!—brought on a sudden moment of irrational dread, a vague presentiment of accident or maiming befalling one of my own children while I am off rescuing Harriet—but in the next moment the yellowjackets came out of the ground and the hapless bee killers scattered in a fine panic across the field, arms flailing and hands clawing at shirt collars. The boy fell to laughing in such a sweet way that when he rocked forward to clasp his knees, the one just above the whittled smooth ash-wood leg and the neat fold and pin of the trouser leg, I forgot all worry for my sons—forgot Harriet, even, in that bubbling musical sound of pure joy.

I had meant to get from Dick Musch his mother's name and address, having the somewhat maudlin idea that I might write to her about this meeting with her son. But it slipped my mind along with the other things, and I didn't remember it until long after Dick and I had shaken hands and gone our separate ways. I will tell you when I remembered it: it was when I was unfolding my blanket-bed on the floor of Florence's cottage just a while ago and from the small bedroom at the back I heard Florence's voice, a wordless moaning, and then her mother's whisper, her mournful comforting words, "Here, here, come here, lay your head down in your mother's lap."

🌰 *A woman of my queer and scandalous habits is seldom made to receive visits or to pay them, for which reason the hours between supper and bed can be entirely given over to the small domestic dramas. When we are not playing duplicate Whist, the boys and I often read aloud, going by turns round the room, and I have made condemned books a particular center of interest: Hardy's* Jude the Obscure *(which was dull and which the boys would not put up with), Balzac, Fielding, Zola, and especially Oscar Wilde, whom the world knows I admire highly. We have lately been reading "The Isle of Caninus," which story we have come through in three days; and though Kingsley's tale is a poor patch on Verne, and his story lifted almost entirely from Welsh tales of the Fortunate Islands, the boys are loyal to any story in which dogs roam in a free state. Even Kingsley's steely-hearted hero, Lord Coquardz, was so struck by the cheerfulness of creatures in their naturally wild condition that—George was reading now—"never afterward would he see fit to confine a dog to leash or crate."*

I've suffered through readings in the drawing rooms of literati, at which it was strictly forbidden to interrupt, but my sons are inclined to break in with shouts or whispers of complaint, corrections, queries, approval, as befits the reader and the story, and I'm inclined to think they're better listeners for it. Now Oscar asked our general assembly, "What's a leash?" Inasmuch as Buster was at that moment lying prostrate and twitching with dream under the dining room table, I intended to make a sour remark, intended to say, Our house is the very exemplar of the Isle of Caninus, as neither the dog nor the children know the meaning of the word "leash." *But George, speaking the words with slow gravity and a considered manner, said, "Old Gus Statmuller, how he ties up his dogs." And the other boys all lifted their eyes to him with an admiring look.*

Fatherless, George has made up his own manhood, and his brothers and friends consider him bold and high flying, cunning, deep. He is sensible of this and plays to it, without veering from his natural character, which is solemn and iconoclastic. He has only recently given up a childhood determination to be a lighthouse keeper and now has in mind a career as a muckraking journalist for McClure's maga-zine. It was George, of course, who authored, printed, and delivered to the neighbors, as well as to every fence post, a vehement and righ-teous broadside regarding Augustus Statmuller's habit of tying his youngest child in the yard with his dogs, a child of an age with Oscar but feebleminded, damaged at birth by a doctor with clumsy forceps. Several neighborhood women of tender sensibilities thereafter begged Statmuller to take the child inside, which accomplished nothing; but the Wahkiakum County sheriff advised him similarly, and people now say he keeps the child tied to a leg of the kitchen stove.

Without a pause, George went on reading down toward the end of Lord Coquardz's adventures on Caninus, but while still pages from the end he closed the book in midsentence and said matter-of-factly, "Any-body would know what happens next," which wasn't true—Kingsley is nothing if not inventive. But Lewis and Frank together trumpeted, "Sure! Anybody!" which forced Oscar to say he knew the end too, and then it was only poor Jules, with a wail of dismay, who begged to be told. There was a brief flurry of cruel lying in which the twins and Oscar advanced an assortment of horrific endings: "His throat is cut by the queen of the Fortunate Islands!" "He buries the treasure in a sack soaked with poison, and the dogs dig it up and they all die!" Jules wailed the louder, and George, who had been looking off with a fine theatrical disinterest, allowed himself to be drawn slowly into the argument. He began to tell an elaborate plot of his own, involving the intrepid Lord Coquardz with, first, Hermaphrodite, then Xerxes, on an archipelago inhabited by dwarfs. It was a meandering invention, intricate and unsolvable, but the other boys followed it with shouts of devotion; and when the end was reached and the loose ends snipped off wholesale, they were satisfied.

Editors, I shall hope—every one of them.

C. B. D.

December 1902

The good ended happily, and the bad unhappily.
That is what Fiction means.

OSCAR WILDE

Camp 6 (in the woods) 3 Apr

I told Melba and Florence to expect me gone by the first light, as I planned to rise early and catch the 5:30 train to Chelatchie Prairie. In the cold half-darkness, as I was putting on my traveling pants and buttoning a wool shirt and jacket and lacing my boots, I heard someone stirring in the little back room, and shortly here came Melba, dressed and clutching both her duffel and a stubborn look. Of course, she is too decrepit to make the trip up the flume and the trail to Camp 8, and we had thoroughly agreed upon her waiting in Yacolt with her daughter while I went up into the woods alone. But since I have long known Melba to be willful and bullheaded, I don't know why I should ever be surprised when she changes her mind.

She followed after me onto the sidewalk and shut the door

quietly on Florence. We went without words through the smoke-gray streets to an open café on Railroad Avenue across from the station landing and drank our coffee in silence and ate our mush in silence while the day paled, and finally I said, "What in the world was the point of my coming up here, then, if you insist upon going into the woods yourself?"

And she put her chin out and said, "What is the point of my staying behind?" Florence, being with child, is absolutely prevented from the trip, but Melba is convinced the duty should fall to some one of the family, which must be her. I let this foolish argument stand out from the shore, and after suffering the silence, she said, "Well, I won't hold you up, if it comes to that. You can put me beside the tracks." Which I coldly agreed to do.

The caboose of the Chelatchie Prairie train, attached to a long line of trucks and flatcars, has doubtless done duty as coach for traveling loggers in various stages of illness or intoxication, as well as all manner of agents and cruisers, wives and *filles de joie*, which must account for the sanguine way the conductor and the brakeman took four of us aboard. His passengers comprised a man with a handlebars mustache and a mild manner, bound for Amboy, bearing with him a little girl in a blue crepe jumper; and us two women, going all the way up the line, one of us well upholstered and getting along in years, and the other a model of immodesty, decked out in trousers which were rucked up into high boots. The brakeman, imperturbable, laying eyes on me without much of a blink, ushered us into the forward compartment as if it were his front parlor. "Ye'll be cold standing out there. Come in to the stove."

The car was stuffy, with a prevailing odor of smoke and leather cushions and grease. The coal bin was built up from the floor of the caboose close beside the long-necked, clubfooted stove. A shovel stood in the coal, and an iron washstand in the corner amidst a litter of soap and soiled towels. Boots with thick worn soles dangled from a hook on one short wall, and a yellow oilskin coat on the opposite wall. We sat on the benches and put our bags behind our shoes.

There was a great deal of shunting from the mills to the station before the conductor and brakeman finally climbed to their high chairs, opposite to each other in the turret of the coach; and at last the engine made up a little steam and bore away from Yacolt. For the first short while, the rails ran past little farms whose few acres have been hewn from the forest. These tracts were once thickly set with trees that rose three hundred feet to the sky and shut out the sun like a lid; now the pale sunrise fell glittery and tender through the haze of mill smoke, and between the stumps in the hop fields, bare winter poles stood as much as twelve feet, and thin as the bones of Longshanks.

Soon the little carved-out fields gave way, and on either side of the tracks stood a desolation of burnt and cutover forests, with the occasional forlorn spar left behind due to puniness or rot, and then unburnt jungly stands, all of it the twenty- and thirty-year-old stump growth and weedy alder that has sprung up where the old hand-loggers cleared out the big trees with ox teams in days long past.

Melba had been fidgeting with her hands and finally she put her head over and confided something to the young girl, after which she lifted her head and declared to the man who had brought her, "You won't let her wander off into the woods," as if this fell in the middle of an intimate correspondence. He was not very taken aback. "I won't. I sure won't," he said with a slight smile, and he gently petted the girl's knee.

"They's a girl took by a orang-utan up in the mountains this week," the conductor called down from on high, which was apparently not news to anyone in the car. A short, interested conversation followed, consisting almost entirely of old rumors and woods-ape stories of years past, and sober speculation among the three men present. I left it to Melba to reveal us or keep still, and she flattened her mouth and kept still, looking straight down to her clasped hands, even while hearing of miners found dead with their heads bitten off. Afterward, when they had gone on to talking of other things, I looked and found her eyes were fixed out the window, her hands loosed from each other, resting separately on her knees.

At Amboy junction the train slacked speed, and the man and his daughter went off there. They walked the ties a short way and then crossed over through the shadow of a small woodlot and took a cross-planked road that pierced the green hills toward the northwest. Once onto the road, the girl began a little skip, and the man swung off his hat and beat it lightly against her stockinged legs; her laugh carried across the air as if it were a bell chiming.

A man I took to be an agent for the Twin Falls Logging Company, or I suppose a little company accountant or surveyor or saw seller, got on board, gripping his bag and carrying in the other hand a yellow novel. He promptly took out the novel and began to read it, and after some minutes of distant and negligent study of the wrapper, I determined that it was not one of mine.

While the caboose sat waiting for the return of the engine, which evidently had gone up the short way to Amboy, a little crowd began to gather. A man carrying homemade prune wine in a pail came out of the nearby pastures, and boys with dogs appeared from somewhere and climbed over the high steps of the caboose, and a shaky old man wandered forth from a building that might have been a brothel, or a saloon, or a café. There was a friendly exchange of information—what price for the wine, what's to be made of this unseasonable sunny weather, and of course some speculation and newsmongering as regards the "orang-utan" who had stolen off with a child in the backwoods—and when the train pulled out, the little boys ran alongside and shouted good-byes quite as if we were all old acquaintances, and even the Twin Falls man looked up from his reading to wave a hand to those left behind. His book, I saw, was *The Ghostly Galleon: A Tale of the Steel-Arm Detective*.

In certain seasons of the year there are shallow-draft steam-boats as can make it up the North Fork of the Lewis River as far as Etna and Speelyei, and therefore Chelatchie Prairie is a town older than Yacolt by some few years, having been settled by Finns and Swedes who put dairy cows on the natural pasture and in years past took their produce the short way north to Speelyei and thence to the Outside. But the logging show has made Yacolt the center of its universe, and Chelatchie Prairie therefore has become a pitiful little town without the look of progress or prosperity about it, the only new buildings being a mill and a railroad station. We loitered on the platform, as pathetic as hobos, before hitching a ride with a little Shay engine going out the short spur line to Camp 6. Spur lines being temporary, they are no more than light rails fastened to flimsy ties on loose and fickle roadbeds, and though a Shay can hunker down and climb a tree if it receives the order, and turn a curve so sharp as to shine the headlight right back over the engineers shoulder into the log trucks hauling behind, it is not the Union Pacific: we were invited to sit on a flatcar, or cling to the bell rope on the forward part of the Shay. We rode the flatcar past the Chelatchie millpond and around the steep north side of a mountain with the Indian spirit-name Tumtum, and so on through the shattered and cutover woods well up the Canyon Creek.

I suppose there are some camps where the little Shay would go puffing in with great drama, rolling straight up to the landing with the sound of axes ringing on every side and the thunderclap of falling trees and the thudding donkey engines rocking the sky, but it is more often the case to find the train has stopped on a level stretch of track where a branch road joins and a few houses show in the distance; and if you're not to waste hours going up the spur to load wood before coming down to the landing, you're advised to jump off into the mud at the side of the track and walk a mile over ties to the camp buildings, where your arrival goes unnoticed and you find all the great woods activity is a distant mutter of sound and fury, off behind a ridge littered with the wreckage of last summer's logging.

Melba wouldn't complain but huffed and wheezed alarmingly as she went up the ties toward Camp 6, and her usual short-legged rocking stride quickly became a sailor's roll. She shifted her duffel from the left hand to the right and back to the left and cast a glance without quite lifting her head from its low-set bulldog stance. "What are those houses there? Have we got to it? I should have thought there'd be more buildings." There were a few houses upon a slight rise standing well apart from the other collected buildings of the camp, which I took for the private houses of the manager and his fellows.

"The camp is up the way yet, Melba. Here, sit down, find a stump. Put down your bag and sit." She was eventually persuaded, and we leant against high old stumps until she had caught her breath enough to peer down the rails and find the buildings that comprised Camp 6.

"Well, there it is," she said with a little cluck of satisfaction.

It was a highballing twentieth-century camp: not an ox to be found, but a shed for storing piles of heavy chains and coils of wire cable under cover, and a great long machine shop where men were mightily engaged keeping the mechanical devices and enginery in working order. In other respects a camp entirely ordinary for its size: the commissariat fifty feet in length; the cookhouse and dining room perhaps ten feet longer than the store, and wide in proportion; five bunkhouses with accommodations each for twenty-five or thirty; to say nothing of meat house, oil house, smithy, stables, filing house, and a tent church of the Northwest Lumbermen's Evangelical Society. Dozens of tents and shacks stood at the perimeter, homes of men who valued solitude or men whose families were with them in camp. I had known of a camp on the lower Columbia boasting rose hedges and walnut trees, as well as a Swiss gardener, but admit to its rarity. Round the buildings of Camp 6, in the more usual way, were desolate stumps of trees and the great litter and disorder of splintered tree limbs and tops, empty casks and tin cans, soiled straw, broken tools, abandoned railroad grades.

A woman stood out from one of the houses in that separate little community of boss places and called to us in a shrill voice, "My dears, are you lost, or looking for work?" which struck me wrong, and I called back, "My dear, we are looking for the rose garden." She stood a moment in silence and then retreated.

"You have a wicked, rude mouth," Melba said, which was delivered as a kind of shocked announcement, and which I did not deny.

We went on leaning upon stumps until Melba had sufficiently

recovered her breath, and then minutes more while she fidgeted and pursed her mouth, which is a habit of hers, and a warning and portent of coming commotion. In my experience she is at such moments often preparing herself to make some troublesome petition, or to lodge some vicious complaint against me or my children or the arduous conditions under which she is made to labor in our home.

"He can be dirty mean, you know," was what she finally brought out, and her slight look, as it passed over me, seemed composed equally of embarrassment and insinuation. Since I didn't know what to make of this, I should have made the safest answer, which is silence, but my own habit is always to toss something out. I believe I said, "Then he's only true to the form," without knowing in the slightest which man we were condemning. Melba knows my radical opinions and the general disrespect with which I like to speak of the male sex, but her round face colored to a fine pink. She said, "Well, most men as I've known were decent to their wives and their children. And I know you don't like to speak of it, but Wesley Drummond was a good husband who never laid a hand on you nor none of the boys, that I ever seen." She nodded tightly as if to draw a line beneath these words, and then said, "Which is more than I can say for Homer, and that's all I wanted to say."

I took this to mean there was a good deal more she wished to say, but though I pressed her, could get nothing further. What was I supposed to make of such dark hinting as this? The worst of several possibilities occurred to me: that Homer had killed his own daughter through beating her too hard, and had buried her in the woods. I don't put this past a man of a certain temperament, and therefore cannot entirely rule it out, but I have got hold of my imagination by now and believe I know what

Melba was getting at, which is only that she blames Homer's harsh ways for causing Harriet to run off and get lost.

We trudged on to the office, where we were received with surprise and courtesy—*the orang-utan—horrible business—hope yet—innocent child*—and made to understand the way up to Camp 8 was *a turrible slog fur a lady*—with a pitying look at poor Melba. Would we like to pack a lunch from the dining room? We would. Have a lie-down until the cook's flunky brought it round? Most obliged. We were then let into quarters at the rear of the store where there were three beds, evidently used by traveling timber cruisers and Twin Falls Company men. One of the beds was in disarray, and upon another lay a man's open shaving kit, as well as soiled socks and underdrawers. This seemed to give our host a moment of fluster, though he recovered in good order and swept the offending articles under his arm as he backed out and left us to our privacy.

Melba sank to the one neat bed as if we'd finished up a trek over the mountains of Tibet. Her face was scarlet, the sleeves and collar of her shirtwaist wilted and wrinkled from damp sweating, her breath a dangerous rale. She lies there now, snoring, while I sit upon the other bed and write these words. I said to her bluntly, "The way from here will be all mud and hills and entirely afoot, seven miles or more, which ought to be all the argument necessary why you're not fit to go on." Her idea of physical conditioning lies in a weekly scrubbing of the kitchen floors and a quarterly beating of the parlor rugs. In recent years I believe she's seldom been called on to walk farther than from one Astoria shop to the next, and the boat that ferries her around Skamokawa is often as not rowed by Stuband or one of my sons, all of which has left her legs sinewless and her lungs enfeebled. She is a stubborn hen, though, and had to be worn down and led by the wattles before finally granting my point. She then argued for waiting on at Camp 6, until made to see that it wouldn't help the cause. We agreed, finally, that I would go on alone, and after lunch and a rest she would take the Shay back to Yacolt and keep a vigil with Florence, which of course had been my original idea; and though I had a keen wish to remind her of this, the set of her face warned me from it. Melba, as I have come to know, can be steered but never driven.

"Why are inferior novels sometimes very widely read?" P. G. B.

Because a good many readers of novels do not know the difference between good and bad work; as a good many people do not know the difference between good and bad architecture, and build ugly houses when they might build beautiful ones. Because crudely written novels often deal with subjects in which people are deeply interested at the moment. Because novels of inferior quality sometimes have considerable narrative interest; there appear from time to time men and women who have the gift of telling a story but no feeling for the art of writing. Because tales of inferior quality are occasionally illuminated by knowledge of character and by humor. Not all inferior novels are hopelessly bad. It must be added that there are some popular novels the success of which is inexplicable; they are cheap in style, clumsily constructed and untrue to life. In the reading public,

as in every other public, there appears to be a
residuum of natural depravity in matters of taste
and intelligence.

HAMILTON W. MABIE,
"MR. MABIE ANSWERS SOME QUESTIONS,"
Ladies Home Journal, November 1905

Melba

The woman clapped the sleeve iron to the shirt front and ran
the heavy narrow nose along the gathered pleat that overlapped
the buttonholes, and then the next pleat and the next, polishing
the tucks to the seams, and she then snatched a hot sadiron
from the stove and smoothed the shirt across the back in broad
strokes, and turned the shirt and pressed the yoke, and turning
again ran across the seams at the caps of the sleeves and pressed
the narrow selvage of the collar band and flattened the lower
sleeves and the buttonhole band, then placed the seven-pound
iron on the stove again and took the little sleeve iron and pushed
into the gathers of the sleeve caps and smoothed the cuffs flat,
turning the tip of the iron delicately into the small pleats at the
wrist.

She was accustomed to the ironing board, which sat the
floor imperfectly and shifted its weight from end to end with
the shifting weight of the iron. She stood before the board with
her hips wide, shifting her own weight from foot to foot without consciousness of it any more than she was conscious of the
shifting board and the slight complaint of the wooden braces.
The irons were nickel plated and polished, three heavy sadirons
and the little sleeve iron ground by perfect machinery, every
iron true, face-shaped, double pointed, though the detachable

wood handle sometimes would release an iron without warning, and always would wobble in her hand, a loose motion on the stroke and again on the pull, which she was no longer conscious of after so many years, the same irons, the same board, every Tuesday the ironing and mending, the women's shirtwaists and then the boys' overalls, the stockings and vests and the boys' blouses and shifts and plain shirts, and the women's skirts, the man's collarless work shirts.

On Mondays she washed and churned. On Wednesdays and again on Saturdays she scrubbed the white pine kitchen floor with a brush, sand, and soap she had made herself of hog fat, lye, and wood ashes. The boards in that floor didn't fit together as tightly as she would have liked, and the cracks were inclined to accumulate dirt and old crumbs of crackers and the dust of flour and cornmeal, which if it wasn't gotten up quickly would bring ants and mice; and as she sat on her shoes spreading a thin lake of water and brushing it hard across the boards and down into the cracks, she sometimes would think of the boys, the youngest two crawling on that floor as babies, how they liked to lick the crumbs from the cracks. Thursdays or Fridays she baked bread and pies, and on the other days or in other hours, and according to the season, sewed curtains, cushions, and lamp shades, made carpet from rags, tended to sick neighbors, took up and beat carpet, cooked the meals, made jell, cider, pickles, and preserves, cut stove wood, blacked the stove, painted the rain barrel, oiled the woodwork, planted and weeded the garden.

For some of these chores she had the help of one boy or another, but she considered the children in her care more trouble than relief. In truth, she had grown too set in her ways to turn over the work to clumsy hands. Her own child, a daughter, was long since grown, and though she was fond of the boys, the little boys especially, she tired of them readily and found her greatest comfort in the long quiet of schooldays, alone in the house. She was accustomed to the lonely and monotonous nature of house-work, as she was accustomed to the loose handle of the iron, and seldom remarked on it.

The entire of her adult life had been lived in remote where-abouts, and inconvenience was something she took also as a matter of course. That women Outside enjoyed gaslights, municipal water, domestic plumbing, commercial ice, coal furnaces, steam radiators—this seemed to her quite unrelated to her own situation. Telephone lines had been brought to Chinook and Ilwaco; at Brookfield, she had heard, the Meglers had an Edison graphophone with wax disc records and a morning-glory horn; in Grays River there was a bowling alley; at Altoona, Hans Peterson ran about the mouth of the river in a gasoline launch. That such things might make their way to her, here at the ragged edge of the Frontier, she found an interesting though airy hope, rather like a Utopist vision, something to be looked forward to in a vague way but not to be counted on. She had little confidence and less interest in the idea of Progress, not having noticed much improvement in people's happiness with the improvement of machinery.

She was fifty-two, with graying hair and weak eyes, a ready temper, and an implacable need for orderliness, both in her sur-roundings and in the daily and seasonal round of her work. The smell of clean pressed laundry, suggestive of starch and heat and soap, satisfied her in a way she could never have articulated.

She carried the bundles of shirts and overalls off to rooms in the house furnished with bureaus and dressers, and afterward, it being Tuesday, she retired to her attic room for a half-holiday.

Her employer was a supporter of the eight-hour workday but
had not made the leap from the general to the particular; the
woman's work as a housekeeper and child-minder ended at
seven o'clock in the evening, with Sundays and half-Tuesdays to
spend at her discretion. Her secret habit, of a Tuesday, was to
read the newspaper through and through while reclining upon
her bed without stockings or corset.

While she read of a cap-makers' strike in New York, and of
the prominent evangelists holding revival meetings in Portland,
and of a rich woman in dread of being poisoned, the pressed and
folded clothes took up the smell of the cedar shavings lying in
white-waisting sachets in the dresser drawers. It was of course
unknown to her that the smell of cedar carried in clean clothes
would years afterward have the power to spark off long wordless flutters of memory in the boys—this woman who had once
been their caregiver returning to them and streaming away
from them as live coals will blow suddenly across the darkness
on a flaw of wind.

Afternoon of 3rd (top of the flume)
I am continually amazed at the paucity of imagination where
the loggers' naming of landforms is concerned, but Canyon
Creek is a plain and apt call, the creek brawling down through
a narrow basalt gorge and Camp 6 lying just where the gorge
flattens somewhat and takes a wider stance. They have cleared
out the trees on the near and easy ground, and now take their
logs from five miles up the reach of the canyon and send them
down to the camp through an arrangement of flumes not much
less pretentious than a Roman aqueduct. At the catch basin,
hallooing over the roar and spout of logs plunging off the end

of the slideway, the men told me I should have trouble walking the flume, as the eight-inch catwalk is a precarious path even for a man, and in dirty weathers a flume tender will slip off every now and then and be killed or crippled. I told them even a woman may slip and be killed, but she would never tolerate dirty weather, and I climbed up to the walk and set off while their brains still scrambled for purchase. When they had got their gears moving, however, they sent a man climbing up after me, doubtless instructed to escort the helpless woman the entire five miles of the catwalk with an intent to ensure her safety, which of course had the effect of endangering it, as I then had to step out briskly to keep up appearances.

Logging of my acquaintance on the Skamokawa sloughs and creeks relies on the splash dam and the spring freshet to move sawlogs downhill, which has kept me from much experience of flumes, but I became acquainted in a hurry. The flume follows the creeks winding course, but being a man-made and wooden river, it clings by a miracle of modern technology to the high wall of the canyon, and the little plank catwalk follows the flume in such a way that the steep rushing trough is always at your hip, the water slipping by with the unremitting thump and scrape of sawlogs caroming hell-for-leather downstream, while catwalk and flume together bridge and rebridge the creek and its shoots, offering at every hand giddy views down to the white rope of the mountain river, and ahead to spindling timbers supporting the next terrible spiderweb of trestle, the next oncoming curve leaping out over the abyss. Walking a flume is just the sort of brisk living as draws the blood right out of my head, and this of course raises Melba's old question: What could have possessed Homer to bring his Harriet up this high-way?

The fellow sent after me had the gaunt and sorrowful face, the pasty complexion of a Russian. I used up my supply of Russian on him and then, clinging to the flume, took a careful look behind in order to collect my reply. He stood at his ease on the skinny catwalk, his long arms clasped behind him on the handle of his peavey hook and his sorrowful gaze going past me, and at length said in plain English, "I don't follow, ma'am, but if you're swearing at me, then I ought to say this wasn't none of my idea."

He was a flume tender, he said when we had made up our quarrel. He had the work of patrolling the lower half of the cat-walk looking for jams or leaks, the bane of flume operators, and of clearing the jams or signaling if there was a break. A log will take a curve too fast and leap right out of the trough, he said, or jam up and divert the following logs over the edge of the flume and down; a turn of logs will pile up on a curve, and the weight of wood and dammed water will cause a flume box to stove in, in which case all the water and wood arriving from above goes spilling down in the canyon until the gap is discovered and the flume rebuilt.

This news of logs flying through the air did nothing to stiffen my manly nerve, but the flume tender himself, following along persistently behind me, was an unexpected comfort. He began by helpfully pointing out waste wood along the route of the flume, which I could glimpse for myself and which led to a tedious redundancy, inasmuch as there was sufficient lost lumber below us to build a dozen miles of trestle or an entire mill town complete with several dining halls and a dance pavilion. In any case I am accustomed to the waste of timber, as the creek banks below the splash dams of the lower Columbia are a tangle of stranded logs which must lie there until a bigger splash moves them along, or until such time as someone invents new machinery to lift them out.

But having a considerate nature, and having evidently guessed or been told the point of my errand, he soon turned to encouraging tales of miraculous rescues and escapes: a baby which fell from its father's arms and flashed down on the flume, where it was snatched up safe in the hands of the surprised flume tender; a runaway train bearing nineteen loads of logs which came down the main line into Yacolt and, going off the end of the track, slid straight on down the county road, traveling fast and upright and gradually coming to rest without encountering a single dog, woman, child, or baby carriage. He supposed I would be relieved and comforted to hear that flumes transport not only the ordinary lumber and sawlogs and shingle bolts but every sort of article from crates of groceries to catches of fish, as well as the occasional injured party borne out to the hospital. Of course, if Harriet must be carried out of the woods with a broken leg, I will hope that she's also catatonic and senseless, for although the Canyon Creek flume is a short five-mile slide downhill at better than a mile a minute and the trail otherwise is a tedious and hard roundabout, I believe, for myself, if I fell on my axe, I should rather take my chances with gangrene and a slow painful jostle carried out on the backs of my fellowmen, than plunge down the flume in a boat having the shape and velocity of a sawlog.

We came at last to the flume tender at the upper end, who, when he'd gotten over his surprise at seeing a woman climbing up the catwalk, scrambled down like a monkey into the complicated geometry of the trestle and hung there while we passed single file over his head. The two men exchanged the most casual of greetings and lengthy summaries amounting to an All's Clear

At Both Ends, and after we had passed by him, the monkey clambered up to the catwalk again and sauntered off downhill, giving the occasional drift-log a cautionary jab with his peavey hook.

My own dear flume tender, as I discovered from a chance remark, was a reader of newspapers, and when I heard this I turned our talk away from close shaves and perilous lifeboats—entirely away from the lurking but unspoken business of a child lost in the deepwoods. We enlivened the air with our fair knowledge of the world's doings and our opinions of how things were being conducted. We argued over the future of capitalism and prospects for the end of the Russo-Jap war, as well as the possibility that as men are more knowledgeable and more advantaged by technology, they may become more rational, and whether this transformation—together with radium power—might bring about the millennium.

We had a vigorous discussion of the mind of the educated woman. Under the old regime, I told him, a woman would pledge her housekeeping and baby-tending services to a man, along with certain social gains and regular sexual relations, all in exchange for economic security. But intellectual development renders a woman less dependent on marriage for her physical support (which I have proven in my own life), and as women are permitted to read Herbert Spencer and work with calculus, there may come an end to their sewing on buttons and embroidering pillow-slips.

I would not have been surprised if a rough and whiskered flume tender living way back in the wilderness had objected most strenuously to such an idea. The vast majority of men, even in these modern times, still require a lisping, clinging creature with a willingness to worship the masculine form. I have no doubt that such men as Homer Coffee or Melba's drunkard husband, Henry Pelton, fear women's access to higher education will create a race of monsters—unsexed creatures with clubbed hair and a blighting power. But the flume tender gave way before my arguments and offered his own mild opinion that a woman with a complete understanding of the clockworkings of the universe is a woman in closer touch with nature.

I wondered then, as I do now, if he might have been a man hiding his lamp under a basket, so to speak. It's well known that the remote logging camps are scattered with educated men—lawyers, doctors, teachers, men who have held important positions in business—who have turned to the hermit life after legal or personal calamity of one kind or another. I asked him nothing of that kind and offered him nothing of my own history: such is the Western way.

I sit now at the top of the flume—having shaken his hand and seen him back down the catwalk—refreshing myself with an apple and sandwich on a stump well apart from the furor of the logging, while I bring events up to date on these pages. On another sheet I have scribbled down the outline of a little story in which the hero is a flume tender of knightly attributes, driven into the wild West by tragic circumstances in the civilized East, and whose heroine is a pretty though stalwart girl, forced to cross miles of precarious and collapsing catwalk in order to save the life of her wounded beloved.

🍂 *If I were writing in a serious vein, I should worry that the literary value and aesthetic considerations of "women's writing" has never been seriously addressed at all. Women with a literary vocation have in times past been banished to the periphery, where they were encouraged to focus upon letter-writing and the intimate diary. But writing is a profession which is now said to be thoroughly compatible with the modern understanding of a woman's role: the "authorine," after all, may work at home out of the public eye, close to the nursery, the sickroom, the parlor, the kitchen, and thus bring into the family a modest income which does not challenge the idea that a woman's first duty is to her husband and children. That she must write, or try to, between visits, dinners, housework, sewing, and so on is understood.*

Of course, while we are told that writing is one of the few careers now open to women on equal terms with men, women who wish to write are relegated to special fields where we will not disturb or occupy the space designated for the male Artist. In men's literature, of course, there may be Human Beings in all their terrible contradictions and distress: men and women who struggle with their ignorance, their doubt; men and women who are overwhelmed and exhausted by their circumstances but who, despite bleakness of landscape, refuse to be overcome by the violence, cruelty, and apparent hopelessness of their societies. Women, on the other hand, should write only about other women and the domestic issues of love and nurturing (and nothing else); in women's literature, women must be incapable of committing evil deeds or even imagining them; in women's novels, heroines should always be good and generous, and when they are unjustly overpowered or attacked, they must seek a male champion.

And since women are rarely mentioned in articles and other works of literary criticism that present a history of literature, these omissions are compensated for by including separate chapters dedicated to "women who write" and preparing collections of stories and essays just for women (that in general are not read by men). One can presume the literary standards in such a "one-eyed, blinking sort o' place" must suffer accordingly.

Of course, I am not great myself—cannot take myself seriously as an Artist. I write Romance, certainly, full of action and a wild, fierce life—stories without much more than a glimpse of the shop or the town, stories in which there are frozen landscapes and fiery interiors, wild mountains, rivers whose sources have never been hunted out— but my writing is frankly "light" and does not try to be anything else: the lower forms of cloak-and-sword, without a glimpse of the Truth.

As to plot, I am in substantial agreement with Haggard: there must be a sacred stone, and in front of the altar a trapdoor under which burns a constant fire into which condemned prisoners are thrown. There may very well be a gigantic volcano beneath which lies a vast limestone cavern illuminated by columns of fire or electrical light from a mysterious source. I am fond of colliding planets, invisible airships, elixirs that confer immortality, and crumbling temples guarded by ancient snares and pitfalls. In my stories, mystics and villains enter a drugged trance, leave their bodies, and travel through the world on a spiritual plane. I am a devotee, like Verne, of the possibilities of science and engineering: bulletproof vests, lie-detector chairs, electrocution machines, artificial men of steam and iron, as well as a proliferation of high-speed comfortable trains fitted up like hotels.

I am, however, no fan of Haggard's priestesses and empresses, who seem to me symbols of the Woman-Monster whom men worship and fear—Vampyres who would suck the vital strength from Men. On the other hand, although domestic novels are useful weapons in women's undeclared war against male society, and while I am sympathetic to plots involving husbands who drink, gamble, and chase, as well as runaway daughters and sons who stray, sickness, poverty, insecurity, and so forth, I would never write them myself. I am thoroughly tired of the Loose Woman, Handsome Seducer, Sick Husband, Other Woman, Brave Wife, Tortured Hero, Tubercular Child, and Martyred Indian Maiden who seem to live upon every page of the magazines women favor—Godey's, Ladies' Home Journal, the Casket, et al.—and in so very many of the cheap novels to be found in women's hands. It is my feeling that the one thing worth doing as a writer is to dwell upon things that arouse the imagination—upon swords and gabled cities and ancient forests, upon temples and palaces, giant apes in their revolt, and imprisoned princesses in their unhappiness.

As a thoroughgoing Feminist and a woman who has herself thrown over the traces of domestication as much as can be done without risking arrest, I do my best to swim against the tide. For heroine of a scientific romance, I will always choose the scientifically inclined daughter or sister of a world-renowned anthropologist; and for the western romance, look for a girl who can ride and shoot, a ranch girl born and raised in the West (though of course not in a trapper's shack—it must be a wealthy ranch, a minor island of culture possessed of cupboards of books, fine furniture, and a piano); and—it will turn out—she has been to boarding school in the East: the cultivated heroine aglow with the strength of the wilderness.

I am, of course, driven by the marketplace. My thoroughly unrepentant, ungenteel tomboys and Amazons must be killed saving the hero's life. And my lovely girl hero, who may exhibit composure, courage, self-reliance, and practical competence until five pages from the end, must ultimately be propelled off the range and into the ranch house—the running of her life given over to a man.

I bore from within as much as may be: in courtship, the dear girl never falls into a romantic swoon but keeps a clear head about her—chooses her husband for his qualities as a companion—and keeps her spunky spirit unto The End. I hope it may be inferred of my girls they would never take mistreatment from a man—would rather pack up the children and move to Alaska, where they would all pan for gold and live in a tent.

C. B. D.

May 1904

C. B. D. (1905; unpublished)

TATOOSH OF THE SEE-AH-TIKS; OR,

A GIRL'S ADVENTURES AMONG MOUNTAIN GIANTS

CHAPTER TWO: THE HORRIBLE SIGHT

A fearful encounter—Helena cast into darkness—
A message sent by invisible means—Helena bravely poses a question—
Journey across the mountains

Having the habit and inclination of a scientist, the brave girl bent her attention to a close observation of this abomination of nature, even as she stood in dire peril from it. Though erect of posture and in other ways resembling a man, the creature towered above the forest floor to a hideously unnatural stature of more than seven feet, its monstrous physique covered thickly with short, black, coarse hair, which had the effect of transforming its appearance to that of a hitherto unknown species of giant ape or gorilla. Its huge, swarthy head was placed low upon immense sloping shoulders, and a thick, bearded chest gave upon a narrowing waist. Its feet were wide and flat, with toes all of a length, and seemingly not possessing the gripping strength of the known great apes of Africa and Asia. Further, there was no prehensile tail. Its hands, while huge, were delicately formed and possessed of fully opposable thumbs. Although Science would have it that no such creature lives in the vast Cascadian forests, nor ever has, the creature's conduct was entirely natural, as though it was native to these environs.

In its upright and naked condition, the creature's masculinity was manifestly disclosed, and though Miss Reed was a seasoned explorer, the sight struck her with such force that a small gasp of abhorrence was wrung from her lips. The monster, which might otherwise have remained unaware of our young adventurer, chanced to hear the telltale sound, and at once it laid flashing black eyes upon her. She glimpsed rows of glittering yellow teeth in a hideously wide red mouth, and the world, in that moment, spun about her in a kaleidoscope of colors. Though she resisted with every fiber of her strength, she was relentlessly drawn down into the helpless darkness of oblivion.

For an indeterminate time, no sound came to her ears, but then she began to hear a musical murmuring voice which filled her with an uncommon sense of peace and tranquillity. "Have I awakened unto Death?" she wondered, without the least sense of fear or foreboding.

"No," she was told by the most euphonious of voices, as if she had spoken her thought aloud. "You are quite alive, safe, and unharmed." The words entered into her very being, in the manner of melodious bells being rung at a distance too far to perceive save in the vibrations of one's soul. She might have believed that she had entered upon Heaven, had she not become suddenly aware of her earthly body. Her eyes opened at last, upon a view of the crystalline blue sky and the overarching verdure of the great forest. It was only when she became aware of the hideous mountain giant, its face now but inches from her, that she recalled all with a rush of apprehension. "Do not be afraid," the magical, musical voice reassured her once again, and as a peaceful quietude reentered her mind, she beheld the deep-set black eyes of the forest beast gazing upon her with something approaching tenderness and innocence.

Realizing she was unharmed, she sat up resolutely and looked about her. Her knapsack had fallen open when she had swooned, and its contents were arrayed on the mossy forest floor: dry stockings and foot plasters, compass and watch, sandwich, strong twine, minnow netting and a folder of trout flies, two-bladed jack-knife, rubber blanket, strike-anywhere matches, and a large tinned coffee cup. When she returned her attention to the mountain giant, its voice—for she had by now realized that the invisible words indeed emanated from the creature before her—spoke once again as if within her very brain: "From the items in your sack I should judge you to be a ready adventurer, and perhaps quite used to startling discoveries and frightful sights such as I must be to you."

Only her father, the renowned explorer James Reed, had ever supported her in her chosen vocation, and she had become sadly accustomed to amusement and doubt arising from both men and women when they first learned of her intention to become the first woman accepted for full membership in the National Geographical Society. Indeed, those who heard of her experiences in Java and Africa were likely to respond with disapproval, even revulsion, as if a woman adventurer were an abhorrent and unnatural thing. The creature's frank and immediate faith in her abilities was both satisfying and unexpected. "Indeed, I am not usually given to such swoons," she said in dismay, and was immediately, though wordlessly, reassured that the swoon was not due to her own weakness, but to an arcane art of the creature before her. What relief!

She now betook herself to stand, and having regained her feet and her aplomb, she spoke again to her monstrous companion: "I have heard certain tales from the native tribes in these regions, describing just such creatures as yourself. In the legends of the Kwakiutls, I believe, there is a hairy giant known as Tzooniquaw, and among the Tsinuks the name given is Hoquiam."

The giant replied in the musical telepathy to which Helena had by now become accustomed: "Among the Indian people, our names are many: Skoocoom, Swalalahist, Om-mah, Sa-sa-katch. Among certain of the Cowelits Indians we are known as See-Ah-Tiks, which in the Cowelits language has the meaning People of the Forest."

Helena, by means of the creatures unspoken words, understood that this appellation pleased him, and she resolved henceforth to address the hairy giants, in word or thought, as the See-Ah-Tiks, the Forest People.

He continued: "I am myself called Tatoosh, which in your language might be said as the Scented Flower." "Tatoosh" seemed completely unaware of the irony of a creature of such masculine girth and strength as himself, bearing such a feminine and pacific name.

"Dear Mr. Tatoosh, I am known as Miss Helena Reed," she replied, and taking a shuddering breath of determination, offered her small hand to the animal. Though he at first seemed without understanding of this human gesture, a mental image may have passed from Helena's mind to his, for he soon took her hand tenderly in his huge fist. The ape's palm was smooth and quite hairless, manlike in every way but for its size.

She had already become quite used to the See-Ah-Tik's animal-like appearance, and with this familiarity had come the realization that what had heretofore seemed horrific and monstrous was in fact well disposed and benign. Indeed, the See-Ah-Tik's teeth, on closer inspection, were the blunt molars of a vegetarian, and his sunken, glittering black eyes were round as a child's and fringed with thick lashes. His huge, delicately formed hands were expressive and gentle in the manner of a refined man of breeding. Most interesting to Helena Reed, his overall demeanor demonstrated neither the animosity of the feral animal to the human, nor the dominion of male over female, but a respectful equality as between two beings of correspondent rank. From what sort of race had this creature come? she wondered. What habits of his culture had encouraged this respect for other species, and indeed for the opposite sex? She became curious to observe the See-Ah-Tiks in their native intercourse, males and females together.

"Are there many such as you?" Helena inquired. "I'm made to wonder why none other than Indians have recorded the existence of a race of such uncommon size and appearance as yourself."

The creature beheld her with a sorrowful smile. "We are not so many as in past times. As your people have advanced upon the forests, we have been driven to smaller and smaller precincts, and though we keep within our own borders as much as possible, there are certain pharmaceuticals which can be supplied only by venturing out." He lifted and showed her a black box-shaped container formed of an unnaturally smooth, indeterminate material, into which he had been gathering leaves of thimbleberry and hairy manzanita. "Inevitably there have been encounters between your people and mine, but our powers of hypnotism have, for the most part, kept us safe from human memory." Again he smiled, with all the poignancy of someone who accepts a bitter destiny. "If one day our hiding place is revealed, we will doubtless be driven to extinction as so many among the species of Indians and of animals have been, and perhaps then we shall live only in your legends."

As a scientist unswayed by sentimentalism, she recognized the bitter truth in what he said. Helena then made what many would think a rash proposition. "Might I return with you to your See-Ah-Tik home in the forest?" she asked the giant earnestly. "May I undertake to examine and record your customs, ceremonies, and usages? If your extraordinary powers of hypnotism are as you describe them, then you shall be as safe from human discovery as you wish to be, for I cannot share the knowledge and memory I will gain, unless with your approval. Indeed, you are wise to be fearful of the White Race of humans, and on that ground I must accept any such restrictions. But it may be that a written record of your society could benefit the future of your race, or of mine, and surely it would be desirable to prepare this record while there is yet a living society to record."

Her gravely ardent face studied Tatoosh for some sign of his sympathies, but the giant's face was a secret mask. At long last he solemnly replied, "It is not in my power alone to make such a decision. But you may return with me to the Gate of See-Ah-Tik, where the Council of Five will discuss the matter and come to a determination."

Our adventurer thus was satisfied. She had every confidence that the rational power of her argument would persuade the so-called Council of Five to allow her to enter the occult society of See-Ah-Tik.

As she hurriedly gathered the contents of her knapsack, her active young mind leapt upon a multitude of questions: Was telepathy their only means of communication, or did they also, among themselves, make use of oral language? On the matter of sexual community, did they recognize marriage and arrange themselves into families? What were their food resources and what the state of their industrial and scientific development?

Tatoosh beckoned her to follow him as he strode purposefully through the trees. The stalwart girl's years of physical conditioning served her well; inured to long tramps across deserts and jungles, she was in good wind, with but little flesh on her bones and her muscles well strung, and had no fear of getting tired. Though the See-Ah-Tik's long, effortless stride equaled three of Helena's, and though he made no apparent effort to slacken his pace for the sake of his young companion, she did not flag but maintained a steady, tireless jog across the rough terrain of hills and valleys, ever keeping the giant ape close before her. Acting against the opinion of some members of civilized society, she had adopted the custom when in the forest of dressing in a man's jumper and boots, and thus was saved the added effort of struggling through the shrubbery with full skirts a-billow More than once she uttered a self-satisfied cry of vindication as her strong young legs, clad sensibly in double-twist blue denim, conducted her with ease through a tangle of brambles or bore her trimly down a steep and rocky slope.

Nevertheless, the distance they covered was considerable, and our noble girl had nearly reached the limit of her endurance when at last the See-Ah-Tik moderated his pace and indicated with a gesture of his long, shaggy arm that they had reached their destination. They had come by a gradual and roundabout route onto the shoulder of a basalt mountain, and Helena was startled to realize that here, amid the impenetrable forest, the mountain had been scored as if with an invisible knife. The resultant ravine just at their feet was so abrupt and steep that the branches of the trees on either side almost touched and concealed it, in such a way that it was impossible to gauge its depth from above.

Though not a word had entered upon the air, she under-stood beyond question that this was the Gate of See-Ah-Tik, and her brave heart trembled with a sudden, awful misgiving.

Camp 8 (deepwoods), midnight of the 3rd

I cannot sleep; and since I wrote in these pages twice today, yet failed to bring the day to its close, I will write a third installment.

I should first report that the camp boss at the head of the flume (Camp 7) was a short Englishman with an impressive scar upon his cheek and a plug-tobacco habit that had stained his lower lip and chin. He had suffered three or four of his crew flying off to the search, he said, and the news that had come back was all of shootings and shouting; as for word of that lost child, he had none. He made me the offer of a trail guide, which I refused, having heard from the flume tender that the way up the canyon to Camp 8 was pretty well beaten in. He walked me as far as the trailhead, though, across a wilderness of windfalls, tall butts, sawed-off tops and branches, roots turned toes-up and looming fifteen feet in the air.

Before we shook hands and parted, we stood at the edge of the logging ground together and watched the donkey engine yard in a log, which is something I've seen before but never will get accustomed to. The donkey engine is a pathetic little thing to look at, a boiler, a furnace, pistons underneath, and the two drums worked by the pistons, drums for winding up the wire cables, which is little enough for a machine to do; but the whole thing is bolted on a great heavy wood sleigh and often moored, besides, by guy ropes into the trees; and when the whistle blows and the donkey puncher winds the lead line taut on the drum and then lets in the steam, and the engine bucks and rises up on its skids like a beast, well, then you begin to see the need for chaining it down.

"'Ere 'e comes now," the Englishman said to me happily, and spat beside his boot. There was a startling uproar in the woods—the sound of a cataclysm—and a log came charging out of the brush from a thousand feet off, hurling stones and earth before it, smashing and gouging its own pathway, bumping and battering over stumps and windfalls. It is quite something to see a log of that size, six feet through, seventy long, hurtling over the ground, lunging for the little donkey as the slavering Grendel after his Beowulf; and then the donkey rocks back and the poor log fetches up at its feet and you see who has the iron hand.

I should have covered the two miles of twisty trail before dusk but was slowed by the corruptible spring weather. It rotted away to the west before I had fairly gotten clear of the log operation, and the clabbering front which overtook me brought a dismal rain and a spate of hail. My lovely ramble through the bright woods, as I had been fooling myself, gave itself over to the sober truth: became a slippery footslog through the gloom, on a mission of dread and torment. I dug out my corduroy jacket and my hat from the meager outfit on my back, and put my head down.

That trail following Canyon Creek is involuted as the streets of Constantinople, and a steep climb followed by a steep downhill followed by the next climb and the next fall, and so on, with the latter in my opinion always much the worse. The path both going up and coming down was mud and runnels, for which reason, being alone, I made my way with caution and deliberation. I crossed over the two miles in something around an hour and a half, which, considering the circumstances was a decent clip. Nevertheless, the daylight went before me, and I blundered the last mile through gathering darkness, searching out the trail every little while with an Everready flashlight of the very latest design: no wires, no chemicals, no oil, smoke, or odor, but a battery in a cylinder made of heavy cardboard and covered with imitation morocco, which lights an electric lamp when the ring on the side is pressed against the ferrule.

My search light and I made out the buildings at Camp

8 precisely as the men came out from their dinner, and they streamed by me in a swearing, bawdy horde without notice at all of one more trousered man standing there in the darkness. I have resolved to give up the little courtesies men tender to women, in exchange for my independence and self-respect; but I was wet and cold by then and yearning for hot supper and a bed, which shamefully weakened my firmness of mind. I plucked at the sleeve of a man pausing to light his pipe and said, "I have just walked up from Chelatchie Prairie," as if this genuinely pathetic lament in the soprano of a well-bred Gentlewoman should be all the information he needed. As indeed it was. In astonished silence he led me round to the boss logger, who led me round to the dining-hall, where the boys cleaning up from dinner beheld in wonder the woman drinking her coffee and tucking away a chop and a plate of eggs.

The boss at Camp 8 is a tall, lank, and athletic-looking fellow by the name of Bill Boyce. He took me through the dark rain to his office at the back of the storeroom and roused up the little stove and unfolded a cot from under the bench and gave me directions to the privy and the pump, and a key so as to lock myself into the office. "They're good men, though," he said. "They won't give you a bit of trouble," which was said in a quiet and sure way that I approved of.

"I should be glad to speak to Homer Coffee," I said.

"Well, I'll see if I can turn him up, but it may be he spent the night out in the woods. There's parties all around, you see, searching for her, and by now they've got far enough out so they don't come in at night. A search party will get tired or short on provision, and then they straggle to camp and other ones go out. Things are in some confusion, with so many hunting, and I don't keep perfect track of who's in and who's out."

I made a trip to the privy and carried back water, made my toilet, and laid out my bed. Then I sat down in my damp clothes and thoroughly cleaned the mud from under my nails and combed loose my hair, which occupied me until Bill Boyce returned without Homer. "He's evidently up around the lava beds," he said to me, while averting his eyes from the improper sight of a woman's hair hanging upon her shoulders. "They're fixing to search the caves up there."

He described this country for me, which is not the Big Lava Bed of general renown, lying some dozen or more miles farther east, but several narrow ridges of hardened magma and hollow tubes of old lava scattered amongst the forestland, extruded in the same manner as the Big Lava Bed, through pipes in the volcanic system, mayhap from St. Helens Mountain, twenty miles to the north. Then, as he turned from the doorway of the little office, I asked him, "What is the prospect of finding her, do you think?" He had impressed me as a steady-minded man, thoughtful and careful and thorough.

He turned to me again and considered it. Then he said, "She could be lying up someplace, she could have found her a good spot in a rotted-out tree or something like that, and stayed pretty dry and kept herself from freezing. There's some edibles she might know about, cow parsnip and so on. We could still get her out. But it's not as likely as it was that first day. It's been five nights, you see, and though we had a lucky spell of dry weather, there was frost that first night, and now we've got rain. And as it continues on to rain, I'm afraid the prospects will get worse." He briefly shifted his look into the darker corners of the room, so that I felt I had glimpsed his true feeling. Then, when he had considered his audience again, he said in a darker voice, "After this much time, there is not a good deal of hope of finding her—not alive, at any rate, though I guess it would be some small comfort to her mother, just to recover the child's body." I had felt myself prepared for this honest assessment—indeed quite expected it—but the words themselves brought a strange flutter to my heart.

He had up to then said nothing of orang-utans or mountain beasts, but finally he did. "We got men swears they have seen her in the arms of what snatched her, but their testimony is suspect as far as I'm concerned. There is something called a skookum, you know, that Indians and maybe some loggers have seen, and I don't know what it is, but I guess I've heard a screech sometimes that is straight from the devil, so I can't entirely discount the idea. If a skookum took her, well then I'm afraid she must be dead, or would wish to be." He petted the doorjamb. "So my hope is that she just went off and got lost, which is easy to do around here." He pointed. "That's probably a pretty handy little device," meaning the fold-up rubber camp basin in which I'd washed my face and brushed my teeth.

"Yes, it is," I said.

As soon as I was left alone, I hung up my damp clothes over the stove and soaked my feet and rubbed my heels and toes with coconut oil and went to bed in my cotton vest and drawers. The rain had quit but there was a wind that had come up, and it searched along the floor and under the eaves, as well as through the tops of the trees circling the edge of the cutting ground, which is a sound very like a moaning, a lamentation of regret. I began to turn over in my mind what Melba had said to me about Homer, his meanness, and this led to an unfortunate train of thought. So now I sit upon Bill Boyce's cot with my flash light illuminating this page, writing, writing, which is a better occupation for my mind.

No, that demon, that dark death-shadow,
leapt out upon young and old alike,
a hideous ambush! In darkness he held
the misty moors. Men cannot know
whither such hell-wights bend their ways!

BEOWULF

❦ *Of course, I have become accustomed to thoroughly governing my own affairs and the affairs of my children, and I suppose I should have some trouble ever turning them over to a man again. And a woman who is believed to have been abandoned by a man is freed from certain concerns: public opinion, fixed by the unalterable fact of the desertion, becomes charmingly irrelevant. I am in those respects well content with my condition. But I never have conquered loneliness. I find as I grow older that its dominion becomes narrower, but there has always been a moment as I am climbing the stairs to bed when I begin to be mindful of my situation and to suffer from it; and in recent months, of course, I have felt this much more keenly than in the past. The lascivious will doubtless think of "the beast with two backs," but I believe what I miss foremost is something less particular, and less definable.*

There is a relief in getting your hair unbound at the end of the day, and when I have escaped the confines of my clothes and put on a loose nightgown, I like to take the pins from my hair and let it out onto my shoulders, put my hands into the thick tangle and pull my fingers through along the scalp until the whole mass of it is loose. I have an ivory comb with wide teeth which will get through thick snarls rather better than a hairbrush, and I sit at my dressing table and comb and comb with slow care until I've got all the day's knots out. Then I take at my head with the brush. I know some women will brush their hair one hundred times or five hundred, with a religious fervor, but I am too impatient to keep on with such a habit. I brush my hair vigorously from the roots until the brush crackles and my scalp burns, and that must be enough. Then I brush my teeth and wash my face, my hands, and my feet, before taking myself to bed. These are habits of years' standing, my accustomed practices carried out in the same order, always, at the end of every day. In recent years it has become also a sort of ritual habit to indulge in self-pity and dreariness while carrying them out. In the daylight I seldom think of the husband I have lost. But I remember him nostalgically at the end of day—dressing for bed, brushing his teeth, carefully soaping his face and scraping away the day's beard with his razor.

And of course, I miss not only the indefinable comfort of ritual nighttime ablutions carried out in each another's presence but the weight of another on the mattress with me, the heat of that person against my spine, the simple solace of another body in my bed. And in these modern days when life is so material and so rushed and there is less and less time for real talks or real thought, I miss especially the murmured words that a husband and wife exchange in their bedroom at the end of the day.

I suppose if I marry again, it will be for this; and not, as I once thought, for the reason that Feminists should hold up their egalitarian marriages as models before the public. (It is spring; even the birds all have mates.)

C. B. D.

April 1906

In the log camp (deepwoods), morning of the 4th

A party is forming, which I've been invited to join, but they are slow in their preparations, so I sit and write while waiting to head off into the wilderness. Whether I'm to be gone for one night or several remains to be seen—there are apparently half a dozen named and nameless branches of Canyon Creek, arranged in a succession of narrow gorges and elevations, and Bill Boyce has been methodically sending his men up one and down another until they have combed them all.

He rose at 4:30 when I heard the faint clatter of the cook's helpers beginning their preparations for breakfast, went in, and cadged from them the first cup of coffee. The cook is a big fellow with a walrus mustache and small eyes resembling those of a pig, which he turned on me with disapproval, but his helpers, who are George's age or a little more, were solicitous and kind, imagining, I suppose, that I might be their mother. I sat out of their way while drinking my coffee and gave the cook as good as ever I got.

If the camp had been working, the dinner gong would doubtless have been rung by 5:00 and the men breakfasted by 6:00 and walking out through the darkness to their jobs in the woods. But as it is, tired men wandered into the dining hall at intervals, which of course made more work for the cook and may have accounted for his ill nature. Bill Boyce came in shortly past 5:30, and seeing I was alone, he politely sat opposite me. "Have you ate?" he said, and though I had done so I ate again, which was only well mannered. I am not an easy talker before I've had my third cup of coffee, which Boyce before long surmised, so we ate in much of a silence save for the scrape of forks on plates and the quiet chewing of hind teeth. "It's been a while since I've been reminded of the little bit a lady eats," he did say at one point, which I suppose was meant to compliment. I had earlier put away hash and ham, a mess of greens, hotcakes, and oatmeal, as well as bread and doughnuts, and upon this second plate had made a dainty arrangement of bacon and potatoes and stewed fruit. My mind briefly turned over the question of how a Feminist ought to answer such a falsity. "I've never suffered the lack of an appetite," I said in the end, which at least was true and might, under the circumstances, be considered neutral.

When we sat over our plates washing all down with our third and fourth cups of coffee, and my eyelids had risen somewhat, he said to me, "Now, what are your intentions, Mrs. Drummond?"

And I replied in the straightest way possible: "I intend to learn whatever details are to be learned about the way Harriet disappeared, and the progress of the search, and to send that complete information by letter back to her mother and grandmother, who are waiting in Yacolt with only rumors and vagueness to comfort them. And I intend to go out looking for her myself."

He bent his head to his coffee cup. It's rare to see a logger without a soup strainer, but he is clean shaven, his sideburns trimmed short and beginning to gray. A small scar in the shape of a crescent moon decorates his naked chin, the skin of which is leathery and thick in the way of men who work out of doors. When he raised his head from studying the bottom of his cup, he said, "Well, as to the first part, here is what I know: Homer Coffee brought his girl up to this camp on Monday morning, which a father will do, you see, to give his child a little adventure, and to show her off a bit, or maybe show himself off. A log operation is a dangerous place, and I wouldn't bring a child of mine here if I had one, but though I discourage it as much as I can, I don't outright forbid them from it. Well, his donkey crew set her on a windfall a ways up the steep hill behind them, which is the safest place, I guess, though no place is truly safe, and the men say she was good as gold, not scared by the noise or the sled bucking when a log comes up jammed behind a stump or a rock, which it will do. And at lunch Coffee took her out to the edge of the cut woods, to where there is a little crick and a glade, and which is out of harm's way, and they ate their lunch together and he watched while she played in the crick, and then he brung her back to her lookout perch on the hill, where she sat all afternoon without a peep. Which was Monday, and the same on Tuesday. On Wednesday, after they'd had their picnic in the woods, she evidently whined and told her daddy she was tired of watching the same dread work over and over, which I don't doubt, so he left her there at the crick to go on playing, and he says he give instruction for her not to leave the glade. But at the end of the day, when he went out for her, she wasn't in the same place.

"He looked awhile, I don't know how long it was, and when he was walking back to get others to help him look, he evidently had a glimpse of something going off through the trees, which was considerable bigger than his girl, as he says, but even so, he followed after it; and when he finally give up and yelled to the others of his crew, the daylight was going in a hurry. They shortly come back here and we all lit lanterns and looked through the night without finding his girl nor the thing he'd seen, which could have been elk, or bear, or I don't know. What was found next day after the sun come up was one of her little shoes, which was about one hundred feet into the trees, and some long tracks going up the slope from the crick about a quarter of a mile farther along, which might only be men's boot prints run together and wore away by rain. We had had a Special Agent up that way the week before, surveying the trees, and they could have been his prints, you see, where he slid a bit, and then much rained-upon. There was no blood and no sign from a bear or a coyote or any of that kind in the grass where Coffee left her, and her own prints was hard to make out from all the tramping through there looking for her.

"Since then we've had more than fifty men out looking, most of which will swear they're looking for a giant orang-utan that ripped her out of her daddy's arms. I don't know your opinion of Homer Coffee, Mrs. Drummond, and this isn't meant to speak ill of him, but he has become as sure as any fool, by now, and is swearing it was a giant wildman or ape that he saw, though he didn't get much of a look that I ever heard about, and at the time it happened couldn't say *what* it was. What we have found so far, for all our hunting, is just a lot of tracks too muddy to make sense of, and stories too excitable to credit, and men with too little sense to keep from shooting at each other in the woods. But we're still looking and will go on awhile yet, until I'm told by the Company that we ought to get back to work. And that's what I know of the circumstances, pretty nearly all of it."

He lifted his arms from the table so as to permit the cook's boy to take away his plate and wipe the oilcloth clean. Then he said, resting his arms again, "As for the second thing, I wouldn't recommend you to strike off on your own, so I wonder if you mean to attach yourself to a search party that's heading out, or perhaps join up with Homer Coffee in the lava beds?"

Since this was direct and not patronizing, I said, "I frankly don't know. It was just my idea that I'd make myself useful." This was the truth, though not all of it. Here is another part: I had imagined I might find Harriet myself, in some little corner overlooked by others.

Bill Boyce took me to see the place Harriet had gone lost from—the little "crick and glade." We walked out to it through a damp, cold grayness, a morning as featureless as an unlicked

lamb. The fog lying along the ground hid a good deal of the logging mess, the tops and trimmings, old cables and broken tools,
but the waste hemlocks that had been left behind on the cutover
fields rose up singly from the smoking ground and brought to
my mind skinny gray pilings standing in a slough. At the edge of
the uncut woods we jumped a piddling little stream, and Boyce
led me a short tramp under the eave of the forest to the channel of a wider creek, or perhaps it was the main thoroughfare
of the piddle. Here had been a burn fifty or sixty years earlier,
for there were slender trees and brush growing beneath a dead
superstructure of enormous whitened trunks. I confess those
great skinned limbs pale as bone gave me a qualm, which I attri-
bute to lack of sleep and to melancholy.

The clearing where Harriet and Homer had eaten their
lunch must receive the sun when the sun consents to shine, and
the industrious browsing of elk and deer had worn the shrubbery down to nubbins and left a jade-green field of vanilla-leaf
and miner's lettuce, now much trampled upon and disturbed;
of course, there was nothing of Harriet's to indicate she ever
was there. We followed the margin of the creek into the primeval forest until the trees standing about us were giants thick
as the Washington Monument and surely standing well grown
when Columbus crossed the Atlantic. Such trees as these were
common around Skamokawa in my childhood but long since
gone to lumber, and I suppose I began to suffer a bit from a
feeling of puniness and anxiety, which must be the human
response to such supernatural forests. We have become too
domesticated—imagining a forest should resemble a park, with
a few judiciously spaced trees whose dead branches have been
pruned away, flowers in weeded beds, grass neatly mown. Here,
the shrubbery was meager from want of sunlight but great

carcasses of windthrown timber lay about in unequal progress toward decay, with infant trees shooting up Indian file along the nurse-logs; and in damp, dark hollows yellow flower spikes of skunk cabbage were all abloom, which gaudy brilliance in the gray light served, contrariwise, to darken my mood more than raise it. There is something about those great fleshy leaves and spathes that always has struck me as repellent, loathsome; and in my low state I imagined them a teratogenic flower garden tended by monsters. Everything was wild. Of course, that is the meaning of forests, that they are wild.

Mr. Boyce pointed out the muddy bank where he said the big rain-slurried prints had been found, but there were no iden- tifiable marks by this time, and the phantom-orchids growing along the edge of the mud were already beginning to make their recovery from a trampling by boots or the feet of giants. We stood and looked a moment and then faced about and made like cowards for the open ground. On the cutover field, the fog having ebbed off, it was possible to see the shape of the bare ground, knobby as an Irish wold, though entirely brown and much torn up, studded with stumps, cut through by the muddy creek; and this view, even though rough and unsightly, I found a great comfort after the dark and supernatural woods.

Where the creek narrowed between high banks, I made out the distant prospect of a splash dam, which is a structure famil- iar to me from operations on the lower Columbia, where they sit on every little coastal stream, and must have been employed here due to remoteness and lack of a railroad spur line. The usual thing is to yard up your logs behind the dam until the pond is full, and then pull away the spill gate and let the freshet wash the whole show downstream, so I said to Boyce, "I suppose logs splashed down this creek must eventually arrive at Camp 7." My knowledge of splash dams had sparked in me the usual glimmer of self-importance, which I will always advertise.

He gave me an admiring look of surprise—oh, a considerable satisfaction—and allowed as how his logs washed downstream to the pond at Camp 7, where they were gathered up and sent down the flume. When I told him the source of my unwomanly knowledge was merely to have lived most of my life on the lower Columbia, he said to me with a lively interest, "So you're an old pioneer, are you? In this part of the country, I find not many people have been in one place longer than last week."

"Last week I was in Skamokawa, amongst all the other latecomers, but my mother's family was among the first to settle up the Grays River, if you know that part of the woods, and my mother was born and raised there, which doubtless makes her an Old Pioneer."

"I do know Grays River, Mrs. Drummond. We never got up that far, but we scouted some timber on Crooked Creek, which I know is in that direction."

"There's now a post office on Crooked Creek, which some fool has named Eden."

"Is that right? There was nothing much but trees in that country when I went through."

"They're making every effort to cut them all down, in the evident belief that Eden was a stump garden. At the present rate of logging, and considering the improvements to machinery, I don't wonder that all the trees in the West, with the exception of Roosevelt's reservations, will soon be cut to the ground. They have brought a steam falling-saw and a crawling tractor powered by gasoline into the Columbia River woods, you know, and at the mouth of the Wallace Slough they are laying a floating cradle which, when finished, will form an

ocean-going log raft one thousand feet long. The world is spinning fast, Mr. Boyce, and you fellows in logging are doing what
you can to keep up."

He took this impersonally. "Well, we're in a land of logging,
Mrs. Drummond; and I recall from my Bible that Eden is a garden, all right, and no mention of a forest."

This was something I could not deny. Muir and the pres-
ervationists would have the ancient deepwoods unaltered by
man, but I suppose Harriet would not now be lost if these
woods were a tamed and beneficent park. In any case, I am a
woman who most admires the wilderness from the comfort of
her civilized home, and in point of practice my Utopist fantasies will every time bring forth a cultivated, pastoral nature,
with ripe fruit dropping from every bough, and not a giant wild
tree in sight.

We had by now come into near view of the camp, which,
being way back in the deepwoods with no milled lumber at
hand, is made of cedar slabs with the bark left on, and roof
shakes thick as a man's fist. The lamps in the windows were
lighted, for it was still dark inside at half past seven, and the
shaggy buildings sitting amongst the usual black stumps and
rubbish piles and outhouses had the appearance of a comforting
cloister. I was struck by this, a pang somewhat resembling nos-
talgia, and quoted seriously to Boyce, "Home is home, though it
be never so homely."

He skipped a look in my direction, evidently wondering
if there was sarcasm involved—we had just then come within
range of the fragrant hog pens. But his reply, when he delivered
it, was sentimental as a cheap romance novel. "Well, it's a con-
solation, Mrs. Drummond, how lamplight and chimney smoke
will give the worst place a cheerful aspect."

I have written these words down, and expect to place them in the mouth of one romantic character or another as soon as I recognize the appropriate moment in my story.

> Our national forest reserves are still to a large extent in a wild, natural state, and it will be many years, in fact, before they shall have become impressed with the stamp of artificiality. Fire-scarred and over-grazed as many of them are, careful treatment can but improve the appearance which large areas in the reserves present to-day. And yet there are corners and ridges and valleys in these reserves that would retain a higher scenic value by being left untouched, if such a sacrifice were possible. Would it not be possible to combine in each of the proposed special reservations the silvicultural aims and the aesthetic ones?
>
> AMERICAN FORESTRY ASSOCIATION,
> *Forestry and Irrigation*, June 1905

C. B. D. (1905; unpublished)
from TATOOSH OF THE SEE-AH-TIKS

By means of that precariously narrow flight of stairs, the party descended to a hidden cleft in the rock, and thence into a labyrinth of dark passageways and narrow lanes, which after some time unwound onto a broad level road paved with bituminized wood and illuminated by electrical lamps. Helena had nearly despaired of reaching their destination when the road at last gave on a splendid gateway of fluted and twisted pillars, beyond which could be seen an immense domed cavern lit not only by clefts in the mountainous roof, through which poured an abundance of sunlight, but also by the phosphorescence of the volcanic stone itself, which caught the sun and mirrored it. The road, after passing through the gateway, sloped downward into a wide valley, the whole of which could be seen from that high outlook. At the center was a circular city built around a vast central piazza, with streets radiating outward, extending into a land of tranquil lakes, open parklands, and neatly groomed orchards. On the lakes were gondolas of a swan design, powered by some unknown means; and on the footpaths, which were paved with stone, strolled a population of See-Ah-Tiks, the naked men and women alike ornamented with bright and colorful jewelry. The roofs of the city, which were adorned with elaborate flower gardens, struck the eye, from this high vantage, as a bright and intricate Egyptian mosaic. It was altogether a startling and resplendent sight.

4 Apr
Darling boys,
This is morning and I am writing to you from the dining hall of a log camp away back in the deepwoods, while Melba is keeping Florence company in Yacolt. You have never seen such large trees as grow here. If one of you—even George—were to hide behind the trunk of one, even though his arms were outspread, you other boys could not see him from the opposite side. You know the stump behind Horace Stuband's milking shed where Lightning hid her kittens last litter but one? With its rooster tail of fern and huckleberry? The trees they

are cutting here will leave stumps such as that—such as I saw
on the Deep River Divide as a child. I must get this note off
to you quickly—not to frighten you with such haste, but I am
setting off directly with a search party, and by tonight shall be
in the black lava caves far up in the mountains, where we are
all hoping to find Harriet hiding, safe and sound. We will see
one another soon. With all the love I can send you,

M

In the lava fields (morning) 5 Apr

One of my fortunes is a resilient constitution—I have had but
five hours of sleep, which has thoroughly restored me—and one
of my deficiencies a smallish bladder, which is to blame for
my awakening this morning before the crack of dawn. After a
private toilet in the woods, and finding myself reconstituted, I
now sit in a cold gray light, writing of yesterday's events while
the men are still moving sluggish and rolling their blankets.

My letter to Melba and Florence was a breathless flurry of
particulars and minor facts which may yet conceal the scrupulous omission of Hope. I sent it by way of a colored man who
was forced to quit the search—evidently he broke his collar-
bone, and in the nonchalant way of loggers with regard to injuries, his friends bound his arm tight to his body and have sent
him afoot and alone over the trail and the flume to Camp 6,
and thence over the spur to Chelatchie Prairie and the rails to
Yacolt, where there is a doctor.

I saw him away with my letter—oh, it was two letters, as I
also wrote to the boys, and asked Melba to see it posted from
Yacolt—and promptly afterward made off into the woods with
six men and two horses, who are taking the search farther up

Canyon Creek and then along one of the many local stream courses to an outbreak of lava which evidently stretches away in a high ridge toward the southeast.

My own particular intent is to put myself in the way of meeting up with Homer, and this is a party that will likely bring me into his locality; we should end up, I was told, joining ourselves to other search parties among the black caves and casts, which terrain the men look upon as the suspected haunt of monsters and orang-utans.

We struck off south-by-east from Camp 8 across the logged-over field and skirting around Harriet's little glade, until shortly we were under the old trees. After my walk at dawn with Bill Boyce, the dark, eldritch woods had gotten more ordinary; or I had gotten over my spurt of unholy dread; or there were now sufficient numbers of us to foster a feeling of safety. I followed the boots of the man before me, tramping stolidly through a common daylight forest whose trees, though tall as the trees of Brobdingnag, had become the barely noticed frame for hard work.

This was ground that had been thoroughly searched in the first days and therefore could be passed through without much attention. We climbed by means of switchbacks, a seemingly circular route, until I was sure we were headed north-by-west and must soon come down again onto the cutting ground at Camp 8. I was grateful for the horses, who suffered under the weight of the greater part of our provender and carried also the heavy tents, which otherwise would have had to be parceled out to the shoulders of the seven hikers, and to my own puny shoulders in particular. In the rainy months this country is generally inhospitable to horses, as the deep ruts, mud holes, and steep embankments will bring on a condition of swelled ankles which some people have colorfully named "mud fever." The two horses in our party, though, are hammer-nosed, short-legged, sorrowful-looking creatures, whose thick ankles are frankly due to inelegant breeding and whose coarseness serves them well, I suppose, in the matter of standing continually in muddy conditions.

They were brought to the search by the three Pierce brothers, whose cinnabar mine lies situated somewhere in these hills around Camp 8. Besides the brothers, and the audacious woman, our party includes a peeler and a faller from Bill Boyce's crew and, lastly, a photographist named Earl Norris, carrying on his back an 11 x 14 Eastman view camera and a high-extension tripod. He has been making his living by photographing every operation in every phase of West Coast logging, and selling his photographs to loggers and lumbermen to enshrine their place in the fast-disappearing Glory Days of Logging. I'm told he came up the flume from Chelatchie just hours ahead of me, and I don't doubt he joined the search in the hope of finding his own glory: a photograph of a genuine Wild Man of the Woods might be expected to make a man's fortune, and, failing that, a gruesome photograph of a lost child's body should butter his bread for weeks.

"The boys" are a rough class but, as is the usual way in this country, would not fail in respect to a lady. While we climbed through the wet shrubbery, I fell into conversation with the youngest of the brothers, who proved to be desperately anxious to talk once he had been spoken to. We batted the shuttle back and forth: I told a fishing tale to do with a flock of geese flying into a boat cabin and shut in by the quick-thinking captain, who served them for supper; he returned with a mining story of fellows who had blown their own house to shreds while drying explosives in their kitchen stove. I then recommended several books to him, Verne in particular, whose work is principally aimed at the working class and the young; he had not heard of Verne but said he would seek him out, on my good advice. Once the ice was broken—and here I suppose I was encouraged by my earlier success with the flume tender—I pressed on him several arguments for women to have the vote, and the sensibleness of trousers when a woman goes tramping in the woods. This drew from him a circumspect nod which I took to be an admission of the validity of certain of my arguments, and afterward a complete silence. It was necessary for the peeler, a Finn named Peter Mer, to rescue us all with an account of a bear who liked to eat tallow off the logs of a skid road.

When we'd gained a certain elevation, our way straightened and became, as I thought, an ordinary matter of following the course of Canyon Creek, which was occasionally visible as a pale glimpse in the draw below us. But the path was confined to a narrow ridge with a precipitous fall on either hand, and I did take a slip—came up handsomely against a tumulus of rock and earth at the uttermost edge of the yawning chasm— and survived only by luck. In my brief flight I made no sound, though some of the boys shrieked; and afterward, having lain a moment on the ground taking survey of my health, I sprang up with a wild joy and shouted out, "Nothing broken—not hurt at all!" and felt about for my hat. It was only afterward, when the boys sat me on a stone and gave me a look-over, and when I peered once again down into the canyon, that the thought of what could have happened came in a rush, and I very nearly was brought to tears over it. (Of course, now that the experience is safely over, it is interesting to think about—my lack of fear, and how Death might have taken me off just that quickly, without notice or warning. I think of Montaigne: "If you know not how to die, never trouble yourself; Nature will in a moment fully and sufficiently instruct you; she will exactly do that business for you; take you no care for it.")

Shortly we were headed downhill again, very steep into the gorge, until reaching the trough of a nameless little tributary, which we turned up, and thereafter became more earnest in our mission. The log faller, a stringy, big-eared fellow named E. B. Johnson, being the senior man present, gave us our direction: we were to distribute ourselves along both steep banks of the creek and beat our way methodically upstream through the brush. Every little while, he said, it wouldn't hurt to send a halloo into the trees.

The boys said I should be placed along the ridge with the horses—that is, at the top of the pitch to the creek, where the going was least troublesome—but I stupidly refused this offer out of an excess of female hubris, and made off down into the gully, where I took a spot between the peeler and the photographist, on the steep starboard flank of the creek. From there I set to work along my strip of ground, hallooing for Harriet every little while and whacking a stick through the underbrush, looking for a scrap of cloth, or a footprint, or the child herself, dead or catatonic.

I believe I began with an irrational sense of hopefulness, as if I did actually expect to be the one to find her, and—even more irrationally—expected it to happen within the first hours. But the day was passed by clambering over and under the tangled, matted wreckage of hundreds of years of windthrown logs, slipping and stumbling around rocks and crevices, falling breast high into brush and tree limbs and the sharp, piercing spines of devil's club. It was impossible to keep footing on the plunging, muddy incline. I floundered along, trying to look as if I was getting across the ground on easy terms, trying to keep the idea of womanly weakness out of the boys' heads, and my own; and they scrambled along on either side of me, whether with ease or difficulty, damned if I knew, but quick enough and steady enough to make me long passionately for a respite. Gradually the reality of the search, the formidability of it, found its way into my body and brain, and the work became leaden, as if I dragged a pointless weight—as if a logger's heavy blocks and hooks and wire tackle were fouling behind me in the brush.

The rain held off, which was the only grace given to us; the air was cold and damp, and at intervals an icy wind brought down spatters of wet from the sodden trees. We stopped once, to light a fire and restore feeling to our fingers and feet. E. B. Johnson took a seat beside me. A faller is the man with whom all logging begins—the fellow who cuts down the trees. In general, such men are known for a certain cleverness and patience, and for stamina—a tree with a hundred-foot girth is not unusual in these precincts, and is the labor of several days. Our E. B. has been in on the search from the beginning, but if he is worn down, shows it not at all. As to his feelings in regard to orang-utans, I have only the evidence of all our hallooing, which, if he believed in savage ape-men, he might have advised us against, for fear of giving the creatures fair warning.

"Say, Mrs. Drummond," he said to me in a sorrowful, slow Swedish drawl, "yur sure holdin' up fine," which I took to mean I was not.

When we had eaten a lunch of ham sandwiches and apples, we began again our seemingly useless and dismal searching, until we had finally climbed above the stream entirely and into the high forest, which country collects rain and snowmelt and sends it downhill to the stream, and is no less steep, and clotted with green shrubbery which must be painstakingly beaten through. And so was the day passed. By dusk I was lagging far to the rear of our chain, which was a fortunate circumstance or I might have been in poor Earl Norris's place. A commotion made its way back to me, and it was plain that some of the boys thought something terrifically funny had happened. Evidently the photographist had flung up an arm and pedaled backward, defending himself from a dark, monstrous hulk among the trees, which proved to be a lava cast at the edge of an escarpment of old black magma. By the time I straggled up to the front of the line, I was quite inoculated against the shapes of mountain beasts rearing up around us in the dimness. My principal shock was in realizing it was still daylight in regions with access to the horizon: a whitish field had begun to be visible behind the lacework of trees—open sky, a rare creature in these thick woods—and it had become evident that this field of sky lay above outriggers of basalt—ground that supported few trees, and those stunted and misshapen.

At the edge of the pillars and spurs and cobbles of stone, E. B. Johnson located a grotto in the talus, paved with bearberry and strewn with lodgepole pines, which was a campground familiar to him from numerous Sunday hunting expeditions and which other parties had made use of in the weeks and months previous: trees had been felled to make way for tents, and the ground layer was much beaten down and muddied. There was an elaborate lava-rock fire pit whitened by heat, in which discarded tins and jars lay unburied. "There is a sinkhole back in here," E. B. said, seeming to mean a lightless shaft among the rocks, and seeming to mean we should get our water from it.

As the packs came off the horses, the middle of the three Pierce brothers said to the general population, "Here, I got corned beef and sauerkraut," which was evidently an offer to take on the duties of cook, that is to say an offer to open tin cans and heat the named foodstuffs. This relieved me of a woman's natural work, and in any case I had by now fairly given in to my fatigue; my legs and arms were weak, shuddering, and would not hold against any force. While one of the boys set about gathering dead thicket and dragging the sticks to camp, I made a pretense of holding this rope or that picket stake while letting the others manhandle the canvas and raise the ridgepole of the tent. When the tent sides were spread and pegged down and personal belongings stowed within, I sank to a stone and waited stuporously to be fed. When finally we crowded into the tent, it was without washing, without brushing teeth; I stretched out in my blankets like a cataleptic, rigid of limb, insensible of lying among the stinking bodies of six men. And oh! what a blessed relief it was.

This morning the boys have—

> The wilderness, I believe, is dear to every man
> though some are afraid of it. People load them-
> selves with unnecessary fears, as if there were
> nothing in the wilderness but snakes and bears
> who, like the Devil, are going restlessly about
> seeking whom they may devour. The few crea-
> tures there are really mind their own business,
> and rather shun humans as their greatest enemies.
> But men are like children afraid of their mother,
> like the man who, going out on a mist morning,
> saw a monster who proved to be his own brother.
>   ERNEST THOMPSON SETON,
>   *Lives of the Hunted* (1901)

In the lava, night of the 5th

This morning I was interrupted in my report by the breathless news of another party camped near to ours (though it is not Homer's, which is said to have gone farther up Canyon Creek, toward its head). This ridge of basalt with its high, violent disarray of stone is in places half a mile wide, and evidently streams away to the south and east, piled high in middens and long wicked drifts among the trees for five miles or more. Such is the size and complexity of the rivers of magma, our camp was pitched along the verge of the lava field no more than two hundred yards from another tent, and our separate groups might have remained ignorant of each other save one of ours encountered one of theirs, each shyly looking for a private place to move his bowels.

They are an odd lot of five people, including three loggers such as one sees everywhere in the woods: argumentative, tale-spinning, superstitious, stand-alone fellows, who must be sprawling, noisy drunks when in Town but apply themselves seriously to their backbreaking work while in Camp. The other two are a Special Agent of the government and, lo! a woman, though the boys do not seem to regard her as much of one. I admit there are few differences between Gracie Spear and any of the boys: she is built like a stevedore, thick armed and broad through the shoulders, wears overalls and a plaid Kilmarnock bonnet, parts her hair along the side, and wears it chopped short around the ears. She has been working as a peeler on a hand-logging crew at the farther end of Pelvey Creek, where, the boys tell me, she holds up her end as well as any man, and therefore is looked upon with respect, though evidently also as something of a freakish monster.

Now. Special Agent Hank Willard is a tall and strongly

built man of the variety that warrants attention. He and his fellows have charge of investigating homestead and forest claims
for possibilities of fraud. I have followed this forestry scandal
somewhat, as any bona fide Westerner is obliged to do. When a
new Forest Reserve is declared, homesteaders whose claims lie
inside the boundary are offered swaps, for "in lieu" claims else-
where. Bribery of government officials, surveyors, and so forth,
to gain advance notice of new Reserves, has of course been
rampant. Land-grabbers pay people to take out land claims of
dubious merit in the soon-to-be-named district and "sell" to the
speculator immediately; then, as soon as a Reserve is declared,
these low rollers hurry to the Government Land Office and
announce they were living on the claim at the time the Reserve
was created—though they have not seen the land, nor lived
within fifty miles of the township, and the land in question
most usually is hanging upon a cliff. Once the useless claim
has been swapped for more valuable land Outside, the speculator's usual course is to sell his fraudulently acquired piece of
the public domain to a logging company for the removal of all
standing timber; which company in turn sells the stump patch
to foolable homesteaders, claiming it to be "agricultural" land,
or cuts the timber and lets the land revert to the state without
taxes being paid.

The slew of Forest Reserves Mr. Roosevelt has set aside in
recent years has attracted criminals at all levels—Land Office
receivers, recorders, inspectors, surveyors, attorneys general,
as well as the odd congressman and senator. However, these
Special Agents report directly to Pinchot and are said to be a
select and dedicated breed. They have largely kept themselves
in good repute; if any have succumbed to bribery, the news has
not made it into the papers. I cannot vouch for his rectitude,

but Hank Willard, in the manner of a dime-novel hero, carries a pistol in a leather holster—land-grabbers have been known to put up a fight—and wears an Army Duck Dryback coat.

He is, further, the sort of man around whom a crowd gathers: we made our two parties over into one, and E. B. Johnson implicitly gave up the helm to him. The Special Agent promptly divided his party of twelve into pairs—this being rugged, disorienting terrain in which a false step can lead to shattered bones—and dispersed us along the front of the lava so as to thoroughly scour and range over the entire rocky ridge; we were instructed to visit, insofar as possible, every dark tunnel and gallery in the black rocks—any that might hold a child. And pointing ahead a mile or two or three through the thicket of lodgepoles to a particular formation standing dimly against the overcast, he proposed that we should all regather at the end of the day at the foot of those rocks, resembling, to an active imagination, a high-backed Mexican saddle.

The youngest Pierce brother, named Almon, brought up the problem of bringing the horses through the lava field, which led to Willard appointing Almon to pack our two camps and lead the overburdened beasts a safe way around the rocks to our new camping place below the Mexican saddle. Almon's withdrawal left our numbers uneven, but Special Agent Willard, who is used to working alone, said he would fire his pistol three times if he broke an ankle or fell into a sinkhole.

I was partnered to another of the Pierce brothers, the middle one, who is thirty or thereabouts and whose name is Martin, a man with some whiskers and some girth, who likes liquor and changes his shirt on the first day of the month. I have known such men all my life, and stayed away from them.

Once we had gone into the rocks there was seldom

opportunity for seeing the horizon nor the Special Agents landmark, and the rough terrain was dislocating. I brought out my explorers compass and demonstrated it for Pierce, so as to encourage his following my lead; but the principle was lost on him, or he was stubborn as regards the proper roles of men and women. Though he agreed we ought to keep each other in view while working roughly twenty feet apart, he struck out directly and kept to his own course, rejecting the reading of magnetic bearings in favor of personal instinct. It soon became my chief task, trailing Pierce to prevent his being lost and left behind in the lava.

Keeping one's partner in view is about all one *can* manage; peering into chasms looking for a huddled child is a matter of wretched difficulty. That broken field of clinkers and boulders and lava mounds is much covered over with lichen and vines, so the careful placing of one's feet becomes the entire center of one's nerves. And the terrain, which is an otherworldly landscape of stone swags and festoons, gaping black hollows, and picturesque columns of basalt, is further complicated by a dense understory of shrubs, viny maples, and small pines, as well as various members of the fern family. Here is the desolate truth, though no one speaks it: a child could find a cavity in the rocks, of which there are thousands, climb into it, and be hidden for a millennium.

Pierce and I beat back and forth across the tumbled ground quite as deliberately as if our hunting might turn something up. What we turned up were castings of delicate tree parts visible on the surface of the frozen flow; a lava sinkhole with logs standing on end as if sucked into it by a whirlpool; natural stone bridges in startling mimicry of those one sees, manmade, in paintings of the Irish countryside; and long, sinuous, caved-in tubes thirty feet wide, the glyphs of molten streams, with ripples and splashes forever imprinted in the stone.

Here and there are the shafts and tunnels which are the old burnt-out casts of standing and deadfallen trees. At their apertures such cavities are carpeted with moss and licorice ferns, and littered within by woody debris and sheets of leathery, grayish-green lichen such as my sons declare to be dragon's skin. And farther inward, midnight darkness.

I shined my Everready light down certain of the black maws, used a long stick to plumb some of them, and cast pebbles down into others, but when I plucked up the courage to crawl into one of the longer tunnels—fully had the intent to crawl in—my body was dead-set against it. An affrighted imagination might very well fill the darkness with ghosts or giant man-eating apes, but mine filled the caves and holes with oozy invertebrates, poisonous spiders, and mutant, cave-blind rodents. I've never had a fear of tight quarters, and do not fear the dark, so this was something of a surprise; one doesn't expect to learn a new cowardice at the age of thirty-five. Pierce, in any case, believed such occupation too brutal for a woman—not only the physical rigor, I suppose, but the possibility of discovering a child's mortified body; and I found myself unexpectedly willing to play the woman's part. I might perhaps have gotten my heart to quit its frantic racing once I had bored through two or three of the stone tunnels (and, of course, assuming I did not put my hand onto a snake or into a slobbery mouth); but it was Pierce who crawled into these forbidding tubes and descended into the long holes; and so my body went on apart from my intellect, in a rigor of instinctual, aboriginal fear.

I lent him my light, and when the batteries gave out, I offered up my little tin match safe. He carried before him into

the darkness one flaring match after another, while I waited at
the opening and kept an eye out for monsters.

I have said nothing until now about this business of ape-
men living in the lava beds, but in fact there's been much agi-
tated muttering among the boys and the sort of nervousness
which, in males, presents itself as blustery wrath and fidgety
swagger. If Martin Pierce is afraid of crawling unknowingly into
a savage den, he never would admit it, but carries a big, solid
piece of wood which he pokes in front of him as he advances
into each black hole. Poor Almon Pierce, who is a mere boy,
younger than his brothers by a margin of twelve or fifteen years,
was plainly afraid to be left alone with the horses and begged
from his brothers the only weapon the three of them own, a
little .22 caliber rifle which I don't suppose could kill a giant ape
regardless. In fact, several of the men possess firearms—even the
photographist packed in a .32 caliber takedown rifle on his back
with the camera case—and now that we're among the lava rocks,
they've begun to sport their weapons about, which to my mind
is only further proof of fear.

I have an energetic imagination which allows for the existence of wild woods-beasts, and a certain giddiness—perhaps it's
my relish for adventure—which may actually be a wish for their
discovery. But when I allow my mind to think of Harriet, it goes
directly to a handful of clear visions: to a little broken body at
the foot of a rocky escarpment; to a barely living child shivering
under blankets of leaves and boughs; to that first, unspeakable
image of her delicate girl's body brutalized and murdered—by a
monster, surely, but in human form—no hairy mountain devil. I
have even, at times, entertained the idea that she lies buried in
a grave dug by an unnatural father. My imagination deserts me
when I try to see Harriet carried off on the shoulders of a giant

ape-man. I could as soon imagine her whisked away to the See-Ah-Tiks by the gentle Tatoosh.

Still, without a doubt this is the wildest, most monstrous landscape I've ever known, which may account for my own uneasiness—a sense of being observed. I was throughout the day painfully on the alert, my eyes and ears on a search, my whole body straining and ready for whatever should occur. Some primeval instinct has evidently been startled into activity—an acute wariness that must ordinarily lie asleep in one's civilized life.

When Pierce and I sat to eat our lunch, it was cold and overcast, but no weather had blown over us—my feet were amazingly dry, which is very nearly all I require to be happy. We occupied a small open depression filled with wild currants, mountain box, and elderberry, amid scanty woods of fir and hemlock grown up thinly on the ridge of magma. Standing off to the east some moderate distance it was possible to see the high back of Special Agent Willard's Mexican saddle.

We talked about the weather—*uncommonly cold*—*wouldn't be surprised to see a dust of snow in the morning*—and I asked after Pierce's mining prospects, which he replied to with vague optimism and more information of cinnabar than I ever yearned to know. Eventually the subject of the explorer's compass was raised, though I don't recall which of us raised it first. I allowed as how a compass is a useful tool in the woods, but perhaps a native sense of direction might be better trusted in these kinds of rocks. Pierce modestly agreed: "Maybe it's the lead ore as takes the compass needle for a spin." Then he said, in a low tone, "This little girl that's gone lost, she's your niece, is that right?" When I corrected his misapprehension, he said quietly of Melba and Florence, "Well, it may be imagined what anxiety they're suffering," which took me aback. I have known the roughest men in the West be made soft and womanish by a child, but it's also the usual case for men to be entirely taken up with their own heroic efforts and think little of the women waiting at home. I said—and perhaps my tone was supercilious—"Well, they are praying," to which he said, "Yes," his voice sinking lower yet; and nothing further. So that I was forced to turn over the idea that his brain might be more complicated than I had thought.

In the afternoon there was a brief flurry of excitement when someone fired off a rifle shot—impossible to tell from which direction. We were, at that time, in view of Gracie Spear and one of the hand-loggers, acting as her partner, and we all four reared up and stood looking and waiting—some of us more reared up than others; but we went on with our business when no further shots sounded. (It proved to be the little Finn named Peter Mer, a peeler from Bill Boyce's crew, who had stepped into a sinkhole and, losing his balance, had fired his rifle accidentally. I don't wonder if E. B. Johnson, who was his partner, considers himself fortunate not to be killed.)

After ten hours of hard tramping up and down a countryside of rough rocks and dense groves of small trees, we are camped once again, with a great crackling fire to hold back the cold and the phantoms; and the older Pierce brothers have demonstrated the wide scope of their talents by cooking up a decent potato soup, macaroni, and *galletta*, which is a hard Italian bread one moistens and heats in a fry pan. Earl Norris has set up his camera and taken several pictures of us plying our forks and chewing. Now the boys are lying about, talking and intermittently spitting tobacco juice while stitching up their torn garments, as well as waterproofing the seams of their shoes. I listen while I write, write, write, catching up these events.

Politeness and propriety are the order of the day in the

presence of two women—or really only one, as Gracie Spear behaves entirely as if a man. Though her natural behavior with her fellow loggers is quite cheerful—much whistling and laughing and humming of gay tunes—she seems to regard me with suspicion, and I am put off by her myself, which I suppose springs from a morbid misgiving. This has put me in a strange way, behaving more nearly ladylike than if I had been alone with the boys. I have abstained from bringing out my tobacco; and earlier, when the youngest Pierce brother pushed a needle through his thumb, I cooed and clucked over him like a mother, and finished sewing up his ragged pants myself. (He has a burn-scarred hand which does not allow of full movement.) Though I suppose this will distance me, in the boys' eyes, from such as Gracie, I have had a low thrill of worry: that my womanly demeanor might make me attractive to her. How appallingly shallow is one's broadmindedness and progressivism!

Gracie

The woman, who wore denim overalls, sat on the veranda steps of the hotel with her forearms across her knees and her booted feet planted exactly as men plant them, immodestly apart. Her hair was cut short and her face, beneath a wool cap, was broad and mannish. She had no work and little money, and had come out here with scant idea of the arrangements usual in such places—a loggers' hotel. She did not wish to announce her ignorance by asking the bartender or the cook, so her plan was simply to wait here on the hotel veranda until work should fall into her lap. In any case, the weather was uncommonly clear, with a slight breeze to carry the smoke away, which she considered the best sort of weather for waiting.

About halfway through the long morning a redheaded man in a logger's get-up came out onto the veranda and stood near her, gazing uninterestedly at the new buildings along the muddy street, the cleared fields, the smoky hills beyond. One of his eyes was swollen and discolored; there was a deep gash which had filled with old, dark blood. He had been hit by the flying end of a broken wire rope.

"You been hurt?" she asked, with the intent of being friendly and in case it might lead to something. She believed he had been fighting, which was the usual course for loggers "blowin' it in" on the weekend.

Now that she had brought his attention to it, he took an interest in his injury. "Well, I s'pose I was," he said, giving an impression of mild surprise. The forefinger of his left hand gently explored the wound, which immediately opened and ran with fresh blood.

The woman brought a clean handkerchief from her vest pocket and offered it up. It was a large and plain-hemmed square, unembroidered, a man's handkerchief. He considered and then accepted it, and pressed it to his eye.

"I just come down from Vancouver," she said, which was a lie. "Have you heard of work for a peeler?" She had last worked as a prostitute in a coastal mill town and so had a general notion of the jobs to be had in the woods. She believed peeling was something she was strong enough to handle, and was determined to bluff her way onto a crew and then, in the Western way, learn the work by watching other fellows out of the corner of her eye, thus not ever having to admit to ignorance.

The man stood with the woman's folded handkerchief pressed to his eye as he went on looking out at the shattered and cutover field in front of the hotel. He was well traveled, well educated; he had made and lost and remade a moderate fortune and had come West to oversee his investment in the logging business. There was still wildness to be found in this part of the country if you were willing to leave the cities and venture into the backwoods, and he had found himself charmed by the loggers' rough and dangerous life. "I could use another peeler," he said generously. He believed the woman sitting on the hotel steps to be a young man. Other men would eventually point out his mistake, and after his first flush of anger and embarrassment, he would flaunt this bull dyke, this gal-boy he had hired, as proof of the liberalism and unruliness of the West—proof of his own Western nature.

He gave vague and imprecise directions to his camp—she understood that it could be reached from the East Fork of the Lewis River, and that she would come upon the river if she struck out roughly north on a particular trail—and he gave her his name, which he said would be sufficient to get her hired. "Tell Mike yur the new peeler, which I said so," he told her, having deliberately adopted the intonation and cadence and phrasing of uneducated Western men.

She shook his hand as a man would and went up into the hotel for her ditty bag. She considered that the redheaded man might be a bull artist and that she might have a six-mile walk for nothing; but she didn't mind the walk, and if this job didn't break well, she would walk back and wait again for what might come along. She was determined not to fall into a woman's usual occupation as housekeeper, cook, maid, laundress; and equally determined not to be a mother or a wife. Her work as a prostitute had been undertaken primarily for the lively income, and as a radical corrective for what her mother had termed an unnaturally masculine nature. The particulars of sexual congress with men had struck her as disgusting, stinking, and dreary; but loggers and millmen were surprisingly simple in their needs, and she had learned from the other women certain useful proficiencies of touch and tongue which made the work less objectionable, and less likely to result in a pregnancy.

Recently she had given up her attempt to effeminize. She had met a woman, a logging camp cook, who had shown her a couple of things about touch and tongue and had encouraged her to follow her own natural inclination. Now her hair was cropped short as a man's, and her dress was manly as well, and though she made no particular effort to masquerade as a male, she was often mistaken for a beardless boy, which had many advantages in terms of freedom and protection. She wasn't afraid of hard work and believed that she would find, in a logger's outdoor life, the liberty and adventure that were denied to the female sex.

As she went up the muddy street in search of the East Fork trail, the redheaded man came out of the hotel outhouse. She lifted her cap to him, and though he was bareheaded, he lifted and gestured to her cheerfully with the bloody handkerchief as if it were a cap. His business affairs were in a hopeless mess and his men had learned to keep their wages drawn up to date, but he was earnest and always set himself to work as hard as his men, which put him in a good way with them. He was pleased with himself for offering work to a boy down on his luck, a boy who nevertheless kept a clean handkerchief in his pocket. She was pleased with herself for snagging work so easily; and generally high in spirits due to the beaut of a day.

She began to whistle "Oh, That Will Be Glory!" which was heard by people in the nearby buildings and understood correctly to be a youthful expression of simple joy.

Morning, 6th

I tried to think, last night and this morning, what to say, what steps to take, and it's come to nothing, nothing, only vain circling around. I keep my head up and look each man in the face, an absolutely cold look. The innocents, I'm sure, must now believe I have overnight transformed into another woman—a Fury without a shred of civility—and the guilty party, what does he think? That he has had a nasty, smutty little victory? I am half crazy to know which man it was and half crazy with dread to see in someone's face the filthy smugness that must give him away to me, and what will I do then? I imagine mayhem—a knife cutting through his smirk—a fire poker swung square up between his legs—but go on sitting here writing as if all is not utterly changed and I am not rocked by humiliation and rage and—*impotence.*

A hard rain fell in the night, the noise deafening inside the crowded tent, and I woke enough to realize the change in the weather—too tired or hopeless to grieve for Harriet, a shameful worry whether we were to suffer flooding, wet blankets—and then slept deeper and woke again—how much later?—pitch black, the rain still loud—to feel something warm and damp was on me, in me, and groggily thought it must be my monthly flow—an inward groan, *oh dear*—and then my brain fluttering to life, something flashing through my lower limbs, an awakening, a realization, and I scrambled in the blankets, trying to get up, to get away, but the blankets tangling, and the man's hand still between my legs—*his fingers inside me*—and I made a desperate sound, I know I did, but not a word, it was a guttural animal noise such as a cow must make when her belly is torn away by wolves, and *he* made a sound, an obscene whispery breath which he may have meant as hushing—he was surprised, afraid to be found out? His fingers turned in me, his arm caught in my twisted drawers as I reared and lurched—I was absolutely desperate—before he slipped from me, or I escaped, and I flung myself wildly from the tent—the blankets pulled to my breast in a bundle—out into the great noise and cold and utter blackness of the rain. Took no more than a few steps before falling—rocks everywhere—broke open the skin of my knee—and so had to creep back into the tent, soaking, terrified, bleeding, pathetically afraid of tumbling to my death out in the weather, the black night. The stupid men went on sleeping, as poleaxed as steers, and the one, the rat, lying awake though quite still among them, while I scuttled around feeling out my clothes—mad with fear of touching, being touched by *him*, by any of them, the men—putting on the tin pants and every other thing, layer after layer, and then sitting shaking in the darkness in a kind of shock, my heels to my hips and the wet blankets drawn around my coat like a squaw, sitting trembling and listening to every small stirring noise, to the wind thumping the tent ropes, and the scratching of tree branches, and the toenails of animals scratching across rocks, and the turning and sighing of bodies in the night. Long, long hours sitting thus.

And now what to do? What to say? And so I do and say nothing, only meet each man's look with a look of my own, stony cold, the sort of dare that is full of false confidence, and otherwise keep to myself, behave as if nothing has occurred except that I am suddenly friendless and reclusive in wild, impossible circumstances, feeling myself to be completely surrounded by men.

That last is unfair, I think, to Gracie Spear. Aside from the clear fact that it was someone among the six men in my tent, not the five in that other party (no one could have crossed the rocky blackness in that rain and crossed back again between our two tents, crawling under the edge and so forth), the arm was certainly a man's—coarse haired, long muscled—and the breathing low and masculine.

The men, in any case, all behave as if I am suffering from an inexplicable female mood; they ignore me as men so often do when confronted by a woman's temper. But Gracie, though her demeanor is thoroughly manlike, is perhaps enough of a woman to have guessed out *something* of what occurred. She early fixed a curious look on me; and when I fled from Earl Norris and his damned camera and sat apart to eat my breakfast, she brought her bowl of mush and sat near me. When she stood to walk away, she bent low suddenly and blurted out, for my ears only, "I sleeps with a gun under my pillow." So I imagine she knows, or guesses; and though we are not friends, I take some comfort from her presence. When she went into the trees to make her toilet, I hurried to follow her and squat nearby—I am so afraid to be alone now—and her look, as we crossed paths afterward, was knowing, and not unkind.

None of the others are free of my suspicion. My improved feelings toward Martin Pierce have evaporated, and I cannot bear the idea of being alone with him, nor with any of the others. There has been considerable discussion on the question of continuing or ending the search, as the rain is no softer and we are, to the last villainous man, wet through and cold. (I am desperately drawn to the idea of returning to Camp 8—oh! hot supper and warm feet!—where I should spend the night in Bill Boyce's office, sleeping not on rocks but upon a dry and comfortable cot, toasting my toes before a sheet-metal stove and with the door firmly locked against all others.) Yet there is a general unwillingness to call a halt. The likelihood of finding

Harriet has diminished in every mind to a thing of naught, but
no one will admit to it and no one wishes to appear shameful—
quitting the field over the issue of our discomfort. Lacking the
courage to be cowardly, we have agreed to go on searching one
more dreary day, though we will quit the lava field (at least this
portion of it—from high vantage one can see another basalt
outcrop off to the southeast) and will scour out the less-steep
country which lies in a narrow crescent between this ridge and
the conical little knob just to the east. I cannot imagine how I
shall get through this long day—and another black night!

Was interrupted, and this is written quickly, just as we are
making ready to head off into the brush. I found a moment
to speak alone to Hank Willard—*horrible occurence—woman's
modesty forbids—would he keep a watchful eye?*—not knowing if I
had made myself understood at all. He began to blush furiously
and look at his boots with a painful frown—this may have been
anger as much as embarrassment. He murmured a few words
as inarticulate as mine but then pressed on me a deer-foot-
handled hunting knife, which I am now wearing in a sheath at
my belt. I have a knife in my kit, of course, a sportsman's folding lock-blade knife, but Willard's big, masculine blade—the
hair is still on the deer foot—confers an odd sort of boldness.
Whatever else may come from my confession to Willard, I feel
my courage somewhat restored.

> At midnight Bauman was awakened by some
> noise, and sat up in his blankets. As he did so
> his nostrils were struck by a strong, wild-beast
> odor, and he caught the loom of a great body

in the darkness at the mouth of the lean-to. Grasping his rifle, he fired at the vague, threatening shadow, but must have missed, for immediately afterwards he heard the smashing of the underwood as the thing, whatever it was, rushed off into the impenetrable blackness of the forest and the night.

THEODORE ROOSEVELT,
Wilderness Hunter (1892)

Alone in the deepwoods, night of the 6th

What is it, I wonder, that has haunted this whole enterprise?

I had expected to spend this night lying awake in my blankets, clutching a knife to my breast—on guard against another assault—but here I lie alone in the woods with only my coat for a covering and I am on guard against other sorts of monsters— there have been screeches nearby, which must be owls, I suppose, or lions. I've built up a fire and backed it with a rotten log, and the sticks are burning well. With Willard's big knife I've cut hemlock boughs for a bed in front of the long line of fire, and recline here now writing and munching upon dried apricots. My clothes have mostly dried upon me, and I suppose I'll spend the night not uncomfortably so long as the rain holds off, and be reunited with my party in the morning. But I am low in mood, weary from worrying and from overexertion. I believe I have heard guns signaling into the darkness, but impossible to tell from which direction.

This morning we took our search away from the lava tableland, bearing off steeply downhill through the brush and trees in slipping wet boots, in a pouring rain, until we had come down upon thickly wooded, flatter ground—not a great expanse of it, but several outspread fingers and tongues hedged in by the numberless ridges. Willard's idea was that a child wandering lost would stick to the low valleys, the flattish ground, and would not be found upon the steep slopes, which idea wore a certain logic; or we had been made receptive to it by virtue of our own exhaustion. Our tents were brought downhill and pitched along the footings of the lava ridge (lying more or less at the palm while we searched up the several fingers of the glove), and the sorry horses were freed of their enormous swaying burdens and left to munch the scant grass at camp while we two-footed fools set off with our rucksacks and ditties, holding such lunch as we had need of, and little else (which of course I now have reason to regret).

Being by this time old hands at the search, we scattered ourselves wordlessly through the trees. I kept as near to Gracie Spear as could be privately accomplished and beat about the brush without any hope of finding Harriet alive or dead. I confess I had in mind only getting through the day without breaking any bones, and speedily tomorrow returning to dry clothes and stove heat and my own house, my own dear children.

The rain went on until we were thoroughly wringing wet and our boots sloppy; until every depression in the ground, every bunker in the rocks, every hollow among tree roots was inches deep with muddy water and floating detritus. Then the sky lightened to Quaker gray, and steam began to rise from the ground—a startling illusion of vulcanism—and it was the end of rain for the time being. (Why do you suppose one feels the clamminess of clothes more miserably when the rain has stopped than while it is still falling?)

Then occurred an extraordinary adventure.

There is a certain science to the spying out of larger holes and caves in a lava field, certain signs and markers I had become alert to while in the field yesterday, and though we had left the lava behind us, such awareness had not deserted me; in the late morning, after the rain had quit, I was drawn to examine a particular hemlock growing oddly askew, which investigation found the tree tilted over a cavernous sinkhole. I am still agile, or as much as can be expected at middle age, and did not hesitate to shinny along the tree trunk to a point that allowed a short drop to a sloping rock ledge, which then allowed of a careful descent, tossing pebbles ahead as I groped into darkness by the insignificant flare of matches. Quickly it was clear: this was a reverberating, pitch-black passage of huge proportions.

My first thought was that we should be prevented from a thorough search of the cave, my Everready batteries being exhausted and the materials for a pitchy torch not easily to hand in this country of sodden wood. But I nevertheless went after the next-nearest person, which of course was Gracie, and when I had explained the point—cave too large, lacking sufficient light—she made a little happy chirrup and said, "I got just the thing." With a self-satisfied flourish she brought from her lunch sack a kerosene oil lamp no more than five or six inches tall, which I recognized, with a glad thrill of commonality, as a bicycle headlamp. (It was a false trail. "Oh, I ain't never rode one of those things," she told me, her mannish face rosy and artless; she had only admired and coveted the lamp's miniature stature.)

So after all, we investigated. I went ahead of her, snaking out on the tree again and jumping down to the slanted ledge, after which she reached the lamp down to me and followed my example. I should guess her to be twenty-five, and of course very

strong, but built too thick and low to the ground for nimble-
ness: she sat astride the tree trunk and leant forward to embrace
it, then dragged herself along it by inches, which got her to the
necessary place for jumping down. I held the lamp before us as
we began a slow progress down the slippery stone chute.

This entrance proved to be a small lava sink littered with
rock rubble, which after one hundred feet or so let into the side-
wall of a very long, high-ceilinged throughway grooved with
flow marks and a whole succession of shallow ledges. At other
places in the lava field there had, of course, been open gullies and
intermittent stone bridge-work, which must be the skylighted
leavings and minor versions of such caves; but this one was a
considerable size—entirely intact. I am no spelunker but have
read enough to know: they are formed by rivers of lava which,
cooling, forms a thick top crust and simultaneously eats away
the ground beneath its molten stream, so that when the eruption
is finished and the lava drains away, what is left is a through tunnel. The small light cast by the bicycle lantern made a circle of
dim illumination that allowed us to see the tube stretching away
in both directions for an indeterminate length, and the ceiling
twice higher than hands reach. I have read of tunnels thousands
of feet long: Ole Peterson's Mount St. Helens Lava Cave, which
cannot be more than a dozen miles from here, is a modestly
famous international destination for tourists and speleologists.

Inarguably, no human child would choose to shelter herself
in such a place—the vast, echoing chamber seemed, even to me,
a gateway to the underworld. But the cave air was somewhat
warmer than the chilly daylight, and dry despite the hard rain
overnight and this morning; I could imagine a wild creature—
bear or wolf, if not orang-utan—happily choosing such a cave
for winter quarters.

Gracie Spear, while saying nothing of apes nor the unlike-
lihood of a child hiding so deep underground, seemed loath to
advance any farther within. For my part, I have seen more evidence of the savagery of men than of savage ape-men, which on
the one hand frees me from fear of cave monsters. On the other
hand, if no phantasmal beast had dragged Harriet to its den
inside, what could be the point of looking for her there? I cannot, even now, divine the answer, but something of a wordless
compulsion came over me. I said to Gracie, "We shouldn't let
this cave go unexplored," and gave her a firm look.

I have always felt occultism to be the realm of fools and
natural idiots; perhaps it wasn't any glimmer of intuition or
clairvoyance that impelled me into the depths of the cave, perhaps it was my scientific bent and natural curiosity. (Lava tubes
are nothing like the limestone caves in France, of course, but they
have their own interest; and a large, dry stone room holds none
of the terrors of the lava rimrock, its small tunnels and chasms
doubtless home to crawling creatures of slime and tentacles.)
What I should report is only that something—*something*—drew
me in. And in the event, though we didn't find Harriet hiding
in the black cave, and no giant orang-utans leaped upon us from
the darkness, we were certainly led to a discovery.

The left-hand of the tunnel was blocked after some two
hundred feet by the rocks and rubble of its broken-down walls
and ceiling. The right-hand, though, went on for as much as a
thousand feet, with a sandy floor of volcanic ash and pumice,
and dark walls glazed and shiny as glass from the excessive heat
of the lava. The walls narrowed gradually, and the ceiling lowered until we were made to crouch, but then opened suddenly
to a roundish vaulted room like the cupola of a house—it was
the furthermost reach of the tunnel, sealed by the breakdown

rubble of the ceiling—and when we rose erect inside this space and lifted the lamp, I was seized with wonder.

There were husks of empty nuts and fir cones on the floor, and a frightening smell which I took to be feral, but the furnishings of long-absent tenants, scattered in disarray, were specifically human artifacts: chipped and flaked bits of stoneware; fragments of carven or heat-shaped wood; a broken strand of twisted leather strung with shells or bone; the unknit remains of what had once been woven strips of cedar bark; moldering feathers fallen into pieces, which one could imagine had been joined into a sort of cape or blanket, though many were now incorporated into a wild animal's artfully arranged nest on a high ledge at the rear of the room.

Gracie, perhaps seeing only that we had reached a blind alley, snuffled through her broad nose and said, "Shee-it, what a stink."

I rate highly any woman who will freely swear and say the word "stink," but on this occasion I would rather have had a woman with an appreciation for ancient relics and mysterious rooms hidden in the deeps of forbidding caves. I held up for her a piece of flaked obsidian which she might reasonably have been expected to recognize as a spearhead, and in the other hand a bit of bone carved into something like a button. "Someone lived in this cave, Gracie—aboriginal peoples. These things are of great age, and valuable to Science."

She retreated a step and arranged her face in a disapproving frown. "They don't look old to me, only wore out; we better not go poking around in here."

I chided her for the foolishness of her reluctance—"Believe me, no one is returning to cook their supper in this room"—but when this did nothing to persuade her, I took another tack. "We have a duty to gather these artifacts and get them into the hands of Anthropology," I said. She took a dim view of this idea as well, and went on standing over me with her reproving look while I took out my knapsack and began to collect into it the partly intact pieces of implements and tools, stone spearheads and arrowheads, and twisted cords tied to bits of carved ornamentation. There were astonishing finds—a well-formed cylindrical stone pipe!—an intact, finely made awl!—and I should still be sailing on the excitement of these discoveries except for the last one, which somewhat capsized me. At the very rear of the room, in the darkness where the stone shelved away in a series of ledges, behind that neat feather bed some animal or other had made, I lifted a fragment of matting or basketry and found lying beneath it a human skeleton.

For one irrational moment I believed it was Harriet, and my heart lurched. But of course, the bones were ancient, and identified by their Indian accoutrements. "Oh, lordy, what's that you've got there?" Gracie said, and brought the lantern. It was the bones of a small person or an older child, short of leg, with the wizened rabbit-fur moccasins still on its feet; and amid the little pyramid which was the piled-up bones of both hands, a fetish of sticks and feathers which had evidently been clasped to its breast.

I am sometimes forced to admit that my childhood inclination toward romanticism remains stronger in me than my adult study of the sciences; and this was one of those occasions. As we two women stood and looked on those bones in silence, I believed I could feel a very old sorrow creep into the room. The arrangement of the body, lying undisturbed on the basalt bench, had a touching posture of peace, and I was struck by the realization that this rock room was no longer someone's dwelling place but had become someone's tomb; I'm afraid my enthusiasm for collecting the ethnological scraps and fragments of a person's life began, in those moments, to desert me.

"I never have heard of the Klickitats, the Cowlitz, and them burying their dead people in caves," Gracie said in a low, somewhat affronted tone. (It's the Western way to pretend a serious acquaintance with local Indian custom.)

"No, I never have heard of it," I said, being Western myself, and also on the firmer ground of scholarly knowledge.

This opened the door to several speculations—the sort of thing at which I am particularly adept. I told Gracie: These could very well be the bones of a suitor who had been traveling with his entire dowry to the village of his betrothed—he had sought shelter from an ancient volcanic eruption—had composed himself to die alone from horrid wounds received in the showers of flaming rock. Or the only survivor of an ancient tribe decimated by disease—her desperate parents had sequestered her in the deep cave, safe from wolves and weather and their own horrid plague—had furnished her with every tool necessary for her survival—she'd lived alone for months or years until at last succumbing to loneliness. Or a feral boy raised by bears—he'd later been killed by an arrow from his own human tribe, but his mother, recognizing her long-lost son, had tenderly returned his body to the bear den for interment, along with certain items for his use on the spirit-journey.

Gracie received these possibilities eagerly and supported them, one after the other, with an embroidery of her own details—a desirable tendency in a companion. When we had thoroughly satisfied ourselves that the anomalous cave burial was capable of explanation, we considered what we should do with our discovery—a brief and agreeable discussion which led to our leaving the bones exactly as we had found them, except that I placed on the stone ledge beside the body a respectful array of the artifacts I had gathered into my sack.

I suppose I should consider this a loss to Science, and a foolish surrender to sentimentality. Had I been with Pierce, or Willard, or especially Norris, the photographist, I don't doubt I would have behaved differently. But we were two women—they are disgracefully sentimental creatures, after all—and Gracie, having her own particular devotion to privacy and the natural rights of ownership (even as regards the dead), may have been an undue influence. I find it difficult, now that I'm removed from the moment, to explain or defend my performance. At the time, not only did I feel in a particularly weakened emotional state due to recent events, but I felt myself inhabited by a strange and intimate awareness of the ancient past as it related to the present—something of a spiritual nature—something which does not readily yield itself to words. If related to my gender, I shall hope it was not womanish sentimentality but intuitive reason, which Science allows is a woman's natural and creditable inheritance. And I should say, as well, that my mind had made a kind of premonitory leap from the bones in the cave to what must be Harriet's dire fate; I blame this on an inclination toward literary metaphor.

When we came out of the lava tube into the daylight—no resumption of rain, as yet, but a cold overcast and an ill wind—we resumed our search without remarking on the futility of it, simply tramping on through the deepwood, zigzagging around the ruins of logs and poking into thickets of hawthorn and thimbleberry.

Shortly we sat to eat our lunch in a lightly forested glen where some others of our party were already stopped. Earl

Norris fussed and fiddled with his camera and tripod from the vantage of a mossy rockfall, while Almon Pierce and E. B. Johnson and an old ox logger by the name of Edward Stanley huddled in gloom around a smoky bonfire which had not even the advantage of rain cover from overhanging evergreen boughs; they chewed dry crusts of bread and hard jerked meat while submitting to their photograph.

It occurred to me that Gracie and I had made no decision as to whether we would share our news—our discovery of the lava-tube cave and its furnishings—with the men. I suppose if Gracie had blurted out the story, I'd have readily joined in; but she did not. I held off, myself, from an indefinable reservation, and perhaps also from grudgingness—not wishing to share our sentimental, private knowledge with the villain in our midst. In any case, due to the general mood of the day, hardly a one of them gave us the benefit of a greeting.

Gracie and I carried our lunches off somewhat from the others and ate together in silence. Our association was transformed, of course, to one of friendship—we were easy in each others company—but the truth is, I was not in a conversational frame of mind, and our differences are profound. While we sat together eating our crackers and cheese and washing all down with the liquor from Gracie's tin of peaches, we exchanged only a few private words on the subject of the local distilled spirits (the Amboy prune brandy, which by now I thoroughly lamented not buying) and, of course, the weather, which is always a safe topic. I was briefly troubled by a wish to confide in her the specific events of the night before, but I suppose such things are best dealt with sub rosa; and in any case, no occasion for intimacy arose from our discussion of fruit wines and rain.

We did discover a common habit: Gracie, having finished off her lunch, brought forth a twisted black pigtail from her shirt pocket, carved a thumbnail-sized plug, and deliberately seated it in her cheek; which encouraged me to do the same. While half reclined against our respective blowdowns, we each gazed upon the other's vile and unladylike tobaccoism with solemn, if unvoiced, admiration. (And inasmuch as spitting women are evidently newsworthy, we were hurriedly made the object of Norris's yellow-journal picture taking.)

In the afternoon, having suffered through a resumption of showery weather and a rising westerly wind, I became much in the mood to quit the search, but slogged on—I admit—for the sole reason that the others were seemingly unremitting, and I would not be the one to suggest our discreditable surrender. My affrighted need to keep Gracie in my sight gradually subsided (I blame increasing lethargy), and though I glimpsed one or another of my party or heard them hallooing to Harriet in a hoarse monotone through the long afternoon, I often labored alone and in silence. I peered into the dank shade along the corpses of old trees and climbed onto the thrones of their rotted stumps; from time to time I poked a stick into a thicket of wild raspberries. But I'm afraid I became more and more perfunctory, doing as little as could be managed without seeming to have given up the search entirely.

I am not as a rule a startlish person, but may have been brought to timidity and trepidation by recent events; I cannot, otherwise, explain what occurred—two events within minutes of each other, and in large part to blame for my present situation. In the mid-afternoon, after I had not seen or heard others of my party for a good interval, Almon Pierce arose suddenly from the brush behind me, which provoked me to a wild-Indian yelp and my constitutional defense against surprise, which is a malicious glare. This astounded and mortified the boy more than might have been expected—his face flashed crimson, and he was gone—had turned and fled into the wet shrubbery before I had quite recovered my poise. I confess, I stood for some little while afterward in frozen apprehension—knew instinctively and utterly that Almon Pierce had been my midnight assailant and that I had just saved myself from a further assault. I cannot account for this now except to plead the overwrought mind of a beleaguered and exhausted woman.

Which must also be blamed for what followed. Having recovered myself (so it seemed), I went on through the trees some few hundred yards, examining the root flares of thousand-year-old cedar trees, and simply became aware, with absolute and sudden certainty—the heaving over of my heart in my breast—that evil eyes were upon me; became sure of the presence of someone else glimpsed only as a shadow, a heaviness, a shape behind the trees, which vanished as I turned my head. I am half ashamed to admit I took out Special Agent Willard's deer-foot-handled knife and brandished it in the air, while fiercely calling out, "Halloo, damn you, who is there?" to which I received in reply the faint resounding of my own rabbity tremolo. Here is the truth, which can only be told in the privacy of these pages: I quite lost courage, believing someone was there—Almon Pierce again, or a beast, and in either case breathing death; and I plunged off through the deepwoods like a deer.

It is humiliating to realize one's base fear lies so near to the surface.

When I had got over my blind flight (not long) and got hold of my senses, I surrendered to a weaker impulse and made off

directly for camp, with every hope of finding at least one or two
of the others waiting (shameful if I should be the first to call it
quits), and the comfort of hot soup, as well as a tent to get in
out of the rain. It was at that time just past two o'clock.

In the neighborhood of four o'clock, having struck no sign
of camp nor indeed of the lava ridge, and no glimpse of Gracie
nor any of the men, I began to fall prey to a certain anxiety
and restlessness. I had been holding the terrain lightly in my
mind, which is a coherent enough map, and I am usually unerr-
ing in the matter of orientation; but we had been keeping to
the flattish troughs, and the whole of our traverse was gradually uphill, which I suppose had led me into a kind of compla-
cency regarding which way was "back"—that is to say, downhill.
I may also have gotten turned around somewhat, while bolting
from shadows. Further, this is a jumbled country, no less so than
the lava tableland—a muddle of ravines and gullies and ridges
which give upon one another in a confusing way. In any case,
subsequent hours were spent casting back and forth deliberately along the low ground until I became aware that, in the
darkening shadows, injury was ever more likely.

I am not worried in the slightest—have certainly spent many
nights alone in the woods and have sufficient flesh on my bones
to stand the loss of one meal (or two, I suppose, in case I do not
find my fellows in time for breakfast; but I have hardtack and
cheese in my pockets). And here is an adventure, after all, and
a story to embellish for the boys when I have regained them as
an audience.

On the Columbia River I have found evidence of
the former existence of inhabitants much superior

to the Indians at present there, and of which no tradition remains. Among many stone carvings which I saw there were a number of heads which so strongly resembled those of apes that the likeness at once suggests itself. Whence came these sculptures, and by whom were they made?

—JAMES TERRY,
Sculptured Anthropoid Ape Heads,
Found in or Near the Valley of the John Day River,
a Tributary of the Columbia River, Oregon (1891)

Almon Pierce

The man had gone out before dawn, intending to be on his stand in the woods when the elk should break from their beds. Now he sat in the rotted-out shell of a cedar stump, holding the rifle across his knees while he waited. The white moon divided the ground into dim stripes of light and darkness, and relumed the shapes of rocks embedded in the earth around him, the round volcanic boulders hurled up from a crater more than twenty miles away. He had never learned to track, and lately his brothers, having given up the effort to teach him, had instructed him to wait on stand, to stay perfectly still, and to look, to look constantly with intent carefulness, until the deer, the elk, should move past him down the hill at dawn or at dusk to feed in the willow and alder along the stream bottoms.

He was uncomfortable in the darkness, disliking its boundlessness; and out of this illimitable dark ocean came a fecund smell and noises he must continually strain to identify: the rubbing of tree limbs one against the other, the creaking of whole trees as they shifted on their feet, the faint rustlings and whisperings which must be animals prowling abroad at night. He was not afraid but deeply wary, as one who is outcast and must be silent.

The stillness deepened, and the loneliness, and he dozed and wakened several times before becoming aware that, for a while now, the dawn had been sliding up gradually into a whitening sky. He became briefly alert, expectant; he carefully shifted his stiff legs and his arms several times to keep from paralysis. His mind moved restlessly, and when he realized this, he tried to corral it, to get it to think only of the elk that might be coming down from the ridge. He knew that his mind would settle, that he would gain a mastery of things, bring things under control, once he had killed something.

But he was cold and hungry, and nothing came down the hill. He was not able to direct his thoughts, and helplessly he began to think of himself as a boy lying in his bed listening to the low animal groaning of his parents as they performed the marriage act behind the curtain of their bedroom some three feet from where he lay, and of himself creeping under the curtain to watch them, their heavy brutish bodies grotesquely white in the darkness, and greasy with sweat, the hair growing wild over his father's back and buttocks. He particularly remembered the smell in the room, which was wild and earthy, and thinking of that now, his body revisited the memory, becoming flushed and hot with disgust and shame.

His mother had been old and peevish—he was the youngest of her children—and for most of his childhood she could not sleep at night, could not digest her food. When she discovered him sitting behind the woodshed with his pants open, abusing himself, she had dragged him screeching into the house and pressed his open palm down onto the stove until the smell of his roasting flesh brought her back into her right mind. He had seldom touched himself since that time, though he often was visited by lewd and violent dreams. He was twenty-two now, and considered himself vulgar—brutish; he felt that women never had time for him, and men had no respect for him.

The sky remained white, faintly suffused with rose; the day would be fair but the sun had not yet climbed high enough to clear the ridge before him. He was no good at judging the time of day by the angle of the light and the shadows that entered the woods. It might have been six o'clock or ten. He put his head down on his hands briefly and then let go the rifle with one hand and picked up a heavy stick and began to poke himself with it about the breast, which he told himself was a means to keep awake and to force his mind away from carnal thoughts and upon the matter of the elk. The stick had a rough point, which he felt only as a pressure through his coat; he fumbled the buttons open and opened a few buttons of the shirt as well, and drove the stick into his bare chest five or six times, a mild jabbing motion, and then deliberately digging the point hard into his nipple so that he had to bite his mouth to keep from crying out; and twice again the impelling motive thrust and the pain; and three times to the other nipple. He had lately begun to practice self-flagellation as a kind of penitence and abnegation, though of course it was also a secret eroticism.

Within a year he would take his own life, and his own blood smell coming to him as he was dying would cause memory to leap up from all the perilous places and flash through his body in a last cleansing tide race; he would experience his death as a kind of intimacy, unutterably seductive, both binding and alienating. But now, as the blood ran down inside his shirt across the smooth, pale skin of his belly, what he experienced was a sticky heat; and in the smell of the blood was a memory of wildness and of the earth.

Alone, the 7th

There is a certain shock that erupts on realizing you are lost. Fear, of course, is not intended by the body to be mentally crippling; it is a scientific certainty that fear arose in the caveman in order to provoke an unthinking, lifesaving response to the sudden onset of danger. My own situation, however, requires not a quick response but a careful conserving of health and strength, a thorough understanding of my surroundings—the smells, sounds, landmarks, as well as oncoming weather—and a plan.

I cannot blame the unsatisfactory events on lack of a plan. Guns were fired again this morning (which surely were signals), and when I could not make out the direction I shouted and shouted and clapped my hands, which hails went unanswered. Upon finally giving up that avenue of rescue, I climbed to higher ground—which was accomplished only with great difficulty— and carefully studied my situation; discovered, to no great surprise, a surround of ridges and gullies all thickly wooded, a green and silent wilderness covered principally with Western red cedar and Western hemlock, which trees stand straight and tall and close, preventing any clear view of the horizon or of landforms which otherwise might have facilitated my orientation. (I had hoped for a glimpse of the conical little knob, at least, or the Mexican saddle, and most surely the lava ridges.) If the others had ignited a bonfire to mark their position, it was impossible to distinguish it from the wisps and columns of fog rising out of the trees.

From high ground there was a lightened aspect at the
edge of the overcast sky where (unquestionably) lay the eastern sunrise. I realized, as I oriented myself, that I must have
wandered roughly southeast of the camp, and that I should
be able to return to known landmarks—the black outbreak of
lava invisible in the forest cover—by traveling west, or north of
west, which was a simple matter, as I thought, of putting my
trust in the compass; which I did, after breakfasting prudently
on an ounce of cheese and a morsel of hardtack.

Of course, straightforward travel is impossible under the
circumstances, what with the fording of streams, dense thickets, jumbles of house-sized boulders, and so forth. (I shall not
recount the miserable procession of mishaps and difficulties and
disappointments.) A compass will lead you straight up a sharp
peak or straight down into a deep canyon, so I made a zigzag
course, returning as I could to the westward direction. In the
early afternoon, for some two miles or so, I followed a seemingly
beaten path which I believed (joy!) to be a man-made trail, perhaps leading to the logging industry along Canyon Creek or the
Pierce brothers' rumored cinnabar mine, but which eventually
twisted off to the north before dimming and quite disappear-
ing. Here is what I think: I may have misjudged my direction
and meandered too far west, which has led to my skirting past
the lava field entirely and into unknown country southwest of
the rocks. I have, for much of the afternoon, kept to the course
of an unknown creek, which at first took me northwest but has
now turned squarely west—proof it is not Canyon Creek as I
had hoped, but some other nameless stream; and therefore I will
leave it tomorrow and turn more northerly.

The weather, as may be imagined, continued showery
and cold throughout the day. In any case, I became rather

wet—impossible to keep from it—and afterward suffered from
bitter shivering; my feet in wet boots became chafed and sore.
This is the kind of discomfort which can lead (I know) to a
fatal weakening of confidence, and thence to hopelessness and
dire thoughts. I therefore gave up my tramp at an early hour of
the afternoon—it was by then already clear that I must spend
another night alone in the woods—and began to make provision for staying (or rather becoming) dry and warm.

I have more than a passing familiarity with the techniques
of wilderness survival—have made a study of them for the sake
of my intrepid heroines, who are very often thrown upon their
own in hostile surroundings. I have no doubt of my ability to
develop a successful plan and survive until I am rescued. I am
certainly not unduly worried, and as comfortable as one can
hope under the circumstances. I have made my camp on relatively flat ground beneath the drooping umbrella of an enormous cedar; have gathered rotten log castings and have cut long
sticks with which I've fashioned a small lean-to with a lapping
bark cover (very like Spanish roof tiles), and then laid cut boughs
over the bark for double protection against the rain; as well as
hemlock tips for a comfortable bed within. The open face of
my little house is out of the wind, with a long fire fronting it,
and I have removed the outer layers of my clothing, which are
hanging to dry slowly while I become dry myself, sitting here in
my underwear.

Firewood has been my most worrisome problem, which is
hardly to be believed, given that I am surrounded by dense forest, and indeed there is fallen timber lying about me everywhere.
But the canyons and gullies are cleft deep—little sunshine can
penetrate—and rain (or snow) falls for all the winter months. So
every bit of wood into which I put my knife was thoroughly wet

or green, dead logs and limbs mostly moss-covered and sodden. I believe there must be few places on earth where a campfire is harder to light in April. I was almost in despair—log after rotten log—before finally discovering a cache of dead alder lying dry (or nearly) along the south side of overhanging rocks—sticks sufficient for the night. And after a slow start, have a strong fire burning. Tomorrow afternoon as I am tramping (that is, if not rescued) I shall have to begin to keep a particular eye out for dry limbs, even to the point of choosing my camping spot for its proximity to burnable wood.

Inasmuch as knowledge is the first step in overcoming the debilitating effects of undue fear, I have just now taken thorough stock of my equipment. The greater part of my outfit—my folding sink!—of course remains in our camp, the whereabouts of which are unknown. And the provisions I had carried on my person have unfortunately been lightened by the first day's blithe lunching and nibbling, and today's judicious rationing, during which I expected at any moment to come to the end of this entire adventure. But in my pockets and rucksack I discovered a remaining small handful of dried apricots and hardtack, a square of chocolate, and a small tin in which reside at this moment five soft soda crackers and an ounce of cheese. I am, in addition, in possession of a collapsible Sierra cup, Agent Willard's deer-footed hunting knife, as well as my own folding sportsman's knife, the explorer's compass, a match safe which is quarter-full of matches, and a tin can opener (though the cans, of course, all remain with my other equipage in camp). I have also a small rubber sheet which I was carrying to keep my rump from getting wet while I sat to eat my lunch, etc. Though as a bedsheet it is too small by far, it now protects my head and shoulders from the damp ground as I am lying here, and I hope may keep me from pneumonia.

My clothes, altogether, are suited to my situation. How very much worse would be my state had I stuck to a woman's decorous and altogether impractical trappings! As it is, I am well furnished in ribbed cotton underwear (a vest and long drawers); a corduroy shirt; tin pants, which of course are not fashioned from tin but from heavy canvas treated with paraffin (thus waterproofed), and held up by a boy's police-style suspenders; a lumberman's sheep-lined coat, which, until it came to be doused in a stream, had seemed impenetrable to both wind and water; double wool mittens with a heavy tufted lining and rubberized inner lining; and a man's corduroy cap with an inside fur band, which in this cold weather can be turned down over my ears. I have, furthermore, a quite damp and soiled handkerchief, and two pair of wet socks. (With great good foresight, I had carried dry socks in my pocket and exchanged wet for dry while sitting at my lunch yesterday noon. Of course, the dry socks of yesterday noon are by now also wet, and both pair steaming by the fire even as I write.)

I am in low spirits—do not doubt my survival and eventual rescue but find my own deficiencies and weaknesses a frightening embarrassment. And of course I am uncomfortable with cold and damp, somewhat peckish with hunger, and smarting from a great many scratches, bumps, and bruises. The night is black beyond the circle of fire, and I have at moments imagined the glowing eyes of beasts—the phantoms of bears or lions eyeing me from between the pillars of tree trunks, their shadowy forms not quite visible against the darkness. The limbs of trees in the darkling forest can easily become grotesque leaping figures, and the wind has the sound of a wild and weirdy scream. I have a new and heartfelt understanding of the classical mythologists, who populated the dark forests of Europe with an entire menagerie of lesser gods and demons—satyrs who ravished women and carried off the children who ventured into their wilderness lairs.

I have thought often today of poor Harriet, and hope she did not suffer much from fear or pain.

My plan is to turn back to the north and strike the lava field at its middle range, then turn southeasterly along its rim until I should find the camp. Of course, I can no longer count on being able to find it—I fear that the great field of rocks strewn with green lichen and stunted trees may remain, like a fairy forest, unseen until one stands at its very edge. So if the lava field remains lost to me by tomorrow night, then I shall abandon the effort to reunite with my party and simply strike out west, which direction will lead (inevitably) to the logging activity along Canyon Creek or (failing that) the North Fork of the Lewis River, which I can follow to civilization.

I am turning every effort toward remaining calm. To feel fear is normal and necessary, but undue fear is usually caused by the unknown. I look carefully at each situation to determine if my fear is justified, and upon investigation usually find that it is not. (A dangerous noise is discovered to be a squirrel or a bird dropping his nut from a tree, which bounces with great energy through the leaves.) I keep my mind busy and plan for tomorrow. My doorway faces east, toward the rising sun, and I will get up as soon as it is light and get under way.

And in snow on the mountain above the lake, a race of man-stealing giants lived. At night, these giants would come to the lodges while people were asleep, put people under their skins, and take them away to the mountain. When they awoke in the morning, they were entirely lost, not knowing which direction their home was.

KATHERINE JUDSON,
Myths and Legends of the Pacific Northwest (1910)

8 Apr

Here I sit—"staying put" another day, as the rain pours, and I fear taking a fatal chill should I venture onward. In any case, my clothes remain damp (at best) and I am thoroughly exhausted and sore from these last few days (and especially the last) of unaccustomed exertion. The bark and boughs with which I made my little shelter served only to confuse the rain until I was snugly stowed away, then the descending torrents found their openings and let in a deluge, soaking my bed and clothes and person. I have necessarily put a good deal of work into improving my roof, which, though it continues to leak somewhat, is now better protection against the worst of the downpour. After desperate searching, have found another cache of firewood—the bole of a lightning-splintered hemlock blown slantwise by later winds, and part of which (the underside, lying toward the south) is relatively dry—slivers can be cut away with a knife as needed. I try to keep a high blaze going, for I fear if my fire is allowed to smolder, the rain will quite put it out. This is a continual struggle. I believe if I should ever come upon an abundance of dry fuel, I would be tempted to build a house on the spot and live in it until civilization arrives at my doorstep.

I have a wish for some of the oddest things: food, of course, which is not odd at all; but oh! my toothbrush! hot coffee! I am

nearly in tears over want of a comb to work out the tangles in
my hair, and a ribbon for tying it back (not for reasons of vanity but for the practical reason of keeping the stuff out of my
eyes, as most of my pins are long lost); and a deck of cards so
as to play solitaire, which I always have found a soothing habit,
a sedative, when confronted by dull depression and anxiety. It
occupies the mind enough to avoid thinking, but not enough
to tire.

Since repairing my roof, I have been mostly lying here in a
gloomy lethargy, staring into the downpour, venturing out only
to get quantities of wood and to relieve myself at a sanitary
distance.

I am fortunate to have this notebook as a place to write
down the details of my adventure, which is an immediate relief
to my feelings and may someday be of use in plotting a story,
which naturally has been forming in my mind. (A girl archae-
ologist, escaping an attack by wild bears, wanders lost in the
Cascade wilderness and is driven by terrible storms into the
deeps of a volcanic cave, where she discovers a secret cache of
golden treasure and artifacts from an ancient civilization, heretofore unknown to Science.) I know I should further make use
of these blank pages to advance the story—here is the unaccustomed solitude and leisure which every woman writer has pined
for!—should try to keep my mind busy, at the very least. I have
two barely used pencils—sufficient to write an entire novel!—
yet as to story, I cannot bring a single worthwhile sentence onto
the page. Even this little report of my condition is written with
difficulty, by fits and starts, as my mind is tired and wishes only
to feel bleak and not be forced to think. I have in times past
waved away crossword puzzles, petit point, and knitting, but
should find them now more restful than writing, which has

usually come easily for me and been my comfort. I am sure I will be ashamed, in later days, in the comfort of my own house, to see the penciled scribbles in these margins—not full-fledged sketches, which could have been excused, but meaningless mazes and chicken scratches and curving scrolls; this is what I do while I try to think what to write down here—shall I say that I am heartily downcast? that I am filthy?—and then another listless sentence, and then more useless scribbling.

The day passes slowly, and yet I dread the night, which shall pass more slowly still. To say that I am homesick, discouraged, and lonely is but a faint description of my feelings.

❦ *The Artist ever has been a man, living in terrible but splendid isolation, far from the comforts of family life, having sacrificed them to his Art. If a woman is present, she tiptoes in and out, bringing his tea on a tray; and in other rooms of the apartment she quiets the children and manages the mundane complexities of the household so that he might devote himself to his great work. Think of Sophie Tolstoy and of Wordsworth's sister—was her name Dorothea? Women may write potboilers, certainly, as a hobby, or in order to fortify the household income, but they are incapable of great Art, not only for the distraction of bringing up children—so very little time left in a woman's day—but for the same reason women are excluded from Science academies, literary clubs, and other places where men discuss the great questions: "Because of their childish ignorance and want of ideas."*

I count on the irrefutable literary power of the Two Georges to eventually put such idiot notions to rest. But I recognize that I am, myself, small beer. Such writing as I have done in recent years has been easy work, a story of three or four thousand words dashed off in three hours—an afternoon's effort. Sometimes I have to copy it, or change it a little, but usually it is written and mailed off as lightly as a letter. This is not, in the artistic sense, "literature"—I cannot make any pretense of being literary.

There was only a short period after the birth of the twins when I undertook to write a serious novel. Of course, I should have been content with finding time and mind for any sort of writing at all—most women, in the first months, give themselves over physically and mentally to a new child. And I was opposed in the undertaking, by my literary agent, whose portion was threatened, and by my husband, who worried that his children would grow up more devoted to their nurse than to their mother. It was generally believed that I might continue to write of pygmies and radium power and trips to the moon, in the afternoons while the babies napped, but that a Mother could never expect to write a Novel of Ideas. Here is the truth: I had had a girlish ambition to be famous, revered, on a plane with the great writers of the day—think of Kipling, of Stevenson—and now that I was so thoroughly closed in the jaws of motherhood I flew into a kind of panic. I began to swim hard upstream, all the while with my legs in the crocodiles mouth and my hands desperately reaching for a drift log, which I supposed must be my serious novel. Or rather several novels, as I skipped from one Great Idea to the next, never quite settling, always convinced (if briefly) that the new one surpassed the old—that now everything would shake together—I would grasp it all and not be afloat with only broken little bits.

There were heady moments when I was taken with my own cleverness—the words standing solidly on the page, this paragraph and that one moving well and sounding well in my ear, the people striking utterly human poses, the inner workings of theme and style seeming well wrought and important. Of course, these moments were inevitably followed by dark fantasies of the book failing in the worst ways—public humiliation—airy disregard. And so on, and so forth.

Days and weeks of feeling the new work to be shabby, and these wild swings of mood, depressions which robbed me of confidence—I believe it was these and not the ordinary problem of the mother and her "work" that eventually drove me back to dime novels and cheap romances, where my aptitude was proven and I might write four thousand words in an afternoon, tearing it off with hardly a pause, the smooth, swift, easy flow, like racing one's bicycle along a country path for the sheer and splendid joy of it.

So if I have given up trying to be a writer of the First Rank, it cannot be due to specifically female "limitations"; my concentration upon the lesser subjects is simply due to laziness, and perhaps to inferior powers, which a man may suffer from as easily as a woman.

C. B. D.

April 1900

9 Apr

Sun came out today, which raised my spirits to a considerable degree. How our bodies and minds are tied to the sky! Had to leave behind my neat lair after so much work to build—this was hard. But if I'm to be found, must get myself nearer the lava field or into the watershed of Canyon Creek or the Lewis River. Therefore heading northerly, sure of my direction now, though did not reach any place today. I'm not wet, which is exquisite relief, but am somewhat weak, as my food is now all gone. Far too early for blackcaps or wild berries, though there were plentiful bushes with tiny furled buds at the edges of a clearing which I at first thought to be made by farmers or loggers but proved to be an open field of blackened stumps and widow-makers, an old forest burn. (I stood in the cleared space with my face turned up to the sun. Oh the heat and light, delicious!

To find the sky! So hard to go into the trees again.) Have left the watercourse I named Sorefeet Creek, and camped tonight beside a meager little rivulet, a mossy rockfall which is a winter stream course for the runoff of rain and snowmelt, and therefore at this season is wet (though barely) and furnishes my necessary and only refreshment. I heated water in the soda cracker tin, which is a poor sort of pot but holds enough water to make a stab at cleaning my hands and face as well as private parts—used the handkerchief as washcloth, which I then washed (alas, no soap) along with socks and hung to dry. As to shelter, since no rain threatens, my lean-to is not so tight as before—a mere roof pole leant from ground to the crotch of a tree, and blown-down branches arranged upon it at a steep pitch. If it rains after all, I'll discover its deficiencies, but I lie here now in relative comfort and warmth. Firewood is a terrible problem, but I have become alert to certain likelihoods: dry sticks lying under rock shelves, splinters in the cores of old stumps or along the undersides of large fallen logs, dead softwood trees leaning to the south, which underside wood and bark ofttimes will be dry. I have a fire going against the base of the tree so as to throw heat back into my little tent, and I am fairly snug and in positive spirits, though hunger is ever on my mind. I sing, to keep my mind occupied.

As I sit here writing, the eyes of beasts watch my activity from the darkness, and there are rustlings in the brush, which do not alarm me—I have become quite used to them. I do not sleep soundly, which I suppose is a sort of blessing, as the fire does not burn unattended for long and has no opportunity to extinguish itself. I have read that one can influence one's dreams with careful concentration and planning, and I plan to dream of Melba's walnut chocolate fudge and of fried lamb chops which are, of course, smothered in cream sauce.

I have never been alone for so long before, nor thought so much. It is an interesting thing that while one part of my brain churns away upon practical matters—improvising to improve my situation—and upon morale—to recognize and overcome the signs of fear and panic—the other half is quite detached and records the circumstances in which I find myself—hardship and danger and so forth—with the impersonal eye of a writer. *Ah, I see, this is the point at which a lost person gives up fretting over possible embarrassment (what if she should be found a stone's throw from the trail?) and devotes herself entirely to a wish for rescue from her jeopardy.*

TWO BABES IN THE WOODS
Oh do you remember a long time ago
When two little babes, their names I don't know,
They wandered away one bright summer's day
And were lost in the woods, I heard people say.

And when it was night, so sad was their plight.
The moon had gone down and the stars gave no
        light.
They sobbed and they sighed and bitterly cried
And those two little babes laid down and died.

And when they were dead, a robin so red
Brought strawberry leaves and over them spread.
And all the day long they sang their sweet song,
Those two little babes who were lost in the wood.

POPULAR SONG OF THE AMERICAN WEST

10th

Hope! Here is Canyon Creek! and Camp 8 must lie very near—I shall be there tomorrow.

Climbed to the top of a high knob today, which was terrible work, with the summit always seeming to recede before me—upon the higher slopes, patches of old snow hardened to ice in certain hollows and tree wells, the wind blowing gusty and fierce, the view of trees and more trees and an infinity of mountains and canyons in which every pointy cone is seemingly of volcanic origins and every one a twin to every other. I was too exhausted to cry. Left the knob by means of a northerly route which started well but was deceiving, and later fell off steeply into a declivity; I despaired of reaching the bottom alive. But the ravine opened unexpectedly into the gorge of a stream which I am certain is an upper reach of Canyon Creek, as it wends away to the northwest (which it should) and is of a familiar size and appearance (caught between steep walls, with whitened logs, stumps, broken branches tangled in debris amidst tumbled lava forms and boulders brought down by the spring freshet). A relief, in any case, to be next to flowing water again.

My camp (the last!) is a poor thing in the hollow stump of a decayed tree, which I share with spiders and centipedes, but tomorrow I will have a soft bed free of vermin, and a hot bath, as well as a delicious rest while someone else tends to the fire; and FOOD. Footsore, infinitely bruised and battered, and of course cold, as rotted wood throws off so little heat, but these things are as nothing beside the simple fact of hunger. (I wonder if the human body exists for the sole purpose of eating, for when sustenance is denied to it, the stomach asserts its importance and becomes the central organ.)

I have imagined over and over again, like a melodrama, the

moment when I shall limp into the log camp and the astonished men call to one another and come on the run, and someone's soft words—*shall ye be carried, miss?*—which offer I refuse with a weary smile and walk resolutely the last steps to the mess hall, where the cook with a nod and look of approval delivers over a hot platter followed by a blackberry pie, and afterward a troop of men escorts me to the boss's cabin, where Bill Boyce—he has lost heart, given me up for dead—beholds, awestruck, the brave woman before him, and stands guard without while I bathe in his own deep tin tub; and afterward he tenderly applies ointment to my injuries and gives up his own feather bed for my sleep.

11th

Lost. Giddy hopes dashed. Cold, poorly, fretful.

> In the midway of this our mortal life
> I found myself in a gloomy wood, astray
> Gone from the path direct: and even to tell
> It were no easy task, how savage wild
> That forest, how robust and rough its growth.
>
> DANTE ALIGHIERI,
> *Inferno*

12 Apr (7 nights lost)

If I wanted to locate a place where no one would ever find me, here is where I would come. I've not been following the banks of Canyon Creek but some other water, which shows no sign of the activity of loggers. In this deep trench all is gloom and dampness, little daylight arrives, and I cannot escape into the broad day, as the climb upward is beyond my present strength; cannot bring myself to go backward, where lies failure and vanquishment; therefore I press forward, which at least is downstream and must eventually arrive at a larger stream which may yet take me to the Land of Men. The way is hellishly hard, clotted with windfalls of ancient and recent origin, and the stream bank frequently eroded, obstructed by dense thickets of brush, jams of drift logs, or bulwarks of stones. I am slowed by these natural impediments as well as my own failing strength. I have spent the greater part of my life in logging country, but never have felt so entirely enclosed by trees. They are *presences*, their limbs a ruffling commotion, like bats in the cavelike dark. Have spent the last two nights cowering amongst the great root structures of one and then another windthrown giant, being in too much despair and exhaustion to improve my shelter beyond a smoky fire and its natural comforts, which are minimal. Tonight is distant thunder, lightning in faint glimmery flashes which enframe the canyon walls. I should have nothing to fear—should welcome the light—trees too wet to catch fire— but the primeval instinct is alarm. In any case my mind circles and circles desperately around the matter of hunger and will not settle upon a survival strategy.

Wilderness is a great reminder of the limits of human perception. Where there are no clocks or roads, time and distance behave differently, and without signs or labels, everything appears able to shift its shape.

> Dzo'noq!wa are people who dwell inland or live
> on mountains. Their houses are far in the woods

or by a deep lake on top of a mountain. They have black hairy bodies and their eyes are wide open, set deep in the head so they cannot see well. They are two times the size of men. They are stout giants. Their hands are hairy. Generally the Dzo'noq!wa who appears in the tales is a female. She has large hanging breasts. She is so strong that she can tear down large trees. The Dzo'noq!wa can travel underground. Their voice is so loud that it makes the roof boards shake, and when a Dzo'noq!wa person shouts, lightning flashes from the place where he stands.

FRANZ BOAS,
Kwakiutl Texts (1903)

Morning, 14th?

Cold, in a weak state, barefoot—boots and much else left behind when at midnight of a terrible storm a bolt of lightning struck at my very head. In such moments we live in the body, not the mind—hair standing on end, felt the electricity, oh so close, so close, the air galvanic, explosive—fled in a feeble panic. This is how people die—fear and stupidity. I have only my clothes (stockings on my feet) and what was carried in the pockets of my coat: this book and pencil and the deer-foot hunting knife, as well as the useless compass. The most dread loss, of course, being the matches, which I thought were safely carried on my person but were not. Have been keeping warm—not warm, rather, but alive—by scraping a shallow hole to lie in and covering over with hemlock branches and mosses. I regret not only the warmth of fire but the light. Nights are utterly black, filled with unknowable screeches and moans and the phantasms of my cold brain. For these two nights (or three?) I have been dreaming of the dead, all the lost dead ones, Mother and Dad and Teddy and Wes and Harriet, of course, and people I have barely known or not known at all, Horace Stuband's wife and infants, Edith's dead babies, Melba's young husbands, even dogs and cows I have owned and my mother's horse Libby—I dream of them lying in the wet ground, every one of them, all that is left of them the white bones, which I recognize as I turn over in my hands. I know that monsters grow out of people by way of dreams, but I am not afraid to die—these dreams don't worry me; only, sometimes in sleep the earth falls away beneath me and my heart flutters strangely. Have become detached from my hunger, getting used to it, I suppose. If I live, I shall have stories to tell and to write.

Mother

Her husband was a big man, some 250 pounds, and he had gone out to the farther edge of his pasture, wading the flooded creek in the darkness to look for the cause of the scream that had come from that way, an animal screaming or a woman screaming, though not quite screaming, a nasal shrill whistling such as he had never heard—though he had heard elk, coyote, bobcat, panther, screech owl—and while he was standing there at the brushy hem of his pasture in the moonless night, in the rain, peering out, he had been struck by surprise, a small firestorm that ignited his bones, a flash of light rising not from the blackness riverward but from inland, inshore, from the intimate geography of his brain and his blood and his heart. And afterward, after she had come out to the field and found him and had propped his big shoulders with a hemlock branch to keep him from lying in the rising margin of the creek, and after she had gone off to get their neighbor to help her carry him to the house, he had slipped down in the water, the flooding pasture, and drowned. The woman and her neighbor, a man who lived alone and had the only house near them, a quarter of a mile to the south along the creek, carried him twenty yards and laid him across a log stomach-down and rolled him back and forth, which drove a thin spurt of water from his mouth and then a scurf of foam, but after that nothing, and they went on with it only a short while before the woman cried, "Oh, you have gone and died on me," and the neighbor stood away from the body of the woman's husband and said, "Missus, I'm sorry."

The woman wept, which was useless in the streaming rain and which discomfited her neighbor. She exerted herself, and though she could not stanch her crying, it became silent. She felt disconnected from herself, scattered, as if she had taken a long fall or as if their cow, Pearl, had shifted weight suddenly and smacked her against the side of the milking stall.

There had been ceaseless rain now for days and nights, and they stood in it, in the uneven lantern light at the center of a pouring darkness, and the neighbor considered the distance to the woman's house. The creek that divided the man's body from his bed was a narrow runoff from the Grays River Divide, a stillish and shallow gutter of water for the cows to drink from, and the deer, but it had spread out over the pasture and ran now in a broad black path, rushing through the blacker brushy margins with a rattling noise of anxious haste. The woman had crossed this creek twice, on the search for her husband and then for her neighbor, and they had crossed the creek together, she and her neighbor, wading through the mud and brush and

uneven stones with the water sucking at their knees, to get to
the dead man, and now must carry him back over the same
way, his deadweight, which problem the neighbor considered
uneasily.

The woman had put on a short wool coat, but the nightgown
beneath it from her knees to the hem was dank and gritty with
mud, the cold wet flannel cleaving to her bare legs, and her hair
had come loose from its braid and hung in dribbling strands
as if she wore a strange skullcap of raveling rope, and she had
begun to shiver without being aware of it.

"He's a heavy man, missus," the neighbor said, and the
woman, as she went on crying silently and shaking, said, "I can
lift his legs."

They carried the dead man to the near edge of the creek
and laid him down there while they recovered their breath, and
the neighbor went back for the lantern and set it near them,
and they lifted the body again and waded out into the water
with it. The body, depending from their hands, sank low in the
stream, and the neighbor began to worry and to struggle harder
to keep the man's head out of the water, which he knew was
foolish but understood also to be consequential. The woman
had stringy muscles in her shoulders and her back and her arms
from a lifetime of wood-chopping and ironing and churning
and clothes-wringing and carrying two babies about and rowing
waterlogged boats up and down the rivers and the sloughs, but
her husband's body was a heavy weight. She staggered, and with
her husband's legs clasped around her hips, her hands straining,
gripping him to her, her mouth began to release a low whistling
moan, a succession of powerful animal noises, as if she and her
husband were engaged in an act of love. She staggered, and the
cold flood ran in along her thighs.

They pitched the body heavily at the sodden margin of the creek and stood over it shuddering and wobbly and taking breath in and letting it out with the same sound a rubber bicycle tire makes when it's suddenly deflated: small paroxysms of rushing air. Then the neighbor waded back across for the lantern and carried it out half a dozen yards nearer the house, and they went on moving the body in short laboring relays, and moving the lantern with them as they went, and standing betweentimes swaying above the body in silence save for the whistle of their breathing and the unbroken beating of the rain.

The woman's children waited within, behind the streaming glass, watching the minute point of light as it intermittently gathered size in the darkness. Gradually there were shapes of things moving in the cast light, and voices carrying across the wet night. The girl, six, began to cry worriedly, though she went on standing inside the house and holding her brother's hand, which had been her only instruction. The boy, who was four, began to whimper slightly in chime with the girl. In later years of his brief life the boy would remember these events only as they were told to him by others; but the girl, in the next few moments, would begin to make out her mother, and a particular image would engrave itself upon her memory, an isolated single engram, her mother standing over a loose dark heap like a hillock of clay slickened and eroded by the rain; her mother standing with her palms pressed to her hips, heaving breath and releasing it in a smoking cloud downward upon the mounded earth. And in addition, the girl ever afterward would carry behind her eyes, within her dreams, an insubstantial image of the shifting shadows of woods spirits against a wet, glimmering darkness, and voices carried whispery across the rain in the language of bears or birds, and which she understood to have a meaning beyond mere loss.

? 16th

Cold. In a weak condition. Rain in the valleys overnight, snow upon the high shoulders. My bones shaking and mind discouraged—utmost exertion necessary to keep from freezing to death. I line my socks with leaves and moss, which has not kept my feet from becoming bloody—they can hardly be stood upon—but I walk and walk by sheer determination of mind and will to live. The walking is all that warms me, keeps me alive. I have been thinking of the vanity of a rich life and feel that I am reaching a true understanding of things perhaps for the first time, which is a return to Reason after being led down the perilous path of Adventure. If I survive these next days I should never again fail to taste and touch and relish life as it goes by, and my children. When I am home again, I should throw off the vampire seductions of ambition and embrace the solid comforts of housewifery.

🍎 *When I am with my children—wholly with them—then I am working very hard all day, which is sheer joy and the satisfaction of hard physical work; and I am without the frustration that arrives when I take the children in small increments—when I am always trying to solve something else in my mind. Of course, inevitably I begin to feel that the "real" me is buried; and I begin to want to give up being a matron at the center of a large family and go back again to being a bad housekeeper and a good writer.*

And when I am entirely submerged in the writing, I have the devil's own time not to neglect the needs of my children. I come to the surface as if rising through ditch water, and am often unable to think what to say when the boys descend upon me, showing off their treasures; or my answers are short and surly, which is bad, I know.

On the morning of the very day in which I delivered my firstborn child, the proofs of my first little book were delivered to me in the mail. In the interval since, I have been reminded almost hourly: the man who has no wife, nor least of all children—who has given himself up to his Art—has an unfair advantage over the woman who has been given more than one encumbrance.

I applied myself to correcting the copy of that book, Blackstone of Boston, the Strong-Hearted Detective, while I lay like a poor spent salmon in the still water between ever-ascending cataracts of labor. I was very young then, innocent of children, but now it strikes me that Blackstone of Boston was like an older child, demanding my attention in a jealous sort of terror, knowing full well the new babe at breast would unseat him from the center of his mother's heart.

A woman's situation is entirely irreconcilable. Not every one of us should be expected to accept homemaking and child rearing as her main purpose in life: Melba is a decent overseer for my children, gives them all they should have in the way of discipline, a tidy house, regular meals, clean clothes. And I am sprung free—have the time, and the necessary conditions, to write and to read (though conditions are never right for writing and you've just got to write anyway). Still, I always feel it's cowardly in me, or lazy, or shirking, to do only the nice part of taking care of the children. Perhaps I should be giving them what she does (and getting from them what she does!); perhaps there cannot be two women important to a child, and either you are that woman or you are not. If you walk away from them and leave them entirely to the housekeeper, how can you know them or understand their problems? There are so many things only a mother can know or do. Writing comes out of life; life must come first.

And yet at times I am certain I would be a worse mother if prevented from following my own occupation. My life does not go well without writing. It is my flywheel, my cloister, my communication with myself. It is my eyes to the world, my window for awareness, without which I cannot see anything or walk straight. Would my children wish to be raised by a resentful and bitter scold? But I suppose the truth of the matter is that my children will grow up, themselves, bitter and resentful—ill raised by a mother who ignored them in favor of her own selfish preoccupations.

I like to imagine that, with only sufficient hours in the day, I could be both a saintly Mother and an uncompromising Artist. But of course I feel pressed and frustrated, as though I must continually choose between love of a book and love of a child. And sailing between Scylla and Charybdis, my boat always will drift toward this perilous truth: though I am often curt and cross when my children surround and importune me, I have never felt besieged by the writing—have never wished to cut and run from my fictions.

C. B. D.

September 1907

Maybe the 17th

Death comes continually into my mind. I always have refused to believe in life after death, but here I am, feeling as if something important is about to happen—a threshold about to be crossed—and find I have an interest in discovering what is on the other side. There is nothing like living close to death to get you used to the idea, which is something Montaigne and others have said and which I am now proving to myself by coming within sight of death every day and at the same time becoming slowly free of distress. I have begun to take a kind of pleasure in growing weaker and letting myself go—which I imagine must be the usual feeling among the dying if provided with sufficient time to contemplate the process. I only wish I did not have to die alone.

I have seen men die in terrible ways. Wilem Frei was felled but not killed outright when Byers Alesson dropped his .22 rifle while climbing over a fence—this happened when Wilem and Byers were shooting in the hills just north of our farm on the Left Fork. When Byers came down to our house, crying and inarticulate, my mother and I went up into the woods and found Wilem with a bullet in his temple, lying gently waiting for us. It was plain that he was mortally hurt. Byers hung back from the scene, wailing and useless, wringing his hands. My mother began trying to stanch Wilem's bleeding, while I had a conversation with him. He was not much more than a boy—he may have been twenty—and I was twelve or thirteen at the time. Sorry about the trouble, was what he said to me, and that he was glad we had come. His only worry, he said, was of dying alone. When I asked him if he was suffering very much he answered no, not very much at all, but how was Byers holding up? He didn't "bear no grudge," he said, because these kinds of things could happen where shooting was concerned. After going on in this vein a short while, he died.

Pain, of course, is useful as an alarum—for the body to take some sort of action against the danger while there's still time for it to do some good; after that, the brain appears to have certain mechanisms for turning off suffering. It's also true, of course, that these mechanisms can be imprecise and slow. When Teddy became ill with typhus it was seven weeks of perilous

living—coming within sight of dying each day—and there was
terrible pain; but on the last day of his life he became like a
mouse dropped from the jaws of a cat—lying there so quietly,
dying without a struggle. And the last thing he said to us (if I
heard it right) was, "I have the true ease of myself."

It is not death but waiting for death that wears one down—
and the prospect of dying alone—and the dread of what one
may become. Have seen ghosts and apparitions and heard their
screams in the night—I *do* fear losing my mind, dying as mad-
women do, tearing off my clothes as I run shrieking through the
dark trees.

Teddy

The boy and the dog wrestled with each other in a rambunctious
way, the boy down on his knees in the dirt and rolling at times
onto his shoulders and his back or neck as the dog rolled too,
his feet scrabbling loosely against the boy or against the earth,
and the two of them springing apart every little while, eyeing
each other as they circled, and then the boy or the dog, one of
them, releasing a sudden high bark and jumping again upon the
other. The boy's tongue was a thick salmon-pink muscle, which,
in an unconscious habit, he pushed out and held flexed in his
teeth as he wrestled. The dog's tongue was long and loose and
slavering, which the boy failed to notice, as he also slavered. He
imagined that he was a Texas Ranger and the dog a notorious
desperado named Wolf Hicks, who had a reputation for deal-
ing death and mayhem. This was not their first encounter, and
would not be their last; they were evenly matched in a fight, and
Hicks, through trickery or the last-minute arrival of henchmen,
always would manage an escape.

The two of them fell apart, panting, and after an interval the dog began to inspect his own genitals. This interested and distracted the boy, who lay on his back in the dry pasture grass, his eyes turned to watch the dog. Under the dog's tongue, a pink tip of penis, shockingly wet and bright, extended itself from the sheath. As the boy lay watching the dog licking his penis, his own tongue extended itself again, as much in imitation of the dog's action as from his big stiff tongue overfilling his mouth: he had an awareness of himself as an animal, as one among the animals. He licked his own mouth and lips, the salt taste becoming the taste of his maleness, his nature, which he apprehended indistinctly.

The pasture was embayed by a long curve of the creek, whose banks were hedged by red alder thickets and its outer limit unambiguously bound by the sudden steep rise of the wooded hills. A cow and an old horse grazed there, and the boy had been sent to drive them in to the barn. In recent nights, a yearling black bear had been reported ambling through the darkness of neighboring fields, and the boy's mother feared the cow or the horse might be killed—shot by certain of her neighbors rushing headlong to clear the world of bears. Wolf Hicks had sprung his bushwhack just as the Ranger drove his herd toward the river, and now that the boy lay daydreaming, the cow and the horse had wandered off to resume grazing.

The dog stood and shook himself and made as if to inspect the grass: he meant to signal the end of their play. The boy, who understood the dog's meaning but objected to his intent, swung his long arm out and grasped the loose skin of the dog's neck in a provoking way. "Hey, Hikth," he said, which was the dog's imaginary name, Hicks, and then, "Bawther," which was the dogs true name—Boxer.

By reason of the shortness of the bridle, or frenum, that attached his tongue to the floor of his mouth, the boy was unable to speak in a completely human way. His impeded, tongue-tied speech was lisping and guttural, a roupy, beastlike articulation as of a bear or an ape attempting human words: a language that could be understood only by members of his family and which kept him isolated and despised by other boys. When the boy hugged the dog and patted him and kissed him, the dog tolerated this, having a dim understanding that he was the boy's only brother, but he was bored with their play and could not be persuaded to wrestle. Eventually the boy gave himself up to the dog's uninterest and he lay down in the late-afternoon light, in the long thrown shadows of the cow, the horse, and became lost in thought.

The boy could not have told anyone what were his thoughts; he had nowhere near an understanding of them. But in the long, feral summer days, he was more attentive than other boys to the smell of the cedar woods, and of dust upon the dry ferns and thimbleberry bushes, of plowed earth, strawberries, lilacs, rotting apples, of barns and cow pastures, of the mud at low tide in the sloughs and along the riverbanks. He had a wild nature, and his understanding of the world was primitive, emotional; he was engrossed with the land and the sky, and though he could not have articulated such things to himself or to the dog, he was aware of the way colors changed and moved in the water at different times of the day, or under different weathers; and the way the air changed its weight, its light, under the shifting presence of clouds. He was lonely and reticent, reclusive, and loved only by his family, but he felt the world to be alive around him, down to the rocks and trees, and felt himself to be embedded in it as completely as an embryo in a womb. Had he

lived long enough, this was something that would surely have
been driven from him—such is the social compact of Civilization; but within the next year the boy would be dead, killed by
an outbreak of typhus that would sweep him up in a windrow
along with seven other children living along the upper reaches
of the valley; and thus he never would be forced to acknowledge
his separation from the rest of Creation.

18th? 19th?
Cold. Very poor. Beasts in the shadows. How much longer?

> The wind and the thunder
> They are the same everywhere,
> What does it matter then,
> If I die in a strange land.

MARY AUSTIN,
"Indian Death Song"

Night
There is something someone things I have seen and not reported
in these pages not wanting to give proof of an insane mind and
so writing now in the darkness where I cannot see the shameful
evidence of my own scribbled words, here is what I have seen,
their prints first and then seen them skulking along, though
when I try to see them better they are gone—shadows—which I
think must be creatures of my imagination (lunacy brought on
by a starving by freezing) but oh—must believe they are actual
creatures as are known to live deeply secret in the woods—so

thick the trees here the darkness—and shying from human scent
of which I have none, being by now a stinking wild creature
myself—which may be a species of bear or Homer's hairy wildmen or Indians of the most primitive tribe their brutish clothes
made of wolfskin and which a human being should fear—I do
fear if they should see me butchery or savage assault—but being
so afraid to go on alone and to suffer alone the cold nights so
densely black in which my eyes strain and strain to see emptiness I must welcome the company even of monsters or ghosts
though I don't get close but watch them watch for them and
follow their great bare tracks (cannot be made by weightless
phantoms but impressed deep in the moss the mud individual
toes distinct) and tonight they lie together in the crevice of
a rock an undercut, I see their great hairy limbs entangled as
animals will do for warmth and comfort sleeping while the very
air becomes saturated—rain not pouring but a thick fine quiet
drizzle—and my own bed a shallow hole scraped in the earth
and pieces of bark leaning over it to direct the rivulets—I am
so very cold and wet—believe I would creep under the rock
and lie down with those wild creatures if not for the smell the
savage reek of their animal nature which I am afraid of and
their hugeness—or if they should prove insubstantial and my
sanity gone afraid to discover it—so lie here shivering alone
sleeping with my eyes open watching them the heavy darkness
of their bodies under the lip of the rock face and the slight
stirring which must be the shimmer of a lunatic mirage or the
twitching of their animal dreams and I hear them their heavy
bodies turning in sleep and murmuring which has made me
think of my brother Teddy and how he whispered to wraiths
every night and thrashed about on his bed and my own fearful
ghosts, how I must fight them off every night every night in

the cold blackness and lying shaking under piles of hemlock
switches with my eyes open listening to the murmuring shapeless mystery of those wild cries in the darkness those sad whim-
pers those troubled dreams—oh it is just a terrible comfort not
to be alone.

> The worst of a true ghost is, that, to be sure of his
> genuineness—that is, of his veracity—one must
> wait the event.
>
> HERBERT MAYO,
> *On the Truths Contained in Popular Superstitions* (1849)

Cold, windy (have lost track of the date)

On the trunks of certain trees they have left the long ragged
slashes of their claws (I believe I have not imagined them) and
in those places I have used my knife to free the tender inner
bark, which I chew in long thin strips, acerbic but not unpleas-
ant. The troop of shadow-beasts, if that is what they are, makes
its way slowly through the primeval forest, not doing bloody
murder but browsing like the very deer and elk upon leaves and
sprouts of thimbleberry, horsetail, nettle, clover, which I have
begun to eat also, going slowly after them, taking their example
as to what is edible, though it may be the advice of deluded
belief. Where they have nibbled the young twigs of blackberry
bushes, I peel and eat the shoots raw. I've seen the marks of
their digging, the long scrapes in the mud, where must be wild
carrots and wild onions as well as roots of ferns, which my
fingernails cannot get at—have begun to whittle a stick slightly
curved with a crutch handle, a digging tool, which will also

serve for clearing the stones and roots where my bed is to lie each night. I have had a dream in which I located the matches and the lost soda cracker tin—my forlorn pot left behind with the boots, etc.—a dream in which I heated water and cooked snails (as the French do?) with the addition of fiddlehead ferns, and thus made soup which was meager and salty though not vile, and its warmth so very welcome, and then the tin became a deep tub of steaming water which I sat in, tenderly washing with soap and a soft cloth every filthy orifice and weeping sore upon my body. I believe I could eat a fish raw, chewing small bites slowly, before eating grubs or ants, but catching them is a work of patience which I have tried and tried and failed. Today I did put a dead beetle in my mouth and swallowed whole, though afterward imagined horrible hatchings within my belly (They eat slugs, which I cannot do, not yet, and sowbugs, ants, caterpillars, which they scrape from rotted trees, or turn over old logs and excite the bugs with a stick, which they lift to their mouths and lick with long gray tongues curling around the twigs. I have seen them at evening, at the edges of talus where colonies of white moths were roosting among the rocks—gathering the bodies of the ghostly butterflies into their mouths by the handfuls.)

The goddess made a man taller and more powerful than Gilgamesh—a wild beast of a man, unconquerable, which was shaped from clay. The goddess spit upon the clay to keep it soft as she shaped the man. He was unkempt and savage in his looks—two horns sprang from his head. She

left him asleep in the forest and when he woke he
didn't know where he was. He ate fruits and drank
water, befriended wild creatures, and learned to
eat grass and the petals of flowers.

THE EPIC OF GILGAMESH

Sun glimpsed today through white cumulus

Through the trees and from hiding, I have watched the others
fishing. Sometimes they muddy the bottoms of small pools at
the edges of the stream by stamping or using a stick, and as
the fish rise to the surface seeking the clear water, they catch
and throw them into the shore-brush with their humanish
open palms. Or they muddy the end of a deep pool where it
empties to a shallow, pebbly rapids—then go to the upper end
and stamp, which sends the fish in panic down into the mud-
cloud, where some will be stupid and dash through the dark
water into the current, where they can be caught in the shingly
shallows; which I have tried myself but too slow (weak) and my
hands too slow or too small. Desperate to catch fish, so today
for a line I raveled a thread from my underwear, and a clumsy
hook carven from a sliver of wood, and for bait, the worms and
grubs which lie beneath any rotten log. (This is how Teddy and
I fished as children!) One slow-witted trout of small dimensions
came to my poor tackle, which I ate within moments of landing,
discarding only entrails while munching bones and skin all with
industrious appetite, though other people not having been in
these circumstances will doubtless think me savage. The meat
was chewy, not slippery in the mouth as I had feared, and salty,
which I welcomed.

C. B. D. (1906)

FROM "DARK THINGS"

IN A DESOLATION, AND OTHER STORIES

In the flood season several years before, the creek had changed its course, tumbling its long field of boulders into the new channel and allowing to grow in the old stream bed muskegs of cattails and bulrushes, skunk cabbages, arrowhead weeds. The child found this stillish sidetrack, its fetid plant life and extravagance of insects, more exotic and more inviting than the creek running quick through its lunar waste of bare and tumbled rocks. She lifted and stirred the fleshy leaves of skunk cabbages, whose inflorescences attracted carrion beetles, and captured the insects with her hands, then placed them delicately beneath a long piece of cedar bark and stomped upon the bark, which made a crackling noise against the beetles' stiff black carapaces. She turned over discarded leaves and bark until she found the hiding place of a salamander in the mud underneath. They looked each other in the eye for a moment. Then with a sharp stick she opened a hole in the salamander's body and, after examining the result, released the creature to the ground. It became perfectly still, invisible against the mud save for the thread of orange intestine trailing from the puncture. But in a moment it twitched and disappeared into a jumbled field of rocks. The track it left on the mud was thin and wavery as a thread, and the child imagined it was a secret rune—telling the way to faeries' land.

In the duff under an ancient spruce she found the hiding place of a banana slug, its albino skin ghostly and translucent like a spill of white candle wax against the brown humus. When she had sat down on the ground and unlaced her left shoe, she stood again and deliberately pressed her bare sole down onto the slug, which oozed and was cold.

The child, who in other circumstances, other environments, might have demonstrated that she was coming to terms with a civilized environment, had become, in this environment, a savage child of nature, directed by instinct rather than volition and devoid of all those acquired tastes and patterns of behavior which are part of our adjustment to civilization. After cocking up her thin little leg to spy out the pulp and slime on the bottom of her foot, she took some onto her finger and delicately tasted of it, and afterward became bold enough to eat worms and pill bugs, which she turned up in the rotted corpses of old trees.

She waded carefully in the stagnant pools, setting her feet down among the sharp sticks and wood knots, the stinging nettles, the left-behind stones, the one shoe and one bare foot imprinting in the black clay a dim sequence of unequal pugmarks which would later spring back and vanish, as unmade as the child herself.

Cool, cloudy

They have left the stream. Though I feared to follow, my greater fear is to be left alone—the company of beasts or of phantoms preferred to solitude—so went after them up a rocky chute to the top of the ridge, which was accomplished only at great cost to my strength—stockings long ago worn to nothing and my poor bare feet flayed and bruised and bleeding. I could not keep up, but they seemed to slow and slow further, browsing uphill in their easy fashion, and I must wonder if they are deliberately leaving for my discovery the desiccated fruits of highbush cranberry still clinging to bare winter twigs, as well as old hips of wild rose, which are sour but strengthening.

They must know I am here: the trees upon the high ground are thin and scant, growing out of the very rock, and so we wandered along the ridgeline in sight of one another, though each intent upon our foraging, and pretending not to notice the other; or I am alone after all, pretending not to notice the creatures sprung from my wild imagination. But they pull the branches of bushes toward them and strip the leaves with their teeth; their lips curl back flexibly around the twig as they eat, and I have been near enough to see (or dream) that their teeth are yellowish and small and even. Here is what I think: they are real—must be real—and I have begun to wonder if Harriet might yet be alive, perhaps taken into the company of such creatures as these, or following in their trail as I do.

Though walking upright and having a humanish form, I believe they must be (if not phantoms) neither Indians nor the hairy wildmen of loggers' tales but great animals of a species as yet unknown to Science—apes or erect bears of immense size. There are four: the elder female (if they were bears I should call her the sow), perhaps eight feet in height and weighing nearly three hundred pounds, built very stocky with open, flat-nosed features, and her hairless dugs very pendant; a juvenile female (this I presume to be the sow's young calf from last year or the year before), half again smaller but still a child giant of four and a half feet or more, and having soft cinnamon-colored hair; and two younger male calves, twins I should call them, still suckling at the sow's teats and evidently but a few months old, though they are about the size of a two-year-old child. All in this family walk with a distinctive long-legged gait, the knees bending upon each footfall.

I do not seem to frighten them, even when coming within

a dozen yards. Or I am the one not frightened, as my mind has been cut loose from its moorings and now follows its usual course, adrift in a wild beast fable: they are Mountain Giants from the hidden caves of the See-Ah-Tiks, and I am the intrepid Girl Explorer, Helena Reed.

🍎 *My mother came from a family of mad book-lovers, and the greatest gift I have from her is the passion for reading, which is a cheap and consoling entertainment, bringing knowledge of the world and experience of the widest kind, as well as moral illumination and, of course, adventure. The backbone and foundation of my mother's bookshelf was Emerson and Montaigne, but her taste ran out to the further extremities:* Grimm's Fairy Tales, Dickens, Scottish Chiefs, Ivanhoe, Days of Bruce, Victor Hugo. *I remember especially a little book called* Paul and Virginia *by Bernardin de Saint-Pierre, which was a romantic story of two nature children, and which I read over and over until the pages were worn thin. And I read Poe when young, which scared me ill because I believed in it—the fantastic seeming perfectly natural to a child and simply the way things were.*

During the years I lived with my aunt, everyone in our circle of acquaintance was literate as a matter of course, and my aunt and her radical friends were the beginning of my real education, which is to say they offered their own ideas for reliable reading (Irving Lowell, Hawthorne, Woodberry, Carlyle, Arnold, et al.) and passed me pamphlets and articles which addressed the great questions of the day. My aunt has a pure and classical literary taste, none better. She presented me with Pilgrim's Progress *and saw me through a dozen books of the* Iliad. *She was fond of fiction more than anything, but her tastes were of the old school—no poetry worth reading since Byron, no novels since Scott.*

It was the New York Public Library which was my University. No one within those walls ever told me what to read or not to read—it was all there to be consumed, as and when one wished—and I had the necessary curiosity to seek out the things I most wanted to know. I followed my interest in biology and anthropology to Huxley, Spencer, and the scandalous Darwin; learned enough of history (Lubbock's Origins of Civilization, Rawlinson's *Five Great Empires) to discover its amusing limitations; from White's* Warfare of Religion and Science *learned the cultural importance of religion as well as the absurdities and contradictions of the world's repeated attempts in this line; and from Gray's three-volume* Nature's Miracles, *enough of astronomy and electricity, radium, and so forth to get a clear idea of the whirling wonder of the universe. I don't suppose I could have passed a college examination from such independent studies, but there is something to be said for studying from a strong desire to know.*

As for novels, I became an admirer of Miss C. Bronte for keeping her sentimentality firmly bridled, and of J. Austen for her great and good common sense, but I never have bothered to read the modern, petty little stories of continual melancholy, in which men are mewling about the futility of action and women are wringing their hands. I should always prefer to read about sound, active, healthy women, and not always the wearisome sameness of spoiled marriages, and spinsters who should have married and did not. I should always prefer to read tales in which men (and women, though they are rare) have stout hearts and hands instead of nervous conditions and inherited feebleness; tales in which the author finds it sufficient to give his boys and girls a fault or a weakness, and a precarious situation, and turn them loose to win through.

My own strongest inclination as a reader has been toward the romance: that is, toward Kipling and Scott, Stevenson and Dumas. I am an admirer of Stanley Weyman and of Anthony Hope. Of the women, of course, the Two Georges. (When an American woman writes a decent story of adventure, without too much sentimental love in it and without the eternal feminine virtues—why must women always be modest, pure, civil, and reticent?—then I will begin to hope for something great from them.)

I have not mentioned the lowbrow scientific romances, ghost stories, and beast fables, to which I have always gravitated rather more than toward the "high," especially literary, kind of fiction. I shouldn't have to apologize or explain my affection for the bizarre and the fantastic, but I will mention that such tales have always had to overcome a certain disreputability before I could applaud them: my preference is for the writer whose language is gorgeous, whose characters are real as life, and whose stories take my poor little assumptions and give them back to me transformed; I prefer, then, Verne and Griffith, Poe's short tales and Mary Shelley's Frankenstein, over the dreadful penny dreadfuls. There is, of course, an element of shame in listening to tales of the unreal—similar to paying to see a two-headed child—but the extraordinary has an allure of its own that can transcend intellectual considerations.

C. B. D.
August 1902

Evening, cool

My stool today greenish and soft and small, but the first in—how long? Though I am continually cold and often wet and though more or less continually hungry—craving both sweetness (Melba's doughnuts) and salt (Stuband's smoked hams and bacons)—I find I am somewhat in better strength and not entirely starving, from eating shoots and leaves and roots as well as bark and so forth throughout the day, and imagine I could go on in this fashion for an indefinite time—until I am rescued—especially as the summer arrives and certain berries and nuts begin to ripen, as well as Indian camas.

I am weak in my mind, though, and close to tears much of the time. Today was thinking of Gracie Spear and her cheerful whistling, and without quite realizing it I began to pipe "Crossing the Bar." The beasts' own call is a sort of whistle, tuneful in some of its aspects, which I have begun to recognize and follow as they whistle to locate one another in the deep forest, and my wordless melody brought the two youngest through the trees, though when they saw it was the Other they scurried for the protection of the sow, who was browsing only fifty feet from me. This was a startling vision—being so much like my own little boys, who are incurably shy of strangers—and I fell immediately to sobbing for my children, fatherless and now motherless; and I suppose some tears for myself, being the one lost, and living like John the Baptist among the wild beasts of the wilderness. (I have striking weaknesses and must try to defeat them.)

The sow turned her head and gave me a stare—attentive to the safety of the infant cubs, I am sure, but perhaps also curious as to the sound of human weeping, which I should imagine she has never heard before. This being the first straight look I had received from one of the creatures, it quite dashed my tears and hiccoughs—frightened me into silence—and after a moment I lowered my own eyes as one does when unarmed and confronted by a wild beast. However, I should say of her stare that it was not so much threatening as inquiring—a very humanish look—and it was some time before she shifted her own gaze and returned to the serious business of gathering miner's lettuce into her huge grayish maw. During the moment her eyes were upon me, I felt oddly as if we were two women: in another woman (even though a stranger) I should have taken such a look to be a silent, sympathetic invitation to confide one's troubles. Such is the deficient state of my mind. But I think of Montaigne: "What we call monsters are not so to God, who sees in the immensity of his work the infinity of forms that he has comprised in it."

Morning

Rain overnight, which I am nearly hardened to, but then heavy wind, which seemed to fill the night with devils—shrieking and whining in the limbs of the trees—the wild forest animate. The decrepit trees began to groan and fall all around, which quite drove me to desperation—I crept through the wet dark to their denning place, a mere shallow hole in a dirt embankment, which they had lined with dead grass and leaves for insulation— their smell very strong and bestial, but I was more afraid of the wild night—and insinuated myself among their heavy bodies as any poor orphaned cub. They must normally shun human contact, but they only shifted their weight and moaned faintly or sighed, while otherwise seeming to take no notice; and as I lay in that feral dampness and stink, believing I must not sleep but lie awake all night in a rigor of fear, I took slowly into my very bones the heat of their massive bodies and quite let go of the world—oh so cold for so long, day and night—slept deep and dreamless until the dawn.

They now thoroughly tolerate my presence, as indifferent to me as the rhinoceros is indifferent to the oxpecker roosting along his spine. I have learned to pass among them with some degree of casualness and confidence, though I am cautious of abrupt movement, as one must be with untamed beasts, and conduct myself submissively, which is behavior familiar to any housebroken woman.

The wind has died away. It is very much warmer and a haze covers the sky.

> When much in the Woods as a little Girl, I was
> told that the Snake would bite me, that I might
> pick a poisonous flower, or Goblins kidnap me,
> but I went along and met no one but Angels, who
> were far shyer of me, than I could be of them,
> so I hav'nt that confidence in fraud which many
> exercise.

> EMILY DICKINSON,
> *from her letters*

Morning clouds breaking through to a fair afternoon

I have given each of them names, which is only for the convenience of my mind and this notebook.

The adult female I have named Cleo, and the infant twins (whom I cannot tell apart) are Pit and Pat. The female cub, who I now guess to be almost Oscar's age (though in size she already stands nearly equal to me), I have called Dolly. On a naked humanish anatomy they have a thick growth of hair two or three inches long, moderately coarse to the touch, and varying in color from near black to near red, leaving bare only the face, feet, and hands, as well as knees and elbows, and also the female breast and the male genitalia of the twins, which are small and carried close to the body. Their necks are short and faces broad, noses somewhat flattened below a beetled brow, and mouths wide and lipless; nevertheless they possess a star-tlingly human range of facial expressions; and their bodies, as well, can be expressive of emotion in the same way a dog's tail or his hanging head will tell you his feeling.

Overall, though, the emotions of these beasts are not so near to the surface as a dog's—they have a calm demeanor as befits creatures large enough and strong enough to brook no enemies. The screams of lions at night do not turn their hair; today and yesterday we have crossed the heavily used trails of bears, which they ignored as beneath interest, and equally so a bear of mam-moth proportions, which gazed on us from a rockfall ridge and which would have stopped my heart if I had not been in the company of giants. Yet they are shy, and in certain ways much alike to any small animal—as if prey to every bloody-toothed beast of the forest. They continually turn to look behind them and to all sides, as if fearful of being followed; and their dens are made in the deepest brush, among thorns and tangled vines. They never fail to bury their dung—not in the fastidious man-ner of cats, but with the furtiveness of thieves, as if seeking to conceal evidence. Of course, it must be this shy behavior which has kept them unknown to Science, glimpsed only by the occa-sional Indian and the rare woodsman, and it may show a jus-tifiable and intelligent fear of discovery by humans—quite as if they've gained secret knowledge or occult warning from the American bison, the passenger pigeon, the sandhill crane!

As to language, the beasts' whistles and chirrups are a rudimentary form of communication which I am beginning to severalize. At home I have made a study of Buster's various vocalizations—have been able to distinguish seven individual barks of quite different meaning, even to the point of whether the person coming up the path to the front of the house is

Known to the dog or Unknown. In similar fashion I've made out simple meanings in the calls of the beasts—incitements to play, for instance, and a particular whistle which seems to express surprise and puzzlement, as well as alarms such as any animal uses to alert his fellows to the presence of unexplained sounds or events. And there are, as well, two distinct calls the mother uses to locate her children, one a sort of routine inquiry and the other more urgent, a kind of alarmed imperative which infallibly brings the twins and Dolly racing in from wherever they are. In addition, they communicate by dumb show—gestures of a primitive sort but plain to understand—finger pointing, for instance, and a raised hand which I take to mean, "Stand and be still!"

In most scientific circles it is forbidden to say that animals love. (Human beings alone believe they know what love is, and esteem it highly) On the subject of their society, I should say only that there is a bond (or the appearance of it) between the members of this family of beasts. Cleo puts up with her children's rough play to a remarkable degree; her patience when bitten, knocked about, pushed, and pulled I should call saintly in a woman. (Hair pulling is a favorite torment, which she tolerates as I never would from my own children.) She further demonstrates great attachment to her children, becoming anxious-eyed—looking searchingly around—when one or another of the young twins is briefly missing, and when the baby hoves into view his mother bounds to him, overjoyed, and anoints the top of his head with her long gray tongue.

In addition, they touch one another far more than is usual among the Scandinavians or even the Italians and Spaniards of my experience—gentle strokes and petting of a seemingly affectionate sort, as well as grooming of the hair. I should like to know—shall have to investigate when I am returned to civilization—by what measure Science differentiates the love of a human family from the evident affections of a family of beasts, when the chief observable difference lies in less argument and rancor among the beasts.

> In his latest article (Feb. 1892) Prof. Garner says
> that the chatter of monkeys is not meaningless,
> but that they are conveying ideas to one another.
> This seems to me hazardous. The monkeys might
> with equal justice conclude that in our magazine
> articles, or literary and artistic criticisms, we are
> not chattering idly but are conveying ideas to one
> another.
>
> SAMUEL BUTLER

Sun, glorious sun!

We have come out upon a floor of grassland with a steep rock-fall along its flank. Though snow remains over the high trails, upon this gigantic rock garden spring is in full cry: white fawn lilies and mission bells, red-maids and chickweed, buttercup, wild larkspur, starflower, red columbines, bittercress—I name the few I know, though I cannot name nor even count some hundreds more.

We climbed down onto the cliff garden and have spent the whole day happily digging thistle and avalanche-lily roots and peeling their young stalks, nibbling the leaves and flowers of buckbean and wild parsley, as well as tiny yellow monkeyflowers marked upon their lower lip by reddish brown freckles—too exquisitely lovely to eat, though I ate them all and hunted for more! In the afternoon we drank deeply from the cold lacework of water falling along the edge of the rocks, and afterward the others waded in and played as dogs will do, with a great deal of tussling and romping and screeching, and I was so desperate for a bath I did strip off my clothes and splash in and out—the water so very cold, straight off the glacier—and now we are sunning ourselves amid the continual coming and going of bees and butterflies. As long as the sun shines, I shall not have to put on my filthy duds, which is a wonderful relief. As I lie here writing, the twin cubs tumble and play in the stones, while Cleo and her daughter are sprawled and dozing upon the meadow-grass, and I wonder: What is happiness? Perhaps not a State, as we seem to think, but a Moment—perhaps the moment when one stands from one's browsing and straightens into the sunlight, into the heady warmth of the scented air, and one's gaze rises— oh!—across the dazzling field of flowers to the white dome of a far-off mountain perfectly drawn above the dark mountain trees, luminously bright against the violet-blue of the sky. And I wonder: In such a moment, could even Eve in her garden have been more content?

> The female Dzo'noq!wa carries away children in her arms to her house inland, or she puts them into a basket, which she carries on her back. When young girls walk about in the woods, they are enticed away by her or carried away in her arms. (When enticing away a child from a house, she assumes the voice of their grandmothers.) Little children are frightened into obedience by

being told that the Dzo'noq!wa will come and carry them away. (When she has stolen a child, she keeps it as her daughter and picks salmon berries for her.)

FRANZ BOAS,
Kwakiutl Texts

Evening, under a fair sky

I woke thinking: Is it possible that, after all, I am to go on living with the wild beasts while in the greater world others are hunting out the peaks of the Himalayas, the dark heart of Arabia, and the secrets of the Poles—while in the civilized world electricity is spread to every corner, and the flying machine is invented—while in the laboratories and academies and astronomical observatories, by telescope and spectroscope and microscope, others are to discover the minute secrets of Life and of the Universe—all this while I am living ignorant as a savage in the wilderness?

We have left the high meadow and the rock garden, after burying scores of lily bulbs in several holes lined with cedar boughs. No attempt was made to conspicuously mark these winter caches as I would have thought—with cairns of small rocks, for instance, or other indicators. I hope they may find their bulbs again when this field is transfigured by the changing of season; what, after all, will be recognizable when leaves have fallen and snow is on the ground? I suppose there can be no particular intelligence in recovering stored food, only a sort of rote memory, for which even squirrels and certain birds have shown an uncanny knack; and it may be that the beasts will keep in mind particular large and constant landmarks such as coniferous trees or sizable rocks. Or they may be intelligent enough to think of returning to this ground once or twice more—as leaves fall, as snow arrives—to strengthen their memories.

We have been following the grown-over marks of an old trail that I believe has never seen the footprint of a man, a meandering route taking in every thick brush patch and pond-lily puddle and all the soft muskegs which lie in low swales— food to be found in each, and though I am never filled I am not starving. We are seeming overall to take a northerly route. I wonder where we are bound—afraid it must be farther and farther away from the company of other human beings. (I am now struck by this thought: I should expect to be either dead or rescued before they return finally to that high meadow and uncover their lilies.)

This afternoon, met a stream boiling down over boulders which could be crossed only with caution, leaping from rock to rock with the care of a cat. (Proved I am catty.) Then a slow and tiresome climb through an old burn, where the second growth and the trees fallen in tangles made an impenetrable thicket, which of course we must penetrate. Camped tonight under cover of ancient trees, the sky only glimpsed in rags and tatters, which is usual.

I am reminded how rarely I have seen the sky since leaving behind Home and Family and the lower Columbia. Last night, while lying upon the high flower field, I may have had my only unencumbered view of the moon, pale and thin, a merest shaving of the flesh of an apple, yet even that dim light was like a wondrous gift, and filled me with gratitude. I felt I was seeing the night sky, the dense field of stars, for the first time—really *seeing* it—and its beauty. Of course, I should have preferred different company for sky watching—should have asked for a female astronomer with a sense of the aesthetic! But while it may be true dumb animals neither see nor reflect upon the vault of heaven, I did not feel this loss particularly last night, lying with them under that vast canopy of stars—was consoled by their warmth—found it easy to imagine, in their silence, a kind of awestruck meditation.

According to Science, animals are without culture, having neither poetry nor music. Yet I think of the wolves which used to skulk about the hills of my childhood, and their moon singing, which even then struck me as a kind of polyphonic fugue—intricate and exact as any human concert. (How long since I have thought of wolves in the Skamokawa Hills, or seen them? Not for twenty years or more. They would shy away at once if Mother came out to the field with her rifle, but would stand and look with curiosity if we were unarmed, which must demonstrate an animal's instinctive understanding of human intent. Old Lars Larsson claimed to trap the last one, starving, infested with parasites, the year my mother died.)

I believe the beasts have minds, though what they think and feel is another and more difficult question. What goes on in the animal brain? When they lie in the dark with the flower-scented wind in their nostrils, as they look out at the moon and stars or the streaming clouds, what are they thinking about? They make their living in these remote and inaccessible parts of the forest without benefit of metallurgy or agricultural lore, and are curiously compounded of human and animal traits: Cleo commonly carries one or both of her twins upon her hip, washes and grooms them, and if she feels there is a threat to their safety, rushes over and snatches them up. On the other hand, she seems to delight in feeding them the living fish before it is dead, as well as garter snakes, which is a beastly thing to watch; and she examines and explores her own genitals (the cubs looking curiously on) whenever and wherever she receives the impulse. I am not prudish, but this is the shameless indifference of dogs or monkeys.

I wonder what they think of me—if they imagine my corduroy coat, my paraffined trousers, are a furred covering—if they believe I am a singularly ill-trained orphan whose frail size must be due to unknown hardships and abuses! But Cleo is solicitous, sometimes to the point of sending one or another of her children back to locate me if I lag too far to the rear of the column. Like any orphan, I am grateful to be adopted, even if this kindness is driven by animal instinct.

> They are called monkeys (Simia) in the Latin language because people notice a great *similitude* to human reason in them. Wise in the lore of the elements, these creatures grow merry at the time of the new moon. At half and full moon they are depressed. Such is the nature of an ape that, when she gives birth to twins, she esteems one of them highly but scorns the other. Hence, if it ever happens that she gets chased by a sportsman she clasps the one she likes in her arms in front of her, and carries the one she detests with its arms round her neck, pickaback. But for this very reason, when she is exhausted by running on her hind legs, she has to throw away the one she loves, and carry the one she hates, willy-nilly.
>
> FROM A LATIN BESTIARY
> OF THE TWELFTH CENTURY

C. B. D. (1906)

FROM "THE FORKS"

IN A DESOLATION, AND OTHER STORIES

The woman, who had been alone but now was in the company of a small band of wild people, came out of the burnt trees into open meadows and from the grass flushed the first spring birds—juncos, sparrows, robins. There would be woodpeckers and yellow warblers in the lower valleys by now, but she and the others had climbed and climbed high up, where spring had barely sprung. In the wet places skunk cabbages were blooming, which the woman had learned a taste for, but other animals, beavers or raccoons, had been ahead of them, digging in the mud for the tender roots.

They went up to a low, open ridge and below it was a very pretty lake, small and round, hardly more than a pond. Though there were patches of ice on the lake, the snow was entirely gone from the grassy meadows, and the trails of bear and of deer going down to the lakeshore were well used. There were fresh beaver cuttings everywhere, and as the beaver had mowed down all the brush, there was good going around the edge of the lake, with grassy swales and narrow marshes spaced among low ridges, and knolls crowned with dwarfish noble firs and bare-limbed larches.

The wild people fished the lake bare-handed. Along the undercut banks they placed their big hands in the water and reached slowly along the bottom until they had touched a fish, then worked fingers gently along the fish's belly to the gills, where they grasped suddenly, lifting from the water with the swift motion of a long arm, which action the woman studied and attempted to imitate without accomplishing it.

She knew that she might come in for a share of fish the others had caught, but in recent days and weeks she had learned also a rigorous self-dependence. After three or four failed experiments she managed to make a line from twisted strands of her own hair, which she fastened to a thorn and baited with grubs. This was very light tackle, but the lake water was so very clear even a human hair must appear a heavy cable to the eye of a vigilant fish. She caught the stupid small ones, which satisfied her.

She understood that the wild people with whom she traveled had once been human, or had once been animals, and now abided in shadows. She was ignorant of their language, however, and the wild people, in return, believed the woman to be mute and a lackwit. She held to the belief that her inventive fishing contrivance must astound them—that it must represent to them an ingenious technology. In fact, their surprise had to do with her caught fishes, which seemed to them unexpected proof of her native intelligence.

At a shallow place along the upper end of the lake, wet gravel and stones showed where a bear had been feeding upon the grass meadows and then had watered in the lake, twice crossing the round gray cobbles of the gravel bar. A long narrow point of spruce timber divided the upper and lower meadows, and when the woman and the others were crossing through the long spring grasses of the upper meadows, a shadow moved out from the thick edge of the timber and became that bear. He quartered toward them steadily, but stopped suddenly and stood looking straight at the woman and perhaps also at the wild people who were with her. He was large and brown, his pelt ragged, and in his flank and shoulder were several holes, open sores, the result of fighting. Years before, his left ear had been torn loose and now dangled in a comic way, attached by a narrow strap of cartilage.

The bear had been returning to a bloody winterkill which he had taken possession of from coyotes and ravens, and which the woman now smelled and then saw lying upon the grass—a shape which may have been a deer, though by this time much disfigured and dismembered. The wild people saw or smelled this carrion also and crossed toward it as if the bear were not standing there, for they intended to take possession of it themselves.

As a child, the woman had once sat in a wagon waiting while a black bear held the center of the road, a sow standing erect and fixing the wagonload of people with her stare while twin cubs safely crossed behind her from one brushy shoulder of the road to the other. At another time, still a girl, she had met a bear coming up a trail right toward her as she went down it. When the bear was near enough to see and smell the person with whom it shared the path, it started and tripped backward over a deadfall before scrambling off into red alder thickets in an embarrassed way that seemed to her quite human. In several places where the woman had lived, bears had been both prevalent and unapparent, staying under cover for the most part and having nothing to do with human beings except for their rubbish heaps or the old apples left behind in their orchards. If the bears of her childhood environs once had been predators, they had long since stopped being so; she considered them agreeable models for wildness. They appealed to a side of herself which was grumpy and solitary—unsociable.

She now lived in another place entirely, and had lately discovered in herself an unconquerable, instinctive dread of being eaten. In dreams, she had seen the shining interior wilderness of her own ribs and spine and viscera, the glistening scrapple of her brain, lying unfolded upon the somber green of sword ferns and mosses, and carried in the beaks of ravens and the sharp mouths of bears. She had become less afraid since coming into the company of the wild people, who were giants and untroubled by bears or lions. But while she went on crossing the high meadow in front of the big bear—crossing with the others, who were unconcerned—her heart began to trot, in the same swift way a coyote trots, its blurred feet scarcely touching the ground.

The bear's vision was poor but he was gifted with an extraordinary sense of smell. He blew air, chuffing and licking his nose and blinking as he watched the woman cross before him. Then he lowered himself to four feet and continued on across the grass toward the salmonberry shoots and pea vines which had sprouted in the sunlight along the lower edges of an outbreak of rock. It was his belief that the woman was, if not inhuman, at least wild, the dark tocsin of her human scent having been by this time muffled, ameliorated. The woman herself, eating of the old, spoiled, and bloated carrion, disciplined herself from casting a look backward. She was at that time still days away from an understanding of her own wildness.

Drizzling morning, bright afternoon

Cleo's character puts me in mind of Edith Eustler: a cheerful disposition and capable hands. We frequently browse near each other, and she has taken up the habit of "talking" to me in a low, lighthearted warbling which I find not only musical but companionable. I occasionally whistle or chirrup in reply, though my tuneful rendering of "Thou Art So Like a Flower" seems merely to puzzle and amuse her.

At times it seems possible to learn and translate their language. Their whistles and clicks and chirrups can be very like the human voice, with risings, fallings, inflections, clots, and stops such as we use. At certain odd hours of the gray morning I have amused myself by imagining their shapeless noise made over into coherent Roman letters, and thence into English. And along another line, I have wondered: by not speaking aloud for days, for weeks, what is the consequence to ones voice? If I opened my mouth and spoke now, what would emerge? Perhaps furred sounds, unpalatized, or a fluent unshapen pouring. (I think of Teddy.) My prolonged muteness has begun to seem the natural state; I am driven back upon my undeveloped senses, where the important thing is not to name the flower but to look at it—*look* at it—until the yellowness and the minute grains of pollen at the tips of the pistils completely enter one's consciousness and *become* its naming; and afterward, one may wish to christen the flower with a two-note whistle.

Today we have been keeping near a little creek which runs down through a valley of Western red cedar—in my childhood people called them canoe-cedars—such as I am sure Bill Boyce and his fellows would love to get their hands on, the majestic and vigorous trees rising each from its own great hillock of discarded needles and cones. I should guess these ancient trees to be a good five centuries old and moss-covered on their northerly sides, but nevertheless still healthy, having live branches low enough for Pat (or Pit) riding high upon my shoulders to reach playfully with his hands.

I suppose such giant trees as we have in this part of the country owe their immensity to a kind of botanical good fortune: mild climate as compared to the Great Lakes country, or to Maine, where Paul Bunyan's matchstick white pines were

but a puny three feet in diameter; and the nourishment of rain-
fall amounting to a hundred inches or more in a given year (of
which I must believe ninety-nine have fallen on my head since
going lost in the woods); and I suppose also to individual acci-
dents of location with respect to soil, fire, slope, shade, and so
forth: this is Science. The Transcendentalists, of course, would
make of such trees a natural church for Man, which I reject out
of hand as being steeped in the rhetoric of religion; but I admit
that today I was struck by a sense of something grand and beautiful in the accident of Nature. The trees did not intrude upon
one another but stood forth alone, vast and mysterious and still.
It is a different adventure to walk upright through a primeval forest, among the great buttressed and fluted trunks with
their aromatic, pendulous limbs, than to creep through woods
which were logged over or burnt years before and now are over-
grown with a thick tangle of brush and weedy trees and must be
threaded only as the bears and deer do, down on all fours.

A warmish spring day: wildflowers growing upon every bit
of ground where the canopy admits a glimpse of sunlight; the
young limbs of the trees lifting joyously upward, the old ones
downspread with the utmost grandeur; the bright green of springs
growth making a great show at the ends of the branches. As any
gentlewoman on a gentle ramble through the countryside, I took
in the scenery and meditated upon it. I wondered who could look
on the lacy foliage of the canoe-cedar, those flat sprays forked
and forked again along their axis—drooping from their parting
like the mane of a horse—without seeing a small gesture of grace.
I wondered why there was such pleasure in the sound of one's feet
crunching the diminutive cedar cones underfoot. I wondered if
the soft purl and sibilance of the downhill creek must be what
Thomas Fuller had in mind when he said that music was nothing

but wild sounds civilized into time and tune. When Cleo placed her huge feet with deliberate care so as not to trample the tender white shoots of Indian pipe thrusting up from the forest duff— well, this is the sort of thing that supports a poetic invention: I wondered if the beasts of the forest have a sublime, unspoken appreciation for the delicate beauties of Nature.

I don't let such thoughts out on the air—have a lingering fear of my human voice startling the others—have become accustomed to my own silence and theirs—but this book is my dear companion, a good listener to the workings of my mind.

> Though the lower animals have no language in the full sense as we understand it, they have a system of sounds, signs, touches, tastes, and smells that answer the purpose of language, and I merely translate this, when necessary, into English.
>
> ERNEST THOMPSON SETON,
> *Lobo, Rags, and Vixen* (1899)

Late afternoon, spring weather

Today we followed a creek upstream through dense spruce and hemlock until it came tumbling white out of a canyon; we crossed on a foot log, lingered there for a brief rest before tackling the steep, switchbacking climb to the break of the falls. On top, the creek appeared resting for its wild shoot down the canyon—there was a sloughlike stretch of dead water which we followed back through brush to a logjam one hundred feet wide and solid as a dam—the creek impounded behind it in a narrow lake half a mile long. Not the work of beaver but snowslides, I think, for the steep slopes all around were banded with bare vertical stripes where in years of deep snow, avalanches had swept great swaths of timber down the slopes and into the creek.

We fished the slough and the narrow lake, and in the afternoon were eating quantities of dockweed and salmonberry shoots when Cleo suddenly reared her head in alarm—I felt this before seeing it—a bright startle that went right through to my bones. I ran to the twins and Dolly, whether to protect or to be protected, not clear in my mind, but the twins climbed into my lap and Dolly and I huddled together. Then Cleo gave a new cry, a sort of hooting call which I heard as bright and animated; she broke for the near trees in that sloping gait which is so distinctive to her species, and here came from the brush two beasts standing upright and crossing swiftly over the rocky ground with the same long, loose walk—a jolting realization—others of her kind, two males of monstrous proportions.

I was struck suddenly by something like shyness—it was not fear but an exquisite awareness of my smallness and oddness among these wild giants. I made myself smaller yet, crouching with Dolly and the twins, who were shy themselves and did not follow their mother but went on hiding with me and watching from the thickets of salmonberries. Cleo ran full tilt at the elder male—quite bowled him over—and I thought they were fighting or play fighting, though quickly I realized they were copulating—utterly indifferent to their audience, the younger male squatting only just barely out of their way and watching the mating with a look I can only describe as intelligent bemusement; and of course the children.

When they had separated (and after scrupulously cleaning or examining each other's nether parts with long gray tongues) Cleo brought the males round to "meet the family," as it were.

The older male has coarse hair, yellow-gray, about a broad dark face; and the younger male (I should think him George's age) is lean and muscular, with that look of intelligence, though missing one forelimb, which was evidently torn off in a battle or an accident and the stub healed in an ugly fashion just above the elbow. The twins crawled from my arms into their mother's arms and clung to her while the males tenderly examined and petted them—I was reminded of a human being warbling and cooing to an infant, for the males kept up their peculiar soft whistling and clicking, which seemed intended to communicate tender feelings. Dolly was not long in her shyness (I wonder if she remembers them from past meetings), and shortly the twins had taken her lead: the entire family (for I should call them that) began a playful tussling and grooming and a chattery communication that was humanlike in its aspect, quite as if pouring out a pent-up year's worth of news and events; and I went on squatting apart from them all with a painful consciousness of my separation and loneliness.

After some little while, Cleo brought them round to me. These giants are frightening of stature, some ten feet in height and three or four hundred pounds, but having a calm demeanor from which I took comfort. Cleo (I believe) began to tell them everything she knew of my history, all the while stroking the arm of my corduroy coat with evident affection, and sometimes placing her huge hand upon my head. (She no longer makes an attempt to groom my hair, which is impossible of taming—I fear the hair being yanked out by the very roots—have learned to yelp like a puppy, which startles and stops her from her intended ministrations.) The males were interested in the strange orphan, but not so much as in the children, and soon had wandered back to the twins and Dolly. Cleo, having settled her great body on the ground beside me, did not immediately follow them but sat watching her family with an entirely human look of absorption and pleasure, and all the while her great hand resting upon my arm as if we were two companionable women, which gesture moved me deeply and reassured me of my place as her friend.

🌰 *I have published one or two articles of the sort designed to get me in trouble with my neighbors and which are inevitably taken to be a defense of my own sordid history, or perhaps an exculpation of my husband: plain, unvarnished truths about the sex question and denouncing formal, monogamous marriage as hypocritical. Compulsory love, I have written, is not love—it must arise unfettered by state or church or by any law whatsoever; and when love ends, marriage ought also to end. I never have advocated lewd, open, and notorious adultery, but rather the right of couples to love as they choose and to separate when love dies. It is a common understanding of Enlightened Women that releasing women from the need to marry would release them from economic and sexual slavery.*

Of course, these are questions proposed and addressed by a rational mind, and my own practice could be said to be rational: I have quite deliberately chosen a celibate life for its warranty of continuing independence (though this entirely runs counter to the common man's belief that a "professional" literary woman is likely to be promiscuous, and without a doubt indecent).

But there is something darkly compelling in one's body, something that is of raw nature. When the Moon is full, a certain blood-gorged Beast rises from its lair and takes possession of me—I am forced to accept its sexual attentions, as any woman must when abducted by savages. In those hours of my imprisonment, feverish and wild, in a transport of delicious agony, I must write what the body dictates.

As an adherent of free love, I should not be ashamed to admit of prurient desires. But when I am released from the grip of the Savage I cannot look on his bestial dictation without a shudder of mortification. I keep the pages awhile, folded carefully within other pages, and reread certain passages in shameful secrecy—indeed, I edit and sharpen the prose as if the work were intended for a wider audience— as if I had not a fixed design to mislead. But eventually I always burn such sordid erotica and add the ashes to the pail, where they will one day make soap; which use seems to me ironically appropriate.

C. B. D.

November 1903

C. B. D. (unpublished)

(UNTITLED)

Trembling, though otherwise incapable of movement, she gazed upon the war chief's dark hands as they tenderly opened the buttons of her vest and drew back the thin, damp cloth to bare her shoulders. He had begun a low, mesmerizing chant, according to the seductive custom of his people, and she was utterly adrift and helpless, unable to resist. At the dark flash of his eyes—the magnetic burn of his gaze upon her womanly nakedness—her breath quickened, her own eyes fluttering closed; and as he took the rosy protuberances of her breasts into his hands, her flesh rose irresistibly to meet his palms.

Bright day

Today we have not strayed from the same spot—perhaps this is a favorite feeding ground?—and in the afternoon I went down below the lake to a relatively private sanctum behind tumbled blowdown, where I peeled to the skin, engaged in a few moments of brief, frantic splashing in the relatively warmer water of the "slough"—only barely warmer than ice—and immediately put on my filthy clothes again, alert for the males of the species, whose eyes are too nearly human. (Of course, afterward I was struck by the foolish contradiction of my modesty, for I should have trouble ever again lying down in a tent next to men; whereas lying in the darkness of the den beside those great beasts smelling of their maleness, I was entirely comforted and at peace and without a qualm.)

I have, of course, given them names and developed a theory as to the relationships between them all. The elder male is Freddy, and I should call him Cleo's husband, father of her twins, and presumably also of Dolly. The one-armed young male is too old to be sibling of the twins, so I suspect he is brother to Freddy or, alternatively, the younger brother of Cleo—in either case he is Uncle Max.

Today while watching the children and adults all playing together—a catch-and-hold game which resembled Tag, though with much mouth-fighting and tussling and pulling upon arms and legs, as well as fierce calls and pretend growling—I was struck by the thought that their state of wildness might not be irrevocable—might be amenable to change through enculturation—and then, having turned over this idea once or twice, my brain recoiled from it. A wild animal's life is without possessions, but also without humdrum toil and burden. I don't indulge the fantasy that here is my nation of See-Ah-Tiks, but the others are shielded from political skulduggery, at least, and free of certain familiar vices—lying, treachery, avarice, narcissism. Poor Cleo! Poor Freddy! Imagine them tamed and encouraged in the habits of human culture!

I have a romantic bias, though, and the Wild Man of medieval lore, once captured from his wilderness hideout and returned to civilization, was said to have made a better knight than ordinary persons, his wild upbringing giving him exceptional strength, ferocity, and hardiness, as well as innocence and an innate nobility. If it were possible to imagine Max in leather chaps and spurs astride a mammoth mustang—a knight of the West, free and undomesticated as any cowboy—I suppose I should have to reconsider the whole idea. But I would be harder pressed to think of Cleo in a human world, where a woman of strength and independence may only find herself called a Freak of Nature.

I wonder if we might more easily become like animals than animals become like humans. As a species, we human beings seem no longer fitted for life in the wilderness—have been weakened by centuries of civilized life—but there may yet be something inherent in our natures, some potentiality which wants only the right circumstances to return us to the raw edge of Wildness. Think of the Mountain Man of the early West, how quickly he o'erleaped those centuries of civilization and developed the necessary woodcraft, the physical and mental traits to live in his difficult surroundings. I feel this same potentiality in myself; feel I am daily learning to inhabit (body and mind) the wilderness in which I find myself. And as the Mountain Man was tutored and aided by the indigenous Indian, so I am led by the wild Mountain Giants.

They inhabit these forests so comfortably and inconspicuously—are enough like us to have shrewdly escaped our notice; but have not our territorial competitiveness or would long since have come out of hiding and waged war for the diminishing woods. Perhaps they are not lower animals after all, but an evolutionary advance—have grown beyond poor *Homo sapiens* and understand the world well enough that they have no need to construct a civilization upon it.

> I think I could turn and live with animals, they are
>   so placid and self-contain'd,
> I stand and look at them long and long.
> They do not sweat and whine about their
>   condition,
> They do not lie awake in the dark and weep for
>   their sins,
> They do not make me sick discussing their duty to
>   God,
> Not one is dissatisfied, not one is demented with
>   the mania of owning things,
> Not one kneels to another, nor to his kind that
>   lived thousands of years ago,
> Not one is respectable or unhappy over the whole
>   earth.
>
>   WALT WHITMAN,
>   "Song of Myself"

Rainy and gray

This morning a thin-bodied deer stepped into plain sight while we were still bedded, and began to feed intently as a cow in summer pasture. The others, I believe, are too large and lumbering to meet with success as deer hunters; I am too small and slow. We have, for the most part, a simple vegetarian diet, which is augmented by such insects and fish, frogs and snakes as fall into our hands. They will avidly eat carrion (I will eat it too—I am determined I shall not starve) but show little interest in stalking anything larger than a squirrel. They will watch deer, though, with a curious single-mindedness, and we all sat upon the grass gazing at her as she browsed. It was possible to pick out the individual hairs on her flank and the tufts of winter fur that hadn't been rubbed free. I could see the rise and fall of her delicate ribs, as well as the shadowed hollow at the base of her throat where a pulse shimmered. Once, she lifted her head and met Freddy's eye. He became completely still, and I discovered in that moment a sudden awareness of him as a predator, his body and mind shaped for killing. I was sure that he was furiously struggling with the problem of how to stalk and kill her. Then the deer lowered her head and resumed feeding, and Freddy's attention fell away. Perhaps he was only caught, in that moment, by her loveliness, her grace, her perfect nature.

I realize how little I know of their inner lives. Books and scientific knowledge—those things I have always believed in—cannot tell me what the world looks like and smells like and sounds like to them. Oh! I should like to enter their consciousness. I have a strong yearning to visit their minds, know their thinking and feeling—have them look at me and see something like themselves.

C. B. D. (1906)

FROM "THE FORKS"

IN A DESOLATION, AND OTHER STORIES

The woman and the wild people with whom she was traveling slept below a bold, bare granite peak, its precipitous incline streaked with slides and breaks of jumbled rock; below the long talus slopes stretched a great waist-high field of snowberry and mountain grape into which an entire troop of small ponies could have disappeared without a trace—such shrubbery as makes desirable bedrooms for shy animals such as these. When the woman opened her eyes the sun was just coloring the peaks with a faint purplish glint—the mountain face still completely in shadow and the foredawn as crisp as a bright green apple—but there was a swath of pure radiance below, where the sun had clawed above the rock slope and a long field of grasses and wild-flowers lay soft in the new day.

The woman crept down through the velvety umbra of the mountain to the edge of the light, where the sun had already taken the chill off but left the long grasses shining for a while yet, heavy and bent with damp; and she shed every stitch of her ragged, filthy clothes and lay down upon the wet ground. It was something she had often seen the wild people do: lying down in the grass and rolling shoulder over shoulder with great sighs, chattery calls, and whistles, and afterward rising up, casting off the wet from their pelts with quick whole shudders, leaving the hair lying close to their bodies silky damp and shining and smelling briefly of licorice-fern or wild sweet-peas. She had supposed this act to be merely their own primitive bath; but as she laid her bare body along the dew-drenched earth and began rolling, rolling—sloughing off the worst of the filth, which was her only intent—she felt the whole of her skin become as a rose petal upon which the damp and rosy dawn lavished itself. As she rolled and rolled over the vetch- and pea- and clover-covered meadows (roots tangling far underground, and at eye level the working shoots and the mold of leaves living and dead, the trails of skinks and slugs, the creepings of millipedes and sowbugs), she became dizzy, gloriously besotted, crazy with joy. Where are the words to describe the inexplicable, transforming powers of morning dew upon one's naked belly and hips and thighs and breasts? Where are the poets to write of the good delights of rolling naked in the morning dew?

Shortly, a wild woman came down the hill and with a soft moan of pleasure lay down her great body in the band of sunlight nearby and began to roll back and forth across the damp grass; and then the wild children. And when the wild men came down to the grass and lay with the others, the human woman went on rolling, rolling, under the magical influence of the early morning dew, rolling leafless as Eve—no more clothes than a frog—rolling as one among the great naked beasts, and joining in their wild whistling and chirping, which seemed to her a joyous sort of singing and which seemed linked to her happiness and to every other happiness in the world in a continuous symphonic chorus.

And afterward, as she lay gasping on her back and feeling herself to be still giddy, still turning over in the bright play of light—there was a singular moment when she believed she felt the dignified slow rolling of the earth beneath them all.

MISTAKE WILD MAN FOR BEAR AFTER CLAMS
Indians Near Quilcene Take a Shot at Hairy Monster, Which Makes Off Shrieking

Victoria, B.C. (Special)

Captain Owen, pilot, reported today that Indians had seen and shot at the wild man, previously reported to have been seen near Qualicum. The creature, which was naked and covered with hair, was engaged in digging clams with his hands when the Indians came, and thinking him a bear shot at him and wounded him. The man ran away shrieking. The Indians returned to Union much frightened, and reported having wounded the wild man.

Search parties sent to look for the creature have failed. Residents of Union and that vicinity believe in the existence of the wild man. Some allege that he is a young man who disappeared twelve years ago.

Seattle Daily Times, May 1, 1905

Horrible events

A child dead and my mind in turmoil—how to make sense of it? I have lost my bearings, may not be able to tell the truth even to myself.

When you have seen no other person for days on end, you begin to forget what you look like, which is my only blame—I hope is my only blame—and the rest falling on the men, who must have been startled—I must look a strange creature with wild untended hair, filthy red mane tangled with twigs and mosses, and from that distance my mud-daubed coat and trousers maybe mistaken for an animal's thick fur—and I shrieked when I saw them, the two men strolling suddenly out of the dense brush—men!—but in my throat after so long no human language, a wordless animal cry of pure astonishment, which turned their heads, of course, knocked them back, but my God! To kill! The one in a plaid shirt—his pants were stagged, high-lace boots, a miner's getup—lifted his rifle so quick with no thought in it, just fired, and I was utterly taken by surprise, could not speak, stood paralyzed while the other one—suspenders, a mustache, a foolish canvas hat—took his aim deliberately and tried to kill me, and if I had formed a thought—to speak humanly, to make myself known—it was driven out of me by the bullet whizzing past my ear—I bolted like a rabbit for the cover of the woods.

I'm ashamed to admit I took no thought for the others, the instinct of fear and of individual survival at that moment being paramount, but behind or offside to me such a cry arose, a screeching moan which recollected me, and the grief in the out-cry so unmistakable—my heart tearing in my breast, for I knew in an instant, knew absolutely, and throwing a look around—Oh! the cub, the child, one of the twins, lying in gore and the men coming to it on the run, and the mother, the poor mother, stumbling away with the other twin clasped to her hip—must keep safe the living child—but peering back to the lost one and crying, crying—I will never forget that moment, that cry, that horrible glimpse as I ran.

I have only a dim recollection of the next minutes—believe I threw myself headlong downhill—ran and ran—clumps of trees, brushy thickets, a pumice slope—tumbling and falling, stagger-ing up to run again—in certain terror that I would be left behind, that the long strides of the others—my family, my friends!—would carry them far ahead and leave me bereft, abandoned to evil. But the grieving mother staggered yet farther to the rear, carrying her lone child, moaning, moaning, which I bore and then could no longer bear, going back through the trees despite fear, a shaking heart, to find her, to comfort and console her—impossible of course, but I touched her great shuddering body, stroked and petted her, which she did not shy from, and finally we went on together, we two women, desolated and grieving (and the baby in terror clinging to his mother), until we had found the others, our family, whistling for us from the green darkness of the hemlocks.

The husband seeing his wife coming with only the one child, oh! his look was so broken, and he came to her, keening, taking the living child in his arms, rocking from foot to foot, and she let her heavy body slump and began a low whistling moan, which the others took up, which I also took up, though we could not stand there long but must go on swiftly and dangerously down into a rocky canyon and halfway up the vertical opposite slope—I was staggering, exhausted, they hauled me bodily up the cliff—where we crept into a deep hole together and lay in terrible silence while the men thrashed through the brush far below us and called to each other in murderous, excited tones. Their voices became gradually distant and quarrelsome, but we went on lying there mournfully until a crescent moon rose above the edge of the mountaintops, and then we climbed down, trembling, into the steep canyon again and up out of it and through the dark trees, the faint glimmering moonlight, to the body of the child—to the place where the body had been. There was a cold black stain on the grass. The mother began to rock her weight to and fro, though her wailing was silent in the night, beyond the range of human ears, and we stood with her, all of us, while her husband moaned softly in the wordless language which is grief, which is unspeakable sorrow, and then we went on uphill following the broad track in the duff and the thin smear of blood where the child had been dragged along the ground, the men's boot marks in the track and their human smell still rank where they had worked and sweated to haul the child's heavy body uphill. We followed them up through the trees onto a high outcrop of rock, where their rough little house was standing beside the open black mouth of a mine, the place

where they had brought the child, and oh! God! He was evis-
cerated and flayed, the naked shape so white and so thin in the
darkness, the body of a child (the body of one of my own sons or
my brother), butchered and hanging from the branches of a tree
by the bloody sinews of his bare feet, while his bloody fleece
was nailed in cruciform upon the bole; and if I had any thought
yet of speaking to them—of making myself known to them—if I
had formed that thought in any part of my mind, it was driven
out now by wildness.

It always has been my belief that murder is a primitive
instinct not common to women's hearts, but I would have killed
them, I know, if the tools had been in my hands, murdered the
men and brutalized their bodies, which I should be ashamed
to write but am not, being still bloody-minded as I put these
words down. The child's mother—not having the tools to do
manslaughter—lifted a great stone and with a grievous howl
threw it clattering against the door, and this we all took up,
the huge flung rocks booming against the roof of the house and
rumbling down. The men would not come out, but scratched
the chinking from between the logs and poked their rifles
through, firing blindly into the night, which made us more
wild, more unafraid, and we went on with that terrible, useless
rock-throwing, that terrible despairing screeching and crying,
until our murderous impulse was spent. Then the child's father
climbed up into the dark tree and took down his son's naked,
mutilated body, which the child's mother, keening, received
into her arms; and he undid the nails from his son's fleece and
we enfolded the child in it and together we carried him away
from there.

This is dusk, and we are camped along a narrow shelf among
the dense brush of salmonberries, and the dead child lies with

us. We have all day been keeping to the oldest trees, the deepest canyons, not stopping to eat, going swiftly north, carrying the twins, the one who is dead and the one who is living, in the arms of the adults, who must spell one another of the weight; and the orphan woman ignobly carried too, whenever too weak to climb or to clamber her puny limbs over a windthrown trunk. I am so tired, so hungry, but it is my mind and my heart that shake. I have been wondering all day how to write what happened, and who will read it. When you have been so long without speaking, without encountering another human being, you may forget who you are; in this wild state, this wild life, I do not write to be read but to clear my mind and my path, to gain strength.

The mother of the dead child looks out at the country with a stunned expression, as if the world has been made desolate and hostile, as if she has been set down suddenly among the rocky craters of the moon. She does not speak. I think I must be writing for both of us—writing as women have always written—to make sense of what the heart cannot take in all at once.

Grief

I shall be glad if no one reads this, for I must write what cannot be written. My help, my only help, is in these pages, where I take myself to heal grievous wounds; where my woe and my weakness and my anger and my doubt are received in silence.

This morning we ate the body of the child. We afterward buried the fleece, broke apart his skeleton, crushed his skull—scattered the fragments of bone in the forest.

The civilized world will suppose this to have been cannibalism, and an act of savage nature. Indeed, what I have seen and done is unspeakable, never to be erased from the mind, but I believe it was a desperate act of love—it was the sacrament by which this child redeemed the lives of his family. His corporeal body will be found nowhere—he is buried within the bodies of his mother, his father—and thus their lives, their objective existence, undivulged, shall remain a secret closely kept from the brutal world of Men.

I should write further—of my feelings, my spirits, the state of my mind—but find some feelings do in fact elude language. Here I am at the uttermost center where lies the inner being, the hearts core, and which is without words altogether.

Rain today and yesterday

In three days' relentless travel we have left behind our fear of pursuit. At evening of the first day we crossed a river (it may have been the North Fork of the Lewis), which was a dangerous undertaking, the spring freshet having made of it a white cataract running rough with driftwood and entire trees. We scouted back and forth along the river shore for miles (a "basket ferry" at one place and raw new pilings of an unfinished boat landing—terrifying to think of being seen) and briefly tried two or three places which might have done for the others but which I could not have managed alive; then finally made our crossing where the river ran in two streams either side of an island. The near side tore swift and gray over a wide gravelly bed, the water nearly hip high even on the men, and the splash at my chin— must not think of losing one's footing—death if an uprooted tree should come rafting down while we stood precariously in the middle of the rushing flood. I waded across clinging to the others like one of their children, and holding this notebook aloft in my hand to keep it from drowning or being swept away. The far stream was narrow, pouring around a hard curve, with the lap and race tearing at the bank in a wild brown surf—layers of cobbled rock and basalt and sand eroded into raw shingles and shelves. There were trees lying broken across the channel, which we made use of as precarious and slanting bridges, though their yet-green limbs lifted and waved dangerously like the flukes of a whale. This crossing I managed without help—became the helper—showed them how to place one foot warily in front of the other. I have, in a dim and former life, walked miles of six-inch catwalk above a bottomless abyss.

When the moon came up behind the black trees to the east, we denned in the hollow left behind where a giant spruce had fallen, its root mass tearing out of the ground as it went down. Our river crossing had of course been a thorough soaking, which was untroubling to the others—they possess a double guard coat over a dense undercoat which no amount of cold or wet can penetrate—but I am pathetically poorly covered and was, by that time, shaking with cold, my drowned clothes clinging to me, wicking the heat straight away from my body. I shucked every waterlogged rag and in a state of nature burrowed down among the others, where I slowly became warm.

We went on to the north, through narrow canyons choked with cedar, where the cool and sunless ground was groomed and carpeted with an old brown duff of leaves and needles. When we climbed out upon the ridges we could see thin snow on the blue ranges all around us, and white peaks of a mountain chain rising into cloud to the east and to the north.

In the afternoon we passed through the ruins of an old logging camp: huge old stumps with high notch cuts, moss-rotten fence posts leaning about an ancient ox shed, and rusted chains and dogs and jackscrews in the wreckage of an old "boat" fallen down along the dim swath of the skid road. An heroic fir stood at the edge of the old yard, the last of its generation, which I must guess was left for a boundary mark, or for some other reason no one can now know, as the woodchoppers who felled the other trees are dead or long ago gone to the pursuits of old men. These lone, left-behind trees I have heard the loggers call wolf trees. I know that in the old world, where many generations of a clan lived under the shade of one ancient tree, their traditions told and retold the circumstances of its planting and the events that occurred within its witness; and such trees were venerated. And I know that the memory of a tree is real and concrete—it registers in its flesh, in concentric layers, the years of drought and of flood, of fires and volcanic event, and the fall of meteorites centuries old. From miles away we could see the lofty head of that wolf tree, a landmark, towering above the thick stands of blackberries and alder which had grown up again in the cleared field.

We drove doves and quail up out of the grass along the ridges. A coyote stood in a meadow and lifted his head and watched us pass. We crossed a shallow, silty stream that ran to the west, and a heron stood utterly still in the water, not rising to fly from us. We scarcely ate. In the evening we denned under the brink of a gravelly caprock.

Today we have at last stopped our running. We went up slowly through steep, high country, the rock ridges dotted with noble fir, and the columbines in scarlet bloom along the south-facing slopes. We ate mushrooms and cattail roots, maple seeds and leaves of nettle, chewing deliberately as one must do, breaking a fast. When we crossed a barren pumice plain and climbed above it and looked out over the country to the south, cloud shadows were streaming over the land and a hawk was turning in the dark air below us. Tonight we are lying under the shelving roots of an immense fir which was undercut by a rock slide and clings by muscular tendrils to the shorn and gravelling bank. We have had rain and wind in spates since yesterday.

Cool, springlike
Their own word for themselves is two notes of plaintive minor quality coming down the scale, and a following trill. I believe it might be written, in Roman letters, *seqwa'tci*.

C. B. D. (1906)
FROM "DARK THINGS"
IN A DESOLATION, AND OTHER STORIES

After her death, the child lived for a time in the tops of the old trees, among owls and woodpeckers. She swung her bare legs, heels wigwagging, on the springy limbs very high above the society of plants and animals living in the ground story. She and the birds hid laughs behind their elbows when the bears or wolves of that world shuffled beneath them, eyes directed downward. She let loose her hold of the trees from time to time and flickered through the green air, her body an intermittent shadow, a wraith against the canopy of branches. A man, glimpsing the child one day, believed he had seen a nightjar or a crow; but on another occasion a woman's eye caught a flashing of white high up in the trees, which she understood to be a ghost, translucent and insubstantial as a child's bones, lifting and turning above her. The sky was huge that night, with clouds rising like mountains in it. Of course, the child, by then, had been dead for days.

A gray day

We are in the broken foothills of a mountain which can be glimpsed only rarely, though I feel it rising heavily into the sky like a massing of cloud to the north. It may be St. Helens Mountain, though they have named it to me a slow and strong note which I would write as *n'wascht*, and I believe this is the name with meaning and truth in it.

Yesterday we came into the yard of an old homestead long abandoned, and we dug up and ate all the daffodil bulbs which were rampantly growing there. The smell of those people was gone, but something remained in the air about the ruin of their cabin—something cold and disheartening. We passed through a field of lava casts yesterday, too, climbing through a low pass where an avalanche had mowed a wide swath through the forest. This was land as barren and rugged as the moon, so it was startling to hear the faraway gabbling of geese. Presently the high, excited clatter of their voices mounted through the pass, and we caught sight of them as they streamed across the face of the pale sky. Humans envy few things among the animals, but flight must be one of them.

When we came down from the high volcanic valley, here was drier country, with stands of pinewood among the fir and cedar. The resinous cones of pines have palatable, nourishing kernels which I relish more than maple seeds or the needles of Douglas's fir, which are bitter, but we went through this pine forest without eating much, for there was a small natural prairie which we could see below the trees, and we hoped to find camas growing there. We were coming down onto this grassy plain when we

saw a family of Indians who were there ahead of us, already on
hands and knees with their digging sticks—a mother and father
and three children and perhaps an aunt or uncle—a family such
as we were. They squatted back on their heels and looked at us
in silence. We stood still and looked back. Then we went up
into the timber again. The adults after a short time went on
quietly with their digging, though the little children stood up
and watched us as we climbed the hill.

Last night I went onto a ridge to watch the sun set over
the mountain, and shortly afterward the mother of the twins,
carrying her living child, climbed up to this same place to sit
nearby me, settling her heavy body to the ground with a low
groan. Since the death of her other child she has lost her radiance, moves slowly, is thin within her great coat, and though
she may have answered to other names in the past (I once igno-
rantly called her Cleo, which word I now realize has a frivolous
sound, as if she were an infant or a pet), the name by which all
of us now greet her is three descending notes—something like
e'neth'kee, which has a somber meaning I understand and feel
but have no desire to translate—it is enough that I should feel
and understand it.

In silence we two women and the baby watched the sun
set and twilight fall. There was blue sky above the mountain
but long gray strokes of rain upon its earth-hold, and the westward clouds bound in vivid mauves and golds which gradually
purpled and took on dimension, piling high in vast caves and
outcurves, with the hems trailing off in thin whips of fringe. A
mantle of rose pink fell over the summit—it became a pyramid
of soft flame—and while the ranges below it fell away to darkness, the fires on the crest burned on, deepening from gold to
burnished copper. The mountain slowly became separated from

the earth, became a veil of light floating above a black skyline, and slowly afterward dimmed to a silhouette upon the night. Then the witchery: the eastward sky paling to ghost white with the black mountain limned against it, and suddenly from the summit the full moon breaking forth, flooding the lower world with brightness.

I felt that we had climbed high above thought; here we could sit distracted, holding nothing in our minds but the glory of the sky—the miracle of the cold moon upon the white peak of the mountain. Of course, I was mistaken in my feeling, for the black masses of trees stepping away in numberless ridges westward a hundred miles to the sea brought my mind westward until I was suddenly thinking of my children. For a moment I felt unable to recall their names—not only their names but the meanings of their names, which seemed vastly more important—and when I did recall them it was faint as breath or the indecipherable gabbling of geese—a clamor thin and distant. I began to cry, which I have not done for oh so very long—whether for my nameless boys or for my situation or for all the dead and lost children, in truth I cannot say.

The baby was startled by my human crying but the mother almost certainly understood its meaning, for she began to join me in mourning, raising her voice in an opening phrase—a long, low, quavering whistle—which, after a pause, rose quickly and fell slowly and then rose again, ethereal and flutelike. Upon the third or fourth phrase, from the den in the canyon below us the others began one by one to take it up, their sorrowful croons and hums and whistles sounding a chorus as complicated and graceful as any opera. I am disharmonic and my understanding of their language is in its infancy, but even a dog cannot resist the impulse to howl with the wolves—there is release in it perhaps more satisfying than tears—so in a moment I gave up my weeping and joined my own warble to theirs. By such small increments the old lines that set me apart, that defined me, are erased. The sky by then was dark as a bear's mouth, and our keening song, unearthly, wordless as water, rose up into it and was swallowed whole.

> The greatest poets never write poetry. The Homers and Shakespeares are not the greatest—they are only the greatest that we can know. And so with Handel among musicians. For the highest poetry, whether in music or literature, is ineffable—it must be felt from one person to another, it cannot be articulated.
>
> SAMUEL BUTLER

Rain

This is toward the end of a raw, wet day, and we are in a rough country where every step is difficult: in such territory we are surely safe from Men. Here are otherworldly valleys of scraggly, broken, and limbless dwarf pines, mosses, and lichens; pulverized pumice washings and debris gulches washed out by melted snow; steam caves and fumaroles, and cascades of snowmelt over vertical precipices; and yesterday we passed through a high field where great angular rocks large as houses had settled on the snow—these must have been hurled from the crater in ages past, and I suppose under the snow is a field of pumice and volcanic glass. There have been, as well, grassy ascents, and valleys of old trees, and small undulating prairies, but invariably cut by ledges of smoke-colored rock, or steep gulches and chasms, which if they are narrow we can leap—or I should say the others can leap, and lift me over with the children. But as often as not we must take a tedious way around: there are breaks in the earth too wide even for giants to bestride.

Marmots and gophers are thick, their whistled alarms remarkably like our own. We have seen mountain goats and blacktail deer, as well as pikas and coyotes.

Once today while we were climbing a gravelly steep ridge, the sky lifted and the valleys of the Columbia and the Willamette were visible far to the south—streaks of silver on a groundwork of velvet—and though the several white summits of this range were invisible in the overcast, we could see all their connecting ridges and intervening valleys, a vast forest stand seeming entirely whole save for Indian meadows and old burns and the brown scoria of ancient pumice and ash flows.

When we began to climb again, our feet started rocks, which fell five hundred feet to the valley below—a great reverberating sound and a haze of gravelly dust.

March 26th.—When we arrived at the mouth of the Kattlepoutal River, twenty six miles from Fort Vancouver, I stopped to make a sketch of the volcano, Mount St. Helen's, distant, I suppose, about thirty or forty miles. This mountain has never been visited by either Whites or Indians; the latter assert that it is inhabited by a race of beings of a different species, who are cannibals, and whom they hold in great dread; they also say that there is a lake at its base with a very extraordinary kind

of fish in it, with a head more resembling that
of a bear than any other animal. These supersti-
tions are taken from the statement of a man who,
they say, went to the mountain with another, and
escaped the fate of his companion, who was eaten
by the "Skoocooms," or evil genii.

PAUL KANE,

*Wanderings of an Artist Among the Indians of North
America from Canada to Vancouver's Island and
Oregon Through the Hudson's Bay Company's Territory
and Back Again* (London, 1859)

Clear evening

Today we passed down a shelving ridge through a stunted forest of lodgepole and white pine and thence through steep and
ancient woods until suddenly we stood before a vast crescent of
a lake, from which the timbered ridges rose steep-to all around.
The others have told me, this lake lying in its green amphitheater
ever has been a safe hold, as men consider it spirit-haunted: the
old trees stand deep in gray pumice, and there is a silence which
lies along the ground with the scoria. There were the vines of
ripening wild strawberries growing upon the cinders and volcanic glass, and currants in a head-high thicket along the south
shoreline, which crops we were happy to bring in.

I intend never to be lost again nor left behind if I can help
it, and in any event have become as scrupulously wary as the
others, so have learned to keep an eye out—to lift my head every
short while and take a vigilant look at my surroundings. I don't
know why I kept looking out to the choppy water of the lake
except drawn by the wisps of white vapor rising from it, which

I've seen often enough along the Columbia River sloughs, but which appeared here as altogether remarkable—as if the lake had been set fire or had come alive and was steaming, as an overheated horse will do, or a wet dog. I looked and looked at it through the long morning, and in the afternoon when I looked, oh! upon the vaporous water half a mile out rode a stubby barge with men and equipage and piles of rock ore, and on the north shore perhaps three miles off (a small wind had sprung up which cleared out the fog a little) the evident wrack and ruin of a mining operation and a veil of smoke gray as death rising and spreading above the timber.

I stood a moment in stunned surprise watching while the barge made its slow way over the water, and then I began to shake—here was mortal danger. The faces of the men were too distant to distinguish one from another, but I have little doubt they were the type of men "hatched behind a stump," as my mother would have said: fellows whose spare-time pursuits are fistfighting, drinking, gambling, and debauchery, and who would, of a Sunday afternoon, shoot bears for their recreation and sell the orphaned cubs to the circus. I never would have been afraid of such men in the past, but my life has recently been broken in two—I live now in the second half, which is a new world, wild and terrible. And I have learned, like any cub or fawn, to startle and bolt from human beings.

We fled up the ridge again, finding we must skirt around a clearing where a raw new sawmill and a horse shed stood beside a steep corduroy road. A man came out into the muddy yard and shouted after us, which made my heart seize, but he could not have had more than a glimpse of the others, must have seen primarily the orphan trailing behind them, her hindmost quarters pushing uphill into the trees, and perhaps he believed he was shouting at some one of his crew, a fellowman. This is what I hope.

We made off west-by-southwest without stopping to browse until we had come out above the tree line. The sky was a ceiling of dish-pan blue, and when clouds coasted over the sun, the air became abruptly colder and the shadow hurt our eyes. The summit of the mountain stood bright white above us, seeming oddly both smaller and more real—more earthbound—from this near perspective. I supposed it to be only a half mile away, but after an hour of climbing it stood no nearer. Away to the east and to the north the snowy peaks of other mountains rode above the woody valleys, remote and extraordinary, like illustrations in books of fairy tales.

We ate unripe strawberries and the leaves of purslane; I dug wild carrots with my curved stick. Several times we found we must skirt around meadows where sheep were grazing—the shepherd unseen but his smell in the air, and the others raising a silent alarm which I felt as a bright flame in my blood.

We crossed through an old glaciated field bounded on its east edge by a ridge of pumice and rock, and where there was a slight break in the moraine and a steep gorge falling away abruptly, we climbed through the gap and down. The others treated this as an old secret passage, but we were all startled to find at the bottom the broken timbers of a buried cabin, the wooden bones cocked skyward from among the clay and boulders of a rock slide. There was the reek of human smell in the air there, and no telling if men lay dead inside or if they had walked away and built a new house nearby, so we scrambled hurriedly away, back up onto the plain and across it, through a windy pass. (It is an odd and perhaps ominous thing, how I traveled alone for so many days without signs of men and desperately anxious for them, and now I am afraid to be seen by men, and around us the land seems beset by them.)

We are camped now beside a shallow marsh in steep country below a glacier. The ice is evidently slowly receding, as the skeleton of an ancient animal was lying exposed along the bare rock at the glacier's edge. A few hairs were still attached to the bones, as well as scraps of frozen flesh, which, though it might have been four hundred years old, we cautiously smelled of and ate. There are white trilliums here, and a red-tailed hawk has been hunting over the ice field. It must be a lion which has left its droppings at the edge of the marsh, with an entire mouse skull intact in one turd.

We are high up on the peak, and at times, lying down on this high ground, I can feel a slight susurration enter my body, which must be the troubled inhale and exhale of the mountain in its restless sleep. It is windy and cold, but the half-moon is a dim bedside lamp by which to write. My friend e'neth'kee has been wading in the marsh hunting frogs, and while I have been watching her, the stars have come out in the shallow water and now they are moving quietly about her ankles. I believe it was my mother who used to say, when the long shape of the half-moon lay shivering upon the river: *There goes a boat sailing for the faerie isles.*

Bright day, cool and clear

In the deep of night, the mountain became a living animal, a beast of irascible temperament turning and moaning in its sleep, and this morning in the gray daylight there were flakes of ash falling out of the sky (which I at first took to be snow), and above the peak a cloud of steam rising a mile into the heavens. I have dipped into the study of vulcanism—the Cascade volcanoes unpredictably explosive—Helen in particular having blown her top two or three times in the hundred years since Lewis and Clark—but the others have neither History nor Geology and are seemingly indifferent to or insensible of the danger. If I had been alone I might have fled below the timber-line at least, where the canopy of trees would have furnished a little protection in case of eruption, but we spent the morning high on the shoulder of the mountain browsing upon the deer lilies. The ground periodically shuddered beneath our feet, and the sky precipitated soot and ash. Three or four or five times, in expectation of showers of fiery lava, I could not keep myself from singing to them the one-note word of alarm—made desperate hand signals (how does one gesture the spewing of lava and rocks?!)—which they answered unexcitedly with whistles and songs I could only dimly construe. E'neth'kee consoled me with her petting hands; and after so much has happened I do feel myself numbed to the prospect of death.

I wonder if the others' experience of dying, and their understanding of it, is different from the human process. Perhaps it is the curse only of humans: to have a clear awareness of the inevitability of one's own end, and therefore to fear and anticipate it and strive mightily against it. I should be ashamed to tell them, we have scores of books about dying and special shelves set aside for such titles in bookshops—as if the ability to die properly is something one must be specially trained to do.

Grief is another thing. I can more easily think of my own death than the death of that poor butchered child, yet his mother, for the most part, has recovered her spirits. In a human female I should think this unnatural and precipitate, but I am reminded of certain farm women of my childhood, and how they seemed to take the death of a baby as a terrible thing, but not much more terrible than the death of a sow upon whose piglets they had hoped to eke out a living through the winter; and how even my mother, losing a firstborn infant daughter, and then a husband and a son, never became death's handmaid—our house always was filled with laughter. I suppose it is our modern way of soft living which has made grief such a prolonged event. I suppose, among those who live in the old way, the realities of death bring about a more "natural" acceptance, and if I am to go on living wild I shall have to learn this myself.

Today we flushed a single crow from the foot of a basalt cliff and found a yearling deer lying dead under the low brush there, the flesh still very warm, the bright eye only just beginning to cloud. The poor thing was very thin, unmarked save for the crow's work; perhaps a weakened winter condition had kept it from thriving.

I have become devoted to carrion for its strengthening properties, preferring it to worms and grubs, and was glad to eat of meat not yet soured nor infested with flies. I was struck by a certain sorrow, though, or perhaps only by an irony: the poor fawn to have survived that first critical year, and then to give up the ghost just as the earth has finally swung nearer to the sun, and every rocky bank and open field is a pasture.

Now we have made our den in a deep-cleft canyon, which I imagine was carved out by an earlier eruption and must soon again serve as a channel for flowing magma. (I have been remembering certain Indian tales: In the interior of the earth, in volcanoes, subterranean gods were often supposed to reside. Craters were inhabited by beings mightier than men, who sent forth fire and smoke when they heated their sweat lodges or cooked their food.)

There is a lake country we have seen to the northwest, which

I suppose we must turn toward in the morning, if men are not there ahead of us. Of course, if we live until tomorrow I shall be very much surprised, but I have given up trying to communicate my worries to the others. Animals are seemingly unafraid of death—oh, they fear pain, yes, but not death—and when they are dying make no effort to live. Their bodies accept death with a kind of grace. I hope, if I am to die, that it shall be "naturally," like a field mouse dangling tail-down from the teeth of a cat: patient and accepting.

Coyote was going along in the valley of the Willamette River and she met some human people who were living there. Those people told her there was a cave monster who was frightening all the people. Every night it would come from its cave, seize as many people as it could carry, and return to its cave to eat them. The people asked Coyote, "What can we do?" and Coyote said, "When the old moon is gone, I will kill the monster."

The monster could not endure daylight. So on the first bright day, when the sun was very high up in the heavens, Coyote took her bow and arrows and went onto a mountain-top. She shot her first arrow into the sun, and her next arrow into the end of the first one, and so on until she had a rope of arrows that reached all the way from the sun to the mountaintop. She pulled hard on the rope until the sun came down into her arms, and then she ran down the mountain and hid the sun in the bottom of the river.

Now everything was dark, and the monster thought night had come again. He left his cave to catch someone to eat. Just as he was about to seize a child berry-picking in the woods, Coyote let go the rope that held the sun down and it sprang up into the sky again. In the sudden bright light, the monster was blinded, and Coyote quickly killed him.

Many years afterward, white people found the bones of the monster and began to carry them away. The Indian people who were still living there told them that evil would come from moving the bones of a monster of the age-old time. But white people turned away from this warning and no one knows where those bones are now.

A COMMONLY REPORTED LEGEND OF

CHINOOKAN TRIBES

It is hard to write this down so that it will mean anything. Houses unlived in quickly become warrens for mice; pastures unmown go to woods. This is how I have been thinking of myself—like a farmstead gone wild—and now someone, a stranger, has hacked a trail through the brush and is setting up house inside my body again.

Returning to live among men after living for a while among mountains, I am sensible of human beings as a Wild Child raised among wolves might be sensible of them: the nervousness of their faces, and the way their hands fidget, their fat-encumbered necks and the bleat of their voices. I have been a wildwoman for so long that I feel myself out of accord with this world, unable to like or understand much that I see. It takes such a very great effort for me to enter the consciousness of human creatures—to look at the world as they do, smell it the way they do—to understand their ways of thinking and feeling. I find I must exert a very great effort just to have them look at me and see something they recognize—a person like themselves. Perhaps, after I am home, then everything will shift, become familiar and natural and well understood again, as it was before. Perhaps I'll even have a hard time remembering the mountains at all. This is why I try to write it down, so that afterward, when everything is returned to itself, I can remember what this all must have been like.

Sunday 21 May '05 (on the Lewis River)

Oh! it is an odd and unnatural thing—the ascribing of dates to the days of one's life—which I shall not easily get used to again. And this date they have given me seems not to be believed: all that has happened can hardly have happened in such a brief time, hardly six weeks since going lost from Canyon Creek. Surely the larger part of my life has been lived as a child of nature—years and years, or so it seems to me. (My former life—the books and the boys and so forth—seems a distant adventure, something I remember only dimly, something glimpsed through the wrong end of a telescope.)

They have brought me down to a place on the river where there are a few raw buildings and a sawmill and a ferry that draws itself back and forth between wooden loading platforms. Prospectors and timber cruisers and the occasional latecomer to the homesteading game all cross the river here, along with tourists and sportsmen bound for the fishing at Trout Lake or up on the mountain to "rusticate" for a while and to hunt bears. They have put me in a clean, cold little bedroom from which I cannot see the mountain, only the steep and muddy logged-over hills behind the river. I am waiting here for—what? It is very hard to write. I am sore and sick, of course, but beyond that, the ferryman's wife is an Irishwoman with a flapping tongue who, being convinced that I am mad or mute or wild (which all may be true), protects herself from me by an unending flow of talk. She seems delighted not to get any answers and not to be interrupted in her presentment of every scrap of gossip about the neighborhood. I am too much out of heart to stifle her, so lie in her bed and look through the window to the river the whole time. The ferry platforms slant down to the level of the boat deck at low water.

It was the ferryman's wife—she told me her name, I have forgotten it—who oversaw my bath, in the forceful grip of two large Swedish women whose homes evidently lie nearby; and who gave me a flannel gown to put on, though I cannot get accustomed to the naked feeling of my bare legs and the flannel twisting around me in the bed. I suffer terrible insomnia, being without the comfort and warmth of the other bodies tangled with mine—an agony of solitariness—I wonder if I shall ever again be able to sleep alone. A clean and pressed shepherd's-check dress (too large by half) has been neatly laid out on the chair "for when you are recuperated" and my own clothes have been burnt, I think, or buried, to keep me from attempting to put them on again. There has been a good deal of effort made to locate me a pair of shoes, but apparently none to spare among this impoverished frontier community; so my feet remain free though the rest of me is prisoner.

It was an odd thing, the bath. I'm sure that, at an earlier time in my life, and after so long filthy, I would have gratefully accepted fiery death in a volcanic explosion in exchange for a hot tub bath, but as I was held in the water and my musky rind scrubbed off with a brush—how white the skin looked with the dirt washed off—I felt like one who was being skinned alive; and through the reek of the lye soap I got a noseful of my own fear-stench.

I must present a grotesque sight—not only the scabbed line of black stitches like a railroad spur from cheek to temple, but my hair cut off close to the scalp on order of the Wildwood Club surgeon and "by reason of the vermin and the blood." I blame my shorn and broken head also for a feeling of light-headedness— my brain disconnected from my body. I have been unable to think at all, neither of the past nor of the future, and only today found any strength for it, and to try to write, if only roughly.

One of the first things I worried about was the fate of this book, whether it went into the ground or was burnt with my ragged old coat and trousers, or whether members of the Wildwood Club had got hold of it and were regaling one another with its monstrous stories while they sat at the fire- side pulling candy. I was afraid to speak to the ferryman's wife about it—afraid to know the truth. But it is here with me after all, was lying in a dresser drawer together with my few civilized possessions—the little stub of pencil, my deer-footed knife, and compass, though not my good carven digging stick, which I cut and shaped myself and carried in my belt for all those weeks, and which I fear I cannot live without.

I've been going over and over events in my mind with a feeling of shock, or not shock exactly—this outcome awaited, dreaded, expected for so long—but rather a lack of feeling, a helpless numbness, as when the fatal diagnosis or the irreversible verdict finally comes to its pass. (I am at the bottom of the cold sea, and anything deeper is death.)

I imagine other outcomes: if we had left the cleft gorge by its western end and gone over the backbone of the ridge toward the lake country, we should never have met the Wildwood Club. But it had begun to rain, and we went down into the cover of the timber along a goat trail that twisted away steeply to the southeast. Though I had had the idea that the trees might defend us from an eruption, it came out that we were in as much jeopardy there as anywhere on the mountain. In the afternoon a great wide stream of mud and small rock poured suddenly down through the standing boles of the firs, with a slight rushing and rattling noise such as wind makes in the winter limbs of cedars—mud thick as pudding, brickyard red, slipping down the hill with not enough force to push over the trees but enough, certainly, to take down a woman, or even a giant—and warm and alive, issuing from the boiling heart of the mountain. We were lucky not to be buried or carried off by it, lucky to get away alive.

The muddy stream forced us higher, a climb to get around the broad, steep-sided basin which stood at its head. In the rain, we went up great slabs of shelving rock to a blasted crag where in clear weather we'd have had a wide view over the tops of distant ridges, a view of mountains breaking into pinnacles of bold gray rock too steep for snow to ever cling, and canyons all trending westward in purplish darkness—in clear weather we might have seen the smoke and felled trees which marked the Wildwood Club in their tented bivouac at the foot of a glacier. But we went over the crag in fog and rain onto ground that was mostly bare basalt, as smooth and polished as a tile floor. We

were coming down off this bench into a park of stunted hemlock and dwarf huckleberries, through the weathered ghosts
of dead trees standing singly in the fog, when the heads of a
mountain-climbing party rose out of a knoll on our left hand.

The alarm I felt was a bright and electric showering of light
that spun away to the ends of my limbs—the others veered off
into cover of the rocks with their great twelve-foot strides, sudden and silent as gulls in flight—we might have gone unseen, all
of us. But I briefly stood there, charged with fear, staring across
at the climbers as they swung their alpenstocks and labored
over the knoll in the rain—stood there alone and still as death
until their startled, greased faces lifted to me beneath their cart-
wheel hats—and only then did I break and run. So it is my own
fault to be here. I am wild, but not wild enough.

I can remember the slapping of my feet across the basalt
floor, and the way the wet stone slanted off obliquely under
me; I remember the gravel scattering when I pressed my heels
into the rock to make myself run faster, and how my eyes teared
against the wind, and how the rain fell into my open mouth. I
remember that I looked back to see where the climbers were,
and whether they would shoot me—some of them had dropped
their packs and were shouting and sawing the air with their
arms, brandishing their axes or their climbing sticks—I realized
some of them were women—and I remember flying over the
top of the ridge, the broken lava-rock crag, and seeing below
me the others bolting down the wet slab-rock shelves into the
concealing darkness of the trees. I remember all this clearly, and
even e'neth'kee, the swing of her long powerful arms, her heavy
legs in that reaching, deliberate, loose-kneed stride, and then
her head turning across the great muscled and caped shoulder,
turning to gain a last look backward, inconsolable, walleyed,

and then gone into the trees; and my feet sliding in the rocks, and the slow fluttering jerk of my body as I fell.

The air smelled of blood and mountain sorrel, and there were twigs and stones inside my shirt, down the back of my neck; this is what I remember. And dirt in my mouth which I tried to tongue out. I lay still and listened to the rain ruffling across the rock. I was thinking how funny it was, to have escaped death and then to be killed anyway, all in the same day.

Someone spoke and I looked over to see who it was, and a great rush of noise and pain sprang up behind my eyes; I believe I also felt something give way in my heart. Those people, the Wildwood Club people, stood over me, speaking to one another in hushed voices in a language that I did not recognize, and one of them, a man with no chin whose nose was streaked with white grease, squatted down beside me and touched my shoulder and spoke earnestly to me. I could not make out the meaning of his words, which drifted and faded in and out. Behind the molten pain I was thinking about the others, and whether the climbers had seen them, and how to keep the climbers occupied with me, to keep them from going down the rock shelves into the trees.

The chinless man was a doctor. He directed things with a good deal of talking and gesturing, and eventually they picked me up, four of them, in a stretcher formed of their linked arms. My vision swung—there was a leap and blaze of brightness—I vomited, which fell half on my own collar and the rest on the boots of the doctor. They carried me, staggering up over the crag and onto flatter ground more convenient for surgery, which I do not remember, or not much of it—a needle and thread and some workmanlike sewing, while certain of the club women reinforced one another in their resolve not to faint. I closed my eyes but did not sleep, and what I remember after that is a shivering that began in my knees and rolled up into my shoulders and arms, and a great swollen grief that pushed into my throat.

My face was stiff and throbbing, and voices argued in a low mutter, and it was very late in the day—the sky in the west was heavy and dark, the swollen clouds streaked with purple veins. The smell of the rain had a very cold edge, as if it were not a spring rain—as if the earth had rolled over on its back and now was facing into winter. They were carrying me down from the mountain, and I was aware of the awkwardness and thinness of my bones in the arms of the men, aware of my body's lightness and its yearning to sink down to the earth. The men often stopped to readjust their grips on one another's forearms, or to shift me to four new burden bearers. At several points while we were stopped like that, a certain woman with a long forehead and long eyes put her face close to mine and repeatedly asked me something, the meaning of which I eventually guessed out. I answered her with my name song, which is two repetitious notes and then the call note, and which I will write as *tuq'tuq'tsqa*. She received this information with a painful look I imagined to be confusion and sorrow.

It seemed to me we were descending through the darkness into a field of yellow stars and constellations of moons in various phases. Shadows fluttered and shifted in the rain, and I heard a wild voice, a whispery crying that faded in and out, muffled by currents of air—my heart in terrible throes. I became suddenly very afraid of being lost, and whistled softly to myself a song for nameless places. Gradually there were a great many bivouac tents, luminous and lit from within, scattered upon a wide clearing in the trees, and several bonfires with which the Wildwood Club meant to keep out the unknowable darkness and the beasts of the wilderness. Shadows began to be people moving among the fires and coming in and out of the tents. Then the wild cry became a woman singing, and I suddenly recognized phrases of the song, which was "Crossing the Bar." Something gathered motion in my head and then collapsed downward, as the edge of a steep riverbank crumbles under the downpour—I felt flooded with language, the several human languages of which I had once had an acquaintance.

I was two nights and a day with them. (They had made elaborate preparations for a three-week trek and were tremendously reluctant to cut it short, whether on account of volcanic eruption or the unexpected capture of a wildwoman.) There were, as it turned out, fifty-some men and women in the expedition, the greater number of whom had remained at the bivouac that day, glissading on icy slopes and fishing glacial streams. They had evidently argued about the probabilities and perils of an eruption, and finally only twelve had been reckless enough to attempt the scaling of a mountain which might at any moment shower them with fiery rocks. When I imagine other outcomes, here is one that often rises to my brain: they might all have stayed back from the climb.

They are a recently organized band of newfangled conservationists who believe in the virtues of the strenuous life—doctors, lawyers, businessmen, broker's agents, librarians; not a farmer, logger, or fisherman amongst them. The rules for the expedition were elaborate and precise: Each person a pack sack of no more than thirty-five pounds, as well as one hundred feet of rope, an axe, and an alpenstock—the most popular form being a stout staff six feet long with an iron spike on one end and, upon the other, a goat horn blackened and polished by hand. All to wear stout boots when hiking and to carry hobnails and the tools for driving them into the boots, as needed for crossing dangerous ice. The women to wear bloomers on the trail but skirts over their bloomers while in camp. Reveille at 4:30.

A makeshift flagpole was erected in the center of the clearing, upon which Old Glory was mounted each dawn and dismounted each dusk. Days were spent in glorious outdoor pursuits; evenings involved a good deal of singing and joke-telling; on most nights, at most fires, corn was popped; and on Friday nights, I was told, half a dozen groups presented skits and sketches before the entire company.

There were several doctors among them, all of whom looked in on me at one time or another, while leaving my hourly care and mental health in the hands of a rotating force of women. While lying in the tent, I fixed my eyes on the ridgepole. While out of it, sitting on a brown duck folding camp chair and swaddled in blankets, I looked toward the east edge of camp, where a great ice-scoured basin rose and opened into the damp belly of clouds. The women spooned soup into my mouth and chattered at me dutifully and concealed my bare scalp and stitches from view of the men, by means of a carefully arranged turban made from their neck scarves. They had not the facilities for a warm bath, and my frail condition precluded a dunking in a cold mountain stream, so they satisfied themselves with wash-ing my hands and feet, head and neck. They could not get my old coat and trousers off without a fight, and all were frightened of me, so my clothes stayed on—they anointed the walls of the tent with lavender oil and cologne.

There was considerable argument over what had brought me to my condition, whether a loss of mind, an upbringing among beasts, or outrageous hardships. The women generally ignored my peculiarities, believing that, with their tender care, I should shortly rise out of my lethargy and silence and tell them all the events of my life in the wilderness. Among the men, the more usual belief was that I represented a strange relative of *Homo sapiens*, a grim and pungent commentary on the bestial side of human nature—a reminder that there are basic and primitive impulses still battling for control of the human spirit.

By the second morning it was felt that I had recovered enough strength to walk off the mountain by short stages, so they sent me downhill the six-mile hike with three disinclined jailers—two gentlemen and a lady, the latter in her climbing clothes—who spoke to the captured wildwoman with exaggerated kindness and in slow, measured tones, supposing her deaf and feebleminded, or driven insane by her years of hermit life in the wilderness. I supposed them anxious to get back to their candy pulls around the campfire, and consequently went quietly.

Now I have been told by the ferryman's wife that word has been sent out to the world—a lost woman recovered—and they are hopeful some one of my family or friends will soon get the news and arrive to take me down from the woods. I am meanwhile lying still and silent day after day, doing nothing because there is nothing for me to do except this writing, which is the work of emptiness and loss. I feel myself becoming suspended and pale and insubstantial, like those souls in Dante drifting about between Heaven and Hell. And at night, like a ghost, I call-howl softly until the moon rises behind a curtain of cloud.

I have been thinking of something I read once—was it in Boas?—how in the winter, for the spirit dances, medicine men would put on long heavy masks carved of cedar and decorated with teeth and feathers, which represented certain demons and immortals such as Raven, Coyote, and Hare; and how sometimes a dancer, crouching and circling with great leaps and

bounds, howling and shaking the heavy cedar-bark fringe of
the mask, would find that his body had become inhabited by
the spirit of the mask. I suppose a dancer who was overtaken
by the spirit of a Dzo'noq!wa mask would run into the woods
and take up a wild life with the other mountain people.

Monday, 5 June (at Etna, waiting for the Mascot*)*
Stuband came as far as Woodland on the sternwheeler, and
under other circumstances he would have transferred to the
small-draft ferry, which draws but a scant foot of water and
even this late in the year might have gotten him up the river as
far as Etna; but I suppose the stately pace of the sternwheeler
had given him too much time for worry and useless conjecture,
and he was therefore impatient of the smaller boat, of its many
delays and unscheduled stops while farmers drive their wagons
into the stream and make a swap of passengers and freight without the formality of a loading platform. People in Woodland
had heard the story of the lost woman who had been found at a
remote location up the river, and they were anxious to help him
get there in case she should turn out to be the woman he was
looking for; so he was offered a ride with a timekeeper who was
pedaling a rail-mounted four-wheel cycle up the spur line to a
logging camp near Speelyei.

    In Speelyei he was saved from having to walk the last half
dozen miles, for I was already there, the impatient ferryman
having sent the lost woman down on the back of a postman's
mule as soon as getting word her family might be coming. She
was sitting on a porch waiting for him, her face skeletal and
pale, a webwork of scars and scabs, and her shaven head now a
half-inch bristle of silvery white hair, but he knew her at once,

and his first feeling almost certainly one of astonishment—he had secretly believed this trip might be all that remained to settle, in his own mind and the minds of the woman's children and friends, that she was lost to them forever.

He went up to her and took her fleshless fingers into his hands. "Do you know me?" he said to her. The woman wore her silence like a coat, but when her eyes flooded with tears, he correctly took this to be an answer, and he was overcome—they both were—by an exquisite sense of deliverance, a surcease of sorrow.

Ours is not a relationship of devotion, but Stuband and I are long acquainted and have old knowledge of each other's losses and successes, burdens and fortunate outcomes. I believe we have a dim understanding: like a tough plant that survives drought and flood and snow and sun, our relation to each other must be deep-rooted and stronger than a relation that is tender and looked after.

It was a bright day, the air warm and the sky moving with thin cloud. We rode back down to Etna in the back of a saw salesman's buggy, over a road that is passable only during the four dry months of the year. In my former life I was perhaps glib and judgmental, and if I had been so now, Stuband might have retreated into quiet himself, which is his own natural condition; but his voice flowed easily into my emptiness, and he talked to me of things as they occurred to him, comments upon the weather and the rough farms and logging camps we were passing by, as well as trivial events recently reported in the newspapers. The breathless speed of the rail cycle had been a revelation, he told me: heart stirring and distracting. He had no experience of traveling in an automobile or on the seat of a bicycle—he was a boatman and a dairy farmer—but he found that the swift steady hum of the spinning axles and the light clack of the wheels on the rails filled his mind with empty sound, freeing him of the need for thinking. He had craned his head forward, peering watery-eyed over the timekeeper's shoulder into the made wind. Perhaps he would learn from me how to ride a two-wheeler, he said.

Where my scabbed hand rested flat on the tailgate between us, Stuband sometimes placed his own hand over it gently and delivered a light stroke. He paid little attention to my silence, not requiring a response to his meaningless flow of talk, and I was aware of this and grateful for it. I have lived a wild life in the woods and consider myself now like a feral dog, needing to be reaccustomed to men's voices and the possibility of peaceful intention in their touch.

"I don't know how I shall get used to wearing shoes," I said, turning to him suddenly. This was in the midst of something he was saying about hair oil, and startled him so much he laughed, the wordless fluent sound endearing him to me beyond any words he could have said. He pretended to notice my bare feet for the first time—they are horribly deformed from calluses and half-healed scars. (I know that my appearance is appalling. Of course, he may have imagined abjectness and illness—it was on this very account he must have been sent up the river alone, to spare my young sons the shock—but his imagination always has been meager, and I think he half expected to find me in need only of a solid meal and a long nap.)

"You always have done whatever you liked," he said with a broad smile—this was at least a partial truth—"so go on barefoot if you want to." I examined his smile for something which I could not have explained. His long mustache had seemingly gone white since I had seen him last—white as my own cropped head—and beneath it, his mouth was generous in its shape.

The road was rough, switchbacking in and out of ravines and around rock promontories and the muscular roots and stumps of trees that were cut down decades before. This country was burnt over in the same terrible summer as the Yacolt fire; there were blackened widowmakers at every hand. All the homes and camps faced the river, not the road. At intervals, greased log chutes hung down the steep riverbank, and wherever the camps were working, logs would shoot down to the river unexpectedly with all the speed and thunder of a rocket. It was necessary to drive under or over the chutes, and the salesman, being well acquainted with the hazards of this road, would hold well back, waiting for the whistle punk's all-clear signal before making his crossing. The horses were skittish going over the greased chutes at ground level; but they went under them, as under the strad-dling legs of a giant, quite without fear.

While we jolted along the road, Stuband went on talking of insubstantial things; I looked out at the half-tamed countryside and did not ask him anything. He may have believed the woman was drowsing, her head nodding with the jerk of the wagon, but she was listening for certain quiet and soft words which could be heard every little while between the steady flow of his language. The spirit of an animal power had come into her body while she had been lost, and since coming out of the wild woods she has been able to do certain things she hadn't been able to do before: to hear and apprehend the voices of other creatures, especially birds, speaking in their own languages. Of course, very soon she would understand that this was a sign of starvation and madness—perhaps she already knew it. But in the weeks and months ahead she would hold on to the notion that it was also a gift.

It has long been a tradition among novel writers
that a book must end by everybody getting just
what they wanted, or if the conventional happy
ending was impossible, then it must be a tragedy in which one or both should die. In real life
very few of us get what we want, our tragedies
don't kill us, but we go on living them year after
year, carrying them with us like a scar on an old
wound.

WILLA CATHER

(1896)

Tuesday, 6 June '05 (on the Lurline)

Stuband tries to spare my feelings and my health by giving over
the news in tiny increments, which is agony—there is too much
of it, and I would rather be smote by a club than stung to death
by ants.

"Well, the center of Yacolt has been burnt out this week," he
said, when I first asked him for news of my missing life, "perhaps by Prohibitionists trying to close up saloons." He then put
his hand into his hair and tugged down the forelock as if he
believed this would keep his scalp from flying off in the wind—
we were standing at the rail on the foredeck of the boat, where
it was too blustery for the tourists. The Lewis and Clark Fair
is in full cry in Portland, which must account for the terrible
crowding aboard: they have seen the Exposition and are now
bound for Astoria to see the ocean. (I suppose it was the more
adventurous among them who were debarking the *Chester* at
Etna—going off to tour Ole Peterson's Lava Cave and take in
the fishing at Trout Lake.)

My brain worked slowly—I had to think of Melba's daughter's name—but after gathering all the words into my mouth I said, "I shouldn't care about the burnt buildings of a town I've been to but once, except I know Florence Coffee has her house there."

He looked down with intent concentration upon the water breaking before the bow, and shortly admitted, "Hers was somewhat singed." There followed another long period of thinking, after which he told me quietly, "In the excitement—or maybe without it—not entirely unexpected—she was delivered of a stillborn child."

No, not entirely unexpected.

We went on standing together in the gusty breeze, looking out at the water and at the clay bluffs sliding past the boat, until I was able to get out the next words: "What is known of Harriet?"

This evidently distressed him, which was its own answer. But when he had pulled his hair down harder and given me a cautious and sidelong look—I felt he was judging whether I had a good grip on the rail so as not to be swept into the water by the terrible thing he had to say—he said both plainly and gently, "She was found lying in a grave not more than a hundred yards from the place she went lost."

I felt an old hollowness and stillness, empty of anguish.

On the thirtieth of April, very early in the morning, loggers returning to their work at Camp 8—they had laid flat the trees around Harriet's little creek the day before—saw a great wolfish animal, long legged, gray as ash, standing amid the tangled trunks and piles of brush. Wolves have rarely been seen in the woods of western Washington for the last twenty years or more, and there was something immediately strange about the way the creature stood, its head low and flat, staring over at the loggers. The men were all of them loaded down with their saws and wedges and springboards, and so they merely stood and watched. It slowly dropped its muzzle—"a kiss" as one of them said—to something which lay on the ground amid the broken limbs and shattered bark, and then slipped silently into the woods behind. This was how Harriet's little body was found, dug up by animals, without a tooth mark upon her flesh.

She had a broken nose and a broken bone in her neck as well as bruises upon her legs and chin; one foot was bare and the other shod; she had been laid in the grave in a tender posture, which the wolf had not disturbed—with her little hands folded across her chest and her face covered by the soft crown of her daddy's hat.

There are unthinkable voids and immense wildernesses in the human heart.

I steeled myself to ask where was Homer now, and Stuband, who always has been a religious man, gave me a grim look and said, "He is in Hell, I'm afraid."

Bill Boyce, the foreman at Camp 8—I remembered him as soon as Stuband said his name—had brought the news to Homer by asking him in a most careful way if he had anything further to report about the last occasion when he had been with his daughter in the woods; and what did he remember of how he had lost his hat? Homer began to swear loudly and turn red in the face; people said he was unsteady on his feet, and that he shook his fist at Boyce, all of which was widely taken as evidence of guilt, though the exact nature of this guilt was a matter for dispute. Boyce sent word down to the constable at Yacolt that he might wish to make an investigation into the circumstances of Harriet's death; but before the constable had traveled up the

flume and over the trail to camp, the men reported that a log
had slipped its chain unexpectedly, had caught Homer's sleeve,
and then, rolling downhill, had tumbled his body along with it.

Stuband did not offer anything more in this line, and my
brain was slow to follow the news backward to the next issue;
only when we were eating our supper out of our laps in the
crowded and noisy salon, I finally thought to say, "This leaves
Florence childless and widowed and her house burnt. How is
she living?"

This seemed to mortify poor Stuband, who was trying so
hard to preserve me from unnecessary worry. He would have
sidestepped—"Folks always look out for their fellow creatures
when such trouble befalls," and so forth—but I pressed him
until he gave up the further news: Melba has taken her sorely
grieving daughter and moved to Seaview, which town was chosen for the well-known restorative benefits of living within
sight of the ocean.

I do not feel myself to be fragile in any way, but the fact
is, I put down my sandwich and cried when I heard this, and
I cannot account for it. Stuband, having failed, as he thought,
to preserve me from agitation, said with a kind of wild over-
anxiety, "Of course, I have seen as many sad and crazed people
living along the edge of the Pacific as anywhere else," which was
unreasonably consoling. And when he'd recovered his thinking
processes, he told me that Melba had acted on the false belief I
was dead—"departed from life," as he said. When I heard this,
I wiped my eyes on my sleeve. "Cannery work will be the only
thing available to her," I told him, "which doesn't suit a woman
in her situation at all. When she's gotten the news I'm alive,
she'll expect me to take her back without a whimper, as if she
had not deserted me and my children, and I suppose I shall

have to find room somewhere in the house for Florence too, who might benefit from being around active boys." I sat back, relieved to the heart.

"Well, there is also a little news of the boys," Stuband said, and his eyes went briefly around the salon looking for a place to rest.

I had been supposing my children to be in the safe care of Edith and Otto Eustler, but Stuband has a transparent face which registers every feeling, and when I saw his look I felt a terrible flutter in the region of my breast, which he must have seen—the truth is, I have lost the will to hide things myself anymore—and he surprised me by be coming suddenly steady, leaning forward to grasp my hands. "Don't worry now, Charlotte, it's all over and the outcome better than expected. There was a siege of diphtheria among the children who live up and down the sloughs, which was evidently caused by the spring flood and sewage getting into the well water. Your boys have all come through it fine"—my heart turning and opening out—he must have seen this also, and yet went on holding my hands, and his face going on serious, which was the worst moment—"but you will learn the truth as soon as stepping off the boat, so I must tell you: Jules has had a very bad case and has suffered a kind of paralysis of his vocal cords, which no one can say if it will be permanent."

I was speechless myself. Then I said, "Some neighborhood children have died from it? Which ones?" in a matter-of-fact voice, before I began crying again. I could not remember the names or faces of any of the boys who used to play with my sons, had not enough memory of my own children—Jules!— but a clear concentrated awareness of my fault, my guilt, and the remorse all coming out in a flood—not to have been there

while he was ill, while all of them were sick, to have been—
where?—gallivanting off in search of dime-novel adventure and
finding—what?—a dark and tangled wilderness, and the ghosts
of the dead.

"Your boys have come through it," Stuband said again, leaning in to me so closely and folding my fingers into his hands.
But I could not stop weeping, bending lower over my knees, and
he leant too, still holding my hands, and kissed my stubbly head
or caressed it with his cheek, and said, "Charlotte, come, come
now, it's all right, be still now," until I became aware of the voice
and his hands, the warmth, and I raised my head and saw him
through the tears, so close, his long sagging mustache not completely white after all but streaked with ruddy brown and bluish
black like the brindle coat of a dog or a dun horse, and the irises
of his sorrowful eyes utterly black, black as a night-dwelling
animal.

People in the salon were watching us—of course, they had
been watching me all along, the wolf-woman with her bald head
and mean scars, her shapeless tent of a dress and her splayed
and ugly bare feet—but I remembered with a sudden stricken
weariness that it was not human to make a public display of
tears. I put my hands over my face like a child, and Stuband
gave me a handkerchief, which I used to wipe my nose and my
eyes. After a while we stood up and went out onto the deck
again, where it was coming toward evening and the wind had
gotten colder. There he told me all that he knew: The diphtheria
had formed a leathery false membrane over the larynx, which
had been removed only with difficulty by the surgeon, leaving a
raw wound and extended paralysis of the voice. More would be
known in another month, and no reason yet to give up hope—
considerable reason to think Jules might regain the faculty of

words. (Of course, I was mute myself once, and I remember it as a resonant stillness—remember that its very formlessness had been a kind of articulation. How to say this to Jules?) Of my five children, Stuband said, it was only Jules and Frank who had been taken ill. Edith had put the two sick boys into her own bedroom, where she and Otto stood watch around the clock (and I think Stuband too, though he did not say so) through the long bout of fever and malaise. George meanwhile conducted himself entirely like a man. He kept himself and Oscar and Lewis healthy by means of strict quarantine and scrupulously boiled water, the three of them spending a tortuous fortnight isolated in the house and reading every book upon the shelves. (And while the boys had been sick, the dreaded word had come down: the search given up for their mother. I knew this without Stuband saying so.) But it was "all over," he told me again and again, and I shouldn't worry.

A pair of wood ducks rose up out of a mud islet and beat across the water, their loud, distressed *wh'eek* piercing my heart. I followed them over the bottomlands into the eastern sky, where a ribbed white cone of a mountain was sliding luminous through the dark light. I wanted to ask Stuband what was the name of this mountain, for I had no recollection of it, but the boat followed the river's turning until the high hills had closed off the view, and the words would not shape themselves in my brain.

I had forgotten how thickly settled was this country. In my childhood, timber grew to the water's edge all along the river, and the early loggers had but to tip the trees into the water and float them to market. But the conquest of the natural world has been the ruling passion of this modern society. Now, in every level embayment there was a house standing in a field of stumps, and every little while a whole town was set down around the mouth of a creek. The deer and the elk, I knew, had been mostly exterminated, and the fish nearly so, which was the cause of Wes's bankruptcy. (I remember times when the silver bodies of sturgeon were piled up as high as a man's hips on the cannery wharf, but it is the same story now as once on the Atlantic: overfishing and damming of the rivers, poor logging practices and wastes from the mills.) I had meant not to think about such things, but here it came: no secret dark hiding places for giants along this part of the river, none for many years. And I stood there wondering how long before the whole of this country was tamed and hedged about, emptied of the last of its mysteries, and the connection between ourselves and the wild world irrevocably broken.

If we had been in the local boat, we'd have put in at Stella, which town was named, I think, for a postmaster's daughter. But the *Lurline* has a high opinion of herself and does not trouble to stop at every village and hamlet. When I saw that we were steaming past the little island at the mouth of Germany Creek, I turned to Stuband and said, "Do you remember? Wes's body washed up here in the year Jules was born." Of course I expected to shock him, but I was surprised in this. He has always had a habit of shyness, an unwillingness to look straight at the person he's speaking to, but he looked directly at me then. "You never wanted to think so," he said very quietly, to which I could make no reply.

Here is another bit of news he told me later, without the least understanding of its meaning: Almon Pierce—this was the young cinnabar miner who had gone up into the woods with my party, and did I remember him?—had put himself entirely into the search for Harriet, and for me, but after all hope was given up, he went home with his brothers, sat down on his bed, and cut his throat from ear to ear.

On getting this news, I had a sudden glimpse of the younger Pierce, his face flashing crimson when we met alone in the woods—and the whole affair in the tent, the groping hand—all of it sweeping through my body like a volcanic wind. (Memory is an odd thing—how you can recall something, bring it into your mind with accuracy, and yet it does not live, is thought only; and another time a door opens and it is all right there; you step through and you are feeling it again, living it again.)

Stuband's gaze was fixed on the darkening eastward sky. He and I had pulled up deck chairs to sit aft of the cabins, while most all of the crowd had gone forward to view the spectacular sunset over the bow. "He was subject to moods," Stuband said softly, "and took everything too serious, I guess. Nobody knows what was in his mind—whether it had anything to do with you and Harriet being lost—so you shouldn't concern yourself too much." He went on a good while thinking these words over, and then he softly added the useless anthem which I had heard a dozen people repeat to him at his own wife's funeral: "There was nothing you could've done."

I am writing these lines while he dozes in his chair beside me. He is swaddled to the chin in blankets, and his face, though quite long and boned like the face of a greyhound, seems child-ishly soft—girlish—as men's faces do in sleep. His weaknesses and sorrows never used to go to my heart, but now the planet has shifted on its axis—I am afraid of people, so much so that I fear I shall always go on like this; and he is custodial, think-ing he should not startle me too much. Once, when the deck became crowded, I leaned against him and reached for his arm, which did not surprise him. I find I am comforted by the simple physical fact of his presence, and he is tender and tolerant of me, unperturbed by my silences. I have begun to remember that he is a quiet sort himself, and that I am not the only one who has lived through storms.

Horace Stuband

The man stood in his yard pitching the ball to himself and swinging at it and walking out to the fence to collect it from the long grass and pitching it again from there, hitting it toward the house and then walking in, hitting it out again, back and forth. He wore several paths in the grass, which at the next rain would puddle and become chutes of mud. When the summer season began, it would be apparent again that he was a decent hitter but could not be hurried running the bases. His legs were long, but there was something lacking in his mainspring: he had failed to find the ground or basis by which the game would assume importance. His neighbors understood this about him, understood that he had experienced a tragedy, or several related tragedies, and therefore they looked on him with a certain forbearance. They always hoped for a hit that was high and deep, over the fence, so that while he trotted around the diamond on his long legs, unhurried and easy, the fielder would be kept busy running down the ball in the brush.

The bat he had whittled and sanded himself from a piece of hard yew was fairly well balanced, a decent bat, but the ball he pitched to himself was made of rags tied up very tightly with string, and it flew unpredictably and made a disappointing pulpy sound when hit; nevertheless he went on using it without thinking of the advantages of practicing with a real ball. He was of a stubbornly sensible mind, his forebears all frugal Danes.

Certain of his neighbors believed him a carrier of bad luck, which was something of which he was unaware. In a small community deeply dependent on the traditions of neighborliness, people found ways to avoid him. A neighbor who had been hoping to ride by his house quickly had once blurted out to him in a fluster, "Can't stop to talk now, got to get the doctor for the wife's mother, she fell and must've broke her arm." The man had immediately gone up to the old woman's place to see what he could do and found her sweeping the kitchen floor, no arms broken. This had baffled him for a while. But though he hadn't seen what was meant by it, he had understood correctly that there was no malicious intent. When he went in to his meeting of the Skamokawa Tribe, Improved Order of Redmen, he had shaken hands with this neighbor and hadn't mentioned the man's mother-in-law or her unbroken bones.

He carried about his person a faint corona, like a lunar halo, an aureola of somberness, which was not grief but its old abraded shadow, and which drew certain kinds of women to him, and children, but kept many men from seeking his company. He was aware of the serious view he had of the world, and the world of him, but not aware of many other aspects of his situation. He believed himself held in the embrace of his community.

In the summer to come, as in summers past, townspeople would charter the *Julia B.* to carry them over to Clatskanie or Rainier or Stella of a Sunday afternoon to play baseball. The man's wife had used to enjoy such outings, but she had been dead now for some time, and it had been a long while before her death that she had stopped enjoying such things. In recent years the man had taken up the habit of bringing along on these trips the sons of a widowed neighbor. He would row himself down to the landing early and tie up his boat and walk to the Methodist church wearing his suit, and then change in the meeting room of the Redmen Lodge and meet the boys at the *Julia B.* and follow them aboard with his bat resting across his shoulder and the homemade ball bulging from the back pocket of his baseball uniform. Coming home late on the boat through the summer darkness, the younger boys would sleep flanking him on the bench with their heads resting hot and damp, one on each of his thighs. He had never had the company of his own children but believed that his neighbors children, requiring little from him and unencumbered with responsibility, must still resemble what he was missing. When he was alone, he had an anxious awareness of his solitude.

The oldest boy came across the field now, tossing a baseball up and catching it in his gloved hand as he came, and so the man left his rag ball lying in the sodden grass, and they began to play pitch-and-catch in the light drizzle, he and the boy, calling out to each other from time to time. The boy, who had just begun to get his height and his sinew, believed himself to be a wise old man, serious-minded, and in truth he carried about his body an aura of somberness, a faint grayish corona, which the man would one day soon, on a summer baseball field, glimpse and briefly recognize with a start of surprise.

After a short while they took to running bases. Once, sliding in the wet grass, they fell together and sat laughing, their trousers striped with mud. Their laughter, rising and floating across the pastures, was heard by other children in the near woods, who were drawn to the sound as iron filings to a magnet. The configuration of their game would soon shift in much the same way celestial charts must be redrawn upon the discovery of new moons; but for a few minutes more the two of them went on playing, unaware, and the other boys, as they were crossing to them over the field, heard their two voices calling back and forth in the simple language of the game.

🍎 *In the popular domestic fictions of my childhood, the heroine always had suffered a great loss that led to her being alone in the world: in those books, the girl's mother or father, or both, always were dead, missing, or damaged. The heroine, having suffered and survived, and now living as somewhat of a social outcast, was often of robust physique, had a will to independence, a desire for education, and the ability to earn a living on her own.*

Such heroines have become quite out of fashion today, replaced by the dainty young thing who faints away at the sight of a six-shooter, squawks when she is startled by a garter snake, and blushes if she catches the eye of a man. It's only in the precincts of the lowbrow scientific romances and western romances that the occasional heroine continues cool under fire; which, if asked, is my rationale for writing them.

A paralyzing apoplexy struck my father down in his own yard when his two children were no more than babies. My mother, who could not lift his weight, raised his head and shoulders out of the mud and propped him against a rock before running to the neighbor's for help, though he drowned anyway, facedown in our flooded pasture, which always has left me wondering if he meant to spare his wife from countless years of caring for an invalid husband. My little brother, Teddy, was killed by typhus when he was but twelve, and Mother herself was killed when I was seventeen, aboard the overloaded Gleaner, which sank while crossing the icy river between Deep River and Astoria. When his business failed, my husband went off to the City without his family, and has not been seen again, which left me to

*raise our five children alone, the youngest of them at the time still an
infant at my breast.*

*I suppose, in considerable respect, I should be a suitable heroine of
my own novels.*

*The truth is, I have never wished to use myself in that way—as
the subject of storytelling. Though the events of my life are sufficiently
poetical, I am neither lovely enough, nor admirable enough, nor sensible enough in my character or in my actions to be an interesting
heroine. And of course I fear coming face-to-face with my Self on the
printed page—it would chill me through to the heart.*

C. B. D.

April 1904

Early a.m., Wedn'y, 7 June (Skamokawa)

I have slept a little (with all the boys, even George, in my bed—
such heat and comfort—the first deep sleep since coming off the
mountain) but woke early and now sit beside them, watching
as they lie tangled all together in the quilts, their arms and legs
seeming so very thin and naked white and their breath hardly
more than the whisper of a field mouse creeping among leaves.
This house is strange and unnaturally still, unfamiliar to me,
inhabited by the ghosts of people I do not know, but I know the
faces of my children as they sleep, and that is enough.

With the boat bringing us so late on the evening tide, I had
not thought to see the boys before today. When we came off the
boat at midnight, I expected Stuband to row me quietly up the
slough in darkness, expected to lie down alone in this empty
cold house and wait for morning, when the boys and I should
be finally reunited, for they've been these many weeks with
Edith and Otto and should have been asleep in the Eustlers'

house long since. But Horace had evidently sent word ahead, for when we stepped onto the landing, oh! there they were, my children together with their dear caretakers—all of them standing in the cone of gaslight on the wharf—standing in a golden shower of fine, lambent pollen which rained from the dark air. The little boys were so shy—I had expected this—and hiding behind Edith; only George stood apart with Otto as if they were two sober men.

I thought my legs would hold. But poor Edith's face became white with shock, and in a moment, when the boys had gotten a good look at me—I am a sight, I know, and they were afraid of me, afraid to discover if I was someone they knew or a wild and shorn and skeletal stranger—Oscar began suddenly to wail, which spread to the twins; and Edith, who had not yet recovered herself, held them to her, crying, "It's all right, it's all right," which meant nothing to them, or everything; but it was Jules, screwing up his face and sobbing in terrible silence, which was more than I could stand. I had to sit down suddenly, or half sit, as Stuband caught me by the arms and I came down upon my knees on the oily boards of the wharf, which I have no doubt frightened my children and which I would have spared them if I could. George had not wept, had gone on standing there shifting his feet in a terrible agony of restlessness, but now with a soft moan he came plunging across the splintered planks to his mother, and I just sat back and gathered him into my lap, my big boy, my giant child, and kissed his dear face, his tears, and he kissed mine.

Of course, then the other boys took after him, rushing across all in a bunch and clambering into my arms, tenderly examining and petting me, and we became as a great mountain of squirming limbs, only barely human in aspect. And while I held them and soothed them, they told me their pent-up news and events of the lost weeks, their thin voices streaming and twining together, but it was Jules I heard most clearly, his voice the wordless, murmurous sibilance of a new-made and ancient language, the language of mothers with their babies and of animals in their lamentation.

Horace, who was naturally worried for my health, soon made the boys get up (they must be lifted from me one after the other), and when he had stood me on my feet again, Edith at once put her arm about my waist. She had got hold of herself and now wore the determined and stern look of a fire warden surveying a burnt woods. "Dear, oh my dear, you've got so very thin!" she said, "I'll have to make you eat pie," and though I am always these days close to tears, this made me laugh; and Horace, who has the most reason to be surprised by such a thing, gave me a wonderfully startled look of happiness.

Otto rowed us steadily away from the river landing, along the path of black water winding between the blacker, brushy margins of the slough. He pulled the oars steadily, breathing through his mouth, his arms straining, and could not be persuaded to let George or Horace spell him, though the tide had begun to turn and the boat was watersoaked and heavy laden. I held Oscar and Jules in my lap, and Edith the twins, the two of us sitting close in the bow of the boat so that our shoulders supported each other. We did not speak. The oar lock cleats were pulling their nails, and I listened to them rattling, and the sweep of oars in the black water. Shortly the stiffness went out of the little boys and they slumped in my arms, asleep. Across Otto's shoulders I watched Horace and George, sitting together in the stern of the boat, their two faces slack with overtiredness; and they watched me. Which went on until the gaslight on the wharf had contracted slowly to a minute point of light and the thickening darkness had made of us only breath and shadow.

C. B. D. (1906)
FROM "TATOOSH"
IN A DESOLATION, AND OTHER STORIES

We began to hear of him in the Moon When Little Fish Are Caught. We had been up the head of the hla'hou river, eating salal berries as they fell ripe, and then we had gone over the shoulder of the ridge to wait down there along the stucallah'wah for those sandbar willows to drop their seeds, and when we came there we learned from stucallah'wah people that he had passed us somewhere in the river draw. The trees all were shining and full of heat that day, and we believed we could see his form still fluttering in the air—it was the form which is taken by human people and certain bears and by ourselves, though those stucallah'wah people said this person wasn't human, wasn't bear, wasn't one of us.

We heard of him again in the Moon When the Adder's Tongue Turns Color, over at kwiwichess, and again at n'sel, where he had passed by the day before, and at last some of us had a glimpse of him at oleqa as we went westward with the ripening camas. Those of us who had seen him told the others this: that his eyes had a startled look, the look of a little wood rat in the mouth of an owl; that his coat was close and pale, the way a hare's coat will look in old snow just before the wake-robins bloom. And we said this: that he walked as human people walk and as we ourselves walk, upended, standing on two of his feet.

Some of us thought he might be a lost person of our family, but some others thought he must be a human whose skin had been blenched in the heat, or an upright-walking bear who had shed his coat or had had it cut from him. We asked the bear people living over along the alimi'ct, but they said they didn't know him, and when we asked the human people at skuma'qea, they said if he was one of them, they didn't know his name or his tribe; they said that none of their people were walleyed, nor sallow skinned. It was human people who pointed out: tufts of thick, coarse hair sprang from his skull, yes, in the manner of humans, but also from his chin and lips, in the manner of goats and certain lions. As a consequence, lacking a name, we began to call him the Bearded Man.

Some of us have seen the Bearded Man. Some of us have only heard other people tell their stories of seeing him. As a result, some of us have wondered whether he has substance or belongs to another world, the world of Tahmahnawis, which we can glimpse only in coming and going. Between this world and that one, it's not a matter of realness or unrealness, but of eye-mindedness. It's the difficulty of seeing what lies at the edges of things, what lives in the thick shade, what is concealed by radiance. In such matters, all truth is hidden.

People began to say this: that the body of the Bearded Man was made of light. They said he was a vessel some wolf-people had made, a sack of light in which to hold their old stories. In one of those old stories, wild people living under the rocks come out at night to eat children.

. . .

The Bearded Man behaved as if other people weren't already living in this country. He left his foul-smelling scat in the waters where fish-people were living, and pissed upon the houses of weasels and porcupines. He crouched beside fire gathered into holds of rock, and afterward left the scattered embers to communicate themselves to the old trees. He ate from the soft hearts of stone-shelled tubers he had carried into this country from an unknown place, and left behind the bright sharp shells scattered upon the ground like seed, where they lay barren, cankering slowly in the rain and sun.

In those days we had no reason to be afraid of him, but some of us were—some of us thought it was a good thing people were invisible to him. But others said we ought to make ourselves known. They said if the Bearded Man built his fire where tree-people were living, if he fouled the nests of fishes with his shit, surely this was done from ignorance, and if people made themselves known, then this accidental behavior would come to an end. Of course, in those days we thought he was of the world, and in it. We were slow to come to this understanding: that the Bearded Man had cut the cord between himself and the world and now stood separate in his victory, like an embryo which has triumphed over its womb.

In the Small Dark Moon, the Bearded Man was seen at chahulklihum digging up the earth, and people said he must be looking for a path down again, to his old home inside the volcano. Perhaps this was true, for he dug with a furious anger in one place and then another: first at chahulklihum, then ts'nuk, then hullooetell. When we went over there to hullooetell to help him find his way home, he had already moved westward. Across the shoulder of the mountain at k'kwiyai, people saw him going on with his digging, stabbing at the earth as if he meant to kill it with his knife. These people saw the dirt fly up from his blows and rise in a scrim that darkened the sky.

In the Moon When Ice Is in the River, we heard of the Bearded Man again, that he had gone mad and was eating rocks and defecating them, over in the tahweas pass, and when we went up there, we saw rocks in great smoking piles, and a terrible field of shattered trees smeared with blood and effluent. Going down from the pass, we had a glimpse of someone squatting in the old dry lava, and afterward some of us believed we had seen the heavy white body of a giant or a bear or a wildman rising from that place, going down through the rocks and trees; or we had seen a hole opening up, and felt a cold blast as from a cave.

In the Moon When the Grass Turns Brown, word reached us that the Bearded Man had been killing people over on the yoncalla prairie, but when we came there to see for ourselves, Raven had eaten the fleshy parts and flown away, so no one could say for sure what had done the killing. Horns and ribs and vertebrae, the bare white armature of the dead, lay upon a vast field of blood. Blood and death are a familiar thing, but there was something in the air and in the red mud footprints at that place, something unfamiliar even to the old ones among us, something malignant and unappeasable. Some human people at once said this must be the work of Dzonoqwa the Wild Woman, whose face is carved upon their masks and totems; they said Dzonoqwa will steal souls and children; they said she abides in the deep shadows. But Dzonoqwa is known to us—we inhabit the same country—and not many of us who looked upon the yoncalla prairie placed the blame for that killing in Dzonoqwa's mouth. Those of us who visited that field of blood began to say something else. We began to say that a giant had climbed up from the dark center of the mountain and now ran wanton upon the face of the earth.

In the Moon When Tight Buds Unfurl, Wolverine found a lost child belonging to the Bearded Man and brought this child to us. We have been keeping it safe.

ACKNOWLEDGMENTS

The author wishes to thank Literary Arts, Inc., for their financial support during the writing of this work; Cottages at Hedgebrook, for a nurturing residency early in the life of the novel; and the Mrs. Giles Whiting Foundation, for their very generous gift.

Thanks to Irene Martin, who steered me toward a more accurate description of the terrain around Skamokawa (though, of course, any remaining errors are mine).

For helping this poor lost book find its way out of the woods, I am deeply grateful to the Truthful Trio, and also to my literary agent, Wendy Weil, and my editor at Simon & Schuster, Roz Siegel.

Turn the page to read a selection
from Molly Gloss's collection
Unforeseen: "Lambing Season,"
a finalist for the Hugo and Nebula Awards

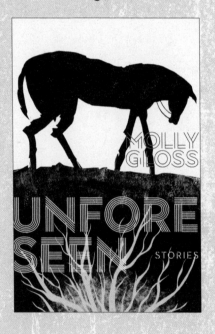

FROM MAY TO September, Delia took the Churro sheep and two dogs and went up on Joe-Johns Mountain to live. She had that country pretty much to herself all summer. Ken Owen sent one of his Mexican hands up every other week with a load of groceries, but otherwise, she was alone; alone with the sheep and the dogs. She liked the solitude. Liked the silence. Some sheepherders she knew talked a blue streak to the dogs, the rocks, the porcupines; they sang songs and played the radio, read their magazines out loud, but Delia let the silence settle into her, and by early summer she had begun to hear the ticking of the dry grasses as a language she could almost translate. The dogs were named Jesus and Alice. "Away to me, Hey-sus," she said when they were moving the sheep. "Go bye, Alice." From May to September these words spoken in command of the dogs were almost the only times she heard her own voice; that, and when the Mexican brought the groceries—a polite exchange in Spanish about the weather, the health of the dogs, the fecundity of the ewes.

The Churros were a very old breed. The O-Bar Ranch had a federal allotment up on the mountain, which was all rim-rock and sparse grasses—well suited to the Churros that were fiercely protective of their lambs and had a long-stapled top-coat that could take the weather. They did well on the thin grass of the mountain, where other sheep would lose flesh and give up their lambs to the coyotes. The Mexican was an old man. He said he remembered Churros from his childhood in the Oaxaca highlands, the rams with their four horns—two curving up, two down. "Buen' carne," he told Delia. Uncommonly fine meat.

The wind blew out of the southwest in the early part of the season, a wind that smelled of juniper and sage and pollen; in the later months it blew straight from the east, a dry wind smelling of dust and smoke, bringing down showers of parched leaves and seed heads of yarrow and bitter cress. Thunderstorms came frequently out of the east, enormous cloudscapes with hearts of livid magenta and glaucous green. At those times, if she was camped on a ridge, she'd get out of her bed and walk downhill to find a draw where she could feel safer, but if she was camped in a low place, she would stay with the sheep while a war passed over their heads, spectacular, jagged flares of lightning; skull-rumbling cannonades of thunder. It was maybe bred into the bones of Churros, a knowledge and a tolerance of mountain weather, for they shifted together and waited out the thunder with surprising composure; they stood forbearingly while rain beat down in hard, blinding bursts.

Sheepherding was simple work, although Delia knew some herders who made it hard, dogging the sheep every minute, keeping them in a tight group, moving all the time. She let the sheep herd themselves, do what they wanted, make their own decisions. If the band began to separate, she would whistle or yell, and often the strays would turn around and rejoin the main group. Only if they were badly scattered did she send out the dogs. Mostly, she just kept an eye on the sheep, made sure they got good feed, that the band didn't split, that they stayed in the boundaries of the O-Bar allotment. She studied the sheep for the language of their bodies and tried to handle them just as close to their nature as possible. When she put out salt for them, she scattered it on rocks and stumps as if she were hiding Easter eggs, because she saw how they enjoyed the search.

The spring grass made their manure wet, so she kept the wool cut away from the ewes' tail areas with a pair of sharp, short-bladed shears. She dosed the sheep with wormer, trimmed their feet, inspected their teeth, treated ewes for mastitis. She combed the burrs from the dogs' coats and inspected them for ticks. *You're such good dogs,* she told them with her hands. *I'm very, very proud of you.*

She had some old binoculars, 7x32 mms, and in the long, quiet days, she watched bands of wild horses, miles off in the distance; ragged-looking mares with dorsal stripes and black legs. She read the back issues of the local newspapers, looking in the obits for names she recognized. She read spine-broken paperback novels and played solitaire and scoured the ground for arrowheads and rocks she would later sell to rock hounds. She studied the parched brown grass, which was full of grass-hoppers and beetles and crickets and ants. But most of her day was spent just walking. The sheep sometimes bedded quite a ways from her trailer, and she had to get out to them before sunrise, when the coyotes would make their kills. She was usu-ally up by three or four and walking out to the sheep in dark-ness. Sometimes she returned to the camp for lunch, but she was always out with the sheep again until sundown, when the coyotes were likely to return, and then she walked home after dark to water and feed the dogs, eat supper, climb into bed.

In her first years on Joe-Johns, she had often walked three or four miles away from the band, just to see what was over a hill, or to study the intricate architecture of a sheepherder's monument. Stacking up flat stones in the form of an obelisk was a common herders' pastime, their monuments all over that sheep country, and though Delia had never felt an impulse to start one herself, she admired the ones other people had built. She sometimes walked miles out of her way just to look at a rock pile up close.

She had a mental map of the allotment, divided into ten pastures. Every few days, when the sheep had moved on to a new pasture, she moved her camp. She towed the trailer with an old Dodge pickup, over the rocks and creek beds, the sloughs and dry meadows, to the new place. For a while afterward, after the engine was shut off and while the heavy old body of the truck was settling onto its tires, she would be deaf, her head filled with a dull, roaring white noise.

She had about eight hundred ewes, as well as their lambs, many of them twins or triplets. The ferocity of the Churro ewes in defending their offspring was sometimes a problem for the dogs, but in the balance of things, she knew it kept her losses small. Many coyotes lived on Joe-Johns, and sometimes a cougar or bear would come up from the salt pan desert on the north side of the mountain, looking for better country to own. These animals considered the sheep to be fair game, which Delia understood to be their right, and also her right—hers and the dogs—to take the side of the sheep. Sheep were smarter than people commonly believed, and the Churros smarter than other sheep she had tended, but by midsummer the coyotes had passed the word among themselves—buen' carne—and Delia and the dogs then had a job of work, keeping the sheep out of harm's way.

She carried a .32-caliber Colt pistol in an old-fashioned holster worn on her belt. *If you're a coyot', you'd better be careful of this woman,* she said with her body, with the way she stood and the way she walked when she was wearing the pistol. That gun and holster had once belonged to her mother's mother, a woman who had come west on her own and homesteaded for a while, down in the Sprague River Canyon. Delia's grandmother had liked to tell the story: how a concerned neighbor, a bachelor with an interest in marriageable females, had pressed the gun upon her, back when the Klamaths were at war with the army of General Joel Palmer; and how she never had used it for anything but shooting rabbits.

In July a coyote killed a lamb while Delia was camped no more than two hundred feet away from the bedded sheep. It was dusk, and she was sitting on the steps of the trailer reading a two-gun Western, leaning close over the pages in the failing light, and the dogs were dozing at her feet. She heard the small sound, a strange, high, faint squeal she did not recognize and then did recognize, and she jumped up and fumbled for the gun, yelling at the coyote, at the dogs, her yell startling the entire band to its feet but the ewes making their charge too late, Delia firing too late, and none of it doing any good beyond a release of fear and anger.

A lion might well have taken the lamb entire; she had known of lion kills where the only evidence was blood on the grass and a dribble of entrails in the beam of a flashlight. But a coyote is small and will kill with a bite to the throat and then perhaps eat just the liver and heart, though a mother coyote will take all she can carry in her stomach, bolt it down and carry it home to her pups. Delia's grandmother's pistol had scared this one off before it could even take a bite, and the lamb was twitching and whole on the grass, bleeding only from its neck. The mother ewe stood over it, crying in a distraught and pitiful way, but there was nothing to be done, and in a few minutes the lamb was dead.

There wasn't much point in chasing after the coyote, and anyway, the whole band was now a skittish jumble of anxiety and confusion; it was hours before the mother ewe gave up her grieving, before Delia and the dogs had the band calm and bedded down again; almost midnight. By then the dead lamb had stiffened on the ground, and Delia dragged it over by the truck and skinned it and let the dogs have the meat, which went against her nature but was about the only way to keep the coyote from coming back for the carcass.

While the dogs worked on the lamb, she stood with both hands pressed to her tired back, looking out at the sheep, the mottled pattern of their whiteness almost opalescent across the black landscape, and the stars thick and bright above the faint outline of the rock ridges. Stood there a moment before turning toward the trailer, toward bed, and afterward, she would think how the coyote and the sorrowing ewe and the dark of the July moon and the kink in her back, how all that came together and was the reason she was standing there watching the sky, was the reason she saw the brief, brilliantly green flash in the southwest and then the sulfur yellow streak breaking across the night, southwest to due west on a descending arc onto Lame Man Bench. It was a broad, bright ribbon, rainbow-wide, a cyanotic contrail. It was not a meteor; she had seen hundreds of meteors. She stood and looked at it.

Things to do with the sky, with distance—you could lose

perspective. It was hard to judge even a lightning strike, whether it had touched down on a particular hill or the next hill or the valley between. So she knew this thing falling out of the sky might have come down miles to the west of Lame Man, not onto Lame Man at all, which was two miles away—at least two miles—and getting there would be all ridges and rocks; no way to cover the ground in the truck. She thought about it. She had moved camp earlier in the day, which was always troublesome work, and it had been a blistering hot day, and now the excitement with the coyote. She was very tired, the tiredness like a weight against her breastbone. She didn't know what this thing was, falling out of the sky. Maybe if she walked over there, she would find just a dead satellite or a broken weather balloon and not dead or broken people. The contrail thinned slowly while she stood there looking at it, became a wide streak of yellowy cloud against the blackness, with the field of stars glimmering dimly behind it.

After a while she went into the truck and got a water bottle and filled it, and she also took the first aid kit out of the trailer and a couple of spare batteries for the flashlight and a handful of extra cartridges for the pistol. Delia stuffed these things into a backpack and looped her arms into the straps and started up the rise away from the dark camp, the bedded sheep. The dogs left off their gnawing of the dead lamb and trailed her anxiously, wanting to follow, or not wanting her to leave the sheep. "Stay by," she said to them sharply, and they went back and stood with the band and watched her go. *That coyot', it's done with us tonight.* This is what she told the dogs with her body, walking away, and she believed it was probably true.

Now that she'd decided to go, she walked fast. This was her

sixth year on the mountain, and by this time, she knew the country pretty well. She didn't use the flashlight. Without it, she became accustomed to the starlit darkness, able to see the stones and pick out a path. The air was cool but full of the smell of heat rising off the rocks and the parched earth. She heard nothing but her own breathing and the gritting of her boots on the pebbly dirt. A little owl circled once in silence and then went off toward a line of cottonwood trees standing in black silhouette to the northeast.

Lame Man Bench was a great upthrust block of basalt grown over with scraggly juniper forest. As she climbed among the trees the smell of something like ozone or sulfur grew very strong, and the air became thick, burdened with dust. Threads of the yellow contrail hung in the limbs of the trees. She went on across the top of the bench and onto slabs of shelving rock that gave a view to the west. Down in the steep-sided draw below her, there was a big wing-shaped piece of metal resting on the ground, which she at first thought had been torn from an airplane, but then realized was a whole thing, not broken, and she quit looking for the rest of the wreckage. She squatted down and looked at it. Yellow dust settled slowly out of the sky, pollinating her hair, her shoulders, the toes of her boots, faintly dulling the oily black shine of the wing, the thing shaped like a wing.

While she was squatting there looking down at it, something came out from the sloped underside of it—a coyote, she thought at first, and then it wasn't a coyote but a dog built like a greyhound or a whippet; deep-chested, long legged, very light-boned and frail-looking. She waited for somebody else, a man, to crawl out after his dog, but nobody did. The dog squatted to pee and then moved off a short distance and sat on its haunches and considered things. Delia considered too. She considered that the dog might have been sent up alone. The Russians had sent up a dog in their little Sputnik, she remembered. She considered that a skinny almost hairless dog with frail bones would be dead in short order if left alone in this country. And she considered that there might be a man inside the wing, dead or too hurt to climb out. She thought how much trouble it would be, getting down this steep rock bluff in the darkness to rescue a useless dog and a dead man.

After a while she stood and started picking her way into the draw. The dog by this time was smelling the ground, making a slow and careful circuit around the black wing. Delia kept expecting the dog to look up and bark, but it went on with its intent inspection of the ground, as if it were stone-deaf, as if Delia's boots making a racket on the loose gravel was not an announcement that someone was coming down. She thought of the old Dodge truck, how it always left her ears ringing, and wondered if maybe it was the same with this dog and its wing-shaped Sputnik, although the wing had fallen soundlessly across the sky.

When she had come about halfway down the hill, she lost her footing and slid down six or eight feet before she got her heels dug in and found a handful of willow scrub to hang on to. A glimpse of this movement—rocks sliding to the bottom, or the dust she raised—must have startled the dog, for it leaped backward suddenly and then reared up. They looked at each other in silence, Delia and the dog, Delia standing, leaning into the steep slope a dozen yards above the bottom of the draw, and the dog standing next to the Sputnik, standing all the way up on its hind legs like a bear or a man and no longer seeming to be a dog but a person with a long narrow muzzle and a narrow chest, turned-out knees, delicate doglike feet. Its genitals were more catlike than dog's, a male set but very small and neat and contained. Dog's eyes, though; dark and small and shining below an anxious brow, so that she was reminded of Jesus and Alice, the way they had looked at her when she had left them alone with the sheep. She had years of acquaintance with dogs, and she knew enough to look away, break off her stare. Also, after a moment, she remembered the old pistol and holster at her belt. In cowboy pictures, a man would unbuckle his gun belt and let it down on the ground as a gesture of peaceful intent, but it seemed to her this might only bring attention to the gun, to the true intent of a gun, which is always killing. *This woman is nobody at all to be scared of,* she told the dog with her body, standing very still along the steep hillside, holding on to the scrub willow with her hands, looking vaguely to the left of him, where the smooth curve of the wing rose up and gathered a veneer of yellow dust.

The dog—the dog-person—opened his jaws and yawned the way a dog will do to relieve nervousness, and then they were both silent and still for a minute. When he finally turned and stepped toward the wing, it was an unexpected, delicate movement, exactly the way a ballet dancer steps along on his toes, knees turned out, lifting his long, thin legs; and then he dropped down on all fours and seemed to become almost a dog again. He went back to his business of smelling the ground intently, though every little while he looked up to see if Delia was still standing along the rock slope. It was a steep place to stand. When her knees finally gave out, she sat down very carefully where she was, which didn't spook him. He had become used to her by then, and his brief, sliding glance just said, *That woman up there is nobody at all to be scared of.*

What he was after, or wanting to know, was a mystery to her. She kept expecting him to gather up rocks, like all those men who'd gone to the moon, but he only smelled the ground, making a wide, slow circuit around the wing the way Alice and Jesus always circled round the trailer every morning, noses down, reading the dirt like a book. And when he seemed satisfied with what he'd learned, he stood up again and looked back at Delia, a last look delivered across his shoulder before he dropped down and disappeared under the edge of the wing; a grave and inquiring look, the kind of look a dog or a man will give you before going off on his own business, a look that says, *You be okay if I go?* If he had been a dog, and if Delia had been close enough to do it, she'd have scratched the smooth head, felt the hard bone beneath, moved her hands around the soft ears. *Sure, okay, you go on now, Mr. Dog.* This is what she would have said with her hands. Then he crawled into the darkness under the slope of the wing, where she figured there must be a door, a hatch leading into the body of the machine, and after a while, he flew off into the dark of the July moon.

In the weeks afterward, on nights when the moon had set or hadn't yet risen, she looked for the flash and streak of something breaking across the darkness out of the southwest. She saw him come and go to that draw on the west side of Lame Man Bench twice more in the first month. Both times she left her grandmother's gun in the trailer and walked over there and sat in the dark on the rock slab above the draw and watched him for a couple of hours. He may have been waiting for her, or he knew her smell, because both times he reared up and looked at her just about as soon as she sat down. But then he went on with his business. *That woman is nobody to be scared of,* he said with his body, with the way he went on smelling the ground, widening his circle and widening it, sometimes taking a clod or a sprig into his mouth and tasting it, the way a mild-mannered dog will do when he's investigating something and not paying any attention to the person he's with.

Delia had about decided that the draw behind Lame Man Bench was one of his regular stops, like the ten campsites she used over and over again when she was herding on Joe-Johns Mountain, but after those three times in the first month she didn't see him again.

At the end of September she brought the sheep down to the O-Bar. After the lambs had been shipped out, she took her band of dry ewes over onto the Nelson prairie for the fall, and in mid-November, when the snow had settled in, she brought them to the feed lots. That was all the work the ranch had for her until lambing season. Jesus and Alice belonged to the O-Bar. They stood in the yard and watched her go.

In town she rented the same room as the year before, and as before, spent most of a year's wages on getting drunk and standing other herders to rounds of drink. She gave up looking into the sky.

In March she went back out to the ranch. In bitter weather they built jugs and mothering-up pens, and trucked the pregnant ewes from Green, where they'd been feeding on wheat stubble. Some ewes lambed in the trailer on the way in, and after every haul, there was a surge of lambs born. Delia had the night shift, where she was paired with Roy Joyce, a fellow who raised sugar beets over in the valley and came out for the lambing season every year. In the black, freezing cold middle of the night, eight and ten ewes would be lambing at a time. Triplets, twins, big singles, a few quads, ewes with lambs born dead, ewes too sick or confused to mother. She and Roy would skin a dead lamb and feed the carcass to the ranch dogs and wrap the fleece around a bummer lamb, which was intended to fool the bereaved ewe into taking the orphan as her own, and sometimes it worked that way. All the mothering-up pens swiftly filled, and the jugs filled, and still some ewes with new lambs stood out in the cold field waiting for a room to open up.

You couldn't pull the stuck lambs with gloves on; you had to reach into the womb with your fingers to turn the lamb, or tie cord around the feet, or grasp the feet barehanded, so Delia's hands were always cold and wet, then cracked and bleeding. The ranch had brought in some old converted school buses to house the lambing crew, and she would fall into a bunk at daybreak and then not be able to sleep, shivering in the unheated bus with the gray daylight pouring in the windows, and the endless daytime clamor out at the lambing sheds. All the lambers had sore throats, colds, nagging coughs. Roy Joyce looked like hell, deep bags as blue as bruises under his eyes, and Delia figured she looked about the same, though she hadn't seen a mirror, not even to draw a brush through her hair, since the start of the season.

By the end of the second week, only a handful of ewes hadn't lambed. The nights became quieter. The weather cleared, and the thin skiff of snow melted off the grass. On the dark of the moon, Delia was standing outside the mothering-up pens drinking coffee from a thermos. She put her head back and held the warmth of the coffee in her mouth a moment, and as she was swallowing it down, lowering her chin, she caught the tail end of a green flash and a thin yellow line breaking across the sky, so far off anybody else would have thought it was a meteor, but it was bright, and dropping from southwest to due west, maybe right onto Lame Man Bench. She stood and looked at it. She was so very goddamned tired and had a sore throat that wouldn't clear, and she could barely get her fingers to fold around the thermos, they were so split and tender.

She told Roy she felt as sick as a horse and did he think he could handle things if she drove herself into town to the urgent care clinic, and she took one of the ranch trucks and drove up the road a short way and then turned onto the rutted track that went up to Joe-Johns.

The night was utterly clear, and you could see things a long way off. She was still an hour's drive from the Churros' summer range when she began to see a yellow-orange glimmer behind the black ridgeline, a faint nimbus like the ones that marked distant range fires on summer nights.

She had to leave the truck at the bottom of the bench to climb up the last mile or so on foot, had to get a flashlight out of the glove box and try to find an uphill path with it because the fluttery, reddish light show was finished by then, and a thick pall of smoke overcast the sky and blotted out the stars. Her eyes itched and burned, and tears ran from them, but the smoke calmed her sore throat. She went up slowly, breathing through her mouth.

The wing had burned a skid path through the scraggly junipers along the top of the bench and had come apart into a hundred pieces. She wandered through the burned trees and the scattered wreckage, shining her flashlight into the smoky darkness, not expecting to find what she was looking for, but there he was, lying apart from the scattered shards of metal, out on the smooth slab rock at the edge of the draw. He was panting shallowly, and his close coat of short brown hair was matted with blood. He lay in such a way that she immediately knew his back was broken. When he saw Delia coming up, his brow furrowed with worry. A sick or a wounded dog will bite, she knew that, but she squatted next to him. *It's just me,* she told him by shining the light not in his face but in hers. Then she spoke to him. "Okay," she said. "I'm here now," without thinking too much about what the words meant, or whether they meant anything at all, and she didn't remember until afterward that he was very likely deaf anyway. He sighed and shifted his look from her to the middle distance, where she supposed he was focused on approaching death.

Near at hand, he didn't resemble a dog all that much, only in the long shape of his head, the folded-over ears, the round darkness of his eyes. He lay on the ground, flat on his side like a dog that's been run over and is dying by the side of the road, but a man will lay like that too when he's dying. He had small-fingered nail-less hands where a dog would have had toes and front feet. Delia offered him a sip from her water bottle, but he didn't seem to want it, so she just sat with him quietly, holding one of his hands, which was as smooth as lambskin against the cracked and roughened flesh of her palm. The batteries in the flashlight gave out, and sitting there in the cold darkness, she found his head and stroked it, moving her sore fingers lightly over the bone of his skull, and around the soft ears, the loose jowls. Maybe it wasn't any particular comfort to him, but she was comforted by doing it. *Sure, okay, you can go on.*

She heard him sigh, and then sigh again, and each time wondered if it would turn out to be his death. She had used to wonder what a coyote, or especially a dog, would make of this doggish man, and now, while she was listening, waiting to hear if he would breathe again, she began to wish she'd brought Alice or Jesus with her, though not out of that old curiosity. When her husband had died years before, at the very moment he took his last breath, the dog she'd had then had barked wildly and raced back and forth from the front to the rear door of the house, as if he'd heard or seen something invisible to her. People said it was her husband's soul going out the door or his angel coming in. She didn't know what it was the dog had seen or heard or smelled, but she wished she knew. And now she wished she had a dog with her to bear witness.

She went on petting him even after he had died, after she was sure he was dead, and went on petting him until his body was cool, and then she got up stiffly from the bloody ground and gathered rocks and piled them onto him, a couple of feet high so he wouldn't be found or dug up. She didn't know what to do about the wreckage, so she didn't do anything with it at all.

In May, when she brought the Churro sheep back to Joe-Johns Mountain, the pieces of the wrecked wing had already eroded, were small and smooth-edged like the bits of sea glass you find on a beach, and she figured this must be what it was meant to do: to break apart into pieces too small for anybody to notice, and then to quickly wear away. But the stones she'd piled over his body seemed like the start of something, so she began the slow work of raising them higher into a sheepherder's monument. She gathered up all the smooth eroded bits of wing, too, and laid them in a series of widening circles around the base of the monument. She went on piling up stones through the summer and into September until it reached fifteen feet. Mornings, standing with the sheep miles away, she would look for it through the binoculars and think about ways to make it higher, and she would wonder what was buried under all the other monuments sheepherders had raised in that country. At night she studied the sky, but nobody came for him.

In November, when she finished with the sheep and went

into town, she asked around and found a guy who knew about stargazing and telescopes. He loaned her some books and sent her to a certain pawnshop, and she gave most of a year's wages for a 14x75 telescope with a reflective lens. On clear, moonless nights she met the astronomy guy out at the Little League baseball field, and she sat on a fold-up canvas stool with her eye against the telescope's finder while he told her what she was seeing: Jupiter's moons, the Pelican Nebula, the Andromeda galaxy. The telescope had a tripod mount, and he showed her how to make a little jerry-built device so she could mount her old 7x32 mm binoculars on the tripod too. She used the binoculars for their wider view of star clusters and small constellations. She was indifferent to most discomforts, could sit quietly in one position for hours at a time, teeth rattling with the cold, staring into the immense vault of the sky until she became numb and stiff, barely able to stand and walk back home. Astronomy, she discovered, was a work of patience, but the sheep had taught her patience, or it was already in her nature before she ever took up with them.